PRAISE FOR THE NOVELS OF KATIE MacALISTER

Memoirs of a Dragon Hunter
"Bursting with the author's trademark zany humor and spicy romance…
this quick tale will delight paranormal romance fans."
—*Publishers Weekly*

Sparks Fly
"Balanced by a well-organized plot and MacAlister's trademark humor."
—*Publishers Weekly*

It's All Greek to Me
"A fun and sexy read."
—The Season for Romance
"A wonderful lighthearted romantic romp as a kick-butt American Amazon
and a hunky Greek find love. Filled with humor, fans will laugh with the
zaniness of Harry meets Yacky."
—*Midwest Book Review*

Much Ado About Vampires
"A humorous take on the dark and demonic."
—*USA Today*

"Once again this author has done a wonderful job. I was sucked into the
world of Dark Ones right from the start and was taken on a fantastic ride.
This book is full of witty dialogue and great romance, making it one that
should not be missed."
—Fresh Fiction

The Unbearable Lightness of Dragons
"Had me laughing out loud...This book is full of humor and romance, keeping the reader entertained all the way through...a wondrous story full of magic...I cannot wait to see what happens next in the lives of the dragons."
—Fresh Fiction

Fireborn

A Born Prophecy

Katie MacAlister

REBEL BASE BOOKS
Kensington Publishing Corp.
www.kensingtonbooks.com

Rebel Base Books are published by
Kensington Publishing Corp. 119 West 40th Street New York, NY 10018

All Kensington titles, imprints, and distributed lines are available at special quantity discounts for bulk purchases for sales promotion, premiums, fundraising, and educational or institutional use.

To the extent that the image or images on the cover of this book depict a person or persons, such person or persons are merely models, and are not intended to portray any character or characters featured in the book.

Special book excerpts or customized printings can also be created to fit specific needs. For details, write or phone the office of the Kensington Special Sales Manager:
Kensington Publishing Corp.
119 West 40th Street
New York, NY 10018
Attn. Special Sales Department. Phone: 1-800-221-2647.

First Electronic Edition: June 2019
ISBN-13: 978-1-63573-073-9 (ebook)
ISBN-10: 1-63573-073-2 (ebook)

First Print Edition: June 2019
ISBN-13: 978-1-63573-074-6
ISBN-10: 1-63573-074-0

Printed in the United States of America

One of the things I love about the Internet is the ability to meet people I might never have had the chance of knowing in person. Christopher Livingston, gamer, reviewer, writer, and an all-around very funny man, is just one such person. Christopher not only feeds me all the latest gamer news, he rides a mean dinosaur. When I was at a loss for lyrics, he kindly lent me his brain for the creation of the verses Allegria sings, and for that, as well as his friendship, I'm profoundly grateful.

I'd also like to thank Jamie Parker for being such a great friend, kickass mage, and fellow fan of bad boys. You do Ciandra proud, Jamie!

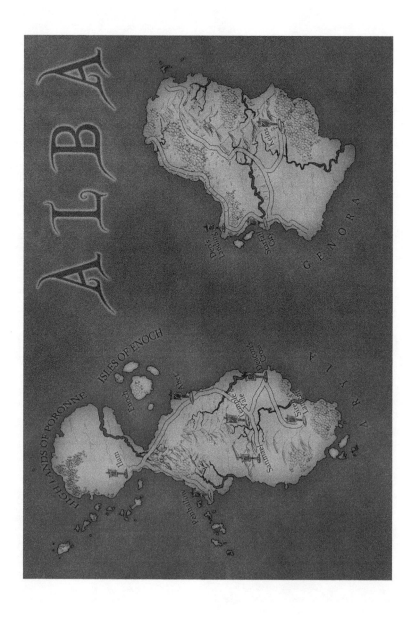

Prologue

"I'm not too late, am I?"

The midwife looked up from where she was carefully cleansing and anointing her tools, mindful to treat them with the reverence they deserved. They had saved—and, goddess willing, would continue to save—many a woman's life.

A tall man strode into the small antechamber, the air that swirled behind him bringing with it the soft scents of the rare night-blooming flowers that grew outside the queen's chamber. The scent drifted through the room, banishing before it smells normal to such domains, instead providing a sense of relief and refreshment. The midwife breathed deeply for a moment, her mind calming and clearing... until those scents native to the impatient man tickled her nose. Horse, sweat, and leather had their places, but not in a queen's bedchamber. Not in a birthing environment.

"The babe is born, if that is what you mean," she answered finally, aware that the man had the decency to wait upon her answer before continuing into the next chamber.

He hesitated. "And Dasa? She does well?"

The midwife unbent a little in her consideration of the man before her. She had judged many a new father on his first words, whether his concern was wholly for his progeny, or if he had a care for the woman who had risked her life to bring a new being into Bellias's domain. "The queen rests comfortably, my lord. She was in labor for half a day, but once the child wished to be born, it went quickly."

"Good." The man reached the door to the queen's chamber in three strides, but he again paused, his hand on the doorknob. "And the babe?"

She knew what he was asking. "You have a son, my lord."

"Thank the goddess," he said, sighing in relief, and without another word entered the queen's bedchamber.

The midwife sidled up to the door and leaned against it, listening for a moment, but the murmur of voices inside was too unclear to be distinguishable.

"Bellias bless and keep the child," she murmured to herself as she returned to the task of cleaning her tools. "And may he be the salvation that we need."

* * * *

Israel Langton, lord of the Fireborn and newly made father, examined the small bundle presented to him by one of the handmaidens. He wasn't overly impressed by what he saw. "Are you sure that's a babe?"

"Israel!"

"Have you seen him?" He gestured toward the child. "He looks more like a boiled frog."

"He does not. He doesn't look anything like a frog, boiled or otherwise."

He pulled back a bit of the swaddling. "Definitely has frog blood. And possibly some sort of mutant pig."

"You are incorrigible!"

Israel smiled to himself and looked over to the mammoth bed where a woman lay draped against a plethora of red and purple cushions, her long black hair washing down over the bedcovers. Her face was pinched and exhausted, but her eyes—silver in color, and right now about as warm as the moon itself—were filled with life.

"How dare you say that about our son? He is perfect in every way."

Israel took the bundle from the handmaiden and brought it to Dasa, carefully easing himself alongside her. Despite the midwife's reassurances, the lines of strain around Dasa's mouth told the tale of just how strenuously she'd fought to birth the baby. "Take a look."

She looked. "Well… maybe not *perfectly* perfect."

"He's red. And blotchy."

Dasa fussed with the swaddling blanket, adjusting it minutely and brushing her fingers against the child's forehead. "He's not blotchy. He just has… different colors to his flesh."

"His head is pointed."

"Yours would be, too, if you were squeezed out of a womb," she countered.

He raised his brows. "I know you think I was born of the lord of the underworld, but my mother tells a different story."

"Then your criticism is null. In time his head will become as round as yours."

Israel considered his son, now nestled against his mother. "He's not very attractive, is he? You are lovely, and I've been told I wouldn't cause a maiden to lose her supper upon viewing me, and yet our child is... not like either of us."

Dasa struggled to speak for a few moments. Israel knew that lies did not come naturally to her and was amused watching her find judicious words to counter his statement. "He won't always look this way," she finally allowed. "You needn't hold his present appearance against him. He's been through a lot in the last hour, and one doesn't look one's best after a battle."

"You always do," he said, shifting his gaze up to her face. "You emerge from even the hardest fight looking as if you could do it all over again."

She gave a half shrug, but he saw one corner of her mouth curl up in acknowledgment of the compliment. "That's different. I am a warrior."

"And he is *my* son—is that what you're saying?"

"Now you are reading an insult where one was not intended," Dasa countered quickly. "I simply said that I am used to battle, whereas our son—Deosin—hasn't had a chance to learn my ways, yet."

"*Our* ways."

Dasa inclined her head. "Our ways. He will be our salvation."

Israel was silent for a few minutes, running his fingertip alongside the pink fists of the babe. Deo was asleep, and for a moment, Israel wanted to wake him up. Would his son have the blue or gray eyes of the Starborn, or would he bear the amber eyes of the Fireborn? "Do you believe that, Dasa? In your heart, do you believe it?"

She glanced away from him and addressed the two handmaidens who lurked in the room, tidying and waiting to be of service to their mistress. "You may leave me. Return in ten minutes."

The women bowed, shot Israel a curious look, and left silently. Dasa waited for the count of twenty before answering. "We made this child because of the prophecy. Do you now doubt it?"

Deo's arm twitched. Israel lifted the little fist and studied it. "It's so minute, so perfectly formed, this hand. It even has tiny little fingernails. And yet it's almost impossible to believe that this blotchy, red-faced little frog could be the one person to bring peace to Alba."

"He had better be," Dasa said with a touch of acid in her voice. "After what I went through bringing him into this world. Not to mention having to consort with a Fireborn in order to do so."

Israel was annoyed for a moment, but decided that she had earned the right to make a few digs at his expense. "You aren't my first choice for a life partner either, my sweet."

She grimaced at the endearment, as he knew she would. "Then it's a good thing we are not wedded, isn't it?"

He leaned close and kissed the tip of her nose. "You may not like me any more than I like you, but that doesn't mean you didn't enjoy the making of this babe."

"Sexual pleasure is hardly a fitting topic of conversation," she said primly, but the corner of her mouth twitched again. "The future is. We should have Deosin's future read now, before the night breaks."

"It can wait. You are tired and need rest, and he is sleeping."

She shook her head, a familiar flash of stubbornness in her eyes. "It must be done tonight, while the moon is still up."

"His future has already been foretold—"

"That was before he was born." She pulled a silk rope hanging alongside the bed. "I have a very good sage. It was she who predicted that your seed would find favor nine months ago. She will cast Deo's fortune and reassure us that he is the one we have waited for."

Israel hesitated for a moment before rising and glancing out through an open window. The goddess Bellias in the form of the moon was low on the horizon, just setting about her path across the night sky, a time when all right-thinking Fireborn were tucked up inside beside fires and family. And here he was, far from home, in the land of his enemies. "And if she doesn't give us that reassurance?"

When he glanced back over his shoulder, Dasa's gaze was on their son, her expression unreadable. "She will. She has to. My people are tired. Yours are decimated. We can't go on like this many more generations before Alba is destroyed."

He said nothing, returning to his examination of the city that lay outside Dasa's stronghold, and his dark thoughts. A tap at the door interrupted those thoughts, and he turned to watch silently as a surprisingly young woman entered the room, bowed before her queen, and shot Israel a worried look.

"Cast your runes," Dasa ordered the sage, who bowed again, and knelt before the side of the bed, one hand on the swaddled bundle.

Interested despite himself, Israel watched as the young woman sketched symbols in the air that glowed first pale blue, then turned silver, before dissolving into nothing.

"Arcane runes?" he asked Dasa.

Her brows rose slightly. "Are there any other kind?"

"Yes. My seers use bones and leaves." He allowed a little grimace to twist his face. "They aren't terribly accurate. They told me that our child was destined for a life of betrayal and sorrow."

Dasa drew the child closer to her in a protective move that relieved some of Israel's worry about leaving his son in the care of the woman against whom he'd fought his entire life. "Your sages are rubbish. Ciandra has never failed me."

"Never, my lady," the woman said, still drawing one-handed symbols in the air. As the last one faded, she shook her head, cast a quick glance over to Israel, and began the process again.

Dasa shifted uncomfortably in the bed.

"Do you have need of one of your women?" Israel asked, wishing to help her, but knowing she would reject any such offer.

"Not yet. I want Deo's future read first; then we will sleep." A little frown creased her black brows when she watched the sage repeating her symbols. "You are slower than normal, Ciandra."

"I know, my lady, and I apologize." She slid another glance toward Israel. "The runes... I'm having some trouble making them understand that it is the child they are to predict for, and not... not him."

Dasa's lips tightened. "I have just been praising you. Do not now make me look a fool for doing so."

"No, my lady." The sage continued to draw symbols in the air, her face tight with concentration, and her arcanist's robes rustling softly with the increased movement of her arm.

Israel turned back to the window, about to resume his contemplation, when the sage gave an annoyed click of her tongue.

"It is not—they won't—I'm sorry, my lady, but the runes are not cooperating."

Dasa propped herself up on one arm. "What is it they are saying?"

The sage lowered her head and stared at the floor, her voice as soft as the night air. "They say a time of great trial is coming."

"What sort of trial?" Israel asked.

The sage struggled for a moment, then spoke one word. "Invasion."

"By whom?" Dasa demanded, her fingers digging into the silken bedcovers. Her gaze found his, and he fought against the need to flinch at the suspicion in it. "From where?"

"I know not, my lady."

"When will the invasion happen?" Israel demanded to know.

The sage made a gesture of frustration. "I... the runes do not give a date. They simply foretell an invasion."

Israel held Dasa's gaze, his face a mask, but inside, suspicion fought with anger. Would the sage lie in his presence in order to hide plans Dasa had to destroy the Fireborn? But no, that made no sense. Why would Dasa want him deceived when she'd just given birth to the one who would, at last, bring the two warring races of Alba together?

"What do they say about my son?" Dasa asked, her eyes narrowed slits of silver when they turned to the young woman. "What do they say about the ending of the Third Age?"

The sage's shoulders quivered for a moment; then she looked up, her face as pale as snow. "They say nothing, my lady. There is no mention of the savior who will bring upon us the Fourth Age. It is as if..." She hesitated, swallowing hard. "It is as if he does not exist."

Israel wanted to snatch up the child and remove him from this place, this homeland of his enemies, and, without thinking, had moved toward the bed, but he caught the expression in Dasa's eyes at that moment.

She was the greatest warrior he'd ever known—goddess knew how many times he'd fought her, a sword in one hand, and a staff in the other—and yet he saw a flicker of fear in her eyes.

The knowledge struck him in the belly almost as if it had been a physical blow: she was afraid for their child. Would she really arrange this elaborate plot if she held such fear for Deo's future? Even as Israel watched, she pulled the babe into the crook of her arm, protecting the swaddled form.

"The runes are wrong," she said at last, her voice as stark as the pain in Israel's gut.

"My lady, I wish they were, but—"

"They are wrong!" Dasa said loudly, and with a jerk of her head dismissed the sage. The young woman scurried out, a strangled sob following the sound of the door closing behind her.

Israel stood helpless, unsure of what action he should take. They had prayed to the goddesses for so long, Fireborn and Starborn alike, and at long last, oracles of both races received identical messages: the joining of bloodlines would end the desolation of the Third Age and bring on the peace and prosperity of the Fourth. But now... he shook his head. "What will you do?" he asked at last.

Dasa lifted her chin, her gaze defiant. "We will do what we always do. We will prepare. We will defend what is ours. And we will survive."

"And the invaders?"

Her lip curled in scorn. "The runes are wrong. But if they come, they will soon learn the error of their ways."

The meaning of her words was quite clear to Israel. He squared his shoulders, reminding himself that although he had drawn up the terms of the accord with the Starborn, it was not to be put into place until their child was recognized by both races, and the Third Age ended.

Now, with the words of one slim girl, that fragile hope for peace was gone.

"So be it," he said, and, with one final glance at the child, left the bedchamber.

Chapter 1

"Is that a body?"

It took a few seconds for the question to filter through Deo's dark thoughts, but at last the words pushed past the bubbling sense of injustice that had gripped him ever since his father had told him he was too young to attend the upcoming council meeting of the Four Armies. He looked up, his eyes narrowing on the mound in the road ahead, instantly dismissing it as not worth his time. "It doesn't look like a person. It's probably a dog."

Lord Israel pursed his lips in the way that annoyed Deo to no end. "I believe it is a person. How tiresome of the locals to discard their bodies on the road. It will have to be moved. Marston!"

"My lord?" One of his father's men rode up beside them. That, too, annoyed Deo. Why did everyone jump the second his father spoke? They treated him like a god, someone whose every whim must be instantly accommodated.

"There is a body ahead."

"Indeed, my lord, so it appears."

"Have it removed and given to those to whom it belongs. They must inter it properly lest Kiriah be offended."

"It shall be as you demand, my lord."

Deo's lip curled at the toadying steward. Never would the day dawn when he allowed himself to lick his father's boots as the others did.

"Now, where were we? Ah yes, a discussion of your behavior at the Temple of Kiriah Sunbringer. The head priestess, Lady Sandorillan, is an old friend of mine, Deo, and I would have you remember your manners around her."

He ignored his father to continue fulminating over the unfairness of his life. He had seen fourteen summers! Others his age were already out fighting with his father's army, but not him. Resentment simmered hotly, causing his fingers to tighten on the reins.

"I've allowed you to come with me on this visit because I think it's time that you see the true plight of those who we serve. You are a Langton. The welfare of our people must always come first in your thoughts." Lord Israel halted his horse as two of his men moved toward the body lying in the road. "I expect you to remember just who you are, and what you owe to me while you are in the presence of Lady Sandor."

"What do I owe to you?" Deo asked, all but snapping off the words. "You treat me like I'm a child, gullible and unlearned and ignorant, but your own sergeant-at-arms says I am the best of all the fighters."

"You get your prowess at arms from your mother, no doubt," Lord Israel said dryly.

"Then why can't I visit her? She must surely have much more to teach me than I can learn in Abet, and I—"

"It is out of the question," his father interrupted, the words spoken with a sense of finality that further enraged Deo.

"But why? You always say that, but you never tell me why! You never let me do anything! I am my mother's son just as much as I am yours; I should be able to visit her if I want!"

"It's out of the question," repeated Lord Israel. "It's not safe for you in Genora. That is why your mother sent you to live with me when you were naught but a babe, and that is why you will remain here."

Deo thought darkly upon his father's words. He'd always been told that his mother had sent him from his homeland, but why would so brave a warrior as she do that? It had to be a tale his father had concocted to keep him from her. Everyone knew his father hated the Starborn. He had no doubt that the queen would have come to claim him long ago, but for the invaders that blighted Genora.

"But I am *not* a babe now," Deo growled. "I am a man, and I want to learn—"

"Then you will learn here," Lord Israel said firmly. "The invaders who came at your birth are more powerful than you can imagine, and your mother and I agreed that it was best for you to remain with me, where you will learn the ways of the magisters."

He was surprised at that, and for a moment, hurt flashed through him at the thought that his mother might really have been complicit in his removal from the land of his birth; but suspicion about his father's motives immediately flooded back. Israel Langton was born of a long line of magisters and wanted his only child to follow in that tradition.

"Bah," Deo snorted, disgust all but dripping off the word. "The magisters are weaklings. Their earth magic heals, but it does not blast a foe into the lap of Kiriah Sunbringer. It is nothing compared to a good sword."

"There is more to the magisters' art than just healing, which you would know if you took the time to attend your lessons. No, do not continue to argue, as I see by your sulky expression you wish to do. If you want to convince me that you are an adult, and not an emotional boy railing against authority, then you must prove it with your actions."

Deo was about to answer with a surly word or two, but just then the body in the road sat up. The two men-at-arms who were about to carry him off the road recoiled, and shrieked in surprise. A tall, gaunt boy with a shock of silver-blond hair got awkwardly to his feet and faced them, dirt smudged over every available surface. It was almost impossible to tell how old he was, given his appearance, his ragged and torn clothing, and the wary, hunted look about his eyes.

"By Kiriah's breath!" the boy gasped, rubbing his face, and managing to smear even more dirt on an already filthy visage. "You almost ran me down!"

"We thought you were dead," Lord Israel said smoothly, eyeing the boy with mild interest. "Who are you?"

"Hallow." The boy scratched first his head, then his arse, before making a jerky bow. "My name is Hallow."

"Well, Hallow, you might reconsider your choice of sleeping venues in the future. Does your family reside around here?"

"No, they are dead." The boy peered out from under a clump of hair, his eyes watchful.

Deo stiffened when the boy's gray eyes flickered over to him. He knew that to this wild, unkempt boy, he must appear exactly what he was—the pampered child of a powerful leader—and that made him feel intolerably uncomfortable.

"And I wasn't sleeping," Hallow finished, shoving his hair out of his eyes. "I... I haven't eaten in a while, and I fell insensible for a bit."

There was something in the boy's voice, a defiant note that Deo understood well.

"You must have someone to whom you belong," Lord Israel said in what Deo thought of as his (irritating) patient voice. "Tell me where your people are, and I will see to it that you are returned to them."

"They're all dead," Hallow said with a shrug of one of his thin shoulders. "They were killed by the Harborym."

"You've seen them?" Deo asked before he realized he was speaking. "What do they look like? Did you kill them? It is said they have a powerful magic unlike anything known—did you see this magic?"

"Deo!" Lord Israel said sharply. At the same time, Hallow answered, "I was very young. I don't remember them at all."

"A life on the road alone is not one for a lad as young as you," Lord Israel told Hallow, giving Deo a side-look that warned of a lecture in the very near future.

"I am fifteen summers," the boy argued.

"Are you? You look much younger. Well, regardless, we shall have to find someone with whom you can live."

"My lord," Marston murmured, standing at the side of Lord Israel's horse. "If I might suggest, the tavern keeper in the town we just left mentioned there was a traveling arcanist from Genora who sought an apprentice, but no one in the town would allow his son to be given over to such an ill-favored occupation. The boy would be fed and trained with him."

"An arcanist," Lord Israel said dismissively at first, then, eyeing the boy, said slowly, "It is indeed an unsavory magic, but all things have their purpose, or so Kiriah teaches us."

"I would like to learn from the arcanist!" Deo blurted out. "It is the magic of my mother's people. I should know of it just as I know of the earth magic of the magisters."

Lord Israel said nothing of the outburst, nodding down at the man at his side. "Fetch some bread and apples for the lad and have one of the men take him back to Deacon's Cross to deliver him to the arcanist. Better he should learn of arcany than be found dead of starvation on the road."

"But—I don't want to go to Deacon's Cross," the boy protested when one of the soldiers grabbed him by the back of his tattered tunic, although his eyes had lit at the mention of food. "I just came from there. I was driven out of the town for stealing cheese, as a matter of fact, so I really don't think they will want to see me again—"

Hallow's squawks died away as he was hustled in the direction from which the company had just come. Deo felt a pang of mingled envy and regret. For half a second, he wished he could switch places with the boy. What would it be like to go where he wished and do what he wanted? Instead, he was coddled and treated as if he were made of eggshells. The only reason his father had allowed him to train with the soldiers was that Deo had made it clear time and time again that no amount of beating (intended to keep his feet in the schoolroom and out of the training yard) would stop him from learning the ways of an armsman.

In both his build and his temperament, he favored his mother, and he would not let anything stand in the way of his learning how to be as great a swordsman as she was reputed to be.

"There is something I must discuss before we arrive at the temple."

Deo slid his father a look. It wasn't like him to speak with such an obvious note of hesitancy in his voice.

Lord Israel stared straight ahead. "You know that I go to consult with Lady Sandor about the invaders who are at present inhabiting Genora."

"I know that you have done nothing to rescue my mother or her people," Deo said, and for a moment thought he might have gone too far.

But rather than reprimanding him for being so outspoken, his father smiled briefly. "I hope I live so long as to see the day when your mother needs rescuing by anyone, and when the day comes that you see her again, I advise you to keep such an opinion to yourself. But that is not why I speak now to you—Lady Sandor is wise, naturally, else she would not be Kiriah Sunbringer's handmaiden. But she is also suspicious of those of us beyond the temple walls, and she might wish to know if you are in agreement with me regarding the invaders."

"The Harborym," Deo said, rolling the word around on his tongue. He'd heard only whispers of the word before this trip and knew his father had kept all talk of the invaders from his ears. And to think the boy Hallow had actually witnessed them in action. True, it was in the act of slaughtering his family, but Deo would have given much to see them in person.

"Yes." Lord Israel looked stiffly uncomfortable as they rode along the dirt road to the temple. "Your mother entrusted into Lady Sandor's care something valuable, a boon of sorts, to be kept until… well, that is neither here nor there. It is a birthright your mother intended for you, and Lady Sandor may ask if you wish it to be used. Naturally, you will assure her that you do wish this."

Deo stared at Lord Israel in surprise. What was this? A birthright that no one had told him about? And why was his father looking so uncomfortable about it now? "What birthright?"

"It is a boon, as I said." His father waved away the question. "What matters is that should Lady Sandor ask, you must say that you agree to its use now."

"How can I agree if I don't know what it is?" Deo asked, quite reasonably, he thought.

His father evidently felt otherwise. "It is of no matter."

"I think it is, if it is mine to use."

Lord Israel's lips thinned. "Deo, understand me—we must present a united front to Lady Sandor. If she suspects that we are at odds with respect to the invaders, she will withhold all but the most minimal support. Now is an important time. Your mother and I are in agreement that we must act before it is too late, and I will not have you put our plan in jeopardy because of imagined slights and abuses."

"You have spoken to my mother?" Deo was prepared to be outraged at his father for keeping him from the woman who must so desperately want him by her side.

"I correspond with all the leaders of the Four Armies, as you well know, including the Starborn."

Deo pushed down the sting that came with the knowledge that his mother was in communication with his father, but not him. No doubt Lord Israel kept from him any letters his mother had sent him.

"I would have your word on this, Deo. I do not know that Lady Sandor will wish to consult you, but if she does, you must be ready to reassure her."

Deo squared his shoulders, frustration making him want to lash out. "You expect me to show compliance, but you won't tell me what is behind that order? What plan do you and my mother have? Why won't you tell me anything?"

"It is a complicated situation," Lord Israel said through gritted teeth. "One that you are not yet equipped to fully understand. You must trust that I am doing the right thing—ah, we arrive."

The horses halted at the tall stone and wood gates, through which two women and a man were emerging with laden pack mules. A woman in the blue robe of a priestess of Kiriah manned the door, and she lifted an eyebrow when Marston hurried forward to announce Lord Israel's august presence. For a moment, Deo hoped she would refuse his father entrance, but she gave a sharp nod when Marston gestured toward the company of twenty men.

"Lady Sandor is expecting your arrival. The men-at-arms may go to the stable, where they will be brought refreshment. If Lord Israel will accompany me, I will alert Lady Sandor."

"Do not forget what I have said," Lord Israel murmured as they rode through the gates. "This is of more importance than you can understand."

They rode past large fields of wheat, golden under the blessing of Kiriah, and smaller fields with green growing things, the smell of sun-warmed dirt filling the air. Everywhere there were women in blue tunics or robes tending the crops, carrying baskets of goods, or gliding smoothly along well-worn paths with heads bowed and hands folded in front of them.

It looked like a tedious, boring life, and for once, Deo was grateful that his father, while a believer in the power of Kiriah Sunbringer, was a traditionalist, and did not expect his son to learn the ways of the goddess.

They stopped before the entrance to the temple and dismounted, two men taking their horses to the stable yard. Deo stood awkwardly behind his father, uncomfortable in his chain mail with the sun beating down upon him, but he knew a true soldier was always ready, always prepared, and if that meant donning the approximately twenty pounds of padded tunic and leggings, along with the mail armor itself, then so be it. He would suffer in silence. Noble silence, he corrected himself, and lifted his chin.

Those priestesses in their light tunics or robes knew nothing of the hardships soldiers embraced. They would snap like twigs under such demands. With other such smug thoughts, he prepared to follow his father into the temple.

"I'm sorry, but Lady Sandor said only that your lordship was to be allowed into her chamber," the woman from the gate said, holding up a hand to stop Deo.

Relief flickered across his father's face, but he quickly schooled it back to his normal stoic expression. "We will naturally respect Lady Sandor's request. Deo, you may go to the stable with the others if you like, or perhaps stroll around and study how well Lady Sandor runs the temple."

Deo considered feeling insulted that he wasn't welcome in Lady Sandor's presence, but honesty made him admit he really didn't want to have to sit and be polite. He'd much rather see what armaments the temple had, and if there were soldiers to guard the demesne lands. He stood with his back to the temple doors, scanning the grounds. There were numerous small outbuildings in addition to the large stable, but there didn't seem to be any soldiers other than those of his father's company. He was considering his options when he caught sight of a slight figure pressed against the wall of a building, half-hidden behind the stables.

It wasn't so much the figure—a girl dressed in the same blue as the other priestesses—but her body language that intrigued him. He crept up behind her, as silent as an owl's wings gliding through the night air, wondering if she intended ill to the members of the temple. Perhaps she was a spy. Or worse, a thief.

Righteousness rose within him, strengthening his resolve to know the girl's business. Never let it be said that he would allow a possible thief to operate right under his nose!

Chapter 2

"Lala, you may recite. Start with the forming of Alba."

I was on my way past the temple with a brace of freshly caught rabbits in one hand when familiar words drifted through an arched window. I paused at the sound of the words that followed, spoken in a child's high, clear voice.

"First there was the void, where darkness and evil reigned supreme. Then the twin goddesses Kiriah and Bellias decided to bring sunlight and starlight to the void, and so the sun and stars were created."

"The sun, the stars, and the moon," an older voice corrected. That had to be Peebles. No one else had the patience to work with the younger children.

"But there are only two goddesses. Shouldn't there be one for the stars, and one for the moon?" the child answered, causing me to smile to myself. Truth be told, I had nothing but sympathy for Lala, since being tested on the priesthood of Kiriah had caused me many a nightmare. Not only had I never seemed to retain the pertinent facts, but I was always full of questions concerning the contradictions in the lore presented as fact.

"Bellias is both the moon and the stars," Peebles corrected. "Proceed."

"Kiriah created the race of the Fireborn, and they were blessed with the grace of Alba, while Bellias formed the Starborn, and they were not graced with anything, and no one likes them."

"Lala!"

I covered my mouth to keep from laughing out loud at the scornful note in the child's voice. I had only a vague memory of Lala, since my path did not often cross those of the younger initiates, but I liked her spirit. Idly, I summoned up a small rabbit made of Kiriah's blessed light. It hopped along my outstretched arm while I leaned against the wall and listened.

"We do not denigrate anyone, no matter whether they were Starborn or not. Continue."

"But no one does like them," Lala argued. "They are responsible for the Harborym coming to Alba and blighting the Starborn because they were evil and deserved it."

"Now, where did you hear anything so outrageous?" the priestess asked.

"It's true, isn't it?" Lala asked, and I remembered asking similar outrageous questions when I was her age. I frowned at the rabbit and it dissolved into little wisps of sunlight. The memory of the day my parents had left me at the temple brought back intense feelings of abandonment and confusion.

"The Starborn, seeing the grace of Alba given to the Fireborn, were sorely jealous, and complained to Bellias, who demanded that her people, too, receive the powers that were rightfully given to the Fireborn. But Kiriah was a just goddess, and she would not take the grace from us, so Bellias smote the Fireborn with arcane power, leaving only three survivors. And because Kiriah loved us, she turned the power of the sun onto Alba and punished the Starborn until the very streams and oceans screamed for mercy."

The singsong familiarity of the words wrapped around me, the pull of memories separating me from the present. A pair of light does, about four inches high, formed on my boots, then leaped off to frolic, almost hidden, in the long grass before me. Idly, I watched them, my mind tangled in the past. I knew why my parents had given me up to the temple—they were simple people, and unable to cope with a child who had unique abilities— but oddly, I held no grudge against them.

Sandor, though...

"Eavesdropping?"

The roughly whispered question from behind me caused me to spin around, gasping as I beheld the boy who had crept up behind me, "Goddess! You startled me."

I would have mistaken him for a soldier who had not worn his helm, but the spikes of black hair hanging over his amber eyes belonged to a boy, probably one not much older than myself.

"What are you doing here?" the boy asked, his words arrogant, but there was something about the way he rubbed his arms that reminded me of Ham, the blacksmith's son, at his most awkward.

I made a show of looking him over, noting that he wore full armor and had the broad chest and long legs of a fighter. "I could ask the same thing. Who are you?"

"You will answer my question before I answer yours," he answered with haughty disdain. Immediately, he grimaced. "That sounded just like my father."

"Is that bad?" I smiled, realizing who he was. "You're Deosin Langton, aren't you? The others were saying your father was coming to see Sandor, to beg her for help. They said you were a grand lordling, and ride a great white stallion. Is that true?"

"No, my horse is black," he said, turning a little pink. "And I'm no lordling! I'm a warrior, like my mother. What are you doing here?"

"Listening to Peebles and Lala. Peebles is the priest in charge of the young children." I nodded toward the window.

"You can't be much older than a child yourself," he said, with lofty disregard for the fact that I was almost as tall as he was.

"I'm not a child. I'm a priestess. I was so anointed earlier this year, and I have seen the passing of fourteen years. My name is Allegria."

"Alla-GREE-uh," Deo said, pronouncing the syllables carefully, just as if he wasn't sure whether he liked them or not. "That's an odd name."

"And Deosin isn't?" I nudged him with my bow.

He gave a rueful smile. "Most people call me Deo."

"Blessings of Kiriah upon you, Deo," I said formally, and drew in the air the traditional grace of Kiriah.

He bowed awkwardly in return. "And grace of the goddess to you, Allegria."

I turned away from the schoolroom, my stomach rumbling warningly. "Are you hungry?"

He glanced down at the rabbits. "Yes, but those would take a while to cook, and I don't know how long my father intends to stay."

"Oh, these aren't for us. I caught them for Bertilde, the cook. Come on. I have a secret stash of apples that I keep hidden from the younger girls."

Deo followed without objection, and ten minutes later we were seated cross-legged in the hayloft. I tossed him an apple from the homespun bag I hid from the younger initiates.

"I don't believe you're a priest," Deo said around a mouthful of apple. "You're clearly a cook's servant, else you would not be out hunting for rabbits."

"That shows how little you know about being a priest." I pushed my hair, ever wild with curls that refused to be tamed, behind my ears and bit into an apple, savoring its tartness. "I'm very good with a bow, and sometimes, I get some rabbits or birds for Bertilde. Why is your father here? The older priests won't tell me anything, but that's because they're all too busy giggling over him."

"Giggling?" For a moment, Deo looked outraged.

"You know. They think he's *sooo* handsome." I made exaggerated googly eyes and kissing noises before returning my expression to normal. "Sandor says your father's visit heralds a bad omen, that the dealings of the world beyond the temple have no meaning to us, but I think she's wrong. I mean, if the world is destroyed by the invaders, then we're going to be affected, aren't we?"

"My father seeks a boon to use against the invaders," Deo said, reaching for another apple.

"Oh." I was disappointed. I had hoped that Lord Israel would be seeking aid from Sandor. The thought of being able to leave the temple, of fighting alongside the soldiers, had filled my head like nothing else. On the other hand, perhaps this was just the opening I needed. "Has your father raised an army to fight the invaders? Does he have archers? I'm very good with my bow, and if Sandor gives me leave to fight, I could go with him today."

For a moment, I thought Deo might laugh, but with a glance down at the dead rabbits, he gave a shrug instead. "I will ask him, if you like, although there are not many women in his company who are not magisters."

I bit deep into another apple and offered him a third. Juice ran down my chin, which I wiped off with one hand while pressing his arm with the other. "Would you? I know priestesses do not often go to war, but it is not unprecedented. Sandor herself is said to have fought long ago against the giants that sleep deep beneath the surface, and I have begged for the chance to fight the invaders."

I kept to myself Sandor's acid response to my many requests.

Deo leaned back against a beam and said smugly, "I'm going to fight the invaders. I'm going to Genora to fight the Harborym."

"Harborym?"

"That's the name for the invaders, although no one around here likes to say it out loud. I'm going to free my mother's people from their enslavement to the Harborym, and I will live there, and my mother will teach me to become as great a warrior as she is."

I eyed him. "You are big like a warrior. Are you good at fighting?"

"I am," he said with absolutely no modesty, and held up an arm. "I train for seven hours a day."

Obligingly, I leaned forward to feel his biceps beneath the chain mail. Deo suddenly grabbed my shoulder and pulled me closer, a hand on one of my breasts, his mouth warm as he kissed me. I was startled by the gesture, but not fearful, since the blacksmith's son was forever trying to kiss me. Deo's kiss was different from that, though. It was warmer, less wet, and apple-scented. I allowed the kiss to go on for a moment, wondering if this meant that I was smitten with him, before I pushed him back, and picked up my half-eaten apple. "That was nice, but I don't think you should do it again."

"Why not?" He looked wounded, and I wondered if that was his first kiss. The fact that his face was hot and red gave weight to that suspicion, but I didn't want to hurt his feelings by asking. "I thought girls liked to be kissed."

"Some do," I said after considering how best to discourage him.

"And you don't?"

"It's all right, but it's nothing I sit up nights thinking about."

His gaze dropped to my chest in very male appreciation. "*I* liked it. I like all of you. If you want to do it again, I'm happy to oblige."

I thought about it, then shook my head, and chomped into my apple. "You're very handsome, but I'm a priestess, after all. I'm supposed to be above such things."

"If you don't like dalliances, then what is it you sit up nights thinking about?" he asked.

"I think about what you're doing."

Startled, he just stared at me until I took pity on him.

"You get to fight with your father. That's what I really want to do. It's why I'd be so grateful if you asked your father whether I could join his company." I tossed the core aside and got to my knees, clasping my hands together in the manner of supplication to Kiriah. "I could fight the invaders alongside you. I'm fast with my bow, and I've recently convinced the blacksmith to teach me swordplay, so I'm sure I could pick that up fast enough. And I have a special power—"

"Deo!"

The word echoed through the barn with the power of a cannon shot. Below us, the mules whinnied, while outside, the sounds of male voices ordering the company together brought Deo to his feet. "That was my father."

"Who has seen my son? *Deo!*"

"I'll go with you," I said, scrambling down out of the hayloft after him. "I could go with you now, if Lord Israel likes. Right now. I have my bow here. I wouldn't even have to go back to my room to gather my things—I don't have much anyway—if you could lend me a sword."

Deo ran out of the stable with me on his heels. To my surprise, Lord Israel was already mounted, his face red with fury. What on earth had

Sandor done to so enrage him? I glanced toward the temple entrance, but there was nothing to be seen except Feliza, the porter.

"For the love of the goddess, where is my—Deo! I have been calling this past age for you. Come. We will take our leave of Lady Sandor, since she refuses to see reason."

Deo looked as if he wanted to argue but, after a moment, took the reins of his horse and mounted quickly. I hurried to his side, wrapping my fingers around his horse's harness while I made my plea. "Will you ask?"

Deo looked down on me, his eyes shaded.

"Please," I whispered, glancing at his father.

Deo nodded, and turned toward his father, gesturing to me as he said, "There is a priestess here, one who has abilities with the bow—"

"Priestess," Lord Israel snorted, and put his heels to his horse, calling over his shoulder, "I have had enough of priestesses to last me a lifetime."

"I'm sorry," Deo said, watching as the company followed his father. A pale red cloud rose from the dust of the track, drifting slowly toward us. "I will ask again, later, when he is calmer."

Sadness and regret filled me. Reluctantly, I released my hold on the harness and stepped back, feeling that yet again, opportunity was slipping away from me. "Thank you. You won't forget?"

"I will not forget you," he promised, and galloped off to catch up with the others.

I didn't know whether I believed him or not. I knew only that I remained trapped, a prisoner of fate.

My shoulders slumped as I turned to the stable, hopelessness making each step feel like a hundred.

Chapter 3

"Master, you have to get up. You're going to be trampled if you don't move. There is a rider approaching, and I don't like this forest. It has a bad feeling about it."

The man who lay prone across the narrow dirt track did not move. A fleeting memory caused Hallow to recall the time before he had met Master Nix, when he was lost and alone, and so hungry he once passed out in the middle of the road.

"And that led me to you, you old reprobate." Hallow sighed and shook his head before shoving the cart he'd been hauling up a steep bank onto the thin strip of a verge, while also disentangling himself from the rope harness that five years before—when he had been newly apprenticed— had been borne by a horse. "Master! For the love of the twin goddesses, you must move!"

It was clear that, once again, Master Nix had drunk himself into a stupor, this time falling off the cart where he'd been sleeping.

Muttering to himself, Hallow scrambled back down the bank and dragged the once-famed arcanist from the track, one eye on the approaching rider. "If you... Kiriah's love, you weigh more than the loaded cart... didn't drink your weight in wine... erg! It's like shifting a bag full of bulldogs... then we wouldn't have fallen behind... ratsbane, are you made of anvils?... the rest of the convoy." With one last heave, he managed to get his master up the bank and onto the thin strip of grass.

Hallow stood panting a little, casting a glance at the approaching rider. The man appeared to be wearing the armor of a highborn, but these days, it didn't do to trust appearances.

He brushed the dirt from his hands, his back feeling itchy. It was the woods surrounding the road. They had an unhealthy feel, as if a thousand eyes were watching... and waiting.

Hallow scanned, for the thirtieth time since descending into the valley, the line of ash and willow trees that spread like a fan from the winding track. The air seemed thicker here, almost torpid, with a profound silence that raised the fine hairs on the back of his neck. Not even the birds he could see in the trees made a sound.

Something was definitely *not* right.

"The sooner we find Lord Israel, the happier I'll be," he told his master, who had rolled a few feet before coming to a halt against the cartwheel. Hallow stood next to him, scanning the woods once again before shading his eyes to watch the approaching rider. "We'll just let this man pass, and then—by the moon!"

Before his amazed eyes, a scene unfolded just as if it were drawn by one of the traveling artists who used to travel with Master Nix. The rider, resplendent in the white and gold armor of Lord Israel's army, had just passed into a section of the track where the trees crowded oppressively close, when from them burst a half-dozen men. They were dressed in the green and blue of the Harborym, although only one of them bore the squat, powerful form that Hallow had heard the invaders exhibited.

The men leaped upon the rider, dragging him from the horse, attacking him with fingers curled into claws. Without even realizing he was moving, Hallow ran down onto the track, one hand automatically drawing a protection rune on his chest while the other began gathering arcane power from unseen stars above. The first blast bowled down the five men beating the rider in white, while the second was aimed at the Harborym.

"Goddess grant me the power of stars and moon and heavens," he chanted, gathering up more starlight, his mind focusing and forming it into the arcane explosion that would end the attackers who were flinging themselves upon the downed rider. *"Light of stars. Light of moon. Light of heaven, all before me is dust!"*

He released the energy of the starlight, watching with satisfaction as it smote the men who were clawing and beating the rider.

Only the Harborym remained, and just as Hallow turned his attention to him, and began the chant once more, the Harborym released a wave of red power at him—chaos power, Master Nix had called it—but all Hallow knew was that it was made of pain.

Agony washed over him, seeping into his pores, digging with sharp, stabbing spikes into his flesh and blood right down to his bones. He fell screaming, instinctively calling on the power of the moon and stars, but it was midday, when the starlight was at its weakest.

A shadow loomed over him. Blotting out the light of Kiriah's sun was the squat, thickset shape of the Harborym. It filled him with loathing. These beasts, these monstrous invaders, had murdered his village before being driven from Aryia's shores, slaughtering his parents and siblings, and every living being, in the process.

Except him. He alone had survived, and that only because he had been out in the fields watching the swallows.

A bird had saved his life, only for it to be lost now, in a dirt lane in a foreign land, with a drunken master, and an unknown rider. It all seemed rather ridiculous when one looked at it that way.

"I did not survive the purging of Penhallow only to die like this," he roared, throwing upward the power that he'd gathered from the weak starlight. It knocked the Harborym back, allowing Hallow to get to his feet. Although every ounce of his being hurt, he pulled from his scabbard the sword he'd named Nightsong and raised it high.

The Harborym lifted his hands, a red light glowing between them, clearly about to fire more chaos magic, but at that moment, a miracle happened.

The Harborym's head went flying to the right, bouncing off the trunk of an ash tree, leaving an unpleasant red smear on it. Hallow stared for a moment at the spot where the head had come to rest (fittingly, in a pile of rabbit droppings), before turning to look at the man who stood before the crumpled body of the Harborym.

"Nicely done," Hallow said, slowly lowering his sword.

"Thank you. I wouldn't have had a chance if you hadn't distracted him first." The man limped forward, blood staining his white armor, multiple cuts on his head and arms freely bleeding. Other than that, he looked relatively hale. He was tall and narrow of build, but clearly had the strength needed to behead a Harborym.

Hallow narrowed his eyes on the man. His savior had golden brown hair, with eyes a similar tawny color, both of which marked him as a Fireborn, but that wasn't what stirred deep memories too fleeting to grasp.

He gave a mental shake of his head and turned to survey the five inert bodies.

His savior did the same. "Didn't hear them coming. Treacherous bastards. I'd be dead now if it weren't for you."

"I'm happy to help a fellow Fireborn," Hallow said. "But I've never seen men like these."

"That's because they aren't men—they are Shades."

"Shades? They are spirits, then?" Hallow nudged one with the toe of his boot. "Are you sure? They feel all too real."

"Shades are not spirits, although if they could reason, I'm sure that would be their dearest wish." The man eyed him curiously. "Shades are what result when the Harborym are finished enslaving Starborn. You have blue eyes."

Hallow blinked his very blue eyes. "I do."

"But your coloring is wrong for a Starborn."

"I am an arcanist." He wondered if he'd have to explain how prolonged manipulation of arcane power changed the eye color of the practitioner to blue, but evidently his savior was a learned man.

"Ah, that would explain it." He dragged two of the bodies to the side of the road. "These must have been a scouting party."

Hallow assisted, asking, "Are you with Lord Israel's army?"

"You could say that." The man turned and whistled for his horse, who obediently trotted up and nosed him in the back. "I *am* Lord Israel. And the name of my brave defender is...?"

Hallow, in the middle of sheathing his sword, stared for a moment. "My lord, I had no idea. I would have come to your aid sooner had I known—"

"You saved my life," Lord Israel said with a wry smile. "You killed five Shades and distracted the Harborym so I could separate him from his head. There is nothing more you could do to aid me. But I do not know who you are."

Hallow bowed, his hand on his chest. "I am Hallow of Penhallow, in the region of... Hallow."

Lord Israel looked at him with one eyebrow raised.

"My parents thought it was amusing," Hallow said, resigned to the snicker that would follow the telling of his name.

"Indeed." To his surprise, Lord Israel clapped him on the shoulder. "Whatever your parents' odd proclivity toward naming their children, you are most welcome in my company at any time."

"This is not the first time we've met," Hallow said when Lord Israel turned to his horse.

"It's not?"

Hallow was very aware of the amber eyes studying him.

Lord Israel frowned. "I have no memory of you."

"That's likely because I was a young lad at the time. You found me insensible on the road to Deacon's Cross and sent me to my master, Nix of Winyard."

"Ah, I believe I remember something of a boy in the road." Lord Israel shook his head after a moment's thought. "But I thought I sent the boy to be an apprentice to a magister, and no magister alive can control arcane power."

"Master Nix is an arcanist, not a magister. He is most learned in the ways of the Starborn and was taught by the head arcanist of Queen Dasa many years ago," Hallow said with pride.

"Indeed. And where is this most learned man?" Lord Israel asked, glancing around.

Hallow nodded toward the verge. Lord Israel climbed out of the lane to the wagon while Hallow followed, explaining their presence. "Master Nix has taken a bit too much wine, I'm afraid, but I will try to awaken him. We were on our way to Abet when he fell... er... indisposed."

"He might have been indisposed before, but this man is dead." Lord Israel stood up from where he'd squatted next to the wagon. "Judging by the color of his face, I'd say it was due to a fondness for the grape."

"Dead!" Hallow knelt before his master. He checked first for a pulse on his neck, then held a hand before Nix's mouth. There was no stirring breath. "Kiriah's nipples! This will mean the end."

"The end of what?" Lord Israel made a face. "Other than him, that is."

"Of me. Of my career as an arcanist." Hallow sighed, stood, and, with an effort, scooped up the heavy form of his now deceased master, and laid him gently on the cart.

"How did a Fireborn such as you come to bind yourself to this old degenerate?" Lord Israel asked, pulling off his cloak, and despite his harsh words, covering the old man's corpse.

"He wasn't a degenerate when you sent me to him," Hallow said, then smiled. "Actually, I suppose he was. The Harborym destroyed my village when the first of them came to Aryia. Before you drove them out, that is. I was alone—I had no one—so I ran wild for a bit, rather like a feral dog. Then some monks found me and told me I would become a scholar and learn how to wield the grace of Alba, but I..." Hallow stopped, feeling that he was on the verge of saying too much.

"But you did not wish to become a monk?" The look in Lord Israel's eyes was mingled amusement and understanding.

"Not so much, no. I never fit in with them, you see. I wasn't humble, or particularly penitent, and they disliked my high spirits. So I ran away, and was on my own again. I wanted to see Aryia, to have grand adventures, but times were hard, and no one wanted a boy who had no family. That's when you stumbled—almost literally—over me. Master Nix wasn't any too pleased to see such a wild youth, but he taught me the rudiments of arcane magic so that I would never be hungry again." Hallow gave a little smile at the memory and snapped his fingers. In his hand, a little ball of pure starlight glowed. "He told me this trick would get me a meal in any tavern across the land."

"Most unusual," Lord Israel said, and, when Hallow slung the rope harness across his chest, helped shove the cart back onto the dirt track. "I have known of only one other Fireborn who could handle arcane magic, and he died when I was a child."

"There were a few, from what I was told, when Master Nix swore to teach me its secrets. He said only arcane magic could combat the Harborym's chaos by purifying it, and he claimed he was the only one who knew how to do this, since the queen's arcanist had fallen to the Harborym. That's why we were going to Abet, so that he could offer you that information… for a hefty price, no doubt. But now…" Hallow gazed back at the covered form, sorrow mingling with frustration. "Now the knowledge he held is lost."

"Don't be so sure," Lord Israel said and gently buffeted Hallow's shoulder before climbing into the saddle. "Where there is one who holds the knowledge, there is bound to be another."

"In Genora, possibly, but how am I to get there? How am I to find another such arcanist?"

"Come with me. I have need of a man of learning. My magisters are being consumed by their attempts to learn the ways of chaos magic, and you could well do what they cannot."

"Master Nix may have believed that arcanists can purify chaos magic, but I assure you that I cannot," Hallow objected, then—because, at this point, his future held little promise—added, "but it was always my master's intention that we offer our services to you should you go to war. And I will abide by that plan."

"Come to Abet, as you intended, after burying Nix," Lord Israel said, pulling a button from his tunic and pressing it into Hallow's hand. "We will discuss it there. I am convening the Council of Four Armies, and the Master of Kelos should be there."

"The head of the arcanists?" Hallow thought for a moment. Although Nix had had nothing but ill to say about the man who ostensibly led the arcanists scattered across Genora, it might be that under him, Hallow could learn all that had been snatched away by his master's death. He tweaked the cloak over Nix to cover him more fully and, after glancing to the sky, nodded. "Very well. I will meet you there."

"Until then." Lord Israel rode off without a look back. Hallow, still made uneasy by the area, shouldered the rope and pulled the cart onward.

It took Hallow three days to get to Abet. His master had been buried in a graveyard in a busy seaport a day's ride to the north, although it cost Hallow the last of his few precious silver coins to pay for the burial and prayers to Kiriah. He was hungry, tired, and dirty when he arrived in the capital city, its shining blue-tiled rooftops glistening in the afternoon sun.

"This is just about as auspicious as the first time I met Lord Israel," he said to himself, brushing off the dust of the road while standing outside the council chambers, waiting to be admitted. "Except this time, I'm conscious."

"What say you?" a servant at the door asked, turning from where he waited for the signal to admit Hallow.

"I was reflecting on the past," Hallow answered, amused. He knew well the image he presented: travel-stained, in the robes of an arcanist, and apparently with the light eyes of a Starborn. It was clear the servant answering his request to see Lord Israel would have pushed him from the keep, had not Hallow shown the golden tunic button. Even now, he felt that at any moment a group of guards might sweep down on him and throw him into the dankest of dungeon cells.

The door behind him opened, and an upper servant with a sour expression gestured him in, saying in a hushed voice, "Lord Israel will see you as soon as he is done with Lord Deo."

"Is that Lord Israel's adviser?" Hallow asked softly.

"No, it is his son." The servant rolled his eyes dramatically. "Do you know nothing?"

"Evidently not. I'm a stranger to these parts."

"Stay here, next to the door, and when Lord Israel is finished, he will call you forward." The servant gave him a hard look before slipping out the door, leaving Hallow in an antechamber that opened up to a bigger, more spacious room.

It was lit with the dying golden orange light of the fading sun, navy blue shadows creeping eastward from the massive table that dominated the main room. Upon it were stacks of books and scrolls, maps spread wide, held down by mugs and various implements. Next to the table stood the man who had saved Hallow, his arms crossed while he watched a second man pace in front of him.

So that was the famed Deo. Master Nix had mentioned there was a son, but had little to say other than he was the son of the Starborn queen, and his birth was said by many to have heralded the arrival of the Harborym two years later.

The man who paced five steps before turning and repeating the action didn't look as if his mere birth had introduced the destruction of his mother's people, but then again, Hallow mused, what was such a man to look like? This one was as tall as Lord Israel, but broader, with a fighter's rolling gait. He had the Starborn's usual dark coloring, although his eyes belied his mixed blood. That he was angry was quite clear, even to Hallow, stuck in the antechamber.

"Why do you not listen to me?" Lord Israel said, his voice rough with exasperation. "All I ask is that you, for once, heed my warnings."

"Warnings?" Deo snorted and paced past his father, turning before he added, "Perhaps that's because you refuse to explain why I should heed them."

Lord Israel rubbed the spot between his eyebrows. "I've told you at least twenty times that chaos magic is too powerful for those born of Alba. Only the Harborym can control it. The arcanists have no idea how to treat it, and our magisters—"

"Are dead, consumed by their ignorance," Deo finished, turning to stride back past the table and his father.

"Consumed by the very power that you try to control, and that is why I forbid your study of it."

"I am not a magister," Deo said, spinning around and marching over to face his father, his face red with emotion. "They are weak. Of course the chaos magic consumed them—they have no knowledge of its ways, how it persuades one to give control over to it, but I do."

"And you think you can succeed where almost an entire order of magisters has failed?" Lord Israel shook his head. "Of the original forty-seven, only three remain. Deo, I know you believe yourself to be invincible, believe your mother's people to be the chosen ones, but must I remind you yet again that it is those very people who are lifeless husks enslaved by the Harborym? If Dasa's arcanists could not force chaos to submit to their will, you will not be able to do so."

"I will! I have! I have found a way to consume the magic, stripping it of compulsion, and leaving only the pure power. Can you imagine what we can do with that? We can rescue my mother, rescue the Starborn, and drive the Harborym back to their nightmare realm. We will have the power to free the Shades from their bondage, to restore to them that which was lost."

"Chaos is the power of death," Lord Israel said, his shoulders slumping as he leaned against the table. "There is no restoring life with it any more than there is the ability to control it."

"You do not know!" Deo roared. "But I do, and I will show you!"

Hallow's eyebrows rose. Clearly, Deo had dabbled in the chaos power, but surely he wasn't foolish enough to continue if it had proved so deadly to others learned in magic? That seemed like the sheerest folly, a sentiment that

Lord Israel evidently shared, because he grabbed his son's arms and snarled into his face, "I forbid it! You cannot succeed. It will mean your death."

"You have no knowledge of what I can do," Deo said, shaking off his father. "You have not lifted so much as one finger to aid my mother and her people, but I will not sit by and be content to guard our borders. I will save those who have no savior."

"You will become that which you rail against," Lord Israel argued. "Did the destruction of the magisters teach you nothing? You will become a monster just as they did. The power will consume you and turn you, and in the end, just like them, you will die writhing in agony. I would wish a better life for my son."

"What life would that be?" Deo asked in a taunting voice, turning away from his father to look out the window. Hallow saw his face and was disturbed by the harsh lines etched there. Deo's shoulders were slightly hunched, as if he were in pain. "To sit by and do nothing, like you?"

"You are old enough to take a wife. Have children. Then you will see the importance of preserving our way of life for others."

"A wife?" Deo turned to look at his father. "You speak of Idril."

"I speak in general," Lord Deo corrected. "Although there is much to admire in Lady Idril."

"She will not have you," Deo said with a cockiness that for some reason annoyed Hallow. "It is I she wishes to bind herself to, not you."

Lord Israel took a deep breath, clearly desirous of remaining calm in the face of his emotional son. "Do not make me act against you, Deo. If you pursue this path, you will leave me no choice."

Deo returned to gazing out of the window, but the fine hairs on the back of Hallow's neck stood on end. "And what if I already have?"

"It cannot be. I would know if you had." Lord Israel sounded infinitely tired, but it was Deo who held Hallow's attention.

Something about the younger man was wrong. Very wrong.

Deo's voice was curiously flat. "As I said, you do not know what I can do."

Hallow took a step forward at the flash of red in Deo's eyes as he turned to face his father. "The power is within me. It is mine to control. I, alone, will master its ways, and when I have learned how to wield it, you will—ungh."

Deo doubled over and dropped to his knees. Hallow stopped at the entrance to the room, unsure whether his assistance was needed. Lord Israel didn't wait to determine what was wrong, though. He rushed past Hallow without seeming to even see him, and flung open the doors, shouting, "Call for the magisters! Immediately!"

Hallow watched Deo, still on his knees, his breath a harsh panting, his fingers white with strain as he clearly underwent some sort of an internal struggle. "No," Deo said, his voice laced with anguish. "No, I will not allow this... urng. I... am... master..."

"Stay back," Lord Israel told Hallow as he reentered the main room, followed by three men in the red cloaks of Fireborn magisters.

"If I can help—"

"No. I have prepared for this day. I feared it would come." Lord Israel hurried into the center of the room, gesturing toward Deo. "Quickly, surround him. The runes must be drawn before the banishment, lest the chaos consume him."

"Banishment?" The words came out of Deo's mouth with the roughness of gravel. His eyes no longer resembled the amber of his father's and were now as red as a pigeon's blood, while the lines alongside his mouth deepened, his lips twisted into a grim line of agony. Slowly, he got to his feet, his body wracked and twitching as he struggled to gain control. "That is your solution? To banish me so that I might die without witnesses? No, stay away from me! I will not allow you to destroy me!"

This last was spoken to the three magisters who surrounded him, drawing runes in the air.

"Don't be a fool, Deo," Lord Israel snapped. "The runes will protect you. They are the only thing that kept the last magister alive... until the strain was too much for him."

"Let me be. I will control this on my own—" Deo stiffened, and, to Hallow's horror, the same red wave of magic he'd experienced from the Harborym blasted out of Deo, hitting his father full in the chest.

"Hurry." Lord Israel gasped, doubling over. "He must... the only way... will be safe."

Hallow rushed forward and caught his savior as he fell, his eyes on the three magisters as their chanting increased, and their hands danced upon the air, heaping rune upon rune onto Deo.

"No!" Deo bellowed, his back arched in pain as he struggled to resist the magic that was encasing him. "I will not—"

The last word was drowned out by a cacophony of noise triggered by an explosion of air, knocking Hallow onto his arse. Even after the noise stopped echoing in his ears, it seemed to vibrate around and through him. Hallow's eyes widened when he realized that the explosion had caused Deo to evaporate into nothing.

One of the magisters fell to the ground, apparently insensible, blood dribbling from his ears. Hallow had never seen anything like the magic just performed, and looked down at Lord Israel. His face was gray, but his chest rose and fell. A clatter of noise behind them heralded the arrival of several servants and guards.

"He's alive," Hallow told the nearest servant, who threw himself on Lord Israel's legs and began wailing. "But you might fetch a healer."

Lord Israel was carried off, as was the magister who had collapsed. Hallow wanted badly to speak to the other two, but they hurried off with hushed words and furtive looks toward him. In a remarkably short time, he found himself alone in the council room, his mind bemused by the experiences of the last hour.

After considering for a long time what was best to do, he rose, and went to see if there was a bathing hut. He had a feeling he might be in Abet for a little while, and he was covered in the dirt of the road.

It was too bad about Deo, he mused as he went in search of a servant. He would have very much liked to know just how one consumed chaos magic.

Chapter 4

"Die, you fiend!" I whirled, as a blade spun near my head, nearly lopping off my left ear, but luckily only catching the edge. "Ack!"

Instantly, my combatant dropped his axe and pulled my hand away from where I'd clasped it against my head. "Allegria! By Kiriah's blessed toes, what have I done?"

We both looked at my bloody hand. My ear had just been grazed by Thorsin's axe, and although it stung, it wasn't a pain I couldn't bear.

"I'll tell you what you've done," I said with deceptive smoothness, before whipping the tip of my sword to his unprotected throat. "You've dropped your weapon."

He rolled his eyes, shoving away my sword before bending to retrieve his axe. "That I did, but only because you weren't paying attention and almost lost an ear. This is no game, priest. If you wish to spar with me, then I expect you to pay attention. Lady Sandor won't appreciate it if I send you home maimed and bleeding."

The clang of the hammer against the anvil punctuated Thorsin's words. I made a face and reluctantly sheathed my sword. "It was a ploy, a cunning ploy intended to throw you off-balance, and it worked."

"Mmhmm." Thorsin wiped down his massive axe, and gently wrapped it in a clean bit of soft leather before donning the blacksmith apron that protected him from sparks and fire. "If that's true, then there's nothing more I can teach you. You have gone beyond my skills."

"Aw, don't say that." I pulled out a small package, consisting of a loaf of round bread and a hard nub of the cheese my fellow priests made, and pressed it into his hands as payment for the lesson. "You're the only one in Temple's Vale who will teach me. How am I to improve if no one will let me practice with them?"

"You don't need practice, little priest. I thank you for the payment. Did you, perchance, make the cheese yourself?"

I couldn't help but laugh at the idea. "I'm the least domestic person at the temple." I glanced to the west, where Kiriah Sunbringer was beginning her descent toward the distant horizon. "And speaking of that, I'd best be getting back before Sandor ends her afternoon meditation."

"Tend that ear," Thorsin called as I ran off down the dusty red track that led to the temple grounds. "And mind you, say a prayer to Kiriah for missing your daily devotions in order to spar with me."

I raised a hand to let him know I'd heard him, and trotted on, my mind wandering down familiar paths. If only I'd managed to convince Lord Israel all those years ago to take me into his company. If only Sandor understood that I was better able to serve the temple by use of my bow and swords than the endless prayers to Kiriah. If only I was allowed to use the power that had been given to me at birth...

I slipped over the fence where a stream crossed under it, hidden by the sparse copse of trees from the view of the porter at the main gate, pausing just long enough to grab the string of pheasant I'd shot earlier in the day, and hurried past the temple gardens, occasionally nodding and murmuring a greeting when a priest passed me, arms invariably full of produce on the way to the kitchen.

"...and Lady Sandor said that we were not to include them in our prayers, but I think that's wrong."

I stopped abruptly as I rounded the corner of the temple, where voices issuing from the covered walk caused me to hide behind a pillar.

"Well, they are Starborn. Why should we interest ourselves in their welfare?"

I gnashed my teeth for a moment at the sight of Catriona and Geer, two of the older priestesses who frequently looked upon me with disdain and suspicion. They stood between me and the door to the vestry, where I needed to be.

"Because Kiriah's love is boundless. Perhaps if we showed it to the Starborn, they would see the error of following Bellias."

I turned around, intending to enter the temple by the side door, even though the risk of being seen was higher there, but gave a little startled jump at the sight of the woman who stood silently behind me. "Oh! Hello, Sandor. I didn't see you there."

"Obviously not." Sandor glanced at the four pheasants hanging by their feet from a short length of twine. "I must be confused about the day, because I could have sworn you were scheduled to be conducting prayers today."

My gaze slid away to study the temple grounds, a haven of round green shrubs, lush grass dotted with lavender flowers, and the graceful, arched trees that grew in this part of the world. Adding in the sweet scents of the flowers, the busy drone of bees, and the high calls of birds, one would think this place was a veritable paradise, but I knew it was nothing but an attractive prison. "I thought I would better serve Kiriah by providing for the sisters. After all, the initiates are praying today, and surely the goddess doesn't need more than four prayers at a time. Any more than four would be wasteful, don't you think?"

The priestess's lips twitched twice, but she had a firm grip on her emotions, something I knew well given the number of times I'd been sent to Sandor's study in order to receive what was politely called *correctional guidance*. "Your actions do you credit, child, but your intentions could use a little more devotion to Kiriah."

"I know," I said with a sigh. "But it's just so hard. There's a war out there, and people are fighting for their lives, fighting to save an entire race."

"The Starborn have brought this blight upon themselves," Sandor said blithely. "Their queen welcomed the Harborym when they first came, whereas our own good Lord Israel rejected their offer to help us bring all of Alba under the domain of the Fireborn. And if the destruction of the Starborn is not a sign from Kiriah of the wrongness of their ways, then I don't know what is."

"They haven't *all* been destroyed," I argued. "There are still Starborn. I heard from the blacksmith that not all the Starborn were taken in the Consumption. Lord Israel should take his army to Genora again and free them."

"Pfft." Sandor waved away the idea. "Lord Israel tried that once a few years ago."

How well I knew that. I felt again the pain of being left behind when Deo rode off after his father, leaving me with no hope, trapped at the temple, and bound to a goddess who seemed to care little about my happiness.

"And look how that turned out," Sandor continued, turning to stroll toward the main entrance. I fell in alongside her. "His army was decimated, and there are no Starborn left. They've all been turned into Shades and are slaves to the Harborym. Thus, it is not worth his time to save them. The Shades can't be saved, not that he would wish to do so."

"His own son is half-Starborn," I couldn't help but point out. "No doubt *he* feels it worthwhile to help any of his kin who escaped the Harborym." She gave a ladylike snort at the mention of Deo. "And just look what the result of that unholy union was—an invasion that destroyed the race that bore him, and then he went mad with the power of the Harborym and was banished."

"But there was a prophecy that said he would bring about the Fourth Age, and prosperity and peace, and—"

"No, child. It was a false prophecy. That much is clear to us now."

"Even so, is it not our duty to help those in need? If you won't send a group to help find survivors who have escaped the Consumption, what about sending us to battle alongside the soldiers fighting the Harborym themselves? I would be happy to lead such a team—"

Her lips tightened even before I finished speaking. "Your duties lie here, child."

"I'm not a child! I could be of so much more use outside the temple!" I wanted to shout my frustration at the priestess, but held my temper in check. I knew from experience that such outbursts would be greeted with chastisement, and little more.

"You are of greater use here." She started to move past me, clearly having dismissed the subject, but I stopped her.

"To do what? Pray? That's all we do!"

"Prayer is important," Sandor protested. "Without it, how would Kiriah know we needed her blessings in this time of great trial?"

"She hasn't heard us since she smote Alba with the fire of the sun," I said with a bitterness I could almost taste. Oh, I knew well that I should keep such thoughts to myself, but as ever, I was unable to stop myself from speaking aloud. "Both goddesses have turned their backs on us since that time. Everyone knows it."

Ire flashed in Sandor's eyes, and she grabbed my wrist in a grip that I knew would leave bruises. "Everyone does *not* know such a thing. It is heresy you speak, and you will cease doing so this instant, or you will force me to punish you." Her words struck me as if they had barbs. "It is our honor and duty to guard the goddess Kiriah's temple, and guard it we shall. Do you understand?"

"A group to help fight the Harborym would aid much more in preserving the temple," I said, wresting my wrist from the painful grip of her fingers. "There are several sisters who are almost as proficient as I with the bow, and I've been teaching them what I know about how to use a sword—"

Her words shot at me with the force of my own arrows. "I am well aware that you are under the delusion—indeed, you have been since you were first brought to us—that you were meant by the goddess to fight evil, but I assure you that in this, as in many other things, you are incorrect."

I slapped my hands on my legs in sheer frustration. "I am a lightweaver! Even if Lord Israel would have no use for my bow or my sword, I have the power to help!"

"Your power is devoted to Kiriah, and nothing else!" Sandor snapped, making a dismissive gesture. "No! No more protestations. The words you speak are foolish and show me that you have yet a long way to go before you are granted any position of importance. And lest you forget, let me remind you that you were given to the temple for a purpose, and I shall see to it that you serve it, no matter how hard you fight against your destiny. Take those pheasant to the kitchen, and then I expect you at the altar with the initiates."

Dismay filled me at the idea. "But... they are to be in prayer all day and night."

"Exactly." Sandor gave me a look that was about as soft as steel. "A night spent on your knees in prayer to Kiriah contemplating your blasphemies and stubborn nature will do you good."

I opened my mouth to protest, but Sandor held up a hand to stop me. "Not one more word, lest I condemn you to the contemplation chamber for a week of solitude. Go about your business, and do not repeat your opinions on this subject to anyone else. The last thing I need is you instilling such inappropriate thoughts in the sisters' minds."

Sandor bustled off, leaving me bristling with indignation, fury, and a profound feeling of helplessness.

"And I hate feeling helpless," I growled to myself, stalking stiff-legged to the building that housed the kitchens. "It's so wrong. I could be helping people. I could be fighting against the invaders. I could be making a difference."

Bertilde, one of the cooks, looked up when I entered the cool confines of the pantry and slammed down the pheasant. "There, now, Allegria, that's just what we're needing for supper—a nice pheasant pie. Merciful goddess, what has you in such a tizzy?"

"I am to pray," I said abruptly, removing my bow and quiver from where they were slung across my back. "That is all Sandor considers me good for."

"Aye, well, we are a devout order," Bertilde said, nodding. Her face was naturally red, but now it was also dotted with perspiration, no doubt from working over the ovens contained in the next building. "Mind you, I don't say that there's not such a thing as too much prayer, and not enough hard work, but there, I'm not the head priestess. Thank you kindly for the birds."

"You're welcome." I dipped a cup into the water barrel and slaked my thirst before asking (more to stall my return to the temple than anything else), "How fares your brother Jack? Is he still watching the coastline for invaders?"

Bertilde's face clouded. "No, he's run off to join Lord Deo."

"On the Isle of Enoch? How is he going to get to there? The harbors are all watched closely lest the Harborym attack, and no captain would sail there."

"Merciful goddess, what would Jack be doing on the Isle of Enoch? He has no need for such perilous travel, because Lord Deo has returned to Aryia," Bertilde answered, snatching up a pheasant and expertly beginning to pluck it. "Jack said Lord Deo is gathering up a group who will use some form of new magic to free the Shades from Harborym control. Not that I have any hopes such a harebrained plan will work, even if Lord Deo *has* found a new magic. The Shades are past redemption. They are nothing but husks, a shell and nothing more. It's best to let them be, and not try to cross the goddess's will."

My jaw sagged in amazement. "Deo is back? But he was banished! His father banished him to Enoch when he tried to kill him."

"When who tried to kill whom?" Bertilde asked absently, her arms and apron now stained with feathers and blood.

"Deo tried to kill Lord Israel last summer. Didn't you hear about it? That's when Lord Israel banished Deo to the Isle of Enoch, which I have to say was rather harsh. Sandor said there is nothing there but rocks and scrawny goats."

"I can't believe a father would do any such thing to his son, not one he raised since he was a wee babe."

"That was just because Queen Dasa had Deo sent to Lord Israel for safekeeping when the Harborym opened their rift in Starfall City," I said, poking through a bowl of chopped vegetables and popping a couple of pieces of carrot into my mouth. I added, indistinctly because of the carrots, "It doesn't mean Lord Israel was happy to have him."

"Pish," Bertilde said dismissively. "What father isn't happy to have a son?"

"Lord Israel, evidently. Or at least he isn't when his son attacks him."

"I don't remember hearing about any such happening, but I don't keep up much with those higher born." She gave me a complacent smile. "I'm just a simple priest in a simple temple, as are you. Jack keeps me informed of any news fitting for me to know. And Lady Sandor, of course."

I hooked a three-legged stool with a foot and sat down, happy to have an excuse to delay my return to the temple, even if it was to be short-lived. "Well! Ham, the blacksmith's son, says it all came about because Lord Israel wed the woman Deo was betrothed to, a highborn named Lady Idril, who was from the north. Ham said that Deo had a great passion for her, but that Lord Israel wanted to punish his son, and so banished him and wed her himself just to spite Deo."

"Tsk," said Bertilde. "Imagine a father wanting to punish his son so strongly that he took his bride. What must Lord Deo have done to bring that curse down upon his head?"

"I don't know. Ham didn't tell me that. He did say—"

"Allegria!"

I was on my feet and hurrying out past Sandor at the door before she could do more than beg the goddess for the strength to deal with the trials life brought her. I ran back to the temple, Bertilde's news rolling around in my brain. So Deo was back in Aryia, was he? And he was gathering his own force to go to Starborn lands and save his mother's kinfolk? My heart raced at the idea of joining him, of working alongside the man who had so captured my fancy years before as a child. But how was I going to convince Sandor that it would benefit the temple to release me into Deo's service?

The goddess must have been smiling on me, for when I trotted from the warmth of the day into the coolness of the temple, I found a group of three men wearing mail armor clustered together at the entrance, one of them demanding that the porter fetch Sandor at once.

"But Lady Sandorillan is communing with the goddess," Feliza, the porter, said, her long silver hair gleaming in the soft lights of the candles that lined the aisle. I tucked a strand of my own unruly hair behind my ear and wished, for the thousandth time, that I had been graced with the silver hair of the highborn, instead of the bland dirty straw-colored hair of what Bertilde called hearty peasant stock. "She cannot be disturbed for anything."

"This is important," one of the men said, clearly in charge of his group. His voice was as rough as his appearance—his face was scarred, and he appeared to be missing part of an ear—but the mantle of authority sat firmly on his shoulders. "We come on behalf of Lord Deo Langton. He seeks a boon of the goddess, one that was promised him at his birth."

"I don't know anything about a boon," Feliza answered, clutching her hands together and looking as if she was about to burst into tears. "Only Lady Sandor would know what to do, but she is communing."

"Is it true that Deo has returned to Aryia?" I heard someone ask, and was mildly surprised to find the voice was my own.

The man turned his head to give me a look that plainly stated he wasn't the slightest bit interested in talking with me. "Yes, he is gathering his forces now for the transformation." He turned back to Feliza. "Fetch Lady Sandorillan, or I will send my men hunting for her, and I doubt if your delicate little priestesses would enjoy having their temple searched."

The men chuckled as if an uncouth joke had been made. I eyed them, wondering if Kiriah would forgive me for spilling blood on her sacred temple floors.

"Oh, dear." Feliza wrung her hands again and cast a look full of appeal toward me. "I can't do that, indeed I could not. I would lose my position should I disturb Lady Sandor. And you cannot come any farther into the temple. Men are not allowed in the inner recesses of the Temple of Kiriah. It is most forbidden!"

"What transformation?" I asked, using the tip of my bow to scratch an itch on my back. Feliza shot me another pleading look of desperation, but I ignored it. I wanted some questions answered before I threw these louts out on their respective arses.

The headman looked confused at my question.

I clarified. "You said Deo was gathering forces for a transformation. What kind of a transformation? Magical, physical, or something else?"

He dismissed my question immediately, while the other soldiers looked down their noses at me even though they were only a little taller than I. We hearty peasant stock may not have the silver hair or delicate features of the highborn, but we are also not slight of figure, a fact I frequently bemoaned.

"It is nothing a *priestess* like you would understand." The headman sneered while he spoke, clearly trying to insult me. He turned back to Feliza, and shoved her out of the way. "I tire of your excuses. Let us search the temple for Lady Sandorillan."

I whipped the bow off my back, and had the arrow nocked and aimed right at his exposed throat before he could blink. "I am no ordinary priest, *soldier*, and you heard Feliza—men are not allowed farther into the temple. What is this force Deo is gathering?"

He blinked at me a couple of times, eyeing the arrow with the respect that it deserved. His Adam's apple bobbed before he answered. "He is *Lord* Deo to you, priest. And just what are his actions to do with you?"

"I might be interested in joining his force," I said boldly, feeling that it was now or never—the arrival of these men right here, at the moment when I most wanted to make use of my gifts, told me that the goddess Kiriah herself intended for me to walk a different path from the one I'd been set upon.

Besides, I told the anxious voice in my head, it wasn't as if I were leaving the priesthood for good. I was simply taking a little hiatus to do good works out in the world.

To my disgust, all three men burst into loud, obnoxious laughter. They laughed so hard, the headman actually had to wipe moisture from his eyes. At last, when he could speak, he said, "You? A priest? Lord Deo has need of fighters, not those who would spend their days in prayer. Lower your weapon, holy woman, or I will have my men teach you what a grave crime it is to raise arms against us."

The whisper of steel sliding against steel sounded softly behind me, causing me to spin around. I let fly one arrow and had the second on its way before the first landed.

"Kiriah's nipples!" the first man cried when the arrow pierced his mail armor and pinned it to the wooden paneling behind him. The arrowhead caught only the mail and the cloth of the tunic beneath, missing the man's flesh, just as the second arrow did. By the time the headman finished staring at his two compatriots' sword arms pinned to the wall, I had another arrow aimed at his chest.

"It is also a grave crime to pull a weapon in the Temple of Kiriah Sunbringer," I said with a look that by rights should have scared the man half to death.

To my surprise (and no little amount of annoyance), he tossed back his head and laughed a second time. "It seems there is more to you than is first seen," he acknowledged at last, making me a little bow.

"You would do well to remember that," I said, lowering the arrow. "Now tell me about the force Deo is gathering."

I thought for a moment that the headman would ignore my request, but a glance at his men struggling to remove the arrows from where they were embedded in the wall evidently caused him to think again. "You are persistent, if nothing else. Lord Deo seeks an elite group of fighters and those skilled in magic to travel to Genora to free his mother and her people. It is nothing that even a sharp-eyed priest like you could manage, however, so you may stop trying to convince me to take you to him. You do not have the skills he seeks."

"You have no idea what skills I wield," I said softly, my eyes on Feliza, who had been slowly edging away until she was at the metal gate that closed off the main part of the temple from the entrance, where the laypeople prayed. I waited until Feliza quietly closed and locked the metal gate and scurried off, no doubt to tell Sandor of the intruders. At the sight of her pale blue robe fluttering around a corner, I asked, "Where is Deo gathering this elite force that I am not important enough to join?"

"*Lord* Deo won't have you," the man said, shaking his head at me. "Not a priest. You have nothing to offer him."

I thought about the time, many years before, when Deo and I sat in the loft of the stable and exchanged what I knew now to be a very inexperienced kiss. "Where is the force gathering?" I repeated.

The headman hesitated a moment, then shrugged. "In Deacon's Cross. But do not expect to see Lord Deo, and do not harbor the hope that your bow-arm will be needed. He sees no one these days but his body servant, and only the best fighters and magic wielders will be chosen to round out this elite group. We have archers aplenty."

"He'll see me," I said with a little smile at my memories of our time in that loft.

"Don't count on it, little priest," the man said, then turned to see where Feliza had escaped. "Damn me, she's gone. Now we'll have to search—"

"There's no need to make me shoot you where you stand for attempting to breach the temple," I said calmly, and gestured toward the locked wrought iron gate. "I'll bring the boon you seek."

He hesitated, giving me a visual once-over that left me all too aware of my ungainly self, my untamed hair, and the dirt that stained the bottom of my robe. "You won't be rewarded by a meeting with Lord Deo, if that is what you are thinking. As I said, he sees no one."

"He's going to have to be seen sooner or later if he wishes to lead a force all the way to Genora," I pointed out. "But wrangling a visit to his bed is not my purpose, if that is what you are imagining. I offer to bring the boon because I don't wish to have to kill you. Kiriah has blessed this place, and I suspect she would not appreciate blood spilled here for such a trivial reason."

The headman took a step toward me, leaning in until his breath brushed my face. "Do not think your threats hold any sway with me, priest. I will allow you to bring the boon only because I do not have time to search the entire complex for the head priestess. But do not tarry with your task. We leave at the rise of the moon."

I gasped at his words even though I knew it was stupid to be so superstitious. "You set sail under the light of the moon?"

A smile curled his lips, and for the first time, I realized he was actually a very handsome man under all those scars. "Lord Deo is half-Starborn. Do you think he fears the light of the goddess Bellias?"

"No, but…" I made an awkward gesture. "It's folly to sail without sunlight."

"Lord Deo is the child of the greatest queen Genora has ever known, and she is graced by Bellias herself." He gestured toward his men, who finally freed their sleeves from the wall. "Do not be late, or I will be sure Lord Deo knows who failed him. Come, we ride to Colburn to meet with a man who bears Kiriah's grace."

The men left the temple, their boots sounding loudly as they made their way out to their horses. I stood in the doorway, leaning against it as I watched them ride out of the gates, headed to the little town of Temple's Vale.

"Deacon's Cross," I murmured to myself, thinking furiously. If I stole one of the temple mules... no, not steal, that would bring down the wrath of the goddess... if I *borrowed* one of the mules, then I could be at Deacon's Cross well before moonrise. But that meant I'd need to get the boon from Sandor's chamber now, pack the things I'd need, and make my escape while everyone was having their evening meal.

Would Kiriah forgive me for temporarily abandoning her worship in order to bring right to the wrongs of the world? I bit my lip, not sure of the answer, but knowing my heart had already committed to the action.

Spinning on my heel, I rattled the gate until Feliza appeared to unlock it.

"Did you find Sandor?" I asked, picking up the hem of my robe with one hand and clutching my bow and quiver with the other.

"No, she was going out to see to the evening meal, and then go along the stream to pick herbs," Feliza said. Obviously, she would have chatted about the men who'd just darkened our doorstep, but I ran off to my small chamber before she could do more than say, "What did you say to get them to leave—"

I was already planning how I would slip into Sandor's rooms to fetch the boon—which I knew was contained in a gold-chased box that sat in pride of place on a small altar in her bedchamber—and which path I'd take to the stable. "Goddess willing, no one will realize I'm missing until the initiates are done with their prayer tomorrow morning," I breathed, and sat down to write a note of explanation to Sandor, along with a promise that I would return as soon as I could.

Kiriah, I felt, would understand my reasons for taking my fate into my own hands.

Deo was an entirely different matter.

Chapter 5

"Deacon's Cross," I told Buttercup the mule as we jogged along the track heading east to the coast, "is a much bigger town than you are used to. Where Temple's Vale is small and compact, Deacon's Cross is a port city."

Buttercup swiveled her ears around so she could listen to me. Of all the mules kept by the temple, she was my favorite. She was curious, didn't take any guff from the horses she met in our little local village, and made no bones about the importance of keeping her happy. I kind of felt like she was an equine extension of myself.

"I tell you this because I don't want you acting skittish when we get there." I shifted in the saddle, flexing my posterior muscles. I wasn't used to riding for more than the few minutes it took to get to Temple's Vale, and Buttercup's trot was not the smoothest. "Also, I will be finding someone to take you back to the temple, so that the goddess doesn't smite me where I stand for borrowing you without sending you home, and I will expect that you'll behave yourself with whomever I find to do that. None of your 'That shrub is a monster! I must rear and throw off my rider' shenanigans, if you please."

Buttercup snorted disgustedly, but I took the fact that she didn't, in fact, try to throw me as a sign of her compliance.

I looked around as we rode through the country. Rolling fields of grapes undulated to the south, while to the north, the vineyards gave way to lush grasslands dotted with sheep and cattle. The farther east I rode, though, the sparser the land, until at last I started spotting gulls in the air and noticed the faintest hint of salt on the wind.

"Greetings," I said when I rode up on an elderly couple driving a pony cart laden with what appeared to be their household goods. "Blessings of Kiriah on you."

"And to you," the old man said, nodding and bobbing his head. "May the goddess smile upon you this day."

"Thank you. Are we far from Deacon's Cross, do you know? I haven't been there since I was a child, and I don't remember how much longer the trip will take. Since the sun will be setting soon…" I left the rest of the sentence unspoken. There wasn't a Fireborn alive who didn't understand the desire to be tucked up safely inside when the sun went down.

"You're a priest," the man said, nudging his wife, who was dozing. "Old woman, look who I found on the road—a priest from the temple."

"What? What's she doing this far from home?" The woman rubbed her wrinkled round face and blinked rheumy blue eyes at me. "That's no priest, old man."

"She is. She's wearing the robes of a priest."

"She's armed to the teeth. That's one of Lord Israel's soldiers, that is."

"She's wearing the robe," he argued.

"Your eyes are bad, you old coot. She's got a bow hanging off the saddle, and two swords crossed over her back. Those are soldier's weapons!"

"Actually," I said, interrupting the argument, which showed signs of becoming quite heated, "I hope to be both. I am a priest now, but I'm hoping to be taken into Lord Deo's regiment. Do you know how long it will take to get to Deacon's Cross?"

"Another three hours," the old man said, nodding. His head was bald with just the merest fringe of white hair running around the sides and back, but his eyes, despite his wife's opinion, were keen. "You won't get there before sundown. You'd best stop at the next village and spend the night."

"Thank you, but I must press on. I have important business with Lord Deo. Blessings to you both." I sketched a rune in the air, causing the same rune to glow briefly on their respective foreheads.

"Did you see, old woman? She blessed us with good fortune," the man said, nudging his wife again.

"Of course I saw. I'm sitting right here, aren't I?" she grumbled, but flashed me an almost toothless smile and bobbed her head at me. "That was right nice of the soldier to take her time to do that. But don't let that give you ideas, old man! I don't want you gambling at the village just because you bear a blessing…"

I left them arguing about what good a blessing was if you couldn't use it (I hadn't the heart to tell them I'd blessed them with protection rather than fortune) and, humming to myself, continued my journey.

It was a good two hours past nightfall when we made it into Deacon's Cross. By then I was on foot, leading Buttercup in order to give her a break, and I was both excited and a little intimidated by the bustle of the town. The only other time I'd been there, I was a mere child, and in the company of all the other new initiates who were to be blessed by the archpriest. It seemed to me that the town was bigger now, with sprawling neighborhoods in which the citizens were out and about even at night. Tall torches were lit, some set against housefronts, others freestanding, illuminating round patches on the silvery cobblestones, the pungent smell of smoke mingling with those of food, spices, and humanity.

There were food vendors calling their wares and waving bowls, from which emerged tempting smells. There were shops with exotic cloth, the light spilling from the opened doorways and unshuttered windows to highlight pools of ruby, sapphire, and rich plum textiles. There were metalworking shops, with highly polished brass bowls and lanterns that glinted softly in the firelight.

People thronged in the street, laughing and talking and calling to one another, women with baskets over their arms, and shawls draped over their heads against the night air, and men with tunics ornate with embroidery, fancy crossties on their leggings, smoking pipes filled with strongly scented tobacco. Weaving in and out of it all, dogs and children ran amok, along with chickens and geese and goats, which scattered and squawked and bleated.... It was a cacophony of noise and sound and scent, and for a moment, Buttercup and I stood in dumbfounded amazement at it all.

Then Buttercup discovered a bowl of some milky substance and, while I was busy gawking at the activity around us, stuck her nose in it and began drinking noisily.

"Oy!" the vendor said, appearing suddenly and poking a finger into my shoulder. "That'll cost you five silver pieces."

"What?" I looked down to find Buttercup, her muzzle dripping with milk, lowering her head into the bowl again. "No! Stop sucking it up, Buttercup! That's not yours!"

"It is now," the vendor said, sucking his teeth and holding out his hand. "Five silver pieces, that'll cost you."

"For a bowl of milk?" I scoffed at him.

"That was the finest ass's milk, that was. Ladies use it to bathe in. Five silver pieces."

"Two," I said, pulling out the small leather purse that hung from a thong around my neck.

"Four. That whole bowl is spoiled, now that your mare's nose has been in it."

"Three, and not one copper more. You don't have to tell someone who's going to use the milk to bathe in that Buttercup was drinking it. Here, three silver pieces. And next time, keep your bowl up where mules can't find it."

We left the man sputtering about people taking advantage of him, and marched onward, pausing twice to ask for directions. The moon was rising in the sky by the time we found the camp on the far side of town where Deo had set up several tents. We headed straight for the largest tent, set well back from the others. Although we garnered many glances, no one stopped us until I tied Buttercup to a stack of wooden barrels and went to enter the tent.

A man whom I hadn't noticed sitting in the shadow of some packing crates suddenly sprang to his feet and blocked my way. "No one is allowed in there. Go about your business, priest."

"I'm here to see Deo," I said, trying to step around him.

He put up his arms to keep me back. "I said no one is allowed in. Lord Deo sees no one."

"He'll see me."

The man snorted derisively. He was shorter than I, slight of build, but with long golden curls that lay along his shoulders. He was dressed in a rather ostentatious manner, but had a wicked-looking pair of daggers strapped to his hips. "That he won't."

"Tell him Allegria is here and has something he wants."

He sneered openly at me. "I doubt that. Yes, I very much doubt that."

"Don't be so crude. I have the boon that he sent to the Temple of Kiriah Sunbringer for, and I must deliver it to his hands personally."

"Give it to me," he said, holding out his hand.

I ignored the imperious tone. "Just tell him I'm here."

"He won't see you."

"Goddess above, just tell him, or I will call Kiriah's wrath down upon your head for obstructing one of her favored servants!"

He looked as if he was going to refuse but, after a moment or two, slid behind one of the panels that guarded the tent's entrance. In less time than it takes to count to twenty, he returned, a smug look on his face heralding bad news for me.

"As I thought, Lord Deo does not wish to see you. He demands you hand over the boon to me. You will give it to me now."

Hurt flashed through me, followed immediately by anger. How dare Deo refuse to see me? He'd sworn never to forget me!

Had he forgotten? Or had he remembered, but just didn't want to see me? It didn't matter which was true—at the very least, he could tell me to my face that he didn't want my help. I eyed the little man standing impatiently before me, wondered briefly if Kiriah would be displeased if I smote him on the spot, and decided, in the end, to hand over the boon.

"Fine, but do not unwrap the coverings," I said, pulling out of the saddlebag a small, silk-bound object. It felt like a book, and I assumed the goddesses had come together to create some powerful spell for Deo's use in bringing peace to the lands, but which was not given to him due to the invasion. "They are sealed with wax, and Deo will know if they are tampered with."

"I am Lord Deo's personal body servant," the man said with a smile so unctuous, it made my hand itch. "There is *nothing* he keeps from me."

"Somehow, I doubt that." I shrugged. "But if you want to court his wrath and that of both goddesses, then it's on your head."

He paled just enough that I felt confident he'd hand over the boon unopened.

"Be off. Lord Deo has many important things to do tonight," the little man said before disappearing into the tent again.

"As do I," I said softly, and, with a quick glance around the area, led Buttercup over to a spot where a group of horses were tethered. I tried to negotiate with one of the lads tending the animals for her to be returned to the temple, but didn't care for the way he eyed my few precious silver coins. I had a feeling her fate would not be what she deserved should I leave her with him.

"I'll just have to convince Deo to take you with us," I whispered in one of her long ears. "Wait here with the horses. And be polite, no nipping anyone on the rump. I wouldn't put it past those boys to set you loose if you give them any grief."

Buttercup snorted and laid back her ears. I gave her a swat on the shoulder and went back to convince Deo that I was indispensable.

"The trick is to get him to see that fact," I said to myself as I sat on my heels behind the stack of barrels and watched the comings and goings of the camp. Several people came up to Deo's tent, but all of them were met, and ultimately turned away, by the officious little man. He didn't see me when he dashed out of the tent, heading down the hill toward the water, where a dray was being unloaded, clearly on a mission for his master.

I smiled to myself, rose, and strolled toward the tent entrance, doing an immediate about-face when two men ran up the hill to take up guard positions.

"Goddess blast them," I muttered to myself, trying to figure a way to get rid of the guards. After a moment's thought, I trotted around to the back of the tent.

"The thing with canvas is that most people forget it's so easily cut," I announced as I entered the tent, having used one of my swords to cut along the corner seam. "They think there's no way in, when in reality, it's quite easy—goddess! Who are you?"

The man in front of me spun around, and for a moment, I was speechless with surprise. The Deo from my past was a dark-haired god, with beautiful amber eyes.

This man had jet-black hair all right, but his eyes were of matching ebony. He was broad across the shoulders and chest, his tunic strained tight across thick ropes of muscle. He stood taller than I, taller than most men I could call to mind, and reminded me of the tales of the giants who'd lived on Alba before the twin goddesses brought us to it.

"What…" I stumbled back another step, holding my swords out in front of me. "Who are you? What have you done to Deo?"

The man made a deep rumbling noise, and I realized he was laughing.

"What have I done, indeed?" He took one giant step forward and thrust his face into mine, brushing aside my swords as if they were twigs. His eyes weren't true black—there were glints of red in them, as red as the blood that beat so loudly in my ears.

Visible beneath the opening at the neck of his tunic was what I could describe only as a silver harness, inscribed with the most powerful containment runes I'd ever seen. He also wore metal bands on both wrists, these glittering with active protection runes. His hair was pulled back and tied with a leather thong, revealing features that were sharp with suspicion, and that were etched with pain. One hand rose as if to grab me by my throat, but instead, it brushed a strand of my unruly hair back from my face. "Allegria. I should have known you would not take no for an answer. It has been many years, but not so many that I have forgotten your willfulness."

My jaw dropped as the words registered in my stunned brain. "Deo?"

"You didn't recognize me?" His face twisted into a grimace, although his voice carried a note of sarcasm. "Have I changed so much? You hurt my feelings, priestling."

I stared in silent horror. How on earth could this... changeling... be the fresh-faced, handsome boy of my youth, the one I had kissed in the stable loft, the one who had filled my thoughts for so many years?

Was this the man I'd risked everything for?

Chapter 6

"What in the name of the goddess has happened to you?"

Deo studied the woman in front of him just as intently as she gazed at him, albeit without the confusion that crawled across her face. He had braced himself for just such a reaction when he revealed himself to those who had known him in the past, but to see the expression of disbelief on the face of someone he remembered with fondness cut deep.

Allegria gestured at his torso, her expression slowly changing to curiosity. "You're..."

"Transformed." He stepped back from her in order to give her space, knowing his physical presence was overwhelming. He had many fond memories of this little priestling, his Allegria who had spoken so fiercely when they were both young and still possessed an idealized vision of life. They had made many plans in the short time they had together: he would be a great warrior like his mother, a savior of both his father's people and those of his mother, while Allegria would fight at his side, her quick bow helping bring peace where there had been none for an eternity. "You see before you the result of years of experiments with chaos magic."

Experiments? the magic whispered. *Adventures, old friend. What we had were adventures. Grand, glorious adventures wherein you accepted me, and together, we killed the unworthy.*

Deo ignored the voice. He'd found that the more he acknowledged it, the stronger its hold became.

"Chaos magic?" Allegria shook her head, obviously having a hard time accepting the changes in him. "I've never heard of such a thing. There's the arcane magic of the Starborn, and the grace of Alba that magisters wield, but those are the only two types of magic."

"They were once, but not now. The Harborym brought chaos magic with them, and although it has cost me much, I have at last mastered it." Deo felt a grim satisfaction at the words, the memory of years of anguish now but a shadow on his mind.

Who has mastered whom? The chaos magic laughed into his mind.

It wasn't a pleasant experience.

"You consorted with the Harborym?" she asked in disbelief.

"No!" he snarled, then held up a hand when she recoiled. "I'm sorry, Allegria. That reaction was not for you. My father used the same phrase a few weeks ago when I told him that we should be using the Harborym's magic against them."

"I take it he didn't approve."

Deo gave a short bark of laughter. "Hardly. He threatened to banish me a second time, saying I had become a monster for trying to control it."

Fools, all of them. They have no understanding of just what I am.

"But…" She gestured toward his chest, where the harness wrapped him in its tight grip. "But you mastered it."

"A fact that my father did not wish to acknowledge or accept. Do you know why I was banished?"

Allegria shook her head. "There are stories… but I did not believe them."

"I have no doubt there are many tales, but I will tell you the truth. My father said I must be banished so that I could do no harm to others. He said that to *me*, the one who was born to unite Alba in peace!"

We will rule Alba. Soon, very soon.

"What Lord Israel did to you was cruel." Allegria's gentle voice softened the sharp memories a bit.

"Cruelty is no stranger to my father," he said, and pushed away the old anger. It was not time to address the ills done to him.

"And yet, he was right in that this magic has made you…" She gestured again, clearly unable to say words he might find insulting.

"Changed," he said simply. "It took from me the grace of Alba, all signs of my Fireborn blood, and left me as you see. It is a form of corruption—"

I prefer to think of it as an enhancement.

"—but one that will allow me to use the Harborym's magic against them, and finally destroy them."

Mmm, destruction. What a lovely warm feeling that gives me.

"Shut up!" Deo snarled, his patience frayed beyond bearing.

Allegria backed up a step. "I'm sorry—"

"No, that was not intended for you." Deo took a deep breath, embarrassed that his temper had slipped from his control. He'd never admitted to anyone except his three trusted lieutenants the truth about the transformation, but Allegria was different. He felt without a shred of doubt that she could be trusted. "The chaos power... talks... to me."

She stared at him for the count of twenty.

"I know how it sounds." He made an abrupt gesture and turned to walk over to the three wooden chests holding various personal items. "But I assure you I am not mad. Not yet, anyway."

"This power is... sentient?"

Oh, I like her. She's bright.

"Yes. That is, it gives me... urges." He squared his shoulders and spun around to face her again. "Violent urges. But none of that matters, because tonight, under the light of the goddess Bellias's eyes, I will transform an army, who will drive the Harborym from my mother's land, and free her kin from the slavery that has bound them for so long. Once that is done, then the chaos magic will have nothing to power it, and it will disappear on the wind."

I wonder if that's strictly true.

Her wary expression faded, followed swiftly by one of assessment. She eyed him with speculation now, and he knew he'd pricked her interest. He smiled to himself. Sweet Allegria, still the same. "You have not changed, have you, little priestling?"

A flicker of anger lit her brown eyes. "If you mean I have little love for fools, then no, I have not changed. Is that why you refused to see me? You thought that this metamorphosis would alter how I felt about you? Or did you just not want me here?"

He heard the note of pain in her voice and was reminded again of how vulnerable she was. He'd known it years before, when they had dallied so pleasantly in the hayloft, but even then, his heart was not his to give away. It belonged to Idril.

Until she destroyed it by leaving him to wed his father.

And together, we will have our revenge on them both.

Deo ground his teeth. Of all the temptations the chaos power offered, it was revenge against his father that was the hardest to resist.

"Deo?"

The pain was stark in Allegria's voice now, and he hurried to make amends for his moment of introspection. "I am, and always will be, happy to see you," he said with a little bow. "But I did not wish to frighten you with the change that has been wrought in me. Nor do I have time to go into detailed explanations of what I am doing, and what chaos magic is. We have only a few hours before the transformation."

"You're going to turn all of your people into..." She waved a hand toward the harness on his chest.

He smiled, although, to be honest, it wasn't a smile that expressed any joy or happiness. "The transformation was harder on me because I experimented with chaos magic for so long before I could master it."

Again, that word "master." I must protest it. Ours is a collaboration. You give me a voice, and I give you that which you seek most.

Disbelief was evident on Allegria's face.

Despite his statement to the contrary, he found himself explaining, "My force will be transformed, yes, but not to such an extreme degree as you see in me. To take in that much chaos magic would be disastrous for most people—it would turn them into the very beings we are hunting."

That end is inevitable. You know this as well as I do.

"Wait, are you saying you *consume* the magic?" Her forehead wrinkled in disbelief. "You take it into yourself? Isn't that incredibly—"

"Dangerous?" he asked, one side of his mouth quirking up, and for a moment, he felt he was back in the loft of the stable, sharing their goals in between kisses. "Inadvisable? Risky?"

"Stupid," she said, then looked appalled at the word. "I'm sorry, that wasn't kind."

He gave a short bark of laughter. "Perhaps not, but I appreciate honesty, Allegria. I hear it all too infrequently. I have tried the transformation on three others, my lieutenants. They are in Genora, scouting out the locations of the Harborym camps. Their change into banesmen was not so devastating as it was to me—the magic leaches from them the colors of the Fireborn as it has done me, true, but it does not change their bodies, nor does it speak to them."

You are special. You are the end to our means. You are destined to a bright greatness, a brilliance that will shine forth and blind the unbelievers.

"And we have found that runes worn on the wrists and ankles are enough to keep the magic from consuming them and turning them into Harborym," Deo finished, steadfastly refusing to answer the magic that taunted him with such provocative statements.

Allegria eyed him silently for a moment. "The lines on your face show... does it... does the magic hurt?"

He considered shielding the truth from her, but he had always been honest. "Yes."

"Is there no ease for your pain?" She clutched her hands together, clearly in distress. "Is there nothing that can be done?"

"Nothing I have tried has helped, but do not let your empathy get the better of you. I have borne worse pain than what I bear now."

She shook her head as if she couldn't believe what she was hearing. "And you're able to control this chaos magic?"

"By the grace of the goddesses, and the runes that are bound to me, yes. For now, it is in check."

Concern filled her eyes. "For now? Do you mean that someday it might be set free?"

"I have no way of knowing." He gave a shrug, impatient to be under way, impatient to be rid of her so that he might continue pacing in his tent until the time of transformation was upon them, and yet, at the same time, oddly comforted by her presence. She brought with her a reminder of times past, of his youth, when his hopes and dreams hadn't yet been crushed by his father.

She reminded him of what he could have been.

What you will be is so much more interesting.

"I can see that you've mastered it, although if those runes are anything to go by, it's taking tremendous amounts of energy to keep the chaos magic in check. Even assuming we could control this magic, is it wise to consume something so corrupted?"

"We?" he asked, amused. "Is *that* why you are here? Not to deliver to me the boon promised at my birth, but to join my cause?"

She smiled and picked up her swords, sliding them into the crossed sheaths on her back. "If you recall the time we spent in the stable loft, I told you how much I wanted to fight against the Harborym."

He touched her wild golden brown hair, twining a curl around his finger. "You are a priest, Allegria, not a soldier, and even if you were otherwise, I would hesitate to see you sacrifice yourself to chaos magic. You are too valuable to the priesthood to be taken from it."

"I am more valuable to you," she said, giving him a level look. "There's something I never told you, Deo, a secret that Sandor swore me to keep from everyone, but I knew the day would come when I would have to reveal it."

His eyebrows lifted in feigned surprise. "You shock me, priest. What secret could an innocent young woman such as you hold so tightly to your ample chest?"

She gave him a look that let him know she didn't appreciate the reference to her bosom. "I see I wasn't wrong when I suspected in the hayloft that you liked breasts."

His laughter rumbled, even while he briefly ogled her upper half. "Only on women."

"Well, drag your eyes up from mine, and heed this: I am a priest of the Temple of Kiriah Sunbringer, yes, and through her, I wield the grace of Alba, but I am something more than that, Deo. I am a lightweaver."

His eyes widened, genuine surprise taking him momentarily aback. "Are you sure?"

She made a face at him. "Am I sure that I can alter reality by pulling on the power of Kiriah's sun? Oh yes, I am very certain. My parents gave me to Sandor when I was only a few summers old simply because I had a power they couldn't—and wouldn't—understand. She refused to let me use it, though."

A mischievous look flitted across her face, and she held out her hand. On it, a small horse made of golden light—like liquid sunlight—pranced across her palm.

"Sandor doesn't know I still conjure animals. I started doing it as a child, but she told me to do such was forbidden, and a crime against Kiriah, and insisted I bury my abilities deep within me."

"Evidently you didn't heed her," he said, amused despite himself.

"No," she admitted with a wry smile. "But I don't let anyone else see it. She warned me against allowing others to know about my powers lest I be made the target of unscrupulous people. That made sense then. Now... now it's different. I can be of great help to you."

"A lightweaver," he mused, rubbing his chin. "Lady Sandor kept that from my father."

"She was worried that the temptation to use me would be too great," Allegria said slowly, obviously picking her words carefully. She knew, of course, that there was no love lost between him and his father. "I am not blaming Sandor for keeping my ability hidden—I didn't understand at the time why she made such a fuss about my never using it, but I know now it was to protect me. And the temple."

Deo turned his back and walked a few steps to the end of the tent, pulling from a leather chest a tunic made of fine black cloth, embroidered with silver threads. He removed his tunic, hearing Allegria give a quiet little gasp when she saw the scars of whippings long past on his back, visible beneath the harness.

He was surprised the chaos magic had nothing to say about Allegria's offer to join his forces. He wondered if it had finally realized he was not going to pay attention to its insidious whispers, or if something more sinister was behind its silence.

"If you were anyone else, I would send you on your way," he said finally, pulling the fresh tunic over his head before turning to face her. "And as it is, I have the gravest doubts. You understand, don't you, that should you undergo the transformation, I cannot guess what the chaos magic would do to you? That I don't know how it would affect your abilities?"

"Why should it affect my magic at all? It's something inherent in me," she pointed out, shaking her hand so that the light horse dissolved into nothing. "It's as much a part of me as my flesh, and you just finished telling me that the effects of the transformation on your army will not be as great as yours."

He hesitated, glancing toward the entrance of the tent. "It's not just the act of becoming a banesman that poses a risk. It's the chaos magic itself."

"How so?" she asked, just as he knew she would. She had been curious when he'd first met her, and she'd evidently not lost that trait.

"You used the word 'consume' earlier," he said reluctantly. He'd warned the others about the cost of using the magic, so it was only fair he make her understand exactly what she would be taking upon herself should she join his company. "Chaos magic gains its power from the changing of life to death. In effect, it gets power from consuming life. By using it, you risk the magic's consuming you, too."

Allegria was silent for a few minutes before giving a nod toward his chest. "You bear protection runes in addition to containment. Is this consuming the reason why?"

"Yes."

She thought for a few minutes longer, then lifted her chin. "Kiriah has never failed to give me her protection when I needed it. I will trust she will continue to keep me safe even against this magic of death."

Still the magic said nothing to him. He wondered again at that. It was on the tip of his mind to ask, but wisdom dictated otherwise. "I admit a lightweaver would be an excellent addition to the force we will bring against the Harborym, but…" He shook his head. He really should send her packing. But if she truly was a lightweaver, then she would be a strong ally in his fight against the invaders.

Assuming the magic didn't destroy her first.

"No," he said, pushing away the idea of her aid. "It is too risky. You aren't strong enough to control chaos magic. Kiriah may guard you from many things, but this is beyond your abilities."

She gave him an odd look, as if she was seeing beyond his external features, and stepped forward, her hands glowing with the golden red light of the sun. "Let me show you what else I can do."

He watched silently as she placed her hands on his chest. Golden light blossomed forth from her touch, surrounding him in a halo of warmth, freeing his chest from the binding constriction of the harness, melting the silver bands, and pulling from him not only the pain he had learned to live with, but the chaos magic itself. He was reborn into the man he had once been.

"Kiriah's nipples!" he said on a gasp, holding out his hands to examine the cuffless wrists. He stretched in bliss, his body whole and uncorrupted, without pain or scars or the black spots that ate away at his soul. He touched the edges of his eyes, pulling up a shield to look in it. His eyes were amber, holding the light of the sun and moon within them. "You can change me?"

"No. I mean, I don't know for certain. I just thought that I must be able to do something to help you, to take away the pain. I don't know how long it will last," she said with obvious regret, and brushed back a strand of his hair, allowing her fingers to trail down his arm. "I did this once before, when one of the temple cats was ill, and it was better, but only for a short time. This may last an hour or only a few minutes. The light animals only last for that long. I fear I don't have the control I need to make the changes last longer, or even become permanent, but I hope someday to find someone who can teach me to do that."

He whooped with joy and gathered her into his arms, the warmth of the sun filling him. "It is a miracle nonetheless. You shall be known as Allegria Hopebringer from this moment on."

She smiled, the light of happiness and warmth in her eyes, and before he could release her, she pulled his head down to kiss him. Her mouth was sweet as if she'd been eating honey, and despite the fact that his heart had been destroyed by Idril, he took pleasure in the kiss. Her fingers tugged his hair, demanding more, and after a moment's hesitation, he gave it to her.

Idril was lost to him. Why not take what Allegria offered? He'd had a fondness for her since the day they first met, and clearly, she wanted to relish this moment when he was in his uncorrupted form. He slid his hands down her hips, his fingers digging into the soft flesh of her behind, pulling her closer to him. Her tongue twined around his while she moved her hands along his chest before trailing lower, her fingers splaying over the fabric across his belly. He was just contemplating taking her to the cot that stood sheltered in the corner of the tent when a noise interrupted the heat of the moment.

"My lord, I have checked the shipment, and find—goddesses' grace!" His servant had returned, and now stood looking first at Allegria, then at Deo, then back at Allegria. "What is—what has happened—what is *she* doing here?"

"I think he's jealous," Allegria whispered, her voice filled with amusement.

Deo cocked an eyebrow at the servant, wanting to both chastise him for the interruption and thank him for the very same thing. Now, he reminded himself, was not the time for dalliances. Not while the transformation of his elite squad awaited. "No doubt. Rixius, this is Allegria. She is considering joining our force."

Is she, indeed?

Rixius gave her a look that was almost comical in its animosity.

Deo—relieved that the chaos magic had at last made a comment, yet annoyed that he cared in the first place—made a mental note to have a word with Rixius when they were next in private.

"But, lord, she is naught but a priest—"

"Does it look like a priest did this to me?" Deo held up a hand to stop the protest that was forthcoming. "No, it matters not what you think, and before you go trumpeting my change to the world, it is not a permanent state." He cast Allegria a swift glance, not wishing to foster hope where it might never blossom. "Although perhaps someday, when we have driven the invaders from Alba... but we are getting ahead of ourselves. Allegria... I don't know what to say—"

"Say that you will have me join your company," she said, her gaze holding his. He read the determination within and relinquished the objections that still held him in doubt.

"Very well, so long as you understand the risk that you will take. Rixius, Allegria will join my forces, and by her goodwill, we shall decimate those who have held the Starborn as slaves for so long."

"I will do everything in my power to bring an end to them," she promised. "You have my swords, my bow, and all my abilities."

He cupped her chin, looking down at her sunny, freckled face. "This is your last chance to change your mind, priestling. I must be sure that you understand the changes that will be wrought if you follow this path. Before you agree to this, search your heart and know that the power you will be embracing will not only demand a constant battle to contain it, but could overwhelm you, turning you into that which we seek to destroy. Should that happen, you will become a Harborym, and my banesmen will show no mercy in destroying you. You acknowledge and accept all this?"

She knelt before him, her hands clasped together. "This I do swear: By the light of Kiriah Sunbringer, my life will be devoted to bringing about the end of the Harborym of Eris. I will be your weapon of vengeance." *This event is... interesting. We must think upon it.* Interesting, how? Deo wondered, but pushed the thought from him before the magic could overhear it. He looked down at the woman kneeling before him, both pleased that she wished to join him and afraid that she would regret this decision.

Nonetheless, it was hers to make.

"Together," he said, pulling her to her feet, "we will bring Alba into the Fourth Age. Your children's children will sing songs to your glory and will celebrate the day we destroyed the Harborym. Rixius, gather the forces together. The time for transformation is almost upon us. We must conduct the ceremony as soon as the moon is at her zenith, ensuring that Bellias Starsong will grant us her favor."

Deo remained in the tent while Rixius carried out his orders. Allegria would have remained, too, but he sent her to write a note of explanation to her priestess. She didn't wish to do it, but he insisted. If she died in battle, or had to be destroyed as a Harborym, he wanted her order to know what she'd done, and why.

Almost an hour later, Allegria's magic wore off, and Deo stood surveying forty men and a dozen women gathered in a field to the west of the encampment. At his emergence from the tent, there were a number of shocked gasps from those who had known him before he had been banished, but no one cried out that he was a monster incarnate, as he'd half expected.

"You see before you the results of my struggle to tame the power of chaos magic," he told the gathering. A few people looked a bit shaken and did not meet his black gaze, but for the most part, the soldiers he'd chosen stood stalwart in the face of what was to come. To the side, watching with a half smile, Allegria stood easily, holding her bow in one hand.

"It has taken from me the grace of the Starborn, but given me the power of Eris itself. Upon your chest is the mark of this power, the mark of the Bane of Eris." He gestured toward his own tunic, identical to the ones they wore. "The crescent moon rising over a blazing sun signifies the unity of both Starborn and Fireborn in combating the darkness of chaos. Wear it with pride, my banesmen, and know that you alone are uniquely equipped to bring down the Harborym where all others have failed."

A cheer met this statement, the faces of his small army showing no signs of doubt now. "The step you take today will have repercussions felt around all of Alba. Generations of Fireborn and Starborn alike will revere your names. Your sacrifice here, today, on this field, will forever after be known as the Day of Transformation, the day when Alba took back her own, the day when the banesmen lifted high their swords and swore that all should be free of tyranny!"

They all raised their swords to the night sky and shouted their approval.

"Lord Israel led his army upon the Harborym when they arrived on Alba, driving their weak forces from Aryia, but for many years he has been unable to break their hold on Genora. We will succeed where he has not! We will free the Starborn upon whom he has turned his back. We will not set down our swords until the last Harborym has been driven from our fair land. How say you?"

A roar of enthusiasm erupted, the oaths of his banesmen filling him with a sense of victory. At last, he would be able to end the invasion, free his mother's people, and bring about the peace of the Fourth Age. And then, only then, would he look his father in the eyes and demand the respect that had so long been denied him.

Hmm, the chaos magic said, but then fell silent immediately.

Deo was too preoccupied to spend much time wondering about the sudden quiescence of a life-form that had taunted and tormented him since he had forced it into abeyance.

"The servants will pass amongst you with goblets. As you drink the chaos magic, remember your family, your children, your loved ones, and know that you are doing this to ensure their well-being." He lifted a goblet in a toast to them all, although his contained only honeysuckle wine.

Before him, fifty-two hands took fifty-two goblets and raised them high.

"Arise, Banes of Eris! For tonight, we take to the sea and deliver the destruction that all of Alba cries out for. Drink, and become that which you were always meant to be!"

With a great cheer, his force drank deeply of the magic that lay in a red swirl on top of the golden wine. Almost immediately, the transformations began, with men and women alike dropping to the ground, screaming in agony, their bodies twisting and contorting while the magic struggled to take control.

It was a horrible sight, and an even worse sound, as people begged those around them for mercy, and to end their suffering. The servants, many of whom were not to go with Deo to Genora, began backing away at the first signs of distress, and were now fleeing into the night, clearly terrified.

Deo stood watching, the magic inside him recognizing its kind and fighting to break free of his control. He focused on his runes, knowing without even looking that they glowed red as he threw his determination into them, and at last, he was able to turn his attention away from his own struggle.

Roiling bodies filled the field, many of them sobbing for mercy, their faces twisted in agony. To the side stood one figure, still, tall, and with a sense of calm in a storm. He held Allegria's gaze for a long moment; then slowly she lifted the goblet to her lips and drank.

Without realizing he was moving, he was at her side when she fell, catching her and holding her carefully while the magic coursed through her veins, permeating every last part of her being. Her back arched against him, her screams a torment, but there was little he could do.

"It's all right," he murmured in her ear as she writhed in his arms, her nails clawing at his flesh. "It will ease in a moment. The worst is over."

"You..." she panted, her voice as rough as gravel. "You promise?"

"Yes." He stroked her back when she doubled up across his leg, vomiting up the contents of the goblet.

All but the magic. That was taking hold of her as she struggled upright. Her skin, pale and freckled, took on a deeper, dusky hue. Her unruly, wild hair darkened until it was as black as a crow's wing. Oddly, a line of black dots appeared across her brow, as if the magic were tattooing itself into a circlet upon her flesh. Her eyes rolled back in her head as she struggled to breathe, struggled to live with the magic inside her, then they slowly settled, the color in them deepening from a light brown to ebony.

"What... what do I look like?" she asked, one hand touching her forehead. "Am I..."

"You are as lovely as you ever were," he said, noting the signs of the struggle easing within her. Her eyes were more focused now, and the trembling had ceased. The wards on the silver bands at her wrists and ankles glowed golden, an interesting phenomenon. Deo glanced at the nearest newly made banesman, who was still in the throes of the transformation. His runes were glowing red, as were all the others.

Deo considered Allegria, smiling a little to himself. Trust her to do things differently. He suspected it was her own powers that had modified the way the chaos magic took hold of her, and hoped this meant she would have a greater mastery over it than he expected of the others.

Perhaps this was the right decision. Perhaps she would not fall victim to the magic.

"Is the pain easing?" he asked when she pushed back on his leg, obviously trying to get to her feet. "No, do not rise yet. Give your body time to get used to its new powers."

"I don't know that day will ever come, but I know I must get up. It hurts too much to stay still."

He helped her to her feet, running an assessing gaze over her.

"Do I look any different?" she asked, pushing back her mass of hair and examining her arms. "Am I bulky, like you?"

"No. Your body is unchanged, save for the change in your coloring."

"My hair?" She grimaced as she touched her head. "I suppose if that is the worst of it… but why does my forehead hurt?"

"You have a marking there."

"A marking? What sort of marking?" To his amusement, she set about tidying her tunic and leggings, brushing off dirt and grass. "Is it something horrible? Goddess, I don't have horns, do I?"

He laughed. "No. The marking looks like a circlet made up of small pinpricks. Ones of onyx. That is all."

"Oh. I guess I can live with that." She grimaced and made an aborted gesture. "Not that I could do anything about it even if I didn't like it. Is this it, Deo? There's nothing more?"

He knew she was asking about the transformation. "This is it. How do you feel?"

"Odd." A variety of expressions passed across her face, everything from confusion to disbelief to acceptance. "I feel… more."

"More what?"

She waved her hand. "Just… more."

"Does the magic fight you?"

"Not really." She was silent a moment, clearly assessing her feelings. "It's there. I can feel it, feel its power. But it's not telling me what to do. It's not talking to me."

He was relieved, his shoulders releasing the tension he hadn't been aware he'd been holding. "Good. If it ever becomes too much for you, if the power will not heed your desires, tell me. I will add more runes to your cuffs."

"I think it'll be all right." She gave him a ghost of a smile, her black eyes glowing with some inner light. It was a bit unsettling seeing those strange eyes in a familiar face, but he was truly grateful that she'd made the choice to join him. "I think I'll survive."

"You are going to do more than merely survive," he said, turning her to view the mass of bodies. A handful of banesmen had risen to their feet, while the others still writhed in the process of assimilating the chaos into their beings. "You will triumph over every enemy. You will help me eliminate the Harborym and return peace to Alba."

"Let's hope it's as simple as that," she said, watching with concern as the other banesmen fought to contain their magic. "I have a feeling it's not going to be, though."

He said nothing.

He suspected she was right.

Chapter 7

"Did you know that your father is here with his army?"

I spoke the words quietly, but Deo acted as if I'd blown a trumpet in his ear. He spun around, the red lights in his eyes firing to show emotions that ran quick and deep within him. He'd been watching the last of the horses being unloaded from the ships that had brought us across the sea to the shores of Genora.

"He is not," Deo said, frowning. "He left here years ago when he couldn't contain the Harborym. Where did you hear such lies?"

I nodded to one of the black and red tents that had been set up before we arrived. "Your lieutenant Hadrian. My mule was disturbed by the bustle of unloading and ran off, and while chasing her, I came upon Hadrian riding to meet you."

Deo looked past me to the small encampment where his three lieutenants were supposed to be waiting to meet us. Only one was present, however, to greet our two ships loaded with banesmen, mounts, and supplies. Deo had been visibly annoyed, a fact that secretly amused me. In the few days it had taken to cross to Genora, I'd discovered he had a temper as short as a hen's memory. He looked even more annoyed now. "Hadrian should have come to me first, not stopped to dally with you."

I couldn't help but laugh at that absurdity. "It was hardly a dally, Deo. I saw a blood covered man racing toward me with the Bane of Eris insignia on his chest, his horse lathered and clearly exhausted. Naturally, I asked if he needed help, and he gasped out that Lord Israel's army was on the move, and he had ridden all night to tell you."

Rixius had approached as I spoke, barely pausing to give me the glare he had settled on as his method of greeting me. Deo snarled something under his breath before ordering, "Rixius, see to the rest of the unloading. Tell the banesmen to be ready to ride as soon as the horses are fed and watered."

"It shall be as you say, my lord," Rixius said, shooting me a poisonous look. "The stores should be checked for damage before they are loaded onto the wagons. Perhaps the priestess could undertake that task."

I fumed silently to myself. I hadn't escaped a life of humility in the service of the blessed goddess Kiriah so I could now be punished with menial tasks. Not when I'd undergone the most excruciating experience imaginable just so I could fight the Harborym. Unbidden, my hand rubbed my forehead where the line of small black dots crossed it.

Before I could protest, Deo said, "Get one of the servants to attend to that. Allegria has other work to do."

He strode off with me running after him. "Are you speaking generally, or of a specific job?" I asked, somewhat breathlessly.

"Both." He marched on without so much as glancing back at me.

I quickened my pace and buffeted him on the shoulder. The voyage to Genora hadn't given me a lot of time to reacquaint myself with Deo, but it was long enough that we'd fallen into an easy relationship.

With one exception.

He stopped suddenly, causing me to run into him. With eyes blazing, he thrust his face into mine and snapped, "What?"

The words that came out weren't the ones I had planned on speaking. "When you kissed me the night I came to your tent... did you feel anything?"

He stared at me for a moment, then cast his eyes starward before shaking his head and continuing toward the red and black tents. "I knew it would be a folly to bring you along, but I couldn't resist the idea of a lightweaver."

"And that is as it should be," I answered, trotting alongside him. "I can finally use my power as Kiriah intended. But that's not what I asked. Did you... you know... *feel* anything?"

"Like your breasts? Yes, I felt those." His expression was as stark and grim as ever, but faint humor laced his voice.

"Did you feel anything like the time we spent in the hayloft?" I continued, feeling it necessary to have an acknowledgment of the thoughts that had been skittering around the back of my mind ever since the episode in the tent.

"We were children then," he said dismissively, then shrugged. "It was obvious you were in love with me. It's natural you felt things that I did not."

For a moment, I stared in surprise at him, very aware of his large form moving alongside me with the grace of a panther. "I was no such thing! I'd just met you. How could I be in love with you?"

"All the girls in my father's house were in love with me. It made sense that you would be no different from them."

He said the words just as if there were nothing wrong with them.

I fought back the urge to hit him over the head with my bow, reminding myself that I had sworn fealty to him just a few days before, and beating him about the head and shoulders was hardly going to reinforce the idea of my loyalty.

I swallowed back my ire, and instead said, "I grew out of it."

He glanced at me, his eyes flashing amusement. "Yes, your kiss said all of that."

"It most certainly said something, but I doubt if you know what," I answered in a mild tone, and added nothing more, knowing Deo's ego wouldn't allow that remark to pass without comment.

We stopped before the tent of his three lieutenants, only two of whom, Borin and Hadrian, were present. Hadrian had been sitting on the ground while his companion was wrapping a long cloth around his chest, binding a jagged red slash that ran from his armpit down almost to his belly.

"My lord," Hadrian said, struggling to get to his feet.

"Stay where you are," Deo ordered, and knelt beside him. "How were you wounded?"

"A party of Shades patrol the Old South Road. I cleared out many groups, but the last one came upon me suddenly and almost felled me. But that is not of any matter—my lord, your father is once again on Genora's shores."

"My father sits in his manor and complains bitterly about fate," Deo said, scorn dripping from each word. "He gave up on the Starborn at the same time he gave up on me."

"It *was* he, my lord," Hadrian insisted. Borin finished tying the cloth and eased a fresh tunic over Hadrian's head. "The men I saw bore Lord Israel's standard."

"How big a company was it?" Deo asked, his expression changing from ire to thoughtfulness.

"Five score, at a guess." Hadrian looked oddly worried. "I rode through the night to tell you, since I knew you would wish to learn of his movements. But I have never seen Lord Israel out with such a small force."

"Nor have I." Deo rose to his feet, again gesturing when Hadrian attempted to do the same. "If he is here, then something extraordinary must have happened. I wonder if he decided to follow me once I told him my plan. No, stay where you are and rest. I will leave a servant with you to tend your wounds until you are fit to ride after us."

"I am able to ride now," Hadrian protested, "although my horse must have rest before I ask her to travel again."

Deo's shoulder twitched. "Very well. Rixius will see to it that you have a fresh horse. Allegria, Borin—come. I have jobs for you both."

Borin was a small man, slight of build, and with features that reminded me of a ferret. He bore the dark hair and eyes of a banesman, but where my skin—and those of my fellow initiates—now possessed a dusky, faintly blue tinge, his skin was as pale as the moon.

We followed Deo to where the horses were being watered, fed, and saddled. In the midst of all the glossy, highbred beauties, Buttercup munched placidly. She'd worked out her objection to the confinement on the ship with an ill-timed escape, but since that had led me to finding Hadrian, I couldn't chastise her too much.

"What is it you want of us, my lord?" Borin asked.

"Follow the South Road. Verify what Hadrian said he saw. Determine whether Lord Israel is here, and if it is he, follow him. I want to know if he meets with a larger company, and if so, where they are headed. Question any Shades you see before you kill them, and do not let anyone of Lord Israel's company see you. We will follow the coast road to Starfall City. You may meet up with us once you have seen all there is to see."

Borin murmured his assent, his eyes flickering toward me briefly before he bowed and went to fetch his horse.

"Tell me you have something for me that's more exciting than checking stores," I said as Deo stopped next to a stack of three leather trunks. "Not that I'm unused to mundane work, but I had hoped that fighting Harborym would require more skills than counting sacks of barley."

Deo opened the top of one of the trunks, pulling out an object wrapped in a long red silk cloth. He handed it to me, saying, "If you are going to fight under my banner, you'll need better weapons than those temple-made eating knives."

"My swords are not eating knives," I said, bristling on behalf of the weapons that had cost me almost all of my meager funds, but the next moment I was sucking in a breath and saying with awe, "Sun and shadows, these are beautiful."

"They should be," Deo said dryly, looking with satisfaction at the two narrow swords I'd uncovered. Both were chased in gold, with sun runes etched into the silver of the blade, while the hilt was covered in intricate filigreed gold and amber gems. "They were made for my mother as a marriage gift."

I traced my finger down the runes, the warmth of the metal making my skin tingle. My hands itched to hold the swords, to watch the light flash from them as I wielded them against the Harborym. Just the feel of them against my palms gave me a sense of power, a rightness, a measure of invincibility... and then Deo's words sank in. "A marriage gift? I didn't hear that your father married the queen."

"He didn't." Deo pulled out a crossed-back scabbard and handed it to me. "They were to be married upon the beginning of the Fourth Age, but that didn't happen. Instead the Harborym came, and my mother's people were under attack. Put this on and listen closely. A day and a half's ride from here, there is a ruin. An old temple to Bellias called Kelos that the arcanists use. They opened it briefly as a sanctuary for the Starborn when the Harborym came, but most of it was destroyed, and the Starborn enslaved. Parts of it remain still, although in what state, I don't know."

I knelt with him when he pulled out a dagger and drew a crude map in the dirt. "This place is east of us?" I asked.

"Yes. Lief, the third of my lieutenants, tells of a man, a runeseeker, who resides amongst the ghosts of those who fell there. It won't be easy to convince him to join us, but you must do so."

"A runeseeker? What is that?" I asked, immediately feeling that I was in over my head. I had imagined I'd be fighting at Deo's side, using skills I had honed for years, but now... I gave myself a mental shake. I had wanted adventure; I couldn't balk at what the goddess gave me.

"A man learned in the ways of arcane magic. Lief thinks he will be most useful to us."

"I have no doubt he would be, but, Deo, I'm not a diplomat. Far from it, Sandor always said I spoke first, without thinking, and I'm afraid she was right. You have a company of fifty-two; in their ranks there must be someone better suited to fetching this man."

"On the contrary, you are the one who must go. Only you. Do not argue with me, priestling—you are the only one amongst all of us who knows the ways of magic."

I gestured toward my fellow banesmen, all of whom were readying themselves for our march to the Starborn capital. "After the transformation, we are all now *very* familiar with the power of magic, Deo."

He waved away that objection. "Chaos gains its power from death. You hold the ability to draw on life, on the sun itself. Do you not think the runeseeker will be tempted to learn from a lightweaver? No, Allegria, you must go and convince the man to join us. You and no other."

I watched for a moment as Deo pulled his own weapons from the trunk, frustrated by my inability to make him see that I would be useless in the role of a diplomat. "I don't want to seem ungrateful, but surely there is a better task you can give me. One I'm more suited for. I have trained long with both swords and bow, and—"

Deo gave me an annoyed look. I knew I was pushing him well past the bounds of his patience, but I had to start as I meant to go on. "Exodius may well be of help to you in mastering your abilities. He will respond to the unique abilities you bear and listen to you where he would turn others away. Go, Allegria. Free the runeseeker from his ghostly jailers and return him safely to me."

"Very well," I grumbled, knowing my cause was a lost one. I had no idea how I was to convince this man and hoped Deo wouldn't be angry when I failed to dazzle the runeseeker with my brilliance. "But I thought when you took me on to battle the Harborym that I would actually be fighting them, not watching over arcanists like a ewe with her lamb."

Deo laughed as he took my old swords and tossed them into his leather chest, helping me adjust the straps of the new scabbard. "You always were a bloodthirsty little thing. I see that, too, has not changed about you."

"Too?" I asked, sliding the swords into place, crossed on my back where I could grab them quickly.

He leaned in, and for a moment, I thought he was going to kiss me. "I know exactly what your kiss in my tent said. Your emotions are an open book, priestling."

Before I could respond, he was striding away, calling out several commands and leaping into the saddle of a great black charger that had been brought forward for him.

I shook my head even as I strapped my quiver to my side and fetched my bow, saying softly to myself, "I don't think you do, Deo. I don't think you know me at all anymore."

Chapter 8

Hallow reached the ruins of the once grand Temple Kelos just as the sun was beginning her descent behind the line of mountains that ran down the center of Genora. He paused at the crumbled gates, gazing at the remains with a critical eye. "Lord Israel is mad if he thinks anyone living would choose to reside there," he told his horse, Penn. "I've seen pleasanter pigsties."

Penn snorted his agreement and jiggled his bit, while Hallow allowed his gaze to move along land that was starkly gray and black. It was an alien place, devoid of life, with no soft lines, just jagged spikes of broken stone stabbing upward to the sky. It was as if a giant hand had plucked from the area everything green and alive, leaving only death behind.

"The gatehouse," Hallow said, urging Penn forward. The horse picked his way carefully around clumps of fallen dirty cream bricks, now burnished gray from the lifeless soil. The arch of the gatehouse stood, but the rest of it was a heap of stone and brick. A movement flitted across the very corner of his vision, but when he turned his head to look, it was gone. "Ghosts," he said, his voice sounding hollow. "Lord Israel said there would be ghosts. Why did I agree to take on this task? I had no idea that when he summoned his army to invade Starfall City, I would be conscripted to poke around a ruins filled with ghosts. I'm an arcanist, not a spirit talker, Penn. Does it seem reasonable that I should be here, rather than wielding my magic elsewhere?"

Penn paused to relieve himself. Hallow took that as criticism. "I'm well aware that the Master of Kelos leads the arcanists, but according to Nix, this particular master has not been seen for decades. Arcanists being what they are—Master Nix always did say it was like herding squirrels to get a group of arcanists to do anything—Exodius is probably long dead, and no one's noticed."

The muffled thump of the horse's hooves seemed to echo when they rode past the main temple building, little puffs of gray dust rising with every step. The oppressive atmosphere made his nerves feel twitchy, forcing him to speak aloud just to hear something normal. "Lord Israel said this was once a famed center of magic and learning. He said the temple was built in the form of a circle, with a silver dome cut with star-shaped holes so the light of Bellias could shine down upon the arcanists, and that they made their own army they called the Masters of Kelos. What do you think of that?"

Another fleeting movement caught his eye, but it, too, was gone as soon as he looked. Hallow considered what he knew of the spirits of the unquiet dead and drew a protection ward over his chest and head. Then, after a moment's thought, he drew the same over both sides of Penn. "There's no sense in taking a chance, is there, old man?"

Penn snorted again, his tail twitching nervously. Hallow knew just how the horse felt. A strange prickling raised the hairs on his arms as they moved past the partially collapsed temple. In the walls that still stood, high arched windows graced with intricate carvings of the stars and moons gave a hint as to the original glory of the temple. Of the silver dome, nothing remained but a pile of stones that spilled out over one of the broken walls and clogged the faint remains of a road.

"If I were Master of Kelos, where would I hide... er... live?" Hallow considered the smaller outbuildings, most of which had decayed into mounds of gray that reminded him of the massive barrows in his native land. Ahead stood a scraggly tower, once held upright by graceful buttresses, most of which were now missing. Only a few delicately carved archways extended from the tower, ending in midair, giving the whole structure the look of an upended beetle.

Hallow reined in Penn and gave the tower a long look. "That has to be it. Nowhere else is even remotely habit—"

A blob flitted in front of him. It was transparent like a jellyfish, but the edges of the form glowed with a strange bluish light. The blob elongated until it changed into a human form. A male human form.

An *angry* male human form.

"By whose command do you think to invade Kelos?" the spirit demanded, pulling out a wraithlike sword.

Hallow had never seen the unbound spirit of the dead before. He'd heard about the beings from Master Nix, but only in anecdotal mentions, usually ending with Nix besting the ghost in some manner. Therefore, he greeted the watchful ghost with an easy manner and general goodwill, sliding off his horse to make a little bow before saying, "Hail, goodman spirit. I have no intention of invading your home—I am simply a traveler passing through who wishes to locate a runeseeker by the name of Exodius. Do you know of him?"

The ghost's eyes narrowed, and Hallow could have sworn that a shifty expression came over his face, although admittedly he found it difficult to read facial nuances when the subject was made up of nothing but transparent bluish spirit particles. "Why do you seek such a person?"

Hallow waved the question away. Although Lord Israel had not given him a deadline for finding the runeseeker and bringing him back to the company, he felt a sense of urgency. The sooner he persuaded Exodius to join the forces of Lord Israel, the sooner he could get to Starfall City, and there arrange to continue his arcane training. "My reasons will not interest you. Have you seen the runeseeker? Does he reside in the tower?"

The ghost lifted the sword in what would have been a menacing manner if it had been performed by a living man. "If you are a traveler as you say you are, you should leave. The living do not come to Kelos."

"They did once," Hallow said, glancing around. From behind every broken stack of brick, every jagged rock, every collapsed building, the forms of bluish spirits lingered, all clearly emboldened to watch the proceedings. Hallow gestured toward the nearest. "This was once a thriving temple, was it not?"

"It was." The spirit straightened up, squaring his shoulders. "And I was captain of the guard, serving the Master of Kelos until his untimely end. Now I serve his apprentice, and that is all you need to know. Be on your way, traveler, lest I teach you that even the spirits of those who once resided in Kelos are to be feared."

Hallow held on to his temper. Never one quick to anger, he had found in his time with Master Nix that patience with the unwilling (or drunk) was more successful than force. "I will be on my way just as soon as I find the runeseeker Exo—by the goddess!"

To Hallow's surprise—and no little amount of pain—the ghost stabbed him in the arm with the sword. Blood poured out of a gash the width of his hand, staining the gold and white tunic bearing Lord Israel's arms. He glared at the ghost, saying, "That was uncalled for. My sword was sheathed, and this tunic is only borrowed. Now it's stained."

"You are *unwelcome*," the captain said, taking a step forward. Hallow didn't take the time to wonder how a spirit could manifest himself in a physical manner; he simply pulled down energy from the weak starlight that waited beyond the range of the sun, and blasted it at the ghost, sending him flying backward through the open archway of a partial ruin. With a quick order to Penn, he ran into the tower, throwing himself at the iron-banded wooden door.

Behind him, many voices cried out in alarm, filling the silent air of Kelos, and with a muttered protection spell that he knew would last only a few seconds, he pushed with all his might against the door.

The hinges were not rusted, but had been used so infrequently that they were stiff and unyielding. He risked a glance over his shoulder, and saw his horse disappear behind a company of ghosts. Coming up fast behind them was his nemesis with the sword.

"Blessed goddesses of Alba, grant me your strength. Or protection. Protection is good. Might even be better."

He threw himself at the door again, mentally rifling through the spells that Master Nix had taught him. Unfortunately, they mostly concerned manipulating arcane magic, and had little do to with oiling frozen hinges, but just as the hairs on the back of his neck rose, the door opened with a bloodcurdling screech.

He squeezed through, wincing at the pain in his arm when he shoved the door closed again, wondering if the spirits of Kelos could transport themselves through solid objects.

For the count of seven, he held his breath, his sword in hand, ready to battle the captain should he materialize, but evidently, he would not be put to that trial. "Either they cannot move through stone and wood and brick, or they are afraid to do so," Hallow said aloud, instantly wishing he hadn't. Behind him, a marble-floored hall seemed to stretch back forever. His voice echoed in a mocking manner that he felt was wholly unnatural... but he had a job to do. In an unconscious imitation of the captain, he straightened up and squared his shoulders, his sword comfortably in hand.

He passed quickly through the hall, his gaze taking in the centuries of dust and cobwebs that covered every chair, every small table, every once-luxurious couch upon which the priests and arcanists of Bellias had reclined. A small room led off to a dark and cluttered kitchen and buttery, while another door opened to a large hall containing a broad flight of stairs that curved upward.

"Runeseeker Exodius?" Hallow called, moving up the stairs. His voice didn't echo here—in fact, it was muffled, as if he had spoken in a crypt buried deep in soil.

"That is not a healthy line of thought to pursue," he chided himself. "Let us think instead of pleasant things like puppies, and fluffy ducklings, and the joy that a full wineskin and a warm serving wench can bring." He paused near the top of the stairs, noting the dust-caked portraits of long-dead occupants, now tattered so that little canvas remained. The nearest portrait, that of a dark-haired priestess holding a star over her head, caught his attention.

"Those are slash marks," he murmured, touching the damaged painting. It quivered and crumbled under the touch of his hand. With a little shiver, he continued his climb upward, passing through a long gallery, to the foot of another stone staircase that led upward in a circular pattern. He peered up into the darkness, judging that he was in the heart of the tower.

Exodius had to be up there... if he was still alive. In vain, Hallow had argued that the Master of Kelos was likely long dead; Lord Israel simply refused to accept that possibility and insisted that he was needed for the Council of Four Armies. "Foolish," Hallow muttered to himself, but resolutely started up the stairs.

The climb upward took a lot longer than Hallow expected, but at last he stood in front of an iron-bound arched door. He knocked, waited for the count of ten, then tried the door. To his surprise it opened, revealing a circular room. Large floor-to-ceiling windows allowed the dull sunlight to fill the room, making motes of dust dance in lazy swirls upon the air. "Magister Exodius? I am Hallow of Penhallow, and I come at Lord Israel's request to bid you attend the gathering of the Four Armies."

There was no sign of life in the room, but Hallow admitted to himself that a medium-sized war charger would be able to hide behind the stacks of books that rose to the vaulted ceiling a good two floors above. The walls themselves were lined with shelves containing everything from pots and jars filled with mysterious contents, to books, plants, odd mechanical devices, star maps, globes, stacks of yellowed papers, great cones of incense, dried flowers and herbs that waved in the gently moving air, neatly folded dust-covered fabrics, and even... Hallow squinted against the gloom cast by a nearby stack of books. A stuffed dog lay in an extremely unnatural and awkward position. "That taxidermist has a lot to answer for," he murmured, dragging his gaze off the dead beast to further scan the room for the runeseeker.

"Are you speaking of Eagle? He has years left in him, years!" The voice that spoke was not old and creaking (as Hallow had expected), nor did it have the ethereal, hollow quality of the ghosts that lived below.

It also originated right behind him.

Hallow jumped and spun around, causing the stuffed dog to lift up his head and utter a rusty-sounding woof. A man who barely reached Hallow's shoulder shuffled past him, a stack of books in his hands, several long scrolls stuffed into the crook of one arm, while the other bore the weight of a dusty red velvet cloak inscribed with runes in gold thread. Strapped to the man's bent back was a long staff made of unmarked black wood, topped with the figure of a black bird with spread wings.

"Exodius?" Hallow asked, making the elaborate bow that Master Nix had told him never failed to impress. "My name is—"

"Hallow of Penhallow, yes, yes, I heard you the first time." Exodius stopped at a table that was already groaning with the weight of several journals, three pots of ink, countless quills, a mountain of loose papers, and a parrot. Hallow eyed it, half expecting it, too, to suddenly move, but unlike the dog, it was well and truly stuffed. Exodius was mostly bald, with tufts of white hair poking up from around the fringe of his head, and the most prodigious bristling black eyebrows Hallow had ever seen. Tendrils of hair waved from his brows, almost as if the eyebrows were feelers bent on capturing small motes that floated on the air. Exodius cocked one of those alarming eyebrows at Hallow. "Do you think I cannot hear?"

"No, sir," Hallow said, clearing his throat, preliminary to making the speech he'd written on the two days' journey to Kelos. "It is with the greatest respect that I come to ask you—"

The old man froze for a moment, cocked his head, and lifted up a hand. "There is an intruder."

Hallow blinked, unsure of what to say to that.

Exodius shot him a quick, unreadable look. "*Another* intruder."

"Sir, I—"

"Did you not hear me? It is you who have troubled ears, not me." Exodius raised his voice almost to a shout. "GO DEAL WITH HER."

"Her?"

"THAT'S WHAT I SAID." Exodius's voice dropped to a normal level. "The lad's simple as well as hard of hearing."

"Sir, I assure you I am not—"

"GO!" Exodius pulled the staff from his back and tapped it loudly on the floor three times.

Hallow found himself moving to the door, almost as if he had no will.

"I am busy locating the queen's moonstones, which were hidden when the Harborym invaded. Do you understand? DO NOT RETURN UNTIL YOU HAVE DEALT WITH THE INTRUDER. Don't know what this younger generation is coming to. No sense of what's proper, no sense at all. Imagine allowing intruders to roam Kelos at will. They'd be getting underfoot, interfering with the magic, and stirring up the ghosts. ARE YOU STILL HERE?"

"I will gladly help, but—"

"HERE. TAKE THORN." Exodius tossed his staff at Hallow. "She's likely to be trouble. I SAID, SHE'S LIKELY TO BE TROUBLE."

"Thorn is your staff?" Hallow asked, a strange warmth seeming to flow into his palms from the black wood of the weapon.

"'Twas the name of my master, one of a long line of Masters of Kelos before me. He chose the form of a swallow when it was his time to pass beyond. HE'S A BIRD, LAD."

"I have a sword, Exodius." Hallow pulled it out so the old man could see how fine was the weapon that Lord Israel had given him.

"She'll kill him before he can even draw it." Exodius gestured, and the sword was knocked from Hallow's hand. "THORN WILL PROTECT YOU. GO STOP THE INTRUDER BEFORE SHE DESTROYS ALL THE GHOSTS. They won't like that at all, no they won't. The captain will have a word or two to say to me about that, and I simply don't have the time. I'm so close to finding the moonstones…"

Exodius moved a stack of paper that promptly toppled and spilled onto the floor, but he paid it and Hallow no mind.

Before Hallow could open his mouth to ask how he was supposed to stop someone who had the power to destroy ghosts, invisible hands pushed him out of the room, and almost to the bottom of the stairs before he felt his body under his control again.

At least the staff felt right in his hands, as if it were made for him. He squared his shoulders again and, with a quick prayer to both Bellias and Kiriah, opened the door just enough for him to slide out into the dusty gray of Kelos.

At first he thought nothing was awry. The air was still and silent, the sensation of being watched still present, but there were no ghosts about. He walked slowly down the stone steps, glancing around, but no one sprang out at him. It was then that it struck him that Exodius had gotten rid of him with a convenient story of an intrusion. "And really," he told himself, shaking his head and turning back to the door, "how likely is it that anyone else would come here?"

He had his hand on the metal latch when the faint sounds of a woman's voice reached him. The wind shifted then, carrying the noise away, but it sounded to him as if someone was… singing? In this place of death and dust?

He shook his head again, but nonetheless slid the staff into the back of his belt. He walked down the main road, passing Penn and giving him a comforting pat on the neck before continuing. He paused every few feet, twice catching the strains of the woman's voice. He hurried on, watching for—but not seeing—any of the spirits who had accosted him.

It was when he passed around the central temple that he saw her. He stopped in the shadow of the broken wall and watched with amazement.

The woman was clad in black, a simple tunic and leggings, the latter bearing silver crossties. Her hair was as black as the wing of a raven, while her skin had a dusky hue that looked faintly blue in the light of the sun. She was voluptuously made, but that wasn't what held Hallow's interest. It was the way she slaughtered the ghosts who were streaming out of the buildings around her, racing toward her with swords held high, and breathless battle cries lifting upward into the wind.

She held two swords, both flashing silver and gold in the dull sunlight as they cut effortlessly through the ghosts' bodies. She twirled as she fought, her hair flying out in a shiny black tangle, her movements effortless, quick, and agile.

And very deadly.

She sang while she moved, the words now reaching him clearly.

Shadows of black, shadows of blue,
Cast by you who are long dead.
Wraiths of the living who once were true,
Though phantoms, still my blade will rend.
And deliver you your final end.

She moved with the grace of a deer while she sang, her swords flashing, the bodies of the ghosts falling to the ground before dissolving into nothing. Hallow wanted to applaud when, in a show of bravado, she leaped onto a fallen column and slashed her way along it, doing an intricate dance step while disemboweling and beheading her attackers. She was clearly enjoying herself greatly, and she moved as if she'd trained for battle her entire life.

But waiting at the end of the column was the captain who had stabbed him in the arm. Hallow reached for his sword, but found it missing. He pulled the staff from his back instead, ready to run forward and help the woman fight the captain, but before he could blink, the captain's head rolled to his feet.

After two seconds, both the head and the body disappeared in a faint glitter of blue light.

The woman jumped off the column, and stopped singing, looking around to see if any ghosts remained.

There wasn't a sound, not so much as a breath of wind disturbing the temple grounds.

Hallow shifted in preparation to take a step forward, and instantly, the woman was there, her swords spinning toward him. The staff jerked in his hands, blocking them just when they would have taken off his head, leaving him looking into very surprised black eyes.

Only they weren't true black. They were flecked with gold, like pinpricks of molten metal that flared and then ebbed away.

"Who are you?" the woman asked, slowly lowering the blades. "Are you the runeseeker? I thought you were an old man. He didn't say you would be so..."

"Dashing?" Hallow said, relaxing enough to give her a little smile. "Obviously intelligent? Slightly handsome?"

She glanced at the top of his head. "Blond. Only the Fireborn have that shade of silver-blond hair, and yet your eyes are blue, not brown. How did a Fireborn learn arcane magic?"

She thought he was Exodius? That was interesting. At least he could answer her question truthfully before he sent her on her way. He had no desire for another person who was searching for Exodius to find him. "I had a master who was taught by a great Starborn arcanist. My eyes turned blue, as is the way of all arcanists. Why do you seek the Master of Kelos?"

"You are to come with me," she said, sheathing her swords, her manner polite but fairly abrupt, as if she were unwilling to spend any more time in Kelos than was necessary. He didn't blame her. It was a singularly unpleasant place. "You are wanted for a great battle campaign. And... er... a personal one, too."

He leaned back against the bit of wall still standing, charmed despite himself. "A personal campaign for you? Now, what would a..." He eyed her tunic, not recognizing the symbol on the black cloth. She bore silver cuffs on both wrists inscribed with what appeared to be containment runes. "...er...what exactly are you containing?"

"Pardon?" She looked mildly startled.

He gestured to the cuffs.

"Oh, that." She gave him a level look that he couldn't easily read, and said in a haughty voice, "I'm a Bane of Eris."

"A what now?"

She repeated the phrase, then added in her normal tone, "Actually, I'm a priestess of Kiriah, too. My name is Allegria."

"You're Fireborn?" He was surprised by this. Her coloring was all wrong for people of his continent. "Do you have a Starborn parent?"

"No. It's… oh, it's a long explanation. It'll have to wait for the ride back to Deo to tell you. Do you have some things you'd like to take with you? I'm anxious to be away before nightfall." She glanced upward, clearly judging the descent of the sun in the sky. "If we leave within the hour, we should be well away from here before the ghosts return."

"You killed them," he said, shaking his head at the inanity of the sentence. "That is, they were dead already, but you… I guess, re-killed them."

"I only dispersed the ghosts' spectral form. Once they have sufficient energy to regain their corporeal forms, they will return. And I'd really rather not be here when they do so, since they are bound to be a bit testy about the fact that I disrupted their day."

"I'd rather not, as well. One of them is quite antagonistic. What was that song you sang?"

"Hmm? Oh, the song. I call it 'That Which Doesn't Kill Me Had Best Run.' Where are your lodgings? In that tower?" She took him by the arm, clearly intending to urge him on.

"Yes, but I can't go with you," he said regretfully, and reluctantly allowed her to pull him toward the tower. He liked her despite her obvious attempts to impress him, attempts that wilted away and revealed her true personality. He suspected she was as bright and sunny as a priestess of Kiriah should be, but for some reason tried to appear much more grave and dignified. "I have my own campaign, alas. Did you say Deo? As in Deosin Langton, son of Lord Israel?"

"Yes." Her manner became wary, and she released his arm to shove open the door. "He sent me to fetch you."

"Well, now, that's very interesting." He was silent while he followed her up the first flight of stairs, mulling over this news. He had a feeling that Lord Israel had no idea his troublesome and occasionally murderous son was on the same continent as he. Hallow was tempted to ask the runeseeker if he had any ravens available for a message to be sent to Lord Israel, but decided that he would simply urge Exodius to leave that day, rather than spending a few days supplementing his knowledge of arcane magic.

She paused at the damaged pictures, peering closely at one. "That picture has been tainted by chaos magic. Were Harborym here?"

But before he could get Exodius away, he had to get rid of the charming but mysterious Allegria. He decided, since she was somehow connected to Deo, that it was safer to parry her questions. "I don't know the answer to that question any more than I have experience with chaos magic."

"Then you are a very poor runeseeker," she said, and continued across the gallery.

He had to stop her. He couldn't let her get to Exodius, or else he'd have more trouble on his hands than he wanted to face.

"I'm sorry," he told her, stopping her when she looked up at the spiral stone staircase. "I can't go with you, much though I would like to meet Lord Deo. I'm very curious as to what he's doing here. You wouldn't care to tell me, would you?"

"No," Allegria said slowly, her expression guarded. "Do you know Deo?"

"I've never been introduced, but I've heard much about him," he said truthfully, remembering the night a few years before when Deo had been banished. "I have heard it said that he went mad trying to control the chaos magic, which caused him to be banished to an isolated island, but I do not know him personally to say whether that is true or not."

"Well, I *do* know him," Allegria snapped, the gold in her onyx eyes flaring to life. "And he is not mad. He might have been at one time when he was undergoing the transformation, but he's not now. He's quite sane, and very determined to rid Alba of Harborym."

"I would love to stay and talk to you more about this transformation you mention, and what Lord Deo wants with Exodius, but I really must take my leave of you. And in case you don't understand the subtext of that statement, it means you need to leave this tower."

"Exodius?"

"The runeseeker. Who, incidentally, will be coming with *me*."

"You're not the runeseeker?" Allegria stiffened, her hands flexing. He was interested to note that the runes on her cuffs glowed slightly. "Then just who are you?"

He made her a little bow. "I am Hallow of Penhallow, and I am the man who will be escorting the runeseeker Exodius to Lord Israel. If you will excuse my poor manners, I needs must get him moving. I fear it's going to take a bit of time, and I, too, wish to be away before moonrise. I will escort you back to the door—"

"What? No! You can't take him—he's mine!" Allegria reached for her swords, but Hallow was ready for such an objection. He had been gathering arcane magic from the stars while he spoke, and now he cast a quick spell to throw a transportation bubble around her. It would move her only twenty yards or so, but that, he judged, would be enough to shift her outside the tower, and it would keep her confined for almost an hour. He turned and ran up the stairs, determined to get Exodius on his way even if he had to sling the old man over his shoulder and carry him.

Chapter 9

"Just when you think someone has nice eyes and an even nicer smile, they put you in a bubble and fling you outside." I looked down from where the bubble was holding me motionless in the air at a height that was almost two stories up, and surely going to cause me an injury when the magic in it finally faded. "I'm so going to make Hallow of Penhallow rue the day he ever crossed me. The runeseeker is his, indeed. I think not!"

I glared at the tower for a few minutes, hoping he could feel the waves of anger I was sending his way, but quickly decided I'd be better served by focusing my energies on getting out of the blasted bubble and into the tower.

"This is just ridiculous," I said through my teeth some twenty minutes later, sweating profusely as I struggled to somehow break the bubble. I had tried my swords, tried conjuring up a veritable herd of light badgers to burrow through the bubble, tried directing the sun itself to destroy the bubble, but all my efforts did was slowly lower the bubble toward the ground until I was about two yards off a slab of fallen wall. "At least I won't break my leg when I finally get out—what? No! Oh, you bastard!"

The doors to the tower opened and the nice-eyed, but definitely black-of-soul, Hallow appeared with a large bulky object held over one shoulder. It was wrapped in a cloak, and judging by the legs that kicked from beneath it, I was guessing he'd kidnapped the runeseeker I'd been sent to find.

Hallow paused long enough to give a little wave and offer me a smile.

"I'll get you!" I yelled, hoping my voice was audible through the bubble despite the fact that it seemed to filter any sound from the outside. "I'll hunt you down and find you and… and… well, I don't know what exactly I'll do to you, but it will be heinous and unpleasant!"

He mouthed something to me that I could not hear, then, with a little salute, hurried off with the struggling runeseeker, followed by a small, fat dog.

I shook a sword at Hallow as he loped away with his burden. "You'll rue the day you ever crossed... well, shite. At least he could have stayed and let me finish ranting. Right. Enough of this. I have to get out of this blasted thing before he gets too far ahead of me. Since lightweaving won't work, maybe the opposite will."

The runes on my wrists offered no suggestions as to how I was to use the magic that roiled inside of me, but I hadn't gone through the hell of becoming a banesman just to sit back and do nothing.

With a deep breath, I closed my eyes, focusing my attention on the chaos magic itself. It felt much different from the power of the sun; it was darker, absorbing energy rather than pouring it into the environment. Just by embracing it, I could feel it drawing on the death forces around me, the living things that were passing over into the eternal night. I held it for one brief second before it slipped my mental grasp, ignoring all my attempts to shape and use it.

"What an annoying type of magic if you can't even use it. And after it almost killed me taking it in. Oh, I'm going to have a few things to say to Deo about just how he expects us to use this so-wondrous power of his," I muttered darkly some twenty minutes later. As I spoke, the bubble burst with an audible pop, causing me to land awkwardly on the stone slab. I hesitated for the count of seven, wondering if there was any reason to go into the tower and search the runeseeker's rooms, but knowing in my heart that Hallow had taken the only valuable thing. "Blast his pretty blue eyes. And... well, his nice smile. And broad shoulders. Really, his chest was... Kiriah's nipples! What am I saying? The man must have bespelled me!"

I slapped my own cheeks in order to snap out of what was obviously a spell intended to charm me, and ran through the ruins back to where I had hobbled Buttercup. I muttered to myself as I ran, aware that the ghosts were beginning to return, but other than a few cries of anger directed at me, I made it through Kelos without again being accosted.

"Come on, Buttercup. We have a villain to catch." I pulled the rope hobble from Buttercup's front legs, deftly avoiding her nip on my rear when I did so. "First we need to figure out what direction he went. Quickly, now, before we lose the light."

It took another half hour before we found hoofprints plainly visible on a dirt track, becoming a road that led to the south. The road had once been paved, but had clearly fallen into disuse. Weeds sprouted from between the stones, some of which had been dislodged and pushed onto the grass verge. There were patches where the road was missing entirely, but enough of it remained that I set Buttercup to a bone-jarring trot, all the while promising myself any number of physical acts of revenge on the traitorous Hallow. His chest really was quite broad. I had always had a weakness for tall, broad-shouldered men like him, ones who made me feel that I wasn't quite such a hearty peasant behemoth. "Kiriah damn his pretty eyes," I muttered under my breath, and pulled a cloak from my pack to wrap around me against the darkness that rolled out over the land like a velvet rug.

Bellias Starsong didn't see fit to give me much of a moon, but the skies were clear, and although Buttercup stumbled once or twice, and three times shied at shadows that seemed to creep across the broken road, we made our way southward without incident. We traveled all night and well into the morning before I fell asleep and tumbled off Buttercup, then decided it was best to take a break before we both harmed ourselves. I slept fitfully, my dreams disturbed by images of Deo ranting about the need for the runeseeker, and the enticing figure of Hallow smiling, the lines around his blue eyes crinkling in a way that made my stomach feel warm.

"Definitely a charm spell," I murmured sleepily at one point, before turning over and claiming another hour's sleep.

All that day and into the following morning, we saw only intermittent signs that Hallow's horse had preceded us. "Is he going to Starfall City?" I asked aloud at midday. "Deo said that the Harborym hold the city. Why would he take the runeseeker there? Did he lie about Lord Israel? Hmm."

My speculation was cut short when, while watering Buttercup at a small pond, I heard riders galloping down the road. I flattened myself immediately to avoid being seen, but there was no need for hiding—the men didn't so much as glance to where the pond sat partially hidden by a copse of trees. What was interesting was that rather than disappear down the road toward Starfall, they slowed and veered off to the right, up a steep rocky outcropping.

"Those men wore Lord Israel's colors," I told Buttercup, and, after filling a waterskin, I hobbled her where she could graze, and stealthily made my way after the men.

I heard the camp before I saw it. Noises with which I'd become familiar after my short time with Deo filtered down over the rocks. Men's voices, horses nickering softly, the clang of metal, occasional outbursts of laughter— all warned that it wasn't a small group. I crept up the rocks, avoiding the path that wound its way back and forth to the top, keeping to the shadows whenever I could. I reached the crest and paused, surprised to find the top perfectly flat, a field that was filled with white and gold tents, horses, men, pens with geese and goats, and all the hustle and bustle of a small town. The tents were formed into a square, in the center of which was an open area dotted with a couple of tables and chairs, a large fire in the middle, and an aged man with a fringed halo of white hair accompanied by the same small fat dog I'd seen at Hallow's heels.

"The runeseeker," I murmured, and scanned the camp for signs of the annoying Hallow. I couldn't see the entire area from where I was crouched, so shifted to another rock in an attempt to get a better view. As I rounded a large boulder, I ran straight into a man in a guard's uniform relieving himself against the rock. He was as startled as I was, but I was faster.

"Oh! Pardon," I said, and spun around, intending to scramble down the rocks before he could call after me.

"Hey! Who are you? Samson, there's a woman here. Come see!"

The guard's shouts did the damage I had hoped to avoid, and before I was halfway down the rocks, they swarmed after me. Worse, another patrol was coming up the winding path, and before I could do so much as mutter imprecations to Bellias to save me from her blighted land, I was marched into the camp accompanied by a full score of men.

There were several cries of surprise, and a few of a more concerning nature. "A spy!" a couple of men yelled.

"Traitor!"

"Do you see her swords? She's an assassin sent to slay Lord Israel!"

"Get the headsman! Kill her before she tries to kill us all!"

"Wait a minute," I protested, struggling when my swords were removed from my back, and my hands roughly jerked behind me and tied with a bit of hemp. One of my sleeves had come off in the struggle. "I'm not an assassin, and I'm not here to assassinate anyone. I come from Lord Deo—"

"Lies!" the guard nearest me shouted. "Lord Deo is exiled on the Isle of Enoch."

"If you'll just listen to me—"

The guards behind me shoved me forward, and to my horror, someone dragged a low table over. Blood stained the top, gouges showing where an axe had bitten deep.

"She has magic signs upon her wrists!" another man yelled, rushing up and pointing dramatically at me. "She is sent to bespell us all. Kill her before she can drive us from our senses!"

"You odious little runt," I snarled, struggling for real now. Unfortunately, without the use of my hands, I couldn't use my lightweaving powers. But there was still the chaos magic…

The cry of "Kill the spy!" was taken up as a chant, and I fought to keep panic at bay, and to focus my mind on harnessing the dark magic that struggled inside me.

The runeseeker, his attention caught as the guards dragged me over to the low table, looked up from a book he was writing in and squinted at me. "Ah, it's the second intruder. Don't let her near your ghosts. She has no patience with them, none whatsoever. Quite deadly with the swords, according to the boy."

I ignored him, ignored them all, ignored even the fact that I was thrown down onto my belly across the low table, my arms stretched out and tied to the legs. If I faltered now, I'd never have another chance. I calmed my screaming mind and gathered chaos magic, holding it back when it threatened to slip free.

A shadow fell over me, and the scent of death filled my nose. I refused to acknowledge the arrival of the executioner, even as I fought to keep my focus while someone handed him a mammoth axe.

The chaos magic didn't want to be used—it wanted to control me. I fought with it and strained to keep it leashed all the while my heart beat a panicked tattoo, filling my ears so I couldn't hear the jeers of the guards.

Until one voice rose above the others. "What's all this noise—Allegria? What are you—no! Stop!"

A surge of chaos power crested within me, threatening to explode outward.

"There you are," the runeseeker said. "Will you get these men to quiet down? I can't concentrate with all the folderol of the intruder's execution going on."

"Stop! I said stop!"

Two things happened at almost the exact same time. The first was that Hallow's voice rose in a roar that hurt my ears, his words accompanied with a thunderclap of arcane power that wrapped itself around me in another bubble, this time protecting me from the falling axe above my head.

The second, and in my mind more impressive, was that the chaos magic, for a scant second, allowed me to channel it and turn it outside myself.

With a sound that pierced my brain like shards of glass, the power exploded outward, leveling guards, tents, horses, and even the trees scattered around the camp.

I looked up to find the only two things still standing were Hallow and me. He'd been in the act of reaching into the bubble and looked down at me now with eyes wide with wonder and disbelief.

"That which doesn't kill me had best run," I reminded him.

He blinked twice before pulling out a dagger and cutting my hands free. "I'd say that was an overstatement, but given that you've just flattened everything in what is probably a two-acre radius, I'm going to move on. What did you do? Was that the chaos magic? I've never felt anything like it. Who exactly are you? Or rather, *what* are you?"

I was rubbing my wrists where the ropes had cut into my flesh when a voice spoke behind me. "What have you done, arcanist?"

Around me, people were slowly getting to their feet, some shaking their heads, others assisting those who were still lying prone. Lord Israel, who had apparently been coming out of the largest tent to see what was going on, got to his feet and brushed himself off as he strode forward.

"It wasn't me," Hallow answered, his gaze curious. "But I would dearly like to know just what Allegria did. It wasn't like any chaos power I've ever seen."

"You said you weren't familiar with chaos magic," I said, narrowing my eyes on him.

He grinned. "That might not have been the strictest of truths."

"You... you..." I couldn't think of anything horrible enough to call him, so distracted was I by the fact that I had escaped death by a scant second or two.

Lord Israel stopped in front of me, his gaze first on Deo's emblem on my chest, then shifting to the silver bands on my wrists and ankles. "So he has done it," he murmured.

I inclined my head. "Lord Israel."

"You are a Bane of Eris," he stated, holding up a hand when the nearest guards staggered to their feet and made to recapture me. "Hold. I would speak with the woman." His gaze flickered to Hallow for a second before he added, "And the arcanist. Bring them to my tent."

I raised my eyebrows and looked pointedly over his shoulder.

Lord Israel, with an odd, martyred look flitting across his face, amended his order. "Get my tent up as soon as possible. Jalas will be here with Lady Idril at any time—I don't want them thinking we cannot even maintain a simple camp while waiting for the rest of the council to arrive. You there—right that table and take the prisoner to it."

Israel turned and strode over to the runeseeker, calling, "Exodius, a word, if you please..."

"Troublemaker," Hallow murmured under his breath, but loud enough for me to hear.

"I have a few names for you, too," I answered in the same tone. "Like thief. *Underhanded* thief. Lying underhanded thief."

"I just saved your life. You should remember that when you're forming slurs to hurl at me."

"I saved my own life; you merely got in the way. Wait... did he say Idril?" I asked in a whisper when the servants scurried to right the table and chairs.

"Yes." He shot me an oddly questioning look. "Are you a member of the Tribe of Jalas?"

"No, but I've heard of Jalas's daughter, Idril." I was silent for a moment before asking, "What is she doing here?"

"The Council of Four Armies is gathering."

I hated to admit ignorance, but my curiosity was greater than my pride. "I don't know what that is."

"Then you shall have something new to learn." He reached out to take my arm, but the second his fingers touched my bare skin, a shock sparked between us, causing him to jerk back. "By the stars, what was that?"

I smiled and lifted my hands to show him the halo of gold that glowed around them. "It would seem you have something to learn, as well. Did I neglect to tell you that in addition to being a banesman, I'm also a lightweaver?"

His eyes danced with inner amusement when he took my arm in a firm grasp. I tried very hard not to notice his eye crinkles (blast the man, that charm spell must still be lingering) or the heat of his palm against my flesh.

Or the way he strode next to me, his movements not coiled with power like Deo's, but smooth and flowing, like light illuminating the dark depths of water. There was a sense of power about him, too, but his power felt different. Where Deo was dark, Hallow was light; the power of the land and skies were flowing around and through him, becoming a part of him, and reminding me of a brilliant blue gemstone glittering in the sunlight.

"Sit," Lord Israel said when he strode up to us, gesturing toward a single chair on one side of the table. Two others were opposite.

I bit back an oath and took the single chair. Israel sat across the table from me and gestured for Hallow to sit, as well.

Hallow hesitated for a moment, then dragged the chair to my side of the table, and plopped it down next to me, sitting with a defiant air that amused, irritated, and oddly warmed me.

Lord Israel did nothing but raise one golden eyebrow a fraction of an inch. "You will tell me how you came to be in my son's service, and where he is now."

"I don't think I will," I said simply, shaking away the power of the sun from my hands. I was beginning to see that there was a time and a place for lightweaving, and this was neither. "Tell you where Deo is located, that is. For one, I'm not exactly sure, since I've been away for two days now, but mostly because I don't believe he'd like for you to know."

"You speak boldly, priest," Israel said, his words sharp-edged.

My eyes widened.

He laughed at my surprise. "Oh yes, I recognize you. You are Sandor's little apprentice, the one she said gave her so much trouble. The one who chased after Deo the time we visited."

I slid a glance out of the corner of my eye toward Hallow, feeling my cheeks warm. Hallow had been looking mildly amused, but that look faded into speculation.

Irritated with myself that I cared what he thought, I cleared my throat and said quickly, "I was a child then, Lord Israel, not to mention the fact that the visit in question was some time ago. Not that I ever fancied him—"

Israel lifted his hand to stop me. "Lady Sandor promised that someday I would desire you for my company. She never told me why, hinting only that you had an ability that was undeveloped, but which, in time, would help our cause."

"She said that?" I stared at him, unable to believe his words. "But… she always told me that my power was not to be used… and yet all along, she intended for me to join you? Why didn't she tell me? Why didn't she allow me to go any of the hundred times I begged to be released so I could fight? Why did she keep me a virtual prisoner when she told you about me?"

He slapped his hands loudly on the table, causing me to jump in my seat. "I have no time for your foolishness. What Lady Sandor did or did not tell you is of no importance; what I wish to know is why she kept from me the fact that you were a Bane of Eris. How did you come by this power?"

"My lord, I don't think—" Hallow started to say.

"Silence!" Lord Israel roared.

Hallow's lips thinned, and I noticed his fingers curling into fists. I wondered if it was to keep from speaking back to his overlord, or if he was trying to stop himself from casting a spell.

"Now." Israel leaned forward, his fingers splaying across the table. The look in his eyes was almost mesmerizing, and for a moment, I felt just like a mouse cornered by an adder. "Tell me what you know."

I looked at him, really looked at him. No gray touched his hair, although that didn't surprise me much. The Fireborn were extremely long-lived, usually enjoying life spans that stretched to a millennium, unless cut short by war or some violent death. Lord Israel had lived a few hundred summers already, but his face was unlined. He exuded power, the sort of power that was earned through hard-fought battle.

Although a flip answer was ready on my lips, I decided on diplomacy. "I know a good many things, my lord, but what you wish to know is not my knowledge to give."

Lord Israel took a deep breath. I reminded myself that I was a banesman, albeit one who didn't know well how to use her magic, and that although I owed my fealty to Deo, Lord Israel was a very powerful man. I needed to proceed with caution. "Did Deo seduce you? Is that it? You tumbled into his bed and he turned you into this... this monstrosity? Or is it that you expect to marry him and one day rule my lands with him? If so, you are sadly misguided."

All ideas of being circumspect flew out of the window. I got to my feet, allowing my ire to show. "Not that it's any of your business, but no, I have not been seduced or tumbled by anyone, nor do I want to rule anywhere!"

"You are a virgin?" His eyebrows rose high for a moment as he looked me up and down.

Heat flooded my face. I cast another glance toward Hallow, furious with both Lord Israel and myself at my reaction. What did Hallow's opinion matter to me?

"You're not that large that you'd be unwieldy in bed. But that's neither here nor there. Where is Deo? How did you come to be in Genora? He swore he would save his mother, but I did not believe he could raise a company in so short a time. Does he mean mischief? Is he planning on attacking the Council of Four Armies because I would not allow him to be a part of it?"

I crossed my arms, aware that Hallow rose and stood at my shoulder. "You insult me and then expect me to tell you what you want to know?"

Lord Israel shrugged. "I am the leader of the Fireborn, and the council. Your feelings are insignificant compared to the fight we face."

"You're here to fight the Harborym, too?" I asked, unwilling to continue the conversation, but knowing this information would be of interest to Deo. "What exactly *is* the Council of Four Armies?"

He looked at Hallow and ignored my question. "You called her by name. How do you know this woman?"

"Master Nix was fond of visiting temples when we traveled," Hallow said after a moment's silence. "We traveled the breadth of Aryia, and Allegria is an unusual name. It isn't one you forget."

I looked at him in disbelief. He deliberately implied we'd met while at the temple, but I would have remembered a man such as he. Which meant he'd willfully (and skillfully) misled Lord Israel. I wondered why he didn't mention our meeting at Kelos, or that I, too, sought the runeseeker, but I wasn't about to ask him.

Not at that moment, anyway.

"I see. Then there's no reason to keep her alive."

"She clearly has a good deal of power—" Hallow started to say.

"She is an abomination," Israel said, his expression one of extreme boredom. "I do not wish to explain to Jalas and Dasa why one of the very monsters we seek to destroy is here in our midst."

Dasa? Was the queen coming to meet with Lord Israel, too? I wondered if Deo knew that both his mother and his former intended would be in his father's company. I had a feeling he knew nothing about it.

"I am not a Harborym," I said before Hallow could speak. "On the contrary, my sole reason for being in Genora is to drive them from Alba. What I wonder is that you are here, too. Deo said you had given up on the Starborn many years ago."

"Deo knows nothing about what is happening here," Lord Israel said abruptly, leaping to his feet, his eyes glittering like polished amber. "I assume he is in the area if he sent his spy to check on me. Very well, we will take care of him at the same time we destroy the Harborym."

A little pang of guilt worried me. Had I spoken injudiciously? Israel had to know that if banesmen were here, it meant Deo could not be far behind.

"Destroy the Harborym as you tried and failed to do for so long?" I couldn't help but ask, and immediately regretted it. I knew better than to give in to my temper.

"Goddesses above, grant us your grace," Hallow murmured and cast his gaze upward for a moment before he shifted so that he was partially blocking me.

Lord Israel snarled a word I'd never heard around the temple and slammed his fist onto the table before turning on his heel and stalking away. "Imprison her," he snapped as he did so.

"My lord," Hallow called after him, a surprising note of steel in his voice causing Israel to pause and half-turn toward him. "Allegria is not your enemy. She has done no wrong—"

"She is a Bane of Eris. Next to the Harborym, they are the biggest threat to peace in Alba. She must be destroyed with them." He started forward again.

"I am no threat—" I began to protest.

"Let me have her," Hallow called, surprising me into silence and causing Israel to stop once again.

"Why?" Israel asked, his face devoid of all expression.

Hallow shot me a quick glance. "She has knowledge of magic which you yourself said we do not understand. It will benefit me to learn from her."

"She is dangerous," Israel said, shaking his head. "Chaos magic cannot be controlled. My own son proved that to me."

"The knowledge that she holds would benefit you," Hallow said smoothly. "If Lord Deo really has mastered the magic—"

"He hasn't, despite what he claims. Do not believe that because he managed to escape his exile, he has become the antithesis of the Harborym. The magic is using him, just as it will use this priest."

"I will be responsible for her." Hallow spoke so persuasively that I stared at him in suspicion. Why was he so interested in learning about chaos magic? While I wanted to flatter myself that he'd felt an instant attraction to me, sadly, I knew it was Deo who held his interest. No doubt Hallow thought he could use me to get to Deo. "I will guarantee that she does no harm to your people. Think of what Lord Jalas will say when we have mastered this power of hers. Did you yourself not say we needed to use every weapon in our arsenal to battle the Harborym? It would be the height of folly to throw away what Allegria has to offer us."

"Are you insane?" I asked him, unable to keep my tongue still.

Hallow ignored the question, his gaze firmly fixed on his overlord.

"You may keep her until Jalas arrives, but no longer. Her execution will mark the beginning of our campaign. Until then, I do not wish to see her," Israel said after a moment, making a quick gesture of impatience before continuing on to his newly pitched tent.

"You will guarantee I do no harm? And just who are you, arcanist, to keep me from doing anything I choose to do? Do you forget that I am a lightweaver as well—"

"Be quiet, you fool," Hallow said, taking my arm and pushing me toward a row of tents. "The guards have good hearing, and the last thing we need is you giving them cause to kill you."

"Now I know you're insane," I said through my teeth, but decided that he was right about one thing—I wasn't going to announce to everyone just what powers I had. I allowed him to keep his hand on my arm as we wove our way through the tents until we came to one bearing a standard with a flight of swallows. He pulled open the flap and gestured me inside. I glanced around, decided that I wanted to get information from him before I made my escape, and entered the tent.

Once I had what I wanted from him, I'd leave. It was going to be just as simple as that.

Chapter 10

Hallow breathed a sigh of relief when he dropped the cloth flap across the entrance of the tent assigned to him, which, luckily, had just been re-erected. Keeping Allegria from being imprisoned had been a near thing, too near for his taste. He looked at her as she brazenly examined the belongings scattered around the tent before turning to face him.

Goddess, but she was a stubborn wench. Even now, she had her chin tilted in the air just as if she were the wife of a wealthy squire, and he a lowly stableboy. Why he'd gone to the trouble of saving her from Israel's wrath was beyond him.

He shook his head even as those thoughts crossed his mind. There was no mystery as to why he'd saved her from imprisonment or worse—she was far too intriguing and had too much enticing knowledge to be locked away—but why he had risked his own status by guaranteeing her good behavior was an entirely different matter. "I suspect you're going to be far more trouble than you're worth."

She stiffened at the words, and he hastened to correct himself.

"My apologies, that came out wrong. I meant that you were going to cause me more trouble than any knowledge of the magic you wield will benefit me."

"That's just as insulting," she said, her chin rising even higher; then suddenly she was right there in his face, her breath fanning out across his cheeks, her sun-warmed scent wrapping itself around him. "You're no prize either, you know. How dare you treat me like an errant child! Who are you to take charge of me?"

"I had to do something to get you out of that situation," he explained, trying to control a suddenly rising libido. It had been far too long since he'd availed himself of a tavern wench, one distracted part of his mind commented. "We might have only met once, but I knew if I left you to your own devices, you'd end up clad in chains, or minus your head."

"You know nothing about me," she snapped, poking him in the chest. "I am not a child to be rescued. I am not just a lightweaver—I am one of Lord Deo's elite team, and I bear within me the magic of the Harborym themselves. So the next time you think to rescue me, arcanist, remember that."

He smiled. He couldn't help himself; she reminded him so much of Master Nix at his most pompous. "I will admit that the explosion you managed was unlike anything I've ever seen. But the chaos magic you wield—I've seen it in the Harborym's hands, and there it has only the power of death and destruction."

Her chin dropped, and she held up her hands. "That's what the containment runes are for. They keep the chaos magic from using and consuming me."

"But Master Nix said…" He stopped, deciding it was not the ideal moment for a lecture on the origin of magic.

"He said what?"

"Something best left for another day." Hallow was once again aware of Allegria standing so close to him, he could feel her warmth against his chest and belly. "Why did you come here?"

Annoyance flickered across her face. "You have my runeseeker."

"You followed us all the way here from Kelos?" Suddenly, he grinned. "I apologize for the bubble and slight deception, but it was important that I get Exodius to Lord Israel. Or so I thought—the old man has done little enough since we arrived, saying he can do nothing until he finds the queen's moonstones. How long did the bubble last?"

"Long enough for the ghosts to begin to return." She poked him again in the chest before allowing her fingers to spread across one of his pectorals. "They were… the ghosts… they were…"

He felt as if someone had sucked all the air out of the tent. The scent of her, part sun-warmed woman, part something heady like wildflowers, tightened its grip on him, sinking deep into his blood. "They were what?"

"Hmm?" The flecks in her eyes glowed brightly as she spread her fingers wider on his chest, her breath caressing his face, leaving him feeling as if he'd drunk a full skin of wine.

He also had an erection that he was willing to bet was as hard as the finest marble.

"Are you really a virgin?" he found himself asking and was instantly mortified. Could he be more uncouth?

She stopped looking at his chest and met his gaze. "I am a priestess of the Temple of Kiriah."

Again, his mouth spoke before his brain could consider the consequences. "There are many children at the temples I visited with Master Nix."

She made a face; then a little smile curved her lips.

Her pink, perfectly formed lips.

"There are a lot at our temple, too," she admitted. "Lady Sandor doesn't care if the priestesses indulge in dalliances so long as it doesn't affect our work."

"Ah. A wise woman."

She was back to looking at her fingers on his chest, sending little tendrils of heat across his torso as her hand stroked downward to his belly. "Yes, it is. Very nice."

"What is?" Somehow, he seemed to have lost the thread of the conversation. It had to be the flowery scent that clung to her.

"Yes." She put a second hand on his chest, and for a moment, he felt as if he'd been punched in the belly. The heat from her fingers as they trailed down his chest drove almost all other thoughts from his mind. Without thinking about the wisdom of such a foolish act, he slid one hand into her hair and tipped her face up until his lips just brushed hers.

"Allegria," he said, enjoying the way the syllables rolled around his tongue.

Her pupils flared, the gold flecks kindling with a light that seemed to glow.

He kissed the edges of her mouth, tentative, asking her without words if she enjoyed it, and rejoicing when her lips parted slightly, allowing him access to the sweetness inside.

She moaned into his mouth, her hands tugging on his hair. And with that, he deepened the kiss, pulling her hips closer to his, enjoying the sweet torment of her body pressed against his now steel-hard penis.

That all ended when she suddenly slapped both hands on his chest and shoved him backward, leaving his mouth bereft of hers. He was momentarily dazed, wondering if he'd done something wrong.

"You dare!" she said, her voice filled with anger, her eyes glittering like onyx in a sunny stream.

"I'm sorry if you didn't enjoy the kiss—" he started to apologize, but she snapped an oath that dried the words up on his lips.

"Kiriah's toes! It's not the kiss I object to—it's the spell you put on me before you left me in that bubble. I demand you take it off now."

"The bubble?" he asked, confused by her use of pronouns.

She made an impatient gesture. "The spell, you ignoramus!"

Now he really was at a loss to understand. "What spell?"

"The one you put on me to make me notice your eye crinkles, and your shoulders, and your really impressive chest... and the muscles that go down to your belly... and your eyes that look like you're always laughing at a secret joke. I object to the secret joke! If you're going to eye laugh, you should tell me what's so funny so I can laugh, too." She put a hand to her mouth and looked momentarily horrified. "And also the spell that made me tell you all that. Goddess, I didn't say what I think I just said, did I?"

He wanted to laugh, but had the feeling she wouldn't appreciate the fact that he found her utterly delightful and different from every other woman he'd met. "Eye crinkles?" he asked instead, and touched the skin at the edges of his eyes. "You mean my crow's-feet? You like them? Master Nix told me that use of arcane magic was making me look old before my time. I can't imagine anyone thinking they were nice. Or imagining I could cast a charm spell even if I wanted to, and even if a wielder of magic such as you would be susceptible to it."

Now it was her turn to look confused. "You didn't cast a spell?"

He shook his head. "My master never taught me spells of chivalry, saying they were for the highborn, and not the likes of me."

"But..." Her gaze went to his head for a few seconds. "You have the pale hair of the highborn."

"My father came from a family who had some renown in our region, but he was cast from them when he chose to marry my mother."

An odd expression crossed her face. "Was she hearty peasant stock, too?"

"Not quite," he said with a little laugh. Then, unable to keep from brushing a strand of hair from her cheek, he allowed his thumb to linger on the softness of her skin. "I will apologize for the kiss if you like, although I would be untruthful if I did not say I enjoyed it."

She sighed. "I did, as well. Which is shameful to admit if you really didn't cast a spell on me—" She shot him a sharp look.

"I swear by both goddesses that I am innocent of any charm spells."

"—but that's really not important now. What is important is that you explain to me what this Council of Four Armies is."

He took in her earnest expression, the way her eyes avoided meeting his, and the fact that she had moved away to absently caress the pommel of Penn's saddle, which sat on a wooden chest. "I will answer your question if you answer one of mine."

She thought about that for a moment, then nodded. "I want to hear the question first. It's only fair, since you know what I wish to learn."

He settled himself and his rock-hard erection on the cot that Lord Israel had provided, thankful once again for the thigh-length tunic that hid the proof of how profoundly he was affected by the kiss. "I want you to explain to me exactly what a banesman is."

She was silent for a moment, then, to his surprise, sat down next to him, her face thoughtful. "I'll tell you what I know, but only because I don't believe it will do Deo any harm, and it might go far to getting your obstinate overlord to realize a few truths. I'm afraid it's not a detailed history, however. Deo was not very forthcoming on our journey to Genora, and the others were no help."

Hallow was very aware of her sitting so close to him, but even as he told his body to stop reacting to her tempting nearness, the analytical part of his brain was weighing the story she told him about the transformation, and how Deo intended to use his elite army to destroy once and for all the invaders who had enslaved half the world.

"So he has really managed to harness chaos magic," he murmured to himself when she had finished her tale. "I hadn't thought it could be done, although my old master swore it was possible. Still…" He eyed the line of dots along her forehead, touching it with the tip of his forefinger. "It seems to me that perhaps Deo has underestimated the impact of his newfound abilities on Alba."

"Is it… ugly?" Allegria asked, then made an annoyed expression. "The line on my head. Is it… unsightly?"

"No," he said, tracing it. On a whim, he lifted the hair at her temple and peered underneath it. "It's just a narrow line of tiny black spots, like knots in lacework. It looks like it goes all the way around."

She rubbed her forehead and made an annoyed sound. "I don't mean to be so vain, but Deo had no mirror, and from the way the others stared at me, I thought it must be very pronounced. What do you mean, underestimated?"

"I'm not sure yet," he admitted, turning slightly, enough that his leg pressed against her. Instantly, he was hard again. "It's just a feeling that things are not going to go as smoothly as he believes."

"That could be said about many things, Lord Israel's campaign included, which brings us to the Council of Four Armies."

"It does indeed." He was silent, wondering what was the best path to take. He had told Lord Israel he would help fight the Harborym, but that help could take many forms. And now, there was Allegria, enticing him in both physical and mental ways. Was not her presence in his life a sign from the goddesses that he was meant to take another path?

"It's your turn to share," she said, nudging him with her elbow.

He looked at her in confusion for a moment.

"We agreed to exchange information," she explained.

"Ah. Yes." He cleared his throat and ignored the burn of her leg against his. "The council is made up of four tribes, as you must have realized. Lord Israel heads the armies of Aryia. Lord Jalas leads the army from the High Lands of Poronne. The Master of Kelos—who is the runeseeker Exodius—leads the arcanists, if such a scattered and unorganized group of people can ever be said to be led. And Queen Dasa controls those Starborn who have escaped enslavement."

"That is very interesting. So the queen will be joining Lord Israel?"

Hallow shifted, uncomfortable with the astuteness of her question. He made it a policy not to outright lie unless there was a very good reason for it, and now that he and Allegria had come to an accord of sorts, he felt unwilling to do so. Then there was Lord Israel. True, he had sworn no fealty, but that didn't mean he could reveal details Lord Israel would prefer not be shared.

In the end, he told Allegria an abbreviated form of the truth. "The queen's intentions are unknown at this time."

"She's here, though, isn't she? On Genora?" Allegria asked, seeing through his carefully worded statement. "She plans on helping destroy the Harborym?"

"It is my belief she is," he said, and decided a change of subject was in order. He tried to pick something suitably interesting to distract her, but before he could do so, his mouth spoke for him. "Is Deo your lover?"

"No," she answered absently, clearly thinking about what he'd just told her. Then she shot him an amused glance and poked him in the side with her elbow. "I wouldn't have allowed you to kiss me if he was."

"But you chased after him when you were young?"

"As did, according to Deo, every female of tender years. In my case, it wasn't true infatuation. I simply wanted to join Lord Israel's company to fight." Her voice was filled with scorn for a few seconds before she chuckled, a delightful sound that went straight to his groin. He made a mental note to have a lengthy talk with his libido later. "Deo was very handsome then, you know. Not blond like you, but still handsome. I think he probably took after the queen."

Hallow gave a one-shouldered shrug. "And his pretty face was enough to capture your attention?"

"My attention was captured by the idea of fighting the Harborym far more than by Deo," she protested. "Why are you trying to avoid talking about the queen? What is it you know that you don't want to tell me?"

"You're good," he told her. "I knew you were astute, but you didn't let the subject of your infatuation with Deo sway you."

"Sandor—the head of my temple—calls it pigheadedness. What do you hide about the queen, Hallow of Penhallow?"

He sighed. "You weren't distracted."

"I was, but only temporarily."

"I suspect I will regret telling you, but I can see you are going to make an issue out of something that doesn't deserve that attention. Queen Dasa is currently in Starfall City."

"That much I guessed. She's a prisoner, then?"

"No." He said nothing more, just let the word hang there in front of them.

Allegria's eyes widened. "The Harborym hold the city."

"They do."

She sucked in her breath while she made the obvious conclusion, drawing his attention back to her mouth with its delicious pink lips. "She's working with them?"

"So it is said."

Her look was as sharp as the swords she had worn. "You don't know for certain?"

"I have not met her," he said carefully, spreading his hands. "I only repeat what was told to me by Lord Israel's men-at-arms."

"Interesting," she said, and was silent while she chewed over this information. "Well, this has been very useful. Thank you for your honesty. If you would fetch my swords, I'll slip out and let you get on with whatever it is you do. What *do* you do?"

"I am an arcanist," he said evenly. "I'm no sunweaving Bane of Eris, but I have my uses. I take it you intend on simply walking out of the camp?"

"Of course. I can't stay here. Lord Israel isn't what I would call overly stable in the emotional department, and even if he were open to conversation, I really have little skill in the art of diplomacy. I'll just take my swords and be off."

He fought the urge to laugh at her matter-of-fact attitude. "I wish it was that easy, but as you will no doubt recall, I gave Lord Israel my guarantee of your good behavior. I doubt if he'd call your escaping to take tales back to his son good behavior."

"I'm not staying, Hallow," she told him, the lights in her eyes glinting a warning.

"I can't let you leave."

"Then I won't give you the choice—" She rose and her hands started to glow golden. Hallow leaped to his feet, frantically drawing protective wards all around before taking hold of Allegria's arms.

They were so close, her scent enveloped him in a wave of lust, desire, and need.

She had stiffened the second he touched her, but suddenly swayed toward him, her hands on his shoulders, her mouth near his.

Just as he was about to accept the kiss she so plainly offered, the flap to the tent was shoved aside, and a hand bearing a familiar black staff was jabbed toward him.

"Take Thorn," Exodius's voice came from outside the tent. "He wishes to go with you."

Hallow sighed against Allegria's lips.

She gave a little laugh. "It's just as well. I don't have time for a dalliance now, anyway."

The hand holding the staff waggled impatiently. "Take it, lad. I SAID, TAKE THORN. HE WANTS TO GO WITH YOU. You'd think the boy would get his ears checked, but that's the way of the young these days. They know best, they always know best. STOP KISSING THE GIRL AND TAKE THORN. HE DOESN'T HAVE THE PATIENCE I HAVE. Those moonstones won't find themselves, no matter what young Israel thinks."

Hallow pulled aside the flap and confronted the runeseeker. "Where does your staff think I'm going? The council is meeting here, as you well know since I brought you here for that very purpose."

"Ask him," Exodius said, shoving the staff into his hands before shuffling off. "I wash my hands of the pair of you. You can keep him. YOU CAN KEEP THORN. As if I have all the time in the world to take him places. If he wanted to go with the lad so badly, he should have remained alive and not left me to be the Master of Kelos."

"Thorn?" Allegria asked, moving next to him while she watched the old man shamble back toward the center of the camp. "Is that the name of the staff?"

"Yes. Evidently the spirit of the former Master of Kelos imbues it. I gather Exodius and Thorn don't get along well." Hallow arranged the staff across the opening of the tent—on the outside, just in case the spirit inhabiting it had voyeuristic tendencies—in such a way that it would fall should Allegria try to escape without his being aware.

Although how he could not be aware of her was beyond his ken. It was all he could do to not kiss her again, not caress that silky soft cheek, not breathe in her flower scent, the one that reminded him of lying in a field on a lazy summer afternoon with bees drowsily buzzing past him… no. He had to stop thinking about his body's urges and remember that Allegria offered knowledge he had no other way to access.

"Lord Israel would not take kindly to your leaving now," he said slowly, hating the feeling of being caught between his duty to Israel and his sympathy for Allegria's plight. It wasn't as if she were an enemy—she wanted exactly the same thing that the whole of Alba wanted. Was it her fault that she'd decided to achieve that end by aligning herself with Deo? "I don't know Lord Israel well, but I know he would view your escape as a declaration of war against him, both personally and politically."

"Do you think that will frighten me?" Allegria spoke with a genuine note of curiosity in her voice, one hand lifted to touch the side of his face. "You know as well as I do that dedicating one's life to magic means releasing fear of the unknown. Isn't that true?"

He caught her hand and turned the palm to his lips, kissing it before he realized what he was doing. "Yes, but it doesn't mean we should throw our lives away with reckless disregard for those who hold power."

"I'm not going to stay," she warned. "I don't mind a dalliance, because… well, there are your eye crinkles, and I think that even though you've tied yourself to a man who feels the only way to deal with his son is to banish him, you're probably an honorable person, but there is something bigger than Lord Israel's ire to fear, and I've sworn to fight it, just as you've sworn to be at your overlord's side."

Hallow hadn't made any oath to Lord Israel, but he understood her point nonetheless. "You can't leave *now*," he said, having resigned himself to the inevitable. Once again, Exodius had seemed to know what was going to happen before he made the decision. He couldn't pass up the opportunity to learn more about Deo and how he controlled and used the chaos power. His path lay clear before him. "The sun has hours before she sets. The guards would see you if you tried to escape before dark, and that would end in a bloodbath."

She snorted a delicate, if unladylike, snort. "Do you think I fear them?"

"No," he said honestly, and gave her hand a little squeeze. "The blood would be theirs. But I don't think you wish to have the death of innocents on this lovely hand."

She gave him a curious look, her cheeks pinkening in a delightful manner. "Do you think my hand is… lovely?"

"I think your hand is a mere shadow to the rest of your beauty," he said with a suavity that had heretofore escaped him.

She blushed again, glancing around the tent. "I suppose it would be folly to just walk out of here in full view of everyone. Which means waiting for six hours or so here. In this tent."

"Yes." Hallow wondered if it was just him, or if the air was suddenly sucked out of the immediate area.

She slid him a look that raised his temperature several degrees. "Do you have any suggestions on ways to pass the time?"

He opened his mouth to speak, couldn't, and cleared his throat before trying again. His voice came out as if he were being strangled. "We could exchange knowledge of chaos and arcane magic."

"Yes," she said slowly, her gaze drifting down to his chest. A burning in his gut seemed to grow... as did other parts of him. "That would no doubt be beneficial."

"To us both," he pointed out, his body and mind urging him to take her in his arms, strip off her garments, and reveal all that lovely soft flesh.

"Mutually improving," she said, a hitch in her voice giving it a breathless quality.

"Mutual is good," his mouth said on its own, his brain having gone off to visit a land made up solely of lustful thoughts.

"Hallow?"

"Hmm?" He stopped wondering how long it would take to get them both naked and forced his attention to what she was saying.

She held her arms open. "Improve me," she said, and with a mental whoop of delight, he swept her up and gave in to the desire to claim her mouth, which had been plaguing him since he'd first seen her.

Chapter 11

"You're not going to be disappointed that I'm not a virgin, are you?"

My words were muffled, being spoken, as they were, against his naked shoulder while my hands were busy stroking his chest.

And oh, what a chest it was. I thought at first it was the breadth of it that made my legs feel as if they were made of honey, but now that I saw it in all its glory, I decided it was the scattering of golden hair that made hidden parts of me come alive.

He stopped struggling to undo the ties on my under tunic, and looked at me, his eyes glittering like sapphires. "You're not bound to someone?"

"Would I be here now if I was?" I shook my head at the idea that he would even ask. "But I am not a virgin as Lord Israel seemed to believe."

"Ah. Well, as to that, neither am I." He grinned, making waves of heat wash up my thighs and pool in my secretive parts. "I'm not going to insult you by asking if you're sure you wish to do this, but I feel obligated to point out we could spend the time exchanging knowledge rather than…"

"I think the sort of knowledge exchange we're going to perform is much more valuable," I said, and put a finger on one of his pert little nipples peeping out from the golden hair.

He sucked in approximately half of the air in the tent. "Oh, goddesses of day and night, yes! Much more valuable!"

I swore his fingers seemed to trail fire when he helped me out of my undergarments, and at one point, I peeked at his hands, but they were just normal hands—long fingers with blunt tips—and yet, they stirred feelings in me that had been missing from my brief assignations with Sam the groom. At last we tumbled onto Hallow's cot, our clothing strewn around the tent, and Hallow's tunic hanging over the bird carved onto the top of runeseeker's staff even though it sat outside the tent.

"Just in case," Hallow said.

I didn't question him about what he meant; I couldn't do anything but marvel at the sight of him without his clothing.

"Erm..." he said, touching the silver band at my wrist. "On or off?"

"On. I don't think you'd like me with them off," I answered, spreading my fingers wide on his belly, my gaze caught and held by his most prodigious gift from the goddesses. "That's... that's a lot bigger than Sam the groom's manhood."

Hallow glanced down at it. "Is it? I assure you it's a pretty standard size. That is, I've not had any complaints, but then again, I haven't had maidens falling to their knees to worship my ability to wield it."

I couldn't help but laugh, and took him into one hand, enjoying his resulting intake of breath. "Bertilde, the cook at our temple, swears that all men think women worship their man bits. You're very hot. You don't have a fever in it, do you? Does it need doctoring? I was never very good with medicines, but Sandor made me learn methods of alleviating a fever. Do you happen to have any leeches? Or I can make a poultice with fresh dung—"

His laughter interrupted my offer of manhood care. He pried my hands from his fevered part, pulling me down until I lay across his (truly breathtaking) chest. "My heart, I assure you my penis is not ailing, nor does it need a poultice, although it does have a fever... for you."

I stopped trying to remember the dung poultice recipe, oddly flattered by both his term of endearment, and the compliment. "Well, then. If you're quite sure all is well there, then I suppose we can proceed."

"I suppose we can," he said with suspect gravity.

I studied him. His eyes were crinkling away like mad. "What would you suggest I do to take care of this fever I caused?"

"Oh, goddess," he said on a half-moan, half-laugh. "Whatever you want. I am putty in your hands. Do with me as you will."

And so I did. I stroked his chest. I kissed his neck. I even licked his nipples, but it wasn't until I took his man parts in both hands that he moaned and begged the goddesses for mercy.

"Stop!" he demanded at one point, when I was working up a nice rhythm that had him writhing on the cot.

"Why? Don't you like that?"

"Kiriah's nipples, woman!" He lifted his head and glared down the length of his body to where I was kneeling between his legs. "Do I look as if I don't like that? I like it a lot. Too much. And if you don't stop squeezing those, it will all be over. And I mean that in a literal sense as well as a metaphorical one."

"I'm being gentle," I said, giving the plump little sacks of flesh a very slight squeeze. "Sam said that a little squeeze was good, and that it heightened the sensations for men. He also said that sometimes, a finger inserted into—"

"Allegria!"

"What?" I asked, startled by the way he shouted my name with a gargle of laughter.

"I'm going to have a word with this Sam of yours, but until then, stop. No, not because you're not being gentle. You aren't hurting me—at least, not hurting me in the sense you mean."

"Sam isn't mine," I felt obligated to point out. "He wed one of the camp followers who came to the temple in hopes that prayer would rid her of her itch for men. Sandor said nothing but a strong salve would do that, and she'd be better off marrying a man who had the same sort of lust for coupling, and so she wed Sam. Why are you laughing?"

"You're the only woman I know who can hold a man's stones in one hand, his cock in the other, and detail the life path of a former lover. Are you done with the tale of Sam and his lusty wife?"

"Yes," I said, releasing both handfuls of man bits. "Her name was Jenna, by the way."

He shouted with laughter, and before I could tell him he was the oddest man I had ever met, flipped me so that I was on my back, and he was over me, a glint in his eyes that warmed me to my toes. "Now it's my turn. And I can promise you I'll do this without once mentioning any of my former lovers."

"Really? How many did you ha—aieeeee!"

His mouth closed on one of my nipples, just about sending me off the bed with ripples of pleasure that spread outward. "Like that, do you?"

"Why didn't I use my mouth on your nipples?" I gasped, my hands flailing helplessly against the linen covers. "Let me do it now. Wait, after you do the other one. And then back to the first. And the second again."

"I'll do whatever you want," he chuckled, his hands caressing my belly. "But perhaps you might want to hold your list of demands until after I try this."

"What?" I asked, thrusting my shoulders back so he'd notice my breasts, which were missing him. He kissed a path down my belly to the point where my inner parts started. "What are you doing down there? Sam never looked at my parts. Is something amiss? Are there black spots there, too?"

"There are no spots that I see, although I have to admit that I'm glad to be able to show you something Sam never bothered to teach you. Now, you might want to hold on to something."

The warmth of his breath was the only warning I had before his mouth touched the secret parts of me. I grabbed his head, my entire being focused on one spot.

"Maybe something other than my hair," he mumbled into my crotch.

"Kiriah Sunbringer!" I said on a gasp and tugged his hair just in case he wasn't paying attention. "What was that? Do it again!"

His tongue swirled at the same time a finger slid into me. I swear my eyes crossed with the warmth and tension and sense of the coming explosion of joy. The sensation was so overwhelming, I quivered with expectation, and then suddenly, his mouth and fingers were gone, and I was filled with his very solid penis.

"So hot," he murmured, nibbling on my neck as his hips moved.

"I told you... oh, merciful Kiriah!... I told you that you had a fever. Do you mind if I do this?" I flexed my hips to take him in deeper.

He reared back, his hair standing on end like a blond porcupine, his eyes so hot I swore they could set the tent alight. "Not at all. Feel free to do that whenever you have the notion. Now would be a good time."

I flexed, enjoying this new feminine power I evidently possessed. I wanted to tell him that I never flexed with Sam, but felt that bit of news could wait for a later time. Instead, I matched my flexing to his thrusting, and in a very short time, we both lost the rhythm.

"I think... goddess, yes, my breasts like that a lot... I think I'm close... are you—"

"Yes! Yes, yes, yes. And if you move like that again, I'll be over the edge."

I dug my fingers into the thick muscles of his behind and made the little swivel of my hips that I'd been inspired to try. He gave a shout of completion, and made hard, fast little thrusts that pushed me into an orgasm so great, my entire body lit up, glowing with the golden light of the sun.

"This...blessed goddesses, how is there even air left to breathe?... this is different," Hallow panted, pushing himself up on his arms. "Please tell me you're not going to flatten this tent again. I don't mind your flexing your magical muscles, but I really don't want to have to explain to everyone what we were doing."

I looked down my body to where we were still joined. The few times I'd used my lightweaving powers, the light had clung to my hands only, but now here I was lit up like a moon bug in late summer. "I don't know what happened. I didn't do this with Sam, but then, he wasn't nearly as proficient with his body as you are with yours."

"Up," Hallow said, sliding off me to stand next to the cot.

"What?" I looked at him in incomprehension. Was he asking me to leave?

"The cot is too narrow to lie together." He pulled me up then lay down on his back before catching me around the waist and pulling me down on top of him, deftly whipping a linen sheet over our bodies. "I don't have the strength to stand. Or talk. Or even think. Just lie here and let me remember how to breathe."

"You are definitely the oddest man I know," I told him, relaxing onto his body with an exhausted sigh of happiness. "Luckily, I like odd."

* * * *

Darkness fell about us like a silken robe slipping from my shoulders.

I sat back on Hallow's cot, watching as he gathered up fresh garments, and pulled them on, warmed by the heated, sated glances he threw my way.

I laughed softly to myself, well content with my decision to indulge my sensual demands, but at the same time regretting that I had to leave him so soon. A small herd of light tigers formed and wrestled across my legs.

"Are you sitting on my—what on earth is that?"

Hallow stopped rummaging through a small leather trunk in order to stare at the tigers.

"Didn't I tell you about that? I make little light animals. They are amusing, and very forbidden by the head priest at my temple." I held out a hand, and one of the tigers jumped onto it before pouncing on my thumb.

"I've never seen anything like this. Can I touch them?"

"I don't see why not." I placed the tiger onto his hand. A look of delight filled his eyes as the tiger gamboled up his arm, across his shoulder, and down his other arm.

"You truly are made of magic," he said, laughing at its antics.

We watched the tigers for a few minutes until they faded into nothing. I rested my chin on my knee and said, "This changes nothing, you know."

"About what? Your leaving? I didn't expect that it would, although I should warn you, if you think to try to take Exodius, you won't get very far. The only reason he allowed me to take him was because he said Thorn told him he'd find success with Lord Israel."

I glanced over at where the shadow of the staff leaning drunkenly across the flap of the tent was visible. "Does the staff really talk?"

"Not to me. Honestly, I think Exodius is a bit... affected... by living alone for so long. I think he imagines some of the conversations he has with people. And things."

"I wasn't planning on taking the runeseeker. I can see that would be impossible, although I am still annoyed with the underhanded way you spirited him away from me."

"My heart, you never had him," he said with laughter in his voice and eyes. I touched the lines that spread from his eyes, feeling—for the moment, at least—warm and happy and sated to the very tips of my toes.

"Why do you call me that?"

"What? My heart?"

"Yes." I brushed a bit of hair from his forehead. "We've only just met. You can't have developed affection for me."

His lips twisted. "Do you think I bed every pretty wench I see? Of course I feel affection for you. And annoyance. And exasperation. Lest you accuse me of toying with you, however, I will add that in my region, 'my heart' is the term we use for those we are sweet on."

I liked the sound of that. Absently, I traced a protection rune in the air over his chest. I was under no illusion that our lovemaking had changed the fact that we were on opposite sides of the battle that was surely coming, but that didn't mean I couldn't cherish moments like this. "In my town, we say 'sweeting.' I think I like yours better."

As the darkness deepened around the camp, Hallow went out to fetch us food, and left again soon after we devoured it.

"I'll be back in a short while. I want to find out what the guards' schedule is," he told me before slipping out of the tent.

I took the opportunity to visit a privy—aware of the guards watching me while I made my way to the privy and back to Hallow's tent—following which I spent a couple of minutes arguing with myself. My better nature lost the argument, and quickly, I made a search of his belongings for anything to replace the weapons that had been taken from me.

He had a sword that had clearly seen better days, a couple of daggers that glinted wickedly but were balanced wrong for my hands, and several books that looked interesting, but wouldn't help me much in a fight against Harborym. "Which means I need to get my swords back. Not to mention the fact that Deo gave them to me, and I want them. How to get them is another mat—"

A shadow moved against the entrance of the tent, and suddenly, Hallow was there.

"Ah, good, you are awake. I wondered if you might not fall asleep, since I was longer than I expected."

"Why do you smell like horse?" I asked, suspicion growing as I examined him. He was clad not in the white and gold garb of Lord Israel's company, but in the same midnight blue and silver worn by the runeseeker. A cloak was clasped around his neck by a silver brooch, and the black bird staff was strapped to his back. A sword hung from his belt, and in his hands he held a long object wrapped in a black cloth. I frowned and glanced around the tent again. Now I realized what was missing. "Your saddle is gone, and you're dressed as if you are going somewhere. If you intend on escorting me out of the area to make sure I don't try to steal the runeseeker, you needn't bother. I told you I wouldn't take him."

"I'm sure you wouldn't, but I know where the guards are located, and where they aren't located because I bribed them to go elsewhere. Come. We don't have long." He handed me the object, which I was relieved to see was my swords and scabbards. I strapped them on, eyeing Hallow when he rifled through the papers in his chest. He pulled out a couple, folded them up, and stuffed them into the outer folds of his tunic before reaching back into the chest and extracting a black cloak. "Put this on and pull up the hood. The fewer chances we give people to recognize you, the better. Are you ready?"

"Yes." I slid him a look, biting my lip for a few seconds while I worked out what I wanted to say. "Hallow... thank you."

"For the cloak? It's one of my master's old castoffs—"

"No, for this." I gestured toward the bed before pulling on the cloak, adjusting the hood so that it hid my face in shadow. "For the... what did you call it? Interlude? And the food, but most importantly for not trying to stop me. I would fight you if I had to, but this is much easier."

He laughed and took me by one hand, snatching up a lantern with the other. "I like your compliments, Allegria. You don't indulge in any of the showy but meaningless words of the highborn. You speak of things that matter, like how much nicer it is to not have to fight your way out of a situation. This way. You have a horse nearby?"

"I have a mount, yes," I said softly, allowing him to pilot me through the maze of tents. There were a few scattered people amongst the tents, but most of them were in the center clearing, where the evening meal was under way. Hallow paused for a couple of minutes next to a string of horses who were munching oats in their feed bags.

"Guard," he said in my ear, gesturing toward the silhouette of a man leaning against a rocky outcropping. "He should leave in a minute."

I turned my head, his breath tickling my cheek. "Then we'd best stay quiet," I said, tipping my head back so that my lips brushed his.

His arms came around me, pulling my body against his at the same time his lips teased mine. "You are wise beyond your years."

I was about to answer, but the silhouette suddenly stood, stretched, scratched his chest, and wandered off toward the privies.

"Another time," Hallow said, taking my hand and leading me past the horses.

It took about ten minutes, but at last we made our way down the rocky hillside, avoiding both guards and the main road.

"Where's your horse?" he asked once we reached the broken South Road.

"Hobbled next to a pond. I can find her. Thank you for your help." I leaned forward and kissed him. "For everything."

"Do you think you're getting rid of me that quickly?" His face was just a faint oval in the darkness, but I could hear the amusement in his voice.

"I don't need you to help me find Buttercup. I know where the pond is. It's just down the road a bit, and off a side track to the east." Annoyed that he thought I was so inept I couldn't find Buttercup on my own, I started down the road, keeping an eye out for guards who might have come down off the hill.

He said nothing. I glanced over my shoulder, a little surprised at his silence, but he was gone, just as if he'd disappeared into the night.

A pang of disappointment ruined the moment, but I told myself not to be so silly. Hallow had done everything I wanted, and I had no right to feel abused because he'd left without so much as a fare-thee-well.

"Has to be a spell. Maybe a derangement spell, one that makes me feel emotions that have no useful role in my life."

Ten minutes later I found Buttercup grazing near the pond, her tail lazily swishing her fat sides.

"I see you haven't suffered from half a day left on your own," I said, removing the hobble and pulling the saddle out of the spot where I'd hidden in it a squat bush. I brushed off the plant matter, shook out her blanket, and, ignoring her bared teeth, got her bridled and the saddle onto her back before she had time to do more than try to take a bite out of my behind. Getting the saddle's cinch tight was another matter. "I swear, you've gotten fatter. Stop holding your breath."

"Troubles?"

I gasped and whirled around to see the shape of a man on a horse standing behind me. My swords were in my hands before I could assess the threat, the chaos magic in me surging so that the runes on my cuffs glowed.

And it was at that moment that I realized why Hallow had smelled like his horse. He'd obviously groomed him before saddling him. I slid my swords back into their scabbards and said, "What do you think you're doing?"

"Other than startling you? I had to fetch Penn from where I'd moved him earlier. Do you need help?" Hallow started to dismount, but I waved his offer away.

"No, I'm quite used to Buttercup's attempts to avoid being saddled properly. What I want to know is why you're mounted and bear the appearance of a man who's about to take a journey." I returned to the cinch and gave it a hearty tug. Buttercup sucked in even more breath, puffing out her sides.

"Probably because I am a man about to take a journey. Didn't you hear Exodius? Thorn the staff wants to go with me. Which means I am to go with you. Are you sure you don't need help?"

"Quite... sure... " I said through grinding teeth, alternately poking Buttercup in the sides and pulling the cinch tight. "You can't... seriously, Buttercup? How can you hold that much air?... can't come with me. Deo wouldn't... gah!... like it."

I was panting by the time I got the cinch sufficiently tight so that the saddle wouldn't slide around the second I mounted.

"Perhaps not, but I don't see how you are going to keep me from accompanying you. I'll simply follow you to where you're going, and it's much nicer if we travel together. Safer, too." I saw the silhouette of his head turn as he glanced around. "The word from the scouts is that the Harborym have packs of Shades patrolling the South Road."

"They don't worry me," I said, attaching my bow and quiver to the saddle. "What about Lord Israel? Does he know you intend to join me?"

"No," Hallow answered, his voice filled with something that sounded a good deal like remorse.

I glanced at his dark shape, wishing I could see his face better. "You would break your fealty to him so easily?"

"Break my fealty?"

"He's your overlord, and you know he wouldn't want you to come with me. At least, I assume he wouldn't want you to." I had a moment of suspicion that he was acting on Lord Israel's orders, but that suspicion evaporated with Hallow's next words.

"Oh, he will definitely not be happy with my actions tonight."

"Well, you *are* breaking your fealty to him."

A curious note was evident in his voice. "Does that bother you? That I would forswear my oath to my overlord?"

"To Lord Israel? No." I tightened the cinch again, uncomfortably aware that I was lying. "But most people feel that when they take an oath, they should hold true to it."

"You are a priestess of Kiriah. They don't allow you to become such without oaths, and yet here you are a long way away from your temple, with weapons on your back, and the intention to fight," he pointed out.

"I was given to the temple as a child," I said quickly, filling my waterskin and attaching it to the saddle. "An oath was taken, but it was not by me."

"And you don't honor that oath because you didn't make it?" he asked, his voice free of judgment, but I bristled nonetheless.

"Oh, I honor it. When I am done helping Deo, I will return to the temple and continue to serve there. I'm doing this first, though."

"Just so you know, my decision to leave Lord Israel's company wasn't made lightly," he said in that same neutral tone.

"Then why do it? There is no need for you to come with me." I bit my lip, wanting to argue more with him but knowing it would serve no purpose. I did feel disappointed in him, though. He seemed like such a man of honor that finding out he could easily cast aside an oath simply to follow a whim tarnished his character a little.

"On the contrary, there is every need. I can't let you travel by yourself. I know you are well trained with your swords, and you bear two kinds of magic I can't use, let alone understand, but I could not live with myself if I let you travel these dangerous roads alone."

"I told you that the Harborym and their Shades don't frighten me."

"No," he said softly. "But they should."

I finished gathering my things and mounted Buttercup, let her do her traditional "Get rid of the person on my back" dance. Once she settled, I rode forward a few paces until I was next to Hallow. His horse snorted and shied, swinging his back end around.

Buttercup bit him on the ass.

"Sorry," I said when Hallow's horse protested, giving a little buck in the process. "She's kind of cranky around horses."

Hallow broke into laughter. "You have a mule."

"I do, but I don't see what's so funny about it. She's very sturdy, and once you get to know her ways, she's not bad. So long as you don't leave her unhobbled. She does try to run away a lot, and she bites, and she tends to steal food, but all in all, she's quite …"

"Reliable?" Hallow said while I struggled to find a word that summed up Buttercup.

"Noo," I said slowly.

"Pleasant?"

"Not really."

"Tolerable?"

"Eh." I urged Buttercup into a fast walk. "Give me some time, and I'll find a word that wouldn't make Kiriah want to smite me for lying."

His soft laughter seemed to surround me in a cocoon of happiness. Which was an odd feeling considering the mix of emotions I felt concerning him. I had enjoyed my interlude with Hallow, but the emotions he stirred in me made me nervous.

I didn't really want him with me, I told myself. I didn't want him to see Deo. I just didn't want him around.

I sighed softly to myself. I really was not any good at lying.

Chapter 12

They came out of the bushes at the exact moment my attention wandered. We'd been riding to Deo's camp for almost two days, following the South Road that led ultimately to Starfall City, engaging in occasional skirmishes with small packs of Shades, but not encountering any real trouble.

Unless you call resisting the lure of Hallow when I was supposed to be sleeping trouble, but that was a personal battle, and evidently not one he shared when it was my turn to sit watch.

But on the afternoon of the second day, Buttercup was clopping along the road, her head bobbing rhythmically as she daydreamed in the warmth of the fading afternoon. I'd fallen into my own reverie, alternating between desiring to talk to Hallow about his knowledge of arcane magic and vowing that he wasn't going to use me as a way to get to Deo, as he so obviously intended. I would leave to Hallow the unenviable task of explaining to Deo just why a liege man of his father was now in his company.

Hallow was riding ahead of me, and just as I was forming a very pithy explanation of why I wasn't going to help him with Deo, a sudden cry of warning snapped me back to the present. With horror, I saw green-and-blue clad figures that must've been the Harborym, rushing from the tall hedges that lined this section of the road.

Worse, they were accompanied by several Shades, the pale creatures who were formerly Starborn, but who had withered away to shells of their former selves under the control of the invaders.

"By the grace of Bellias!" Hallow bellowed, throwing himself off his horse, the black staff already in his hand. Amazingly, the wooden bird at the top of it took flight, while Hallow began drawing runes in the air, clearly summoning arcane power.

I didn't wait to see how he used the blue-white power that crackled around him—with a cry of my own, my bow was singing in my hands, the arrows catching the first couple of Harborym in their respective throats. The others leaped over their bodies, the pack of about twenty swarming forward with at least as many Shades. I dropped a few more before they grew too close.

"Go!" I yelled to Buttercup when I slid out of the saddle and slapped her on her glossy butt before whipping my swords out of their scabbards. Buttercup didn't wait around to be told twice—she bucked as she ran, kicking out at a couple of Shades as she did so, taking both of them down.

The chaos magic in me came to life with the nearness of the Harborym, immediately fighting me for control. I jumped and slashed, spun and sliced, separating arms and heads and, in one case, both legs from my enemies' bodies. But even though I was holding my own against the attackers, more poured in from the hedge. To my right, Hallow was flinging balls of arcane power into the attackers, sending them screaming to the ground with melon-sized holes in their middles.

I spun around and removed the heads from three Shades, yelling at Hallow, "There's more coming your way!"

"I'll take care of them," he shouted back, and with a cry in a language I didn't understand, he raised his hands skyward for a moment before slamming the staff onto the ground in front of him. The ground itself cracked, a deep rumble sounding a second before fissures opened in front of him, the biggest of which swallowed up a half-dozen Harborym.

I would have loved to watch him fight, the blue and silver cloak flying out as he spun and swung the staff against a pair of oncoming Shades, while the small black form of a bird darted back and forth, weaving a net of arcane magic that bound others, causing them to fall to the ground, screaming in agony.

But I had my own fight to focus on, and just as I cleared away three Shades and two more Harborym, a rumbling could be heard from behind the hedge, and suddenly the bushes were gone, a smoking black mass of burned matter, over which strode the largest being I'd ever seen. He was like a parody of Deo, a massive man the height of a giant, with streaming black hair, his dusky skin glittering with sweat, his eyes red with chaos power. The others parted in front of him, clearly giving way to their lieutenant.

A surge of my chaos magic sent me staggering to the side, falling to my knees and dropping my swords in order to clutch at my chest in an attempt to hold the power inside me. The mammoth Harborym stomped toward me, the ground shaking, a low grating sound emerging from his chest. The monster was laughing.

At me.

Hallow screamed something, and I caught sight of him fighting toward me, a sea of Shades threatening to pull him under. He called for Thorn to assist me, and I watched dully as the little black wooden swallow dove at the Harborym leader.

I struggled to hold the chaos magic, to form it the way I wanted it, but it surged again, slipping my control, spilling out of me in an impotent blaze of red light.

The giant approached, and still I knelt, stunned by my own struggle, unable to even move. In one giant hand he held a bloody object that was dragged alongside him. With a horrible shock, I recognized the tunic on the mangled body. It was a banesman, most likely Deo's missing scout.

And still the rumbling, grating laugh continued, mocking my feeble attempts to master that which I'd so eagerly embraced. It was clear that my fate would soon be the same as my fellow banesman. There was no way I could fight the beast.

"Allegria!" Hallow cried, and before I could turn my head to look on him one last time, a heavy rush of air and light slammed into me, sending me flying sideways, out of the Harborym's path.

I landed at least thirty feet away, bouncing painfully on the road, but the arcane blast had served its purpose. It shocked me out of the chaos power's control and allowed me use of my body again. I pulled hard on the power of Kiriah, my hands lighting up gold as I got to my feet. "By the goddess, I will make you pay for the death of that banesman!" I yelled, golden red light crawling up both my arms and across my chest.

I ran toward the Harborym lieutenant as Hallow approached with the same objective from the other side. There were no other Harborym left alive, the area littered with the mangled remains of their force, and the stones slippery with blood. Several Shades chased after Hallow, but with a backward sweep of his hand, they exploded in a brilliant ball of white.

I leaped as I reached the Harborym, using the strength given to me by Kiriah to form the chaos power inside me, throwing it straight at him. Red and black vines began to grow upward from the broken ground, twining themselves up his thick legs, growing higher to encompass his chest and arms. At the same time, Hallow thrust both hands forward, sending a massive blast of pure arcane magic at the lieutenant, rocking him backward. I had no swords left, but I did have my eating dagger, and without hesitation, I yanked it from the sheath at my hip and slashed at the Harborym's neck before I tumbled to the ground.

The chaos magic continued up his body, spreading its tendrils until it held him in a virtual net. The Harborym, clearly not believing his eyes, at first tried to pull off the vines, then began cursing us in a horrible cracked voice.

"Are you harmed? Did I hurt you? Goddesses of day and night, if I hurt you—" Hallow was there at my side, helping me up from where I'd fallen. "It was the only thing I could do. I had to get you out of his way. Is that blood? It is. You're bleeding."

"I'm not harmed, just shaken. And angry," I said with a voice that quavered noticeably. I allowed him to hold on to me while we both watched the chaos magic wrap itself around the Harborym, the long fingers of red now crisscrossing his head, silencing him, until all that was left was the glittering hate in his eyes.

And then even that was gone, the monster having been consumed by the magic. For the time it took for one second to pass into another, a red shape stood before us; then dissolved into the ground and evaporated to nothing.

"My power... the chaos power... it was trying to sacrifice me," I said, pushing back my hair and noticing my hand came away red with blood. "I couldn't control it at all, not until you knocked me to the side. What am I going to do? How can I be a banesman if the power I'm supposed to wield so easily turns against me?"

"I'm afraid I have few answers," he said, lifting a hand when the last three Shades rushed us. They shrieked and burst into flames before racing off, trailing cries and smoke. "But I will point out that you destroyed the Harborym. Not me—it was all you. Whether or not you first had control of your powers, you certainly did a few minutes later. It's probably just a matter of your getting used to using it."

I glanced at the red stain on the earth, all that remained of the Harborym. I wasn't feeling nearly as confident as Hallow, remembering all too well how easily the power had held me in its grip, ready to let me die.

The moon was rising by the time we finally found Deo, first encountering a pair of guards on the road. They were clearly going to object to Hallow's presence, but I brushed their objections—and them—aside with a perfunctory, "We have to see Deo. We have news."

Deo's camp wasn't nearly as large as was his father's but, to my eye, looked much more effective. Deo stood next to a table, over which were spread several maps. Rixius hovered nearby, while Hadrian was clearly in consultation with Deo.

"Which one is the boyfriend?" Hallow asked in a whisper when we approached.

I poked him in the side with my elbow. "I was fourteen! And we did nothing more than exchange an awkward kiss."

"Hmm. I wonder if he's still a bad kisser."

"No. Definitely not," I said placidly, enjoying Hallow's startled glance my way. We approached, and Deo looked up when we stopped in front of him. His gaze settled on Hallow, a frown pulling his brows together.

"My lord," Rixius announced in a loud voice. "The priestess approaches with a stranger."

"I can see that just as well as you can," Deo said irritably. "I thought the runeseeker was an old man. Lief said he was quite aged and slightly mad."

"This is Hallow," I said, gesturing toward him.

"Of Penhallow," he said, bowing. "Of the region of Hallow."

Deo just stared at him.

Hallow gave a little sigh. "My parents had an odd sense of humor. I come from your father's company."

Deo's eyes narrowed, and I could feel a quick flash of anger roll off him. "So the rumors are true? Where is he?"

"Two days' ride from here," Hallow said.

"Is Borin not here?" I asked, glancing around.

"No. He has not yet returned from his patrol." Deo frowned. "I expected him by now, but perhaps he is still gathering information."

"He wasn't at Lord Israel's camp," I said slowly, the sight of the mangled remains of Lief still horribly fresh in my memory.

"I'm sure he will return soon." Deo eyed Hallow. "You look familiar, although I cannot place you. Have we met?"

"Not formally, although your father did save my life. Twice, actually. He found me in the road and sent me to be apprenticed with an arcanist."

"Ah, you were the boy in the road." Deo's frown grew. "That does not explain why you are here now, in place of the runeseeker."

Briefly, Hallow and I took turns explaining the happenings of the last few days, including the fact that we'd buried the remains of Deo's third lieutenant a short while before finding his camp.

Deo looked somber at the death of Lief. "His loss will be felt by us all. It is good you destroyed the Harborym who killed him, though, as it saves me from hunting him down."

"He was a monster," I said with a little shudder.

"The death of the banesman aside, it is as I warned," Rixius interrupted, shooting me black looks. "Word has been given to your father of your intentions. I believe we know who was so free with your doings."

"You odious little slug," I said, anger making my runes fire up. "I did nothing—"

"Just so," Rixius said smugly. "I said all along that you would have no real use, and now you have admitted the very same yourself."

"Listen—" I started.

"Quiet, both of you!" Deo bellowed.

"I'm not going to stand here and let your servant insinuate that I'm a traitor," I snapped.

"Woman, do not push me!" Deo turned a warning look on me.

"Then tell your little minion to leave me in peace!" I glared right back at him.

Hallow swallowed a hiccup of laughter.

Deo took a deep breath. "Rixius, go attend to your duties. Do not argue with me! Just go do your work and leave Allegria be."

"He's an officious little mud skimmer," I told Hallow in an undertone. "We have a history. A brief one, but he doesn't like me at all."

"You don't say," Hallow said with a suspicious quiver of his lips.

"No doubt my father seeks to gather the Council of Four Armies, believing he can cover himself in glory and be named savior of Alba." Deo's jaw tightened for a few minutes before he managed to add, "He is mistaken. It is my banesmen, and my banesmen alone, who will bring down the Harborym and free the Starborn."

Hallow lifted his hand. "Can you find use for an arcanist?"

Deo eyed him. "Why should I take you into my company? You are more likely to be a spy than Allegria."

"Hey!" I protested.

Deo waved it away.

"What reason do you wish to join me?"

"I want to help," Hallow said simply. "And I have sworn to use my knowledge to end the invasion. Your company is smaller than Lord Israel's, so you will benefit more from my help. Your father will soon have the armies of others to join with his own, and does not need me as badly."

"I don't *need* you at all." Deo didn't look convinced.

I studied Hallow's face, unsure of whether he was telling the absolute truth. I wanted to believe the explanation was as simple as he said, but a small doubt wiggled in the back of my head.

Evidently Deo had similar doubts. "You are Fireborn? How come you to have knowledge of arcane matters?"

"I had a Starborn master," he said simply.

I watched him, troubled now by a new thought. Would Hallow swear fealty to Deo, even though he had just offered to cast aside his fealty to Lord Israel? How could a man seem so honorable, and yet in truth, value his word so little? And why did it matter to me so much that he be the man I wanted him to be? Just because we'd enjoyed a little romp in the cot didn't mean we had anything else binding us.

I needed to accept that Hallow was as he was, and not let his flaws bother me.

Deo shrugged. "If you think you can do good, then you are welcome to fight alongside us. But do not expect protection against the Harborym. We will be too busy destroying them to protect a delicate arcanist."

Hallow's lips thinned a little at the word "delicate," but he said nothing in response, a fact I admired. I wouldn't have been able to resist responding to such a comment, but my temperament was more like Deo's—quick to fire and explosive—whereas I was beginning to realize that Hallow had an analytical mind. He looked at situations from all sides before committing himself to action, and apparently treated most situations with humor.

"If you wish to join my company, then I expect you to tell me what you know," Deo said, turning to Hallow. "Why was the runeseeker in my father's camp?"

"He seeks to recover moonstones belonging to the queen," Hallow said.

"For what purpose?" Deo asked. A sullen Rixius and another servant brought food, wine, and campstools for us, allowing Hallow and me to eat, somewhat voraciously, since food had been scarce while we were on the road.

Hallow was silent for a few minutes, chewing the heel of a loaf of bread, before finally saying, "Exodius did not speak about the moonstones themselves, only that he sought them. Lord Israel wanted him present because Exodius is also the Master of Kelos, and thus the head of the arcanists."

"That tells me nothing." Deo's expression was as hard as granite. "In fact, nothing you have said gives me insight into my father's plans. Perhaps you really are here as his spy."

Hallow looked up from where he was offering me a piece of pear. "I am here because I did not believe it was safe for Allegria to travel alone along the South Road."

That was not entirely true, and Hallow and I both knew it. However, I was willing to let it go. I knew that had I been in his shoes, I would want to join forces with Deo. I could hardly blame Hallow for coming to his senses and seeing that Deo had a better chance of succeeding than his father.

"Allegria is a Bane of Eris," Deo said, giving me a smug look that I didn't return. I remembered too well how the chaos magic had betrayed me. "There is nothing on Alba she fears."

"I'm sure that is so, but nonetheless, I could not be easy letting anyone travel alone with the Harborym on the move. I remain here because, as I've already explained, I believe you will be in Starfall before the Four Armies, and I can do more good with you than with them. They have Exodius. You have no one with arcane abilities. If you do not wish me to stay, speak, and I will leave. Otherwise, I am here to do what I can to destroy the invaders."

Deo grunted acknowledgment, returning to the map spread out under the plates. "We will leave at dawn, and should be at the west gate shortly after noon. If my father is two days' journey away, and awaiting the arrival of the Tribe of Jalas and the Starborn vizier, then we should have the invaders destroyed before my father can take to his horse."

"You are that sure about your company?" Hallow asked.

Deo made mildly outraged noises. "Chaos magic is the very thing that gives the Harborym their power. You cannot understand, because you only have dealings with the magic of the stars, which is fine for court conjurers and entertainers, but we bear the power of death itself. Nothing can stand before us."

"That is insulting!" I said, shoving back my plate and giving Deo a frown. "Hallow is a learned arcanist. You have no idea of the sorts of things he can do—"

Hallow's hand covered mine, giving my fingers a little warning squeeze. "I appreciate the quick defense, but it's not necessary."

"It is if Deo thinks you're no better than a court conjurer—"

He squeezed my hand again, and for a moment, I was distracted by the warmth of his fingers on mine, the memory of just what those fingers could do, filling my body with a heat that was hard to ignore.

That heat stayed with me for the rest of the night, through Deo's debate with Hadrian about the best way to force the city gate open, Hallow's suggestion that we could easily enter the city by one of the lesser guarded bolt-holes that he had learned of from his old master, and Deo's decision—after hours of arguing—that if Hallow knew of such a bolt-hole, it would be wiser in the end to save our strength for the destruction of Harborym, rather than spend it on the gates of the city itself.

I had just emerged from a quick bath in the privacy of my tent when a cough outside the door heralded the arrival of the man who had filled my thoughts. "Are you decent?"

"I'm a priestess. Of course I'm decent," I answered, wrapping a drying cloth around me.

Hallow pushed aside the tent flap and entered, the now familiar shape of him making my heart beat a little faster.

Foolish heart, I told myself. *He's just an amusement, and nothing more.*

"You're wet," he said, his gaze crawling over me in a way that made me want to drop the drying cloth.

"Yes, I am. Did you bathe? I'm afraid my bathwater is not as clean as I'd like to think it was, but I was on the road for several days, so if you wanted to use it—"

"I had a bath in the river half a mile away. Two of the banesmen took me there and laughed uproariously when I jumped in and found the water was ice-cold." He glided forward, that magnificent chest calling to me. "If I'd known you were going to bathe in private, I would have joined you, instead. Do you want me to dry you?"

I pulled the cloth from my body and held it out to him, turning around to present my back, glancing over my shoulder. "Certainly. You can dry all the spots I have trouble reaching."

"Thank you," he said on a breath, using the cloth to pat my back and behind dry. "I think your legs need extra drying."

"That's very thoughtful of you," I said. My own breath stuck in my throat when he tossed aside the cloth, knelt, and ran his hands up my calves.

"You're so soft for someone who fights so fiercely," he murmured, kissing a little path up my thighs. "And you smell like flowers. I've never known anyone to smell like flowers. Is it your soap?"

I turned around when he took my behind in both hands, planting a kiss on either cheek. "I used Deo's soap, so unless he smells flowery, no. Are you going to do that thing you did the other night? With your mouth?"

He smiled up at me, his eye crinkles making my belly contract with pleasure. "If you promise not to pull out all of my hair this time, I will."

"I'm sorry," I said automatically, then glanced down at the top of his head. Unlike many of the Fireborn who were white-blond, Hallow had thick hair, which swept back from his brow, and was cut on an angle in the back, leaving longer strands that sometimes fell down over his brow. "I don't know what you're talking about. You have more hair than most men, Hallow."

"Hmm?"

I knelt before him. "What did you think of Deo?"

He grimaced. "I think your boyfriend is lucky we're here to keep him from wasting so much time on the gates when the bolt-hole offers a much easier solution. If that's the sort of counsel he's been given from his two advisers, he's in more trouble than he need be in."

I pinched his arm. "He's not my boyfriend. If I had one, you would be my boyfriend, but I don't have one, so you're not. Did you like him?"

He tipped his head to the side in a manner that I found wholly endearing. "Does it matter to you if I do?"

"Yes."

"Why?"

"Not because he's my boyfriend." I tugged his tunic over his head. "But he is a friend, and I believe in him. In what he's doing. And I know how much his father has hurt him."

Hallow sat back and pulled off his leather boots, peeling off his breeches just as quickly. I spread my hands over his chest, at the same time he claimed my breasts. "I think he's very passionate. And hotheaded. And before you ask any more questions, do we have to talk about your boyfriend? Right now, I think I'd much rather talk about you, and what you will do to my poor, abused body, and all the things I want to do to yours."

I smiled and leaned back. "Did you notice I have furs?"

He glanced at my pubic area. "I wouldn't exactly call it a fur—"

"You idiot." I poked him with my foot and patted the furs that covered a thin pallet of straw. "These furs. Big enough for both of us."

He crawled toward me, a wicked glint in his brilliant blue eyes. "Now that is an invitation I cannot refuse."

"Then maybe you'll like this, too." I gestured toward the furs, waiting for him to lie on his back before sitting on his thighs. "I was thinking about it, and I decided that what you did to me, I could do to you. Isn't that so?"

"Do you mean—"

I took his penis in both hands. It was erect (causing part of my mind to wonder if he went around in that state all the time; I made a mental note to ask him later if it wasn't uncomfortable to ride like that), and as hot as I remembered. I leaned down and swirled my tongue over the tip, pushing the skin around in a way that had Hallow moaning in ecstasy.

"Well, that's interesting," I said, considering the length of him. "You seem to enjoy that as much as I enjoyed your attentions."

"I do! I really do!" he said, panting a little. I noticed he had clutched the furs with both hands, a fact that pleased me. Clearly I could push him beyond the limits of his control just as easily as he did it to me.

"And if I do this?" I leaned down again, and the combination of my hands and mouth had him arching back, his chest heaving, and a nonstop stream of moans of the purest pleasure filling the air.

"I'm going to want... sweet Kiriah's nipples, is your tongue made of fire? My turn to torment you."

I released him to crawl up his body, kissing my way up his belly to his chest. "And I'm going to want you to give me my turn—"

A cool wind swirled a warning a fraction of a second before the tent flap moved and the large shape of Deo entered, saying, "Allegria, I've been thinking of the arcanist's plan, and I think he could be—ah."

I'll say this for him—Hallow was fast. Before my brain could even register embarrassment that Deo had just caught Hallow and me in an intimate position, I was beneath Hallow with one of the skins covering us both.

I peered out from under Hallow's bicep (the sight of which made my inner self squeal happily) and blinked a couple of times. "Deo! What are you doing here?"

A rare flash of humor passed over his face. "I *had* wished to talk to you about whether or not you trust the arcanist, but I can see that you do. Er... has this been going on for long?"

"Long enough," Hallow answered, clearly annoyed. I couldn't say I blamed him, although I did see the humor of the situation. "Why do you ask?"

"I just wondered if you knew her before she kissed me back in Aryia, or if you'd just met." He turned and paused to send Hallow a look filled with warning. "If you hurt her, I'll kill you."

"A warning you might heed, as well," Hallow said lightly.

I looked at him in surprise. His tone was pleasant enough, but his meaning was quite clear.

"You? Kill me?" Deo tossed his head and laughed, the sound filling the night air as he left the tent.

I pinched both of Hallow's sides until he looked down at me, his arms braced next to my ears. "I am not an object for you to posture over."

"In what way was I posturing—"

"If I want to be hurt by Deo, that's my business." I realized how inane that sounded the second the words left my lips. "That is, I would never want to be hurt by anyone, but I am responsible for my well-being, not you. Now, are you going to lie back so I can do all sorts of wicked things to you?"

"No," he said, licking the tip of my nose. "Now, my defiant one, it's my turn, and I fully intend to make up for that untoward interruption."

I sighed happily and gave myself over to the pleasure that only Hallow could stir.

Chapter 13

We were up well before Kiriah Sunbringer sent the sun to greet us.

"Deo, I have something I want to tell you. Two somethings, actually," I said as the company was preparing to depart. I'd led Buttercup, who was unusually obstreperous that morning, over to where Deo was saddling his large black horse. I gave the horse a wide berth, since he didn't seem to like anyone, let alone Buttercup, who laid back her ears and bared her teeth in return.

Deo muttered a curse at the horse and told him to stop jiggling his feet before glancing over at me. "I had hoped you'd lose that beast in the wilds. I can give you a proper horse, you know."

Buttercup's tail swished with indignation. I patted her neck and said, "There's nothing wrong with her so long as you don't give her opportunities to misbehave. Did you hear what I said?"

"Yes." He tightened his cinch and gave his horse a slap on the shoulder when the animal raised a back hoof in warning. "You have two somethings to say to me. If it has anything to do with what you and the arcanist were up to in your tent, I don't want to hear it."

"Surely you don't expect me to believe you are jealous," I said, amused.

"Not jealous, although it was me you kissed first," he pointed out, and gathered up a leather and metal chest piece. "I will always be flattered to think that I held your affections for all these years."

"You wish!" My amusement faded when I knew the time had come to unburden myself. I glanced around, but Rixius was mercifully off overseeing the packing of the wagons, and everyone else was busy putting on their armor and readying their mounts. Hallow stood with his horse across the camp, chatting with one of the men, who apparently was from a town near Hallow's birthplace. "It's something I didn't mention in front of the others," I said, suddenly unable to find the words I needed.

"If you're going to admit your love for me—" he started to say, clearly still laughing at me.

"It's about Idril."

He stopped buckling a bow to the saddle and didn't move for several seconds before asking, "Why do you say that name to me?"

"She's here, Deo." I watched the muscles in his jaw and shoulders tightening, his fingers white on the leather saddle straps. I took a deep breath and let the rest of the words come out in a rush. "She's coming with her father to the Council of Four Armies. I didn't want to tell you in front of the others, but if the armies somehow make it to Starfall City while we're still there... well, I thought you should know."

Slowly, the tension in his hands eased, and he continued strapping on his bow and quiver. "And the second thing?"

My stomach protested the fact that I'd eaten some bread and porridge earlier. "I don't know if you are aware that your mother is in Starfall."

"My mother is a prisoner of the Harborym. They hold her for a guarantee of good behavior from the few remaining Starborn."

"That might not be strictly true anymore," I said slowly, wishing I hadn't ever opened my mouth.

Deo spun around, his eyes burning red. He grabbed my arm, his fingers luckily finding the silver cuff on my wrist instead of my flesh. "What are you saying, priest?"

"I have heard that she is not so much a prisoner as a guest," I said carefully.

His fingers tightened on the cuff, making the runes light up as the power inside me stirred, no doubt sensing the pulsing waves of anger rolling off Deo. "Who dared speak of this to you?"

"Who said it doesn't matter—"

"The arcanist!" Deo spat the word out, releasing me and spinning around, clearly about to go find Hallow.

I dropped my reins and grabbed Deo's arm with both hands, digging in my feet when he started forward. "Deo, stop!"

"I'll stop him, all right! I'll stop him from ever spreading rumors about my mother—"

"Will you listen to me for a minute?" I pulled hard on the power of the newborn sun, lighting up not just my runes but my hands, using the strength it gave me to jerk Deo around until he faced me.

"You dare!" Deo bellowed. His eyes were black and red with rage, his face contorted in a snarl of frustration. Those nearest to us froze in their actions, clearly startled.

Behind him, Rixius suddenly jumped onto one of the wagons to see what was happening. He leaped off almost immediately and started for us.

"Yes, I dare," I told Deo, not allowing him to intimidate me. I held tight to his arm, speaking rapidly. "Your father's own guards told Hallow that your mother was working with the Harborym, so if you are angry, you can take it up with them. For that matter, you can tell your father he should have better control over his own guards so as to keep them from gossiping. Regardless, it's not Hallow who is spreading the rumors." I took a deep breath, ignoring Rixius's plaintive bleats for people to move out of his way. "You need to know what is being said in case it's... well, if there is any truth to it."

Deo shoved his face in mine, twisted with fury, his eyes all but spitting fire. Worse, the runes along the harness on his chest glowed an ugly dull red. "My mother fought her entire life to protect her people, first from my father, and later from the invaders. She would never betray the Starborn. *Never.*"

I released his arm and put both hands on his chest, calling again on the power of Kiriah Sunbringer to pour the warmth of the sun into him, this time to calm the turmoil that I knew filled him. "Deo, no one said she has betrayed her people, only that she is apparently being treated as a guest rather than a prisoner. I have no doubt, if that is the situation, she has a reason for appearing so. You must see past your wrath and let reason be your guide."

"And your precious arcanist?" Scorn dripped off his voice. My hands went cold, and I pulled them back when he half-turned toward his horse. "You would like me to heed his words in all things, would you not? How quickly your allegiances change, little priest. I had thought better of you."

"My lord." Rixius skidded to a halt in front of us, his eyes going from Deo to me and back to Deo. "Is something amiss? Has this woman annoyed you in some manner? I will be happy to have her sent to the back of the line or, better yet, have her removed from your company—"

I had a sword at his throat before he could so much as blink. I pressed forward, causing him to stumble backward, an odd gabbling sound emerging from his mouth. "I've had enough from you. If you speak to me in that manner again, I'll turn your tongue into a toad. One with warts."

"My lord!" Rixius squawked a plea for help, his expression mingled fear and anger.

"You should know better than to poke a lightweaver if you don't wish to feel her fire," I told the annoying man before sheathing my sword and turning back to Deo. "And *you* should know that once my allegiance is given, it remains as constant as the birth of Kiriah each morning, and her death at night."

Deo grunted something in reply, but the anger was gone out of him, the runes on his bindings once again quiet.

Hallow rode over to me a short while later, when the company was setting forth on the road. Deo rode at the head, his two lieutenants alongside, and Rixius trying unsuccessfully to squeeze in between.

"Trouble?" Hallow asked when his horse deftly avoided Buttercup's teeth.

"You could say that." I rode in silence for a few minutes before I admitted, "I told Deo what you'd said about his mother."

A grimace crossed his face. "Was that what he was yelling about? I'm surprised he didn't try to have me beheaded."

"Oh, he probably would have if I hadn't pointed out that the news came from his father. He realized that it wasn't your fault, and that if the queen was the Harborym's guest in the city, there had to be a very good reason for it."

"One would assume so," Hallow said, but I noticed his voice was devoid of expression. I was coming to realize that when his voice went bland like that, it meant he was trying to avoid saying something that might be unpleasant.

I wondered if he knew more about the queen than he was telling. And then I wondered if I could use my newly found feminine skills to get that information from him.

That thought didn't sit right with me.

"What are you shaking your head about?" Hallow asked.

"Just reminding myself that I'm still a priest of Kiriah, even if I'm not at the temple."

A little smile curved his lips. "Struggling with your conscience? I trust you to do the right thing."

I shot him a startled glance. Had he just read my mind, or was my guilt at even thinking of using my womanly wiles to my benefit making me paranoid?

I didn't have much time for contemplation of my sins, for there were several small groups of Shades patrolling the road to Starfall City, all of which were taken care of quickly. Oddly, there were no Harborym with them, although Hallow said, after the third group was eliminated, "Our enemies don't feel it's necessary to use the Harborym so close to the city. Their power is saved for more distant patrols."

In the distance, the purple and silver spires of the city were just visible above the tops of the low-growing trees. I asked, "Have you been to the city before?"

"No. But my master had lived here before the Harborym came and used to tell many stories about it. In fact, it was he who told me about the bolt-holes. And speaking of which, I had better let your boyfriend know we should be leaving the road." Hallow put his heels to his horse, and rode up to Deo, gesturing to the right side.

The company followed his lead, after a while veering off the road into low, dead scrub and long grass, the only sound that of the horses' hooves thudding on dirt, and the swish of the grass as we passed through. Even the few discouraged-sounding birds who'd greeted the dawn were silent, leaving me with a feeling that the air itself was tainted.

We stopped briefly to position the wagons and their drivers in a copse of half-dead trees, leaving a couple of banesmen there to guard them lest the Harborym come across our supplies. We continued onward, Hallow in the lead now, winding in a single-file path up a sandy cliff. Before us, the walls of Starfall rose upward, the once-white stone now stained green and gray with neglect. I scanned the wall as we rode silently alongside it, but there were no guards visible on the ramparts. Glancing to my right, where the cliff dropped off in an increasingly sheer fall, I assumed that the Harborym did not feel it necessary to guard against threats on this side.

No one spoke as we continued to ride along the narrowing path that ran the length of this side of the city. The path occasionally bulged outward to follow the cliff with enough room for four horses to ride abreast but, more worryingly, sometimes curved inward in a manner that had me holding my breath. Buttercup was sure-footed, but I wasn't so confident in some of the high-strung horses. Hallow must have shared my concern, for the next time the cliff veered away from the wall, he pulled up, and we dismounted. Again, a few guards were left to watch the horses, while the rest of us proceeded up the path on foot.

Despite my worries, we arrived at last at a small wooden door set low into the wall. I pressed forward through the other banesmen until only Rixius, who hovered at the shoulders of Hallow and Deo, blocked me.

"Why should we not break it down?" Deo was demanding in a harsh whisper.

I glanced upward, but there were still no guards visible.

"You can if you wish to alert whoever is inside the tower to our presence, but I, for one, would prefer not fighting the whole of the Harborym's contingent at the same time," Hallow said softly. I could tell he was trying to keep irritation from his voice. "If you allow me to coax the lock, we can slip inside and overcome whomever is in the tower without anyone being the wiser."

"I've never heard of this lock coaxing," Deo said gruffly.

"My lord," Rixius said. "If I may—"

"When I want a locked door open," Deo continued, ignoring his servant, "I simply remove it."

"It's your choice," Hallow said with a shrug, but I knew he was annoyed. I certainly was.

I pushed Rixius to the side and poked Deo in the back until he turned to glare at me. "For the love of the sunrise and sunset, Deo! Just do as Hallow says. We've left ten hunters behind as guards, and I don't think that forty of us—even with Hallow's magic—can take on hundreds of Harborym if they are on us all at once."

"Very well. And stop poking me," Deo said and crossed his arms across his chest.

Hallow raised an eyebrow to me, but said nothing before turning his attention to the door. There was no latch on the outside, no handle, but a lock was sunk into the wood. He bent down to look closely at it for a few seconds, then cupped one hand around it and leaned forward.

"My lord, would you like for me to escort the priest to the rear, where she will not assault you further?"

"You just don't learn, do you?" I whispered in a violent hiss to Rixius.

"I am Lord Deo's body servant. I would die to protect him from people like you," he hissed back.

"Are you in love with him?" I asked, noting the jealous light in his eyes.

He looked scandalized for two seconds before fury took hold of him. "You dare speak of me thusly? You, who are nothing, a lowborn priest from an insignificant temple. You aren't worthy of Lord Deo's notice, let alone his consideration!"

"You really have it bad," I said, wondering if I'd ever feel the same fanatical sort of passion for anyone. "Have you told Deo? Would you like me to do it for you?"

"Will you two quit bickering?" Hallow asked, frowning back at us. "I can't hear myself think, let alone concentrate."

"Sorry," I told him. "Although if Deo could control his minion, that would be helpful."

Deo said nothing, clearly consumed by his own thoughts.

Rixius moved until his mouth was close to my ear, his fingers digging painfully into my arm. "If you dare cross me, I will see to it you are—"

He didn't finish the sentence. The chaos magic within me woke up at the threat that Rixius fairly dripped into my ear, and for once, I let it have its way. He yelped when the hand that clutched me turned red with magic, snatching it back to cradle it against his chest, all the while glaring hate at me.

I smiled. He stumbled backward a step before sidling around behind me to get at Deo's other side, no doubt to tattle on me.

Hallow was still working on the lock. I leaned forward to peer over his shoulder and ask, "Are you kissing it?"

He shot me a quick look, a few of his eye crinkles doing their thing. "No. I'm talking to it. Now hush, and let me work before your boyfr—"

I whomped the back of his head with my elbow.

He glared.

"Sorry. Accident." I smiled.

"What are you two whispering about? Is it about me?" Deo asked, ignoring Rixius to lean in and join the conversation. "Why isn't the door opened yet, arcanist?"

Hallow sighed. "I would open it if I were allowed to work. Is everyone done distracting me? Or are there a few more questions to ask? I can wait. We have all the time in the world. At least, until the Harborym notice forty banesmen pressed up against the city walls, and then we're going to have something to occupy our attention."

Deo frowned at me. I put an innocent look on my face and waited.

After another two minutes, the lock suddenly clicked and the door swung inward with a drawn out, nerve-grating squeak.

Hallow glanced back at us, gave a little shrug, and, with one quick move, shoved the door open all the way. The hinges protested, but we didn't wait to see if anyone would notice—doubling over until our hands touched the ground, we scurried through the door into a dark room. A faint light came from a half-opened door, barely illuminating the surroundings. Silently, we crept across the room, into the tower itself. One Harborym sat with his back to us, his feet up on a table, while nearby two Shades cowered in the corner.

Deo was on the Harborym before I could pull my swords, Hallow rushing past him to blast the two Shades against the wall in a burst of arcane light.

The Harborym's head rolled across the floor. Deo hurled the body to the side, lifting his sword high, and yelling, "Forward, my Banes of Eris! Take no prisoners!"

I tried to keep up with Hallow and Deo, but the surge through the doors leading into the city was too great, and I was pushed back several feet. By the time I emerged into the walkway leading to the tower, I paused for a moment to take in the sight that met my astonished gaze.

Lore had told me that the main city of the Starborn was one of the most beautiful places in all of Alba, with tall, graceful spires capped with crescent moons, curved domes chased with silver bands upon which were engraved constellations, and high arched windows, each of which bore beautiful fretwork of moons and stars and comets entwined. The stone of the city varied from pale lavender to a deeper dusky purple, with white accents touched every now and again by silver that glinted brightly in the sun.

Even the invasion of the foul Harborym could not ruin the loveliness of the city.

At least I thought so, until I looked down at the once-white stone pathways that ran under white lattice archways.

The stone was stained black and green, and the archways were splattered with rusty blood.

I ran after the other banesmen, hearing Deo cry, "To battle, my banesmen! May your swords run with the blood of the invaders!"

We broke into two groups as arranged, the first group going to the left in order to secure the main gates. Hallow, assigned to that group, cast a look back for me. I started toward him, but just then Deo called for me. "Allegria, to me! I have need of your skills."

I paused, hesitating. Hallow's group, catching sight of Harborym streaming out of a building obviously being used as a barracks, shouted and surged forward. Hallow stood still for a few seconds, watching me, the staff in one hand, arcane magic gathered in the other. Above his head, the wooden swallow circled, then dove forward, skimming over the banesmen and heading for the group of oncoming Harborym.

"Allegria!" Deo demanded from my right, his enhanced height giving him the ability to look over the heads of his group. He gestured angrily for me. With a little wave at Hallow, I turned and ran to where Deo was storming down a flight of stairs into a once-beautiful garden. The white statues in it lay broken and stained, the plants wilted and dead in their pots. Corpses of birds were scattered across the brown grass, and bare earth showed through the few weeds that struggled to survive.

We ran down through the garden, a horn sounding somewhere behind us, which was answered almost immediately by one ahead of us.

Deo paused at the sound of it.

"Was that Hadrian?" I asked him. I hadn't seen the lieutenant bearing a horn, but I knew he came from a hill tribe who used such things in battle. "The answer came from ahead of us, not behind."

"The second was the Harborym. The first almost sounded like..."
Deo shook his head. "It matters not. Half of you go to the arcanists'
court. I will go on to the throne room, where it is said the captain of the
Harborym quarters himself. After he is dead, we will spread out through
the city and destroy the invaders once and for all. Allegria, I need you to
release the queen."

"What?" I asked in a near shout, racing after Deo when he took off
with four other banesmen. "How am I supposed to do that?"

"You're a lightweaver—you'll figure it out," was all the answer I got.

"And you are overestimating my abilities—" I started to object, but
was stopped short when a few waves of Shades swarmed us. Although
there were only six of us, we made short work of them, as well as the two
Harborym who followed them. I barely had time to get my swords wet
with Harborym blood before we were passing beneath an arched double
door that led to the queen's staterooms.

"Her quarters are up those stairs," Deo said, gesturing to the left side
of a staircase that split and curved upward.

"Deo, I don't think—"

"Go!" he bellowed, and, lowering his head like a bull, charged forward
when a group of a dozen Harborym rushed at him. Behind them, I caught a
glimpse of a swirling green and black jagged miasma twisting and turning
upon itself, appearing to hang in the middle of the air.

It was the rift in space that the Harborym had created in order to invade
these lands. I knew from lore that another had opened on Aryia, but Lord
Israel had seen it destroyed before many Harborym could come through it.

The Starborn hadn't been so lucky.

All this went through my head in the time it takes to blink, and then I
was dashing up the stairs, trusting Deo and his group to take care of the
attackers below.

A pair of Shades milled around on the landing, both of which rushed
toward me with their mouths open in wordless cries, their fingers curled
into claws, their eyes black, lifeless orbs. The Harborym had learned early
on that although they could control the Shades' will, they couldn't arm
them and use them as an auxiliary battalion. The Shades attacked using
their claws and teeth, tearing and biting, while a droning cry emerged from
their blackened mouths. They were wholly repugnant, and I told myself
as I dispatched the duo that freedom from their hellish existence was the
most merciful way to deal with them.

The hall divided in front of me, both sides taking ninety-degree turns and disappearing from view. I dashed to the right and peered around the corner, but saw nothing but a couple of Shades shuffling their way down the hall. "To the left, then," I muttered to myself, and, spinning around, headed in the other direction. As I turned the corner of that wing, I smiled. Ahead of me, a group of four Shades was clustered outside a double door. They turned and started their shuffling run toward me as soon as they saw me, hissing and droning their mindless calls.

The chaos magic in me surged, filling me with power that allowed me to take the first Shade's head off cleanly, and pierce the heart of the second just as the other two reached me. Their claws dug deep, but before they could draw blood, they both lay dead on the floor. As was my habit, I spoke the words of blessing while releasing them from their torment. "May Kiriah take your spirit unto her. Now, let's hope this is the right door..."

I reached out to open the door, my runes glowing golden, but at the sight of them, I hesitated. Should I knock, or would the queen forgive my breach of protocol? The magic urged me to burst in and slay everything in sight, but I had it well under control. "At least for the moment," I said to myself, then, with a prayer that I wouldn't find a room filled with Harborym, I threw open the door and ran in, both swords in hand.

A small, wizened old woman looked up from where she sat next to a fire, a cup in her hands. "Who are you? What are you thinking, clomping in like that?"

"Binchley, what is that noise from the courtyard?" another voice asked from a connecting room.

"I know not, my lady, but here is a soldier come running into the room covered in the blood of Shades."

The old lady was clearly a servant. I gave her a quick nod of my head and sketched a fast protection ward on her before heading to the open door where the voice had emerged. Just as I got there, a woman appeared, a tall, dark-haired woman bearing a single silver star upon her brow.

I bobbed the curtsy that Sandor had insisted I make whenever local authorities visited the temple, and said, "Queen Dasa? I have been sent to escort you to freedom. If you will come with me now, Deo waits below——"

"Deo?" She looked annoyed, casting a quick glance toward the window. "He is here? Of all the idiotic ideas——"

"My lady, please, you must come now," I said, making shooing gestures toward the hall door. I didn't dare grab her and hustle her out as I would anyone else, not because she was a queen and I was from the hearty peasantry, but because there was an air of the seasoned warrior about her that made me secretly acknowledge she could beat me into the ground if she so chose. "The Harborym are aware of our arrival, and you are not safe here. Lord Deo is most concerned that you be released."

She snorted and strode past me to look out the window, her long silver robes fluttering as if they were made of gossamer. "Don't be ridiculous. You may tell Deo I wish an explanation of what he's doing in Genora without my permission."

"My lady," I said, a distinctly pleading tone entering my voice, "please, you must allow me to rescue you. *Now*. Time is short!"

"Yes, it is," a voice said from behind me. It wasn't a pleasant voice, sounding more like someone was gargling gravel. I whirled around, both swords in my hands, but the man who strode past me simply waved a hand, and I went flying backward, slamming against the wall with enough force to make my vision go black for a few moments.

I slid down to the floor and lay there watching stupidly as the Harborym captain strolled over to the queen, saying, "Your spawn causes much disruption."

He was big, bigger even than Deo's enhanced form, the reddish hue of his skin glistening as if he were oiled. His black hair was long and braided, slithering over his shoulders and back as if it had a life of its own.

The queen made an annoyed gesture. "He is not here by my bidding. I told Israel to keep him well away from here, but clearly he cannot undertake even that simple task."

I shook my head to clear it, clumsily getting to my knees, struggling to stay upright while the floor tilted. The little old lady who'd greeted me had scurried to another room at the appearance of the Harborym captain, and she returned now with a pale pink shawl.

"This changes things," the Harborym said, lifting his hand toward the old lady.

The queen quickly grasped his wrist, her eyes blazing for a second before she said, in a voice that had edges as sharp as a razor, "Binchley is not worth your trouble. Nor, for that matter, is my son. He will bluster and shout, nothing more."

The Harborym lowered his hand, but his eyes, shiny and black, were full of ire as he, too, turned to look out of the window. "You speak with sincerity, but not knowledge. Your son, the one you claimed was in the control of his father, now threatens our plan. It is no longer wise to remain here. I have given the order to regroup."

"I wondered why you had sounded the horns."

"Only one was mine," the captain said darkly.

The queen inclined her head. "I do not agree that such an extreme action is necessary, but if it is your wish to leave, then so be it."

I managed to get to my feet, but almost fell when I bent to pick up my swords, my head swimming. It was the chaos magic, however, that had me worried. Rather than reacting to the captain with a surge of power that left me struggling with it, it had gone dormant, so quiet that I glanced at the cuffs on my wrist. The runes were still present, but lay oddly flat and dead upon the surface of the metal.

It was as if the captain had knocked the magic right out of me.

"My *wish* is as it has been these last ten years: to be allowed to proceed unhampered." The captain's lips thinned. "I have acceded to your desires, instead, but that ends now."

"My lord Racin, I assure you once again that my son's actions will in no way impact our plans—"

"I will not allow them to."

I staggered a few steps, my head clearing enough for me to focus my gaze upon the form of the massive Harborym. The chaos magic still refused to answer me, so instead, I sent up a prayer to Kiriah and drew upon her power.

"Do not think you will remain behind." The captain grabbed the queen by the arm and shoved her toward the door.

"But I have sworn to remain in Starfall!" she protested, struggling to free her arm. "I cannot leave now or all will be undone!"

"That means nothing now." He raised his hand toward me when I stumbled forward. This time, however, I was ready, and wrapped myself in light just before a wave of chaos magic sent me flying toward the fireplace, and once again into a brief oblivion that snatched awareness from me.

Chapter 14

Although I had hit the brick mantel painfully, I was on my feet a few seconds later, rushing after the captain and Queen Dasa. "Stop and fight, you scum!" I yelled, twirling my swords, halfheartedly hoping to goad the captain into pausing in his quick descent of the stairs. He didn't, but I was heartened when he turned toward the throne room, where the sounds of fighting could be heard.

"Deo!" I yelled, hoping to give him a warning. "The captain is here!"

I skidded to a halt inside the room, pausing for a moment at the sight that met my eyes. The room was filled with banesmen and Harborym, the floor littered with bodies of both Harborym and Shades alike. Hadrian's group was here, the long room echoing with cries and screeches that hurt the ears. Blood, both black of the Shades and red of the Harborym, lay in pools on the floor and splattered the once pristine silver and white wall hangings. The few pieces of furniture in the room were destroyed, gore dripping from jagged pieces of wood, the upholstery torn and stained.

And in the middle of it all, striding through the pandemonium, was the captain, with the queen in tow.

"Deo!" I yelled again, and this time saw his dark head turn our way. He was on the far side of the room, slashing at two Harborym who were trying to skewer him on pikes; the air around Deo was red with magic. As I called his name, he slammed a ball of chaos directly into the nearest Harborym, causing him to explode in a rain of guts and blood.

Brilliant blue lit up the room for a moment, followed almost instantly by a percussive blast that knocked half the occupants down. In the center of the blast, Hallow stood with the black staff held high, the bird circling him with joyous swoops.

"Nicely done," I said under my breath, before once again drawing on Kiriah Sunbringer. I slid the swords home in their sheaths, striding after the captain, the way made easier now that Hallow had downed half the Harborym. My eyes were fixed on the back of the massive invader. The light of the sun gathered in my hands, my lips moving as I spoke the words of the goddess's invocation. Around me, banesmen fought Harborym, the noise from the battle terrible to hear. Two banesmen went down as I passed, still gathering power from the sun. Deo, now seeing his mother in the grip of the captain, fought his way toward the center of the room, where the twisting black and green rift continued to turn in upon itself, little tendrils of black reaching out to snap in the air.

It was at that moment that I realized what the captain meant when he'd said they were regrouping—he was going to take the queen through the rift into the Harborym's dimension. She struggled and fought him in a way that spoke of centuries of experience in melee combat, but before she could disable him, he clamped his hand over her head for a second, and she fell limp.

"Hallow!" I dashed forward, ducking when a Harborym swung his axe at me and jumping over another one that was crawling in his own blood toward a banesman. "The rift! They're going to the rift!"

Hallow spun around, took the situation in with a glance, and started forward, but at that moment, a phalanx of Harborym poured through the door and went straight for him. I hesitated, torn between stopping the captain from escaping and helping Hallow. A blast of arcane magic that punched hundreds of little holes in the nearest oncoming Harborym solved the problem for me—Hallow could take care of himself.

I ran forward, toward the rift in space, still drawing down sunlight, the halo of it surrounding and half-blinding me. All around me, the banesmen fought, while Deo hacked his way toward the rift, and Hallow continued to pump raw arcane power directly into the attackers. Dimly, I heard a horn sound, and wondered if yet more Harborym were on the way.

It didn't matter—I had to stop the captain from dragging the queen into his realm. Deo screamed something unintelligible, his face black with agony as he threw Harborym from his path, knocking back others who had flung themselves on him, until they swarmed him, at least two dozen trying to hold him back as he dragged them slowly, step by painful step, toward the rift.

I stepped over a banesman who had lost an arm and was writhing on the floor, my eyes on the twisting black nothingness, the sunlight streaming out of me as if I were Kiriah herself. The banesmen and Harborym alike fell back out of my path, scurrying out of the way of the burning light.

"No!" Deo cried, attempting to free himself, reaching out one bloodied hand in entreaty. "Stop the queen!"

Something in my mind clicked, like a gear slipping into place. Just as the captain reached the rift and stretched out a hand to draw it open, I released the sunlight, a great burning shaft of it coming down from the sky, blasting through the roof and floors above us, until it slammed directly onto the rift. The light grew until it filled the room, the screams of those nearest to it drowned out by the rush of air as the rift was destroyed.

Right after the captain dragged the queen through it.

The light burned itself out, leaving me momentarily bereft of its power, my vision dazzled by the brilliance. For a second or two, I stood there, blinking at the spot in the air where the rift had been, my heart feeling as if it were made of lead.

I had failed. I wasn't in time.

Deo's agonized snarl filled the air, and suddenly, he was everywhere, spreading a wave of chaos magic in front of him, literally melting the Harborym with it.

At the sight of it, the chaos within me burst into being again, filling me with a lust for blood and vengeance. Unable to control it, and with no light left to weave, I spun around, feeling like an animal at bay, and charged the nearest Harborym, slamming bolt after bolt of magic into his body. He, too, melted, screaming a death cry that would haunt me for centuries.

Deo and I ran amok. There's just no other word for what happened—we were like the frenzied giant berserkers of old, wild with bloodlust, chaos power flowing from our fingertips as if it were water. The room filled with the entire battalion of Harborym, their bodies consumed by the magic until just smears of blood were left on the corpses of those who had been killed earlier.

Hallow lit up half the room with another arcane explosion while Deo and I, along with the surviving banesmen, continued to plow through the oncoming mass of Harborym. Just when I thought there couldn't be any more left, the chaos magic began to ebb, allowing the runes to control it again. At that moment, a group of Harborym ran into the room, their eyes wild. We attacked with vengeance until the last one dropped.

I stood panting, my hands and arms dripping red with blood, my swords lost somewhere under the piles of bodies. My head echoed with the screams of the dying, a dull pain growing until it almost blocked my vision, my body shaking with the aftereffects of so much magic. I felt as if I were made of wet linen, and wanted nothing more than to crumple to the ground and sleep for a month or two.

Hallow stumbled forward, fell to his knees, and sat for a few minutes, his hands limp on his stained leggings. He was clearly just as exhausted as the rest of us. The wooden bird circled him twice, then landed on his head. Even it looked drained.

Seven banesmen survived in addition to Deo and me. Two were on the ground, nursing grievous wounds. They, too, were covered in blood, and had a dazed, stunned look that I knew I bore, as well.

I dragged myself over to the side of the room where I thought my swords had been torn from my back, halfheartedly looking for them while trying to cope with a growing headache and sense of exhaustion.

"It is exactly as I expected," a voice said from the side. Dully, I turned my head and saw Lord Israel gesture to the bodies in front of him. Three guards hurried forward and cleared them from his path. His tunic was as pristine as ever, although the sword in his hand was stained black with the blood of Shades. He looked with distaste first around the room, then at me, finally settling his gaze on Deo. "You have truly become the monster I feared you would be." His gaze flickered over to the handful of banesmen who staggered forward. "And this time, you have damned others to your nightmare. Well done, Deo."

Deo stood in the center of the room, where a black stain on the floor marked the location of the rift, his head bowed, his great chest heaving and shining with sweat and blood. The runes that crossed his chest still glowed red, although they were fading with each passing second.

He lifted his head and looked at his father, his face so filthy with gore it was hard to see an expression. "I did what you were too weak to do. I saved Alba. I—and my banesmen—brought an end to the Third Age, as was foretold at my birth."

"And do you expect congratulations for that? For embracing the foulness of the invaders? For becoming as much an abomination as they were?" Israel waved his hand toward the room. "And what do you expect to do now? Return to Aryia and live happily ever after with the taint of Harborym oozing from your every pore? Or do you expect your mother to welcome you to your Starborn kin—those that your kind hasn't yet destroyed—and have you rule at her side?"

"The queen is gone," Deo said, his words as hard as granite, but I heard a thread of pain in them, and guilt grew once again within me.

I'd failed to save the queen.

"Gone where?" Israel asked, his lip curling in scorn. "It isn't like her to leave a battle. Or did she know you were coming and conveniently locate herself elsewhere?"

"My mother is no coward," Deo snarled, limping over to stand in front of his father. "She was taken by the monsters that you failed to destroy for ten years. Ten years, old man! Ten years of you whining and moaning about the invaders, but not one finger did you raise to save my mother or her people!"

"What? She was taken?" Israel looked thunderstruck; then suddenly his face was red and choked with rage. "When?"

"Just before you came," Deo answered, relaxing his aggressive stance a little. I could only imagine his pain at knowing how close he'd been to saving his mother. "You are, as usual, too late to help her. Assuming you wished to do so, which, judging by your actions these last years, I doubt."

"You know nothing," Israel snapped, the words all but bitten in half when he spoke them. His fingers were white on the hilt of his sword. For a moment, I wondered if he would strike at his son, but he had more control than I had given him credit for.

"I know what my eyes see, and that is a man come conveniently to a battle once it has ended," spat out Deo before turning away, as if he couldn't bear to look at his father any longer.

Lord Israel said nothing for a moment, clearly struggling to maintain a hold on his emotions before he moved around the bodies. He stopped in front of Hallow, who still sat on his heels, his shoulders slumped. Even his eye crinkles looked tired.

I wanted badly to wrap my arms around him and lose myself in the comfort of his warm chest, and warmer eyes, but I didn't have the energy to do anything but stand and watch the scene in front of me.

"What happened to the queen?" Lord Israel asked Hallow.

Hallow sighed and slowly got to his feet. He held one of his shoulders higher than the other, indicating some injury of the chest or shoulder. The wooden bird fluttered with Hallow's painful movement, and hopped back to its position on the top of the staff. "The Harborym captain took her through the rift. Allegria called down the fury of Kiriah Sunbringer herself, but..." He slid an apologetic glance my way. "But the Harborym made it through seconds before the rift was destroyed."

"This should never have happened," Lord Israel said, his voice filled with anger. He turned back to Deo. "If you had not been so determined to have your way, we could have controlled the Harborym, and kept them from taking Dasa. If you had heeded my advice—"

"Your *advice*? What would that be? Banishing me to a godless rock in the ocean again? You will forgive me if I chose not to sit and do nothing, as you have done all this time." Deo choked on the last words, and once again turned his back on his father.

Israel's free hand tightened into a fist. I was dimly aware of others entering through the side door that Israel had used: a yellow-eyed giant of a man in amber and gold armor, over which flowed a braided blond beard; the balding runeseeker; and a slim, dark-haired man bearing a purple and silver tunic. No doubt the last was the queen's representative to the Council of Four Armies. Even as I watched, the men parted and a woman stepped forward, tall and willowy, with the bearing of the queen herself. She had the same silver hair as Hallow, and was clad in the amber colors of her father.

Idril, the Jewel of the High Lands. My mind tried to mock the title I'd heard used for her, but I was too tired even for that.

Deo's head snapped around, and for a second, his runes came to life. I started forward toward him, not knowing how I was going to stop him if he'd chosen to attack his father's wife, but it wasn't necessary.

"What do you here, Idril?" Deo said, his words dripping with venom. "Come to watch your husband claim victory? You're too late. We did the job for him."

"My... husband..." Idril glanced at Israel, then returned her cool regard to Deo. "You have changed much, Deo."

A great mocking laughter filled the hall. "And for that, you may thank your husband, for I have no words left for you."

Deo went to the other banesmen, helping them up and conferring briefly. I moved over to slide my shoulder under Hallow's listing side, putting my arm around his waist to help him.

"You are not going to just let him leave, are you?" the blond man asked, his voice so deep it sounded as if it came from the very center of Alba. "Did you not witness the slaughter of which he is capable, the bloodlust that has possessed him? It was a killing frenzy powered by the magic of the invaders. They are nothing but Harborym in disguise!"

Israel said nothing, but his fingers on the hilt of his sword tightened.

"Jalas speaks the truth." The Starborn representative looked nervous and uncomfortable, casting worried little glances between Israel and Jalas. "Now that the Harborym have left... have been destroyed... we cannot allow remnants of their power left behind to taint and corrupt others. My people have suffered enough from the invasion!"

"We don't corrupt others," I said, annoyed despite my weariness. "And your people—what remains of them—are safe now because Deo had the bravery to embrace the only power that could destroy the Harborym."

"It is not the *only* power," Hallow murmured in my ear.

"No, but they don't have to know that," I whispered back. "I won't stand for them villainizing Deo just because he did what they couldn't do."

"I believe there is more to it than that—"

"Far be it from me to command any man to destroy his own kin," Jalas said, casting a glance toward his daughter before addressing Lord Israel. "But you yourself said that you would drive the last vestige of the Harborym from the land. These so-called Banes of Eris are nothing but Harborym in the making. Destroy them before they bring ruin to Alba."

"What?" I gasped, not having expected that the minute we saved the world, we would be damned and destroyed for it. "You're mad!"

"Allegria, do not allow your emotions to gain the upper hand," Hallow said, pulling me back when I started forward. He winced at the movement, and added, "Don't give them any ammunition for calling you hotheaded and out of control. Calm yourself and think this through."

"I *am* calm," I said, glaring at the group that made up the council. "But I'm not foolish. I'm not going to stand idly by while they condemn us. Not when we have done nothing wrong."

Still Israel said nothing. His eyes were on Deo, who had turned to me and gestured for us to join him.

"What say you, Lord Israel of Abet?" the Starborn asked, the formality of his phrasing at odds with his anxious expression. "Will you honor your word, or do you expect the council to countenance the continued existence of these abominations who call themselves banesmen?"

"Oh! I'll abominate you—" I snarled and started forward again.

"Allegria!" Hallow called after me, but it was Lord Israel who kept me from punching the Starborn nobleman in his face.

"Cease, priest," he said, casting a fast glance my way before turning back to look at his son. "Exodius."

"Yes, I'm here." The little runeseeker hurried forward, three pale green stones in his hands. "You should know that, since you summoned me, and sent the lad for me, although that turned out to be Thorn's doing more than anything if you listen to him. And I don't always, because he usually was unbearably smug about such things."

Hallow hobbled over to where I stood, dividing my time between staring pointedly at the Starborn lord and watching Deo. He gestured for us again. I took Hallow's hand and tried to tug him forward, but he refused to move.

"The moonstones," Lord Israel said, his lips barely moving when he spoke. "Use them."

"Now? Here? I will remind you that I do not know whether the stones will cooperate. You did not give me time to consult them—no, you didn't—and moonstones can be very tricky to handle if you don't go about it properly. Luckily, I've always had a way with them, but these three are strangers to me, and thus, I cannot guarantee their efficacy."

Lord Israel's lips thinned. To my surprise, he gestured a hand toward me and said, "The priest's service in closing the rift will be remembered. She will return to her temple, and I will ensure that Lady Sandorillan removes all memory of her from the people and the land."

"You are absolutely insane," I said, pulling desperately, first on Kiriah Sunbringer, and then on the chaos power, but neither answered me. They had both abandoned me, leaving me bereft and empty inside.

"You, arcanist." Lord Israel's gaze was still on Deo even though he spoke to Hallow. "You served me well."

Hallow stood stock-still for a moment before stiffly nodding his head. I stared at him, the words echoing in my head. "What service—"

"Deosin Langton, son of Aryia!" Lord Israel's voice echoed around the room even though it was filled with bodies.

Deo had started for the main doors. He turned to look back toward us, and I fretted momentarily because I couldn't see his expression. I knew he was in pain, both emotionally and physically. I didn't know which needed my aid more, he or Hallow.

What did Lord Israel mean Hallow had served him well? A suspicion began to grow in my mind.

Hallow coughed up a bit of blood, and absently, I sketched a few healing runes on his chest.

"My shoulder, too," Hallow whispered, wincing. "I think it's broken."

I drew several runes on it, my hand still in midair when Lord Israel spoke the words that changed the world forever.

"Lord Jalas is right. The Harborym might be gone, but their foulness remains. Alba cannot tolerate such to taint its purity."

Deo laughed again as he faced his father. "Do you think to threaten me, old man? Are your eyes so feeble that you don't see before you the very proof of my success? Do you not recognize the power that I now wield?"

"Your *power* is an abomination, as are you. And as are those whom you've tainted." Lord Israel gestured toward the banesmen. My fingers dug so hard into Hallow's arm that he squawked. "You and those you have made in your image cannot be allowed to continue if there is to be peace in Alba. The Fourth Age will not begin until you are removed from it."

"We have to stop him," I whispered to Hallow. "We've done nothing wrong. *Deo* has done nothing wrong. This is naught but a witch hunt."

The look Hallow gave me was filled with pity. "My heart, did you not realize all along that this was always Lord Israel's intention?"

"No! He called me a monster before at his camp, but I thought that was because he didn't know what we could do."

"He knew. He knew well the power that Deo—and you banesmen—hold."

"What sort of a father murders his own son?" I thought for a moment. "Or, for that matter, marries his son's sweetheart, and banishes said son to a rock in the ocean?"

Hallow said nothing, but his eyes were grave.

"And how do you intend to destroy me?" Deo asked, striding forward, one hand gesturing toward the council leaders. "Do you think your beloved council can do what an entire battalion of Harborym couldn't? We destroyed them. We fought them hand to hand, and destroyed every last one of them. Can you say as much?"

"Their captain was gone," Jalas said loudly, making an angry gesture. "They lost heart and became easy targets. It was only a matter of time before we would have killed them all. You were simply here before us, nothing more."

The others murmured their agreement, although I noticed Idril said nothing, just stood by her father's side looking pale and delicate and small-boned. No one would ever call *her* hearty peasant stock.

"Do you wish to see just how tainted I am by the Harborym?" Deo called to Jalas in a taunting voice. "Come and I will show you."

"Hallow," I said in warning, my eyes on the harness crossing Deo's chest. The runes were glowing softly. "How fast can you move? Better yet, can you get out of this chamber on your own?"

"No," he said, his fingers closing around my wrist. "Do not interfere."

"I'm not going to let Deo kill his father," I protested.

He shot me a look that I couldn't easily read, and said, with a strange note in his voice, "Stay with me, Allegria."

I shook my head. "There has been enough death today. I'm not going to allow any more."

"If you stay with me, we can teach each other. We could be happy. We—" Before he could say anything else, I slipped out of his grip and moved forward, around Lord Israel and the runeseeker, sending desperate queries to Kiriah, but again she turned her back on me, dooming me to a life without her grace.

"You have done enough," Lord Israel said, and gestured to the runeseeker. "Do it now, Exodius."

"What can a runeseeker do—" Deo started to say, then paused. For a moment, I thought he was merely hesitating; then I saw a thin sheen of ice growing outward along his skin, building layer upon layer, holding him frozen in position. The other banesmen were similarly affected, their expressions ranging from anger to wariness. I stared in horror at Deo, at the others behind him, before turning to look at the runeseeker. He held the stones high, his eyes closed, chanting words I did not recognize.

"No!" I shouted, and would have lunged toward the runeseeker, but Israel caught me and held me back. "Stop it! You must stop. Lord Israel, you don't know what you're doing!"

His eyes held nothing but anger. "I know far more than you, priestling. Arcanist! Take her."

I shrugged my way out of his grasp, backing up when Hallow limped forward. "No one is taking me. I am a Bane of Eris—"

"You will join your compatriots if you don't cease speaking now," Lord Israel said, and without another look at his son, added, "Bury them deep in the earth where their bodies will never be seen again," before striding out of the room.

The others followed silently after him.

I stumbled forward, reaching out a hand to touch the ice that covered Deo, now several inches thick. It wasn't cold, and I realized with a start it was crystal that held him in its grip, crystal encasing him in an airless tomb.

Grief hit my gut hard and hot, causing me to double over, even as I sobbed out Deo's name. Guards swarmed forward, three of them picking up the frozen figure of Deo, while others hauled away the remaining banesmen.

Tears burned hot trails down my cheeks. I made one last desperate attempt to gain the grace of Kiriah, filling her ears with my pleas. If I could just summon the power of the sun, I could break the crystal... but she did not heed my prayers. It was as if she was deaf to me.

"Allegria. My heart—" Hallow limped toward me, one hand stretched out to me. "Let me help you. Come with me. I will do what I can to ease your pain."

I looked first at his hand, then at his eyes, those bright blue eyes in which I thought I'd seen so much promise. The emptiness inside me filled with inky black despair, all the while Lord Israel's words echoed in my head. "You were working for him all along? Even after you left him? You betrayed me, betrayed Deo and the banesmen?"

Hallow said nothing, but the pain in his eyes was clearly visible.

It pierced my heart, that pain, choking me with the injustice of it all. "You came with me, with us, but you were acting on his behalf. You *used* us."

"I acted as I thought best," Hallow started to say, but I wouldn't let him finish. I couldn't. I didn't want to hear any more lies from the lips that even at that moment I wanted so badly to feel upon mine.

Traitorous heart.

I ran away, ran from that room, ran from Hallow and the Council of Four Armies. Ran from the five banesmen who guarded our supplies. I said nothing, just fetched Buttercup, and rode until numbness swept over me, cradling me from all concerns.

THE FOURTH AGE

Chapter 15

"Someone stop her." The words came from Hallow's lips, but they had a strange, alien quality to them. It was as if they had been spoken at a great distance from himself. He tried desperately to move forward, to chase after her, to hold her and ease her pain, but his body failed him.

He stumbled and fell, his broken shoulder screaming at the movement, but it was the dull, hot pain inside that worried him. He mumbled the few protection spells he knew, but they did little good.

Dimly, as he lay on the floor, the filthy, cool stone beneath his cheek, he became aware of hushed voices around him. Lord Israel's men were removing the bodies. When they came to him and tried to lift him, he groaned.

"This one's alive," the man who had grabbed his feet said, dropping them. "Someone bring a stretcher."

He was borne away, his mind muddled with pain and exhaustion, but always in the back of his mind was the need to move, to find Allegria. He couldn't leave her now, when she was vulnerable, when she thought the worst of him.

"Take him to the healer."

The words drifted over him like Thorn flying over their attackers. He slid into insensibility, surfacing only when a sharp pain in his shoulder recalled his wits.

"Ouch!"

"Ah, you awaken. Good." A ruddy face peered down into his. "Lord Israel thought you might have been mortally wounded. This one's ready to go!" The last words were yelled as the man—judging by the golden blond beard, probably one of Jalas's healers—straightened up.

Exodius hove into view, his black eyebrow tendrils waving in agitation. "Is he? He looks like he might expire at any moment. Don't you think he'd be better with you?"

"We have our hands full with our own wounded," the man said, shaking his head. "This one is yours. You must take him, else he'll be left for the Starborn to deal with."

Exodius looked very much as if he wanted to wash his hands of Hallow, but to his infinite relief, the old man heaved a sigh and said, "Very well. Have him loaded into my wagon. I don't say he'll survive the journey back to Kelos, but if he does, I expect I'll find some use for him."

"Thank you, you are all graciousness," Hallow murmured, and tried to sit up, but the pain and effort were too great for him, and the black oblivion swallowed him up again.

When he next came to his senses, it was to find himself jouncing around in the back of a small wagon, his head banging against one of a half-dozen kegs of beer. This time, he did manage to sit up. "I feel like I've been staked to the ground, and a herd of warhorses has run over me. Several times."

Exodius, whose head was nodding as he sat on the front bench, suddenly snorted. "Hrrf? Oh, he is?" The old man swiveled around to look back at Hallow. "By Bellias's belt, you're right. You live, lad. I SAID, YOU LIVE!"

"I'm not deaf," Hallow replied, rubbing his head and wincing at the tender spot that had been hitting on the nearest keg. His chest ached horribly, his shoulder burned, and he felt as weak as a piece of sodden bread, but at least he was alive. "You don't have to yell. Where are we?"

"A day away from Kelos."

"That would explain the urgent need I have to stop. Do you mind?" Carefully, so as not to stress his chest and shoulder, he managed to scoot himself to the edge of the wagon, where he eased himself into a standing position.

"Wouldn't mind a break, myself," Exodius said, and hopped nimbly off the seat to trot over to the grass verge. He whistled tunelessly and scanned the skies as he relieved himself.

Hallow managed to find a semi-secluded shrub and, with much relief, attended to pressing matters. By the time he tottered back to the wagon, he realized just how parched he was.

"Do we have any water?"

"Now, what use would we have for that? What? Oh, yes, I suppose he is. There's a skin of wine in the back, under the fine furs Lord Israel gave me. Drink up."

Hallow had intended to climb up onto the bench next to Exodius, but just the brief foray into the bushes had left him feeling as if he were dragging leaden weights from every limb. He resettled himself more comfortably in the bed of the wagon and sipped at the wine. "How many days has it been since the battle at Starfall?"

"Three. We would have made better time, but this horse of yours evidently wasn't broken to harness. He is now."

Hallow smiled to himself and made a mental promise to pamper the horse just as soon as he was able. "Has there been any news of Allegria?"

"Who's that?"

"The woman who was with Lord Deo."

"The banesman?" Exodius yawned and reached his hand back. "Let me have some of that wine, if you are done with it."

Hallow duly handed the skin forward. "What news is there of her?"

"None," Exodius said after a couple of swigs. "She left. Lord Israel sent a few men after her, but they said she rode like a madwoman, and they lost her trail after a few hours."

Hallow sighed to himself. Just as soon as he was able, he'd have to try to find her. He felt driven to clear his name, to wipe from her eyes the accusations of betrayal that had shown so clearly when Lord Israel spoke.

"It's better you let her go, lad. You've got a lot of work ahead, and a woman'll only confuse you."

Hallow said nothing, busy with thoughts of how to find Allegria. Would she remain on Genora, or would she go back to Aryia and her temple, there to live as an outcast?

"Thorn'll give you such advice as he can—indeed, more than you could want—but you'll want a clear mind and full focus for what's to come. I did not insult you; I simply told the truth. Well, you should not have passed into the spirit world, then. I never wanted the job, and you could have remained—that is a blatant untruth! I never coveted anything of yours."

Perhaps she would remain in Genora. Perhaps... Hallow sat up and turned to look at Exodius, the old man's words finally filtering through his own thoughts. "What are you talking about? For what do I need a clear mind?"

"Kelos, of course. The ghosts are sure to object, and then there are the arcanists. Have you ever seen a bumblepig? They're all over Genora. Small, shaped like a furry potato, little round ears, and black spots on their coats—you know them, yes? Trying to get the arcanist collective to do what they should is just like training a bumblepig: impossible."

"Are you talking about taking me on as your apprentice?" Hallow asked, wondering how he could gracefully refuse the offer. He was flattered that someone as important as the Master of Kelos would want him as an apprentice, and he was sure there was much he could learn, but he felt his time of apprenticeship was over. He had things to do, one of which was to find Allegria and make sure all was right between them.

"Why would I do that? You're clearly not at all apprentice material." Exodius's voice was filled with scorn.

Hallow ignored the insult and leaned back against one of the kegs, relieved.

"You'll want to take one yourself, no doubt, so you can pass on all of the tiresome tasks, but that's your business and not mine. No, Thorn, I did not insult you again! You know full well the only reason you took me as an apprentice was to give me all the unpleasant tasks. Bah. Another lie."

The staff, which was leaning against the back of the front bench, shook with what Hallow imagined must be impotent fury. He was amused by the idea that the staff talked to Exodius, amusement that faded with the old man's next words.

"I'm ignoring you. You're not my problem, any more than the ghosts or the blighted arcanists are, and if the lad chooses to toss you into the nearest fire, he won't hear a word of condemnation from me."

The staff banged around a few more times, almost hitting Exodius in the head.

Hallow shot up so fast that his chest screamed in agony. "What are you talking about? Why would I want to burn Thorn?"

"The real question is, why wouldn't you? But that is up to you. The Master of Kelos may do as he pleases."

"The Master..." Hallow's throat closed. "You're mad. Or I am. Or I'm hallucinating. It's that, isn't it? I'm dead, or very near it, and am having delusions."

"All arcanists are mad to some degree," Exodius said blithely. "It goes with the magic. As to the other, I couldn't say."

"You are talking about making me the Master of Kelos, aren't you?" Hallow asked, desperately hoping for a negative response.

"Yes, yes, I heard. He is quicker of wit than I first supposed, although much good that will do him. I suppose learning will come with time. He's certainly more willing than I was when you took yourself off to the spirit world."

Panic grasped Hallow's insides with cold, clammy fingers. Although he wasn't an overly modest man, he was not given to grandiose ideas and plans, and never once had he thought of obtaining such a high post as Master of Kelos. All he wanted was to have his freedom, to serve where he could, and to continue gaining knowledge in the arcane arts. Being the leader of a bunch of solitary mad arcanists... he shook his head in horror at the thought. He'd never sought leadership, or the bonds that came with it. "Master Exodius, I am cognizant of the honor you do me, but I cannot accept. I have neither the experience nor temperament to lead the arcanists' order, and—"

"You've no choice in the matter, lad," Exodius said. "I made the decision two days ago. I've done my time; now it's your turn. Ha! You can say what you like, Thorn, but when I get to the spirit realm, I shall do more than plague my old apprentice. There is much learning to be found amongst our predecessors, and Eagle and I shall enjoy not being bound to earthly constraints anymore."

"Eagle?" Hallow said, his mind desperately scrambling to find some viable reason why Exodius couldn't carry through this plan. As an arcanist, he was bound by their code to accept whatever the Master of Kelos demanded, but that didn't mean he couldn't find a way to get out of it. "Your dog?"

"Passed on to the spirit realm just after that battle in Starfall, poor little mite. But he's waiting for me, and I promised him it would only be a short while. Now you see why you can't go chasing after that girl."

The next six hours dragged by with Hallow throwing every argument he could think of at Exodius, and the old man, wily and far more cunning than Hallow had imagined, deftly turned away each one.

By the time they arrived at Kelos the following midday, Hallow was more or less resigned to the inevitable.

"I will do as you command," he said, slowly and painfully unhitching Penn from the harness that the horse so obviously felt was beneath his dignity to bear and leading him over to a post. "But you must give me two or three spans of Bellias before I take up your mantle. I have to find Allegria—"

"There's no time," Exodius said, gathering up the staff and one of the small kegs. He nodded toward the wagon. "I must be off to the spirit realm before Bellias lights the sky tonight. Bring in the rest of that, will you? It'll all be yours after tonight, and you don't want the captain finding it. He has a special love of beer, and will want to impose a tax on the goods you brought in."

"But I didn't bring them—you did," Hallow said, a sense of hopelessness filling him.

Exodius said nothing, just entered the tower, leaving Hallow standing with his tired horse, a wagon filled with goods, and, if the glimpses of movement from his peripheral vision were accurate, a ruin full of ghosts.

"If I asked you to run over me a few times to put me out of my misery, would you do it?" he asked Penn.

The horse turned and snorted on him, blasting his chest with snot.

Hallow sighed. "That's about as accurate an assessment of my life as could ever be made."

The ceremony that marked the change in leadership of the arcanists was not at all the impressive occasion Hallow had imagined.

"Here. Thorn is yours now," Exodius said. He shoved the staff into Hallow's hands, then filled his own with various books and scraps of parchment, topping it all off with several small boxes the size of a man's hand, and the stuffed parrot. He peered over the top of the parrot and, with a pronounced waggle of his eyebrows at Hallow, added, "I'm off now. Don't let the ghosts get the better of you—it'll be a nightmare to regain control. Farewell."

"But, Master Exo—" Before Hallow could finish the sentence, Exodius spoke a few words that Hallow had never heard, stepped forward, and was swallowed up by... nothing.

Hallow looked at the spot where Exodius had disappeared. "What—I have never—what was that?"

Summoning the entrance to the spirit world, a voice said into his head.

Hallow blinked a few times and angled a glance up at the wooden bird atop the staff. "You really do talk? It wasn't just Exodius being... eccentric?"

Of course I talk. I would be a very poor Master of Kelos if I couldn't do something as simple as imbuing a staff with my presence in order to lend my support to the current master. Now, listen well, young Hallow, for there is much for you to learn. Exodius was a horrible master and let all sorts of my regulations and policies slide. You shall reinstate them, and order will be brought to the arcanists. First is your apprentice. Every Master of Kelos must have an apprentice. Exodius refused, but pay that no mind. While you were insensible, I arranged for your apprentice. He should be here in the morning. Then there is the general state of decay in Kelos. You need to restore it before you summon all the arcanists to acknowledge your leadership.

Hallow sighed for what seemed like the fiftieth time that day. He had a feeling his new position was going to be even more taxing than he'd imagined. But that job would have to wait until he found Allegria.

It took a full week until he was able to move with any sort of ease, and more than two weeks beyond that before he tracked Allegria to a ship that had sailed a month earlier. He didn't return to Kelos after finding that information, instead taking passage on the same merchant ship, and arriving at Deacon's Cross a few days later.

"Blessings of Kiriah and Bellias upon you. My name is Hallow." He made a bow to the priestess who stood at the gate to the Temple of Kiriah to which he'd been told Allegria was bound. "I have come a long way, an exceptionally long way, to see a priestess. Allegria is her name. Would it be possible to have a message sent to her?"

"No." The woman turned her back, clearly done with the conversation.

"Might I ask why not? If it is against some temple rule—"

The woman clicked her tongue in annoyance. "She sees no one. She has gone into seclusion and has contact only with a custodian."

"I'm sure she'll agree to see me if you could but take a message that I'm here. Not that it is of importance, but I did come all the way from Genora to see her—"

"She sees no one," the porter interrupted.

"By her own choice?" Hallow asked, suspicious that the head of the order might have locked her up for becoming a Bane of Eris.

"Of course! We do not force our priests into solitude. Seclusion in the hermitage is an honor, not a right, and certainly not a punishment."

The porter made it quite clear she was done speaking to him. Hallow considered his options, but short of barging into the temple and searching it for Allegria, he had no idea how to find her.

He spent three days in the small town outside the temple, trying three more times to see Allegria, even going so far as meeting the head priestess, but every time he was met with the statement that Allegria wished to see no one. At last, before he had to leave in order to catch the ship sailing back to Genora, he paid a small girl to smuggle a letter inside the temple and deliver it into Allegria's hands.

"If you find her, give her the letter, and tell her it's from me," he told the girl, a child of one of the cooks. "Tell her that I will return at any time if she needs me. Can you remember that?"

"I think so," the girl said, her eyes on the small bag of coins Hallow held before her. "My mam will know where she is. Can I buy anything I want with those coins?"

"Anything that your mother wouldn't mind you having," he replied, hoping he wasn't bringing down upon his head the wrath of an irate mother. "Mind you deliver the letter first."

The girl snatched the bag from his hand and ran off, scattering promises behind her.

Hallow felt as if his body were deflating, hope having slipped away from him, leaving him as flaccid as an empty wineskin.

"And that is that," he told the horse he'd rented at the stable as he prepared to ride back to Deacon's Cross. "I can only pray to the goddesses that she reads the letter."

Eleven months later, he was still waiting for a response from her, one that he finally admitted to himself might never come.

That thought was uppermost on his mind one morning.

"Master Hallow! Master Hallow, wait! I have news!"

"The morning looks to be a fresh one," the captain of the guard noted sourly when Hallow emerged from the run-down stable, where he had been attending to Penn.

"Master, it is a message!"

Hallow paused to look up at the sky. It did indeed appear to be the start of a cloudless day. "Is it the good weather that annoys you, or the fact that the sun makes you so transparent you can barely be seen?"

The ghostly captain of Kelos glowered at Hallow. "I see *you're* in a mood."

"Master, it is of much importance!"

Your apprentice wants you, Thorn whispered into Hallow's mind.

Hallow smiled at the captain of the guards. "Indeed I am. The light of Kiriah is always welcome in Kelos."

He's chugging toward you at quite a pace, the staff continued. Hallow wondered if, when the day came to leave his physical form behind, he'd imbue his spirit into an inanimate object as Thorn had done. *Lad has to stop filling his piehole with sweets. His face is almost as red as his hair.*

Definitely not. He didn't want to blight whoever was unlucky enough to be named Master of Kelos after him.

Now he's fallen. Oh, he's up again. Boy's got pluck, I'll give him that, but he's not master material. You know that, don't you?

"I do know that, but thank you for pointing it out. I don't suppose you have anywhere else to go? One of the ghosts to visit? A small child to frighten?"

Hahaha. I like you. You're much more interesting than that apprentice of mine. Exodius was mad, quite mad.

"I'm going to be lucky if I'm not the same in a very short time," Hallow muttered. He continued toward the tower, ignoring the labored breathing and dull thump of running feet behind him. It would do Selwin good to get a little exercise. The boy spent too long cloistered in the apprentice's quarters, gaming with the spirits of soldiers long dead.

"Mast... mast... er..." Selwin was clearly at the end of his breath now. Hallow briefly contemplated running up the stairs to his quarters, but decided to take pity on the boy. He paused at the doors, one hand resting on them with a familiar sense of mingled possession and weariness.

He looks like a tick about to pop, Thorn mused.

"Master... a... a..."

"A message, yes, so I gather." Hallow held out his hand, waiting patiently for the boy, now doubled over with his hands on his thighs, to catch his breath.

"Came from... a messenger..."

"Messages so often do," Hallow replied, and sighed to himself when the boy just looked blankly at him. It had been a long week with no one for conversation but people long dead and a new apprentice who was not the sharpest arrow in the quiver.

What's it say? Is it something about Exodius? If he's dead, tell him he can't haunt you. I was here first.

Hallow broke the wax seal and quickly scanned the message.

The words had been written hurriedly, the letters standing out starkly against the cream of the paper. As he read it, Hallow shivered, feeling as if the sun had suddenly gone behind a cloud. He glanced upward, but the sky was still a pale washed blue.

"There's blood on it," Selwin pointed out breathlessly, nodding to the paper.

Oooh. Blood? Who is it from? What does it say?

"So I see." Hallow turned and entered the tower, the sound of his boots on the stone stairs tapping out a rhythm that seemed to echo in his brain.

"Master Hallow, is something wrong?" Selwin dogged his footsteps. Hallow didn't have to see his apprentice to know the boy's face would be twisted with worry—except when gaming, Selwin always wore a worried countenance. It was one of the reasons Hallow regretted taking on the lad against his better judgment—Selwin clearly did not have his heart in magic of any form.

"Something is always amiss somewhere. Remember that, and you stand a fair chance of holding on to your sanity."

Pfft. We're arcanists. We live for battle and strife.

"Maybe you do, but some of us have seen enough fighting to last for the rest of our lives," Hallow told the staff, before continuing up to the room that had once belonged to Exodius.

It had taken a good six months before Hallow forgave the old man for dumping the responsibility of Kelos upon him.

Selwin looked momentarily startled at Hallow's words, but everyone in Kelos knew that Thorn spoke only to the current master. With a hesitant glance at the staff, Selwin hung around the doorway, clearly torn between curiosity and the desire to escape any potential work that Hallow might assign him. Curiosity won, and the boy followed him into the tower room. Hallow had made few changes since Exodius left, although he had cleared out the vast quantities of paper, leaving it to Selwin to sort through the stacks. The books Hallow kept. He went directly to a small writing desk and sat, writing a few lines quickly.

"Is it bad news, Master Hallow?"

Yes, what is it that had you turning so pale?

Hallow looked up, his eyes on the apprentice. He would never be an arcanist, not one of any ability, and it was far kinder to release him from a profession he didn't enjoy than to try to teach him the wonder that Hallow found in manipulating arcane magic. "Do you want to go home, Selwin?"

The boy's face lit up with joy. "For a visit? Can I do that? My father said I have to wait until harvest time—"

"Go home for good, I meant." Hallow sealed the scroll with a blob of blue wax, pressing the Kelos signet ring he wore on a chain around his neck into the soft wax before getting up to face the boy. "It's clear to me that while you have tried your best here, your heart isn't in it."

Good for you. Send him home and get a worthy apprentice. He isn't at all what I thought he would be. I'm sure I can find another, a better one for you.

Selwin's face blanched. He stammered, "Ma-Master Hallow, if I've done something wrong—"

"You've done nothing wrong. Nothing that you could help." Hallow put his hand on the boy's shoulder, giving him an encouraging pat. "Not everyone is meant to be an arcanist. It's an exacting profession, one that takes centuries to learn, and a lifetime to master. There is no shame in trying and deciding it's not for you."

"My father—" The boy's eyes were still frightened.

"I'll tell him I am about to go into battle, and I can't have an apprentice now. Give him a little time, and then broach the subject of your apprenticing yourself to... what do you like to do?"

"Dicing," the lad said promptly. "And eating."

"Perhaps there is a publican you can assist," Hallow said. "That would be a much better life for you than staying with me."

"Are you really going to battle?" Selwin asked.

I hope so. I love a good battle, and it's been far too long since we had any fighting to speak of.

"Yes." Hallow eyed the boy for a moment, then shook his head, and pulled the staff from the sheath on his back. He held the staff at arm's length. "Thorn, I want you to deliver a message for me."

A message? The wooden bird form atop the staff quivered excitedly. "Can you carry one?"

Of course I can. The bird's wings stretched and flapped. *I was the Master of Kelos, the Light of Bellias Starsong, savior of a thousand Starborn, and an arcanist of such renown that my very spirit remains strong when those of others fade into the twilight. I am the—*

"A simple 'yes' will suffice. I need you to take this scroll to Darius in Starfall City. Do you know him?"

Mealymouthed fellow who stands for the Starborn in the Council of Four Armies? Thorn snorted. *What do you want him for? He doesn't have the stomach for fighting. Didn't he let Lord Israel take care of the handful of Harborym who remained after you killed the others?*

"Nonetheless, it is to him I wish for you to take this message. The others, I will deliver myself."

He held up the scroll for the bird to grasp. It did so, making a few swoops through the room before darting out a window. *Don't fight without me! I'll be back as soon as I deliver the message.*

Hallow said nothing, just went to a small chest hidden under a table bearing numerous vials of various liquids. He forgot for a moment that Selwin remained in the chamber. The chest brought back so many memories.

And so much pain.

He opened it, pulling out the scarred and stained sheath that he used for Thorn when he was fighting. "Still usable, despite being locked away for almost a year," he said to himself, and set it aside.

Several garments were next. He took them out and shook them. "Could do with an airing, but there's no time for that."

"Are those the clothes you wore for the Battle of the Fourth Age?" Selwin asked, his tone almost comically reverential. "My father told me that you fought at Starfall."

He touched one of the laces on a sleeve, remembering how Allegria had hurriedly unbound them.

Allegria.

He'd tried to avoid thinking of her over the last few months. He tried not to remember her shining black hair, the way her eyes would light with gold flecks set in onyx, her wit and warmth, and her delight in intimate pursuits. He closed his eyes for a moment, remembering the scent of wildflowers that clung to her no matter how long she'd been fighting. The pain was just as sharp as it had been the day she'd fled the throne room.

If only his body hadn't been so broken.

If only he'd hadn't collapsed trying to follow her, to stop her, to make her see reason.

If only she'd stayed with him.

"So many lost opportunities," he murmured. The sound brought him back to the present, and, with it, awareness of the freckle-faced boy who knelt beside him. "There's no time for sentimentality now, Selwin. We must act."

"All right. Do you want me to do something?"

"Yes. Go home. I'll send the captain of the guard with you to Knellsbridge," he said, naming a town three days' away. "Your father's farm isn't far from there, is it?"

"Half a day's walk, faster if I have a horse," the boy said wistfully.

"Tell the captain to give you the new gray gelding. It can be a gift to your father," Hallow said.

Selwin's eyes widened in excitement. "Are you sure, master? You just bought the gelding."

"I'm sure. I won't have time to train him, so your father might as well have the benefit of him. Now go, pack your things, and send the captain of the guard to me."

Selwin's sandals slapped on the stone floor as the boy dashed from the room.

Hallow rose and commenced gathering a few things into a leather satchel. It had been a long time since he'd left Kelos, not since the day he returned from the fruitless effort to see Allegria, but he went about the business of collecting necessary items almost mechanically. A compass, two canteens, his personal book in which he kept spells he was crafting, some silver coins, a pair of daggers, and… silver glinted from the bottom of the chest. Pain hit him hard in the gut as he removed the two narrow swords, gems at the hilt glowing in the morning light when he held them up.

Allegria's swords. He'd taken them from one of Lord Israel's men who had claimed them, much to the man's dismay. Hallow had been careful to keep the swords from Israel's sight, since Allegria had told him they had been made for the queen.

After a moment's hesitation, he tied the swords onto the satchel and donned his travel clothes.

* * * *

It was a week almost to the hour when the ship traveling from Genora to Aryia landed at Abet, the capital city of the Fireborn. He didn't tarry there to answer the summons he'd received, instead heading south along the coast. Two days later he was on the road to the temple that he had become familiar with the year before. As he neared the temple, his heart started beating faster.

The same porter guarded the door as had been on duty the last time he'd come.

"Greetings," he said, dismounting from the horse he'd bought in Abet. "Feliza, isn't it?"

The porter blinked at him a couple of times, puzzled. "It's... you're Hallow, aren't you?"

"Hallow of Penhallow. Now of Kelos. Master of Kelos, not that I've taken much pleasure in that title. I've come to see Allegria."

Wariness replaced the confusion in the priestess's eyes. "You're back, are you? Well, you know as well as I do that you can't see her. No one sees her."

"I know that. I also know that this time, I'm not going to let her send me away until I've accomplished my goal. Would you tell her that I'm here, and I won't leave until she speaks to me."

Feliza was shaking her head even before he finished the last sentence. "You don't seem to understand what hermitage is. She sees no one, my lord. Not even us—the priestesses. We are forbidden her company."

"She must see someone. What about Lady Sandorillan?"

"No one sees Allegria."

Hallow sighed, then got down onto his knees. "It's not often that I beg, but Allegria touched my heart in a way no other woman has. I must see her. I will not leave until I do so. If you insist on denying me, I will remain here and return every hour to prostrate myself before you, before your goddess, before anyone who can take me to her. Understand, I am desperate. This will happen, or I will die in the trying."

Feliza's gaze softened upon him. "Quickly, get to your feet lest someone see you," she urged, tugging at his arm. "I shouldn't tell you this—goddess knows I shouldn't—but Kiriah is benevolent and rewards those who are pure of heart, and you must surely have a pure heart if you are willing to sacrifice yourself just to see Allegria." She glanced around, hesitated, then said softly, with rushed words, "Some of the others think she may have died. One of the younger girls said she'd seen bones in the cave where Allegria was banished, but Lady Sandor said it was only a goat skeleton."

"Allegria lives in a cave?" That wasn't at all what Hallow had pictured.

Feliza looked him dead in the eye and said blandly, "I don't know what you are talking about, Lord of Kelos. I mentioned nothing about the caves to the north, found in the cliffs that follow the stream."

"No," Hallow said, joy blossoming in his chest. "You didn't. Thank you for not telling me."

She bowed her head in acknowledgment. "Kiriah's blessings upon you." The door set into the great stone wall closed firmly. Hallow didn't waste time—he simply mounted his horse and headed for the rocky cliffs to the north of the temple.

He left the horse at the base of the cliff since the path was steep and narrow. When he finally found the entrance to the small cave, it was empty of all but a chair and small table, a cot, and a chest upon which sat an altar to Kiriah. "At least I know where she *was*," he said to himself, and went out to survey the cliff face. A narrow track wound upward. He followed it, emerging at the top, where a field of tall grass waved gently in the afternoon air. Lying on a flat rock was the figure of a woman, her arms outspread, her eyes closed.

For one brief, horrible moment, he thought she was dead, but as he approached, she wrinkled her nose and rubbed it before resuming her spread-arm position. She looked exactly the same as she had a year before—her hair was as glossy and black as a raven's wing. The line of dots remained across her forehead. Her face was as fresh as if she'd just stepped from a bath.

The memory of the night she'd done just that returned, bringing heat to his groin, but he told his body to stop thinking of that, and attend to the present. "You look just as lovely as you did the first day I saw you."

Allegria frowned, then sat up, one hand shading her eyes so she could look up at him. He watched with interest as her face expressed first confusion, then joy, then despair, quickly followed by anger.

"What are *you* doing here?"

He ignored the emphasis on the pronoun, holding up a hand when she got to her feet. "Pax, Allegria. Do not run off in a snit."

"A snit?" She marched up to him and poked him in the chest. *Hard.* Absently, he rubbed the spot. "I do not have snits!"

"You threw something very like one eleven months and twenty-two days ago, when I was broken and bleeding and could barely stand, let alone run after you."

She blinked a couple of times before saying, "You betrayed me! I didn't run from you in a snit—I ran from you in abject betrayal. You, a man to whom I'd given myself, and with whom I was very likely falling in love."

He was oddly pleased despite the situation. "You were? I was quite smitten with you, too. That's why I asked you to stay—"

"You asked me to stay because you knew Kiriah Sunbringer had shunned me, and thus I would need protecting from your overlord. Whom you *also* betrayed!" Allegria slapped her hands on her thighs and turned to march away across the grassy cliff top.

"How did I betray Lord Israel?" This was not how he'd pictured their meeting. He'd expected anger, perhaps tears, and then a joyful reunion. He had not anticipated Allegria hurling accusations at him and storming off. "Not that I betrayed you, but let's start with Israel."

"You broke your fealty to him," she snapped, swishing her hand angrily through the tall grass. He caught up to her, aware that a sense of life had returned to him, one that had been missing since the moment she had run out of the throne room.

"What fealty?" he asked, perplexed. He had a vague memory of her saying something about fealty before, but he'd paid it no mind at the time.

"Whatever it is you swore to Lord Israel. Whatever it was you threw aside so you could seduce me and join Deo's company. Come to think of it, you *also* betrayed Deo by working all along for someone else. I wouldn't be surprised Lord Israel showed up in Starfall when he did because you told him where we were going."

He took her by the arm and spun her around to face him. He was willing to allow others to think ill of him when it didn't matter, but this did. It mattered a lot. "My heart, I owed fealty to no one."

"Don't call me that," she said, pulling her arm from his grasp. "I'm not your heart." She paused for a moment. "What do you mean you owed no fealty? You were an apprentice. You had to swear fealty in order to take that position."

"My master was dead, and when you and I met; I had no other."

Her eyes scanned his face, obviously looking for signs he was dissembling. "But... you were with Lord Israel's company—"

"With them, yes, because it was a mutually beneficial arrangement." He ran his hand up her arm until he could cup her chin. "I did not betray anyone. I did not tell Lord Israel where Deo's company was, and I certainly did not use you as you assumed I did. I wanted to see Deo for myself, because I'd witnessed his banishing, and heard only that he was mad and enthralled by the chaos magic. What you said about him made me curious, but when I decided to join his company, it was only because I believed in him, not to betray him."

"But..." She rubbed the line of spots across her forehead. "You didn't tell Lord Israel what Deo was doing?"

"No." He grimaced, and admitted, "It's true I kept to myself the knowledge that the Four Armies were setting off for Starfall the morning after we left them, but that was because you said Deo was already on his way there. I knew he would reach it in advance of his father's company. I didn't think Lord Israel would travel quite so swiftly, but that, my heart, is all I'm guilty of."

Her eyes narrowed with suspicion, but he waited while she worked through everything he'd said. After a few minutes, she shook her head, and leaned into him. "All this time, I thought you had used us. Used me to get to Deo, in order to curry favor."

He wrapped his arm around her, taking pleasure in the warmth of her body against his, a pleasure that was increased when he took a few subtle sniffs and found that she still smelled like wildflowers. "I tried to explain, but you ran away."

"You could have told me that I was an idiot and wrong," she mumbled into his shoulder.

"I tried that, too, but only made it to the door of the throne room before my body gave out. It took some time before I was healed enough to travel, and by the time I found your temple, you had been secreted away. I was told you refused to see anyone."

"Kiriah's blood, I feel like such a fool thinking what I did—wait, you said that you came to the temple?"

"I did. Several times, in fact, over the course of about three days. I even pleaded my case before the head priestess. I assume by the look on your face that you were not told I'd petitioned to see you?"

"No." She looked horrified. "I received no message from you. I assumed you didn't want to see me again. I assumed—I thought you—"

"You thought I was a bastard who loved you and left you," he said with a grim smile. "Well, it's not the most flattering thing that's been said of me, but it's not the worst either."

She stared at him for a minute, pain in her eyes. "Sandor must have interfered... but how could she do that to me? Why would she hide your visits from me?"

Hallow didn't feel it was his place to speak ill of the temple's leader, even though it was obvious she had deliberately kept them apart. "I can only assume she acted in a way she thought for the best."

Regret danced across her face. "Hallow, I can't even begin to tell you how foolish I feel, and how sorry I am for not trusting you, and thinking so ill of you. All these months, wasted, and for what? My foolish pride, and Sandor's ill will."

"I don't know that she wished either of us ill, but she certainly did not want us together." Hallow damned his own actions of the past. Why hadn't he pursued Allegria when he was here? Why hadn't he continued to argue with Lady Sandorillan, begging, demanding, pleading to see Allegria? "I could have done more. I could have fought harder."

"This is not your doing. It's my fault, and I will regret it to the end of my days."

Her sadness made him want to sweep her up into his arms, but he steeled himself against such a reaction. He had to stay focused. "Let us share the blame and move forward."

"That's it, be the reasonable one. I've missed that about you almost as much as I've missed your eye crinkles." Allegria slid her arms around his neck and would have kissed him had he not gently pushed her back.

"No, do not make that face," he said, laughing when she looked outraged. "There is nothing I want more than to lay you down on the grass and love you as I've dreamed of these last eleven months, but we have no time."

"Why don't we have time? Time is *all* I have had. There were days when I thought I'd go mad with it," she said when he took her hand and led her toward the cliff path. "Hallow, where are we going? I assure you that the grass is much more comfortable than the cot in my cave."

He stopped at the top of the cliff, where the wind caused her hair to whip around her as if it had a life of its own. He put his hands on her shoulders and, for a moment, reveled in the gold specks in her eyes, shining as bright as polished coins. "They're back, my heart."

"Who's back? What—" Her eyes widened, disbelief filling them, giving his gut a wrench.

"The Harborym have returned. This time to stay, unless we stop them before their full force descends upon Alba."

"But—but the rift that they used—I closed it. It was gone."

"They've opened three more. On Aryia." He hated to see the pain in her eyes, but there was simply no time to ease her into the truth. "One in Abet, one to the west, and one south of here. So far, they've only sent their monstrous soul hounds through the rifts, but it's only a matter of time before the Harborym themselves start pouring through to decimate our land. Allegria, it sounds melodramatic to say you are our only hope, but it is just about at that point. A few Harborym we could cope with, but with three rifts spewing battalions of enemies onto Aryia..." He shook his head.

"We?" Her eyes studied his chest for a moment. "You and Lord Israel?"

He took a deep breath. "The Council of Four Armies and me. I am now the Master of Kelos. I head the arcanists' army."

"Kiriah's toes. *You?*"

She looked so disbelieving he had to laugh. "Yes, but I assure you it was a position I took against my will. Exodius—no, we don't have time for that tale. We have to leave for Abet now. I have tarried far longer than I should have, and the council awaits us."

"No," she said simply, and pulled her hand from his.

"Allegria, I know you blame the council for what happened to Deo—"

"No. That is, yes, I do hold them responsible for his death, and the for the deaths of the other banesmen they encased in crystal and then buried deep in the ground, but that's not what I'm objecting to. I mean no, I can't help you."

Of all the objections he'd anticipated, never had he thought she'd refuse outright to lend her assistance. "You are angry, and I understand that—"

"No, you're not listening to me." She clicked her tongue in annoyance and took his face in her hands, her fingertips caressing the lines that fanned from his eyes. "I can't help, Hallow. Not in the sense you mean. You came to me because I was a banesman once, but I am not one anymore."

He touched the silver cuff on her wrist. "You aren't?"

"No." Sadness filled her face as she let her hands drop and turned away to look down upon the temple grounds. "Not since that day. All my power, my lightweaving, and the chaos magic—it's all gone. Just as if it had never been."

"You were tired after the battle—" he started to say, but she interrupted with another shake of her head.

"I told myself that very same thing, but even after I recovered, days later, I still couldn't feel the power of Kiriah. I couldn't conjure up so much as a single small light rabbit. And where the chaos magic once struggled inside of me, there was only emptiness."

"But you returned to the temple. You must still have a connection with Kiriah, or it would not be possible for you to have returned."

"Hallow…" She put her hand on his arm, the warmth of her fingers giving him comfort despite the hopelessness that threatened to overwhelm him. "I am not on temple grounds. Sandor saw at once that I had been cast from Kiriah's grace, and she sent me to the cave."

"But surely a priest cannot be exiled like that…" He stopped, unable to finish the sentence.

"I wasn't exiled. I was shunned by Kiriah Sunbringer herself. The people of the town, the other priests, even the animals of the area, all feared me. Sandor offered me a sanctuary, not a prison, although I will admit there are times when I would have rather been killed alongside Deo than have suffered this solitary existence." She gazed steadily at him, her eyes so sad, it made him want to weep. "I'm sorry, Hallow. There is nothing left within me to fight the Harborym except my abilities with a bow and sword, and I'm sure you have no shortage of common soldiers. You will have to seek out one of the five banesmen who remain."

"They are gone," he said, giving in to the urge and pulling her to his chest. He kissed her forehead, her eyes, her cheeks. He wanted more, but he stopped before control slipped through his fingers. "Two disappeared. Lord Israel said he 'took care of' them. The other three I sent into hiding so they could avoid capture, but I've lost contact with them. I don't even know if they are still alive. I'm sorry that you've suffered so for these last months, but, my heart, there is no time for comfort. We must leave now and ride hard if we are to be in Abet before moonrise tomorrow."

"I just told you I can't help—" she protested when he took her hand again and started down the path to the cave entrance. "Why are you doing this? Didn't you listen to me?"

He smiled at the note of ire in her voice. He had begun to think that the sorrow of her life had driven away the sharp-tongued Allegria. "I heard. And I wish I had an explanation as to why Kiriah seems to have turned her back on you, her most promising priestess, or why the chaos magic has gone dormant in you, but there is no time to work that out now. We can get into it once we are on the ship."

"What ship? I thought you wished to ride for Abet?" she asked, following reluctantly.

"I do. The ship comes after."

"What exactly is going on?" She stopped. "Lord Israel sent you, didn't he?"

"Far from it." He took her hand again and pulled her down with him to the entrance of the cave. "Do you have things you wish to take with you? Clothing? Books? Weapons?"

"No. My swords were lost in the battle, and my clothes don't matter. What do you mean, far from it?"

He sighed a martyr's sigh and led her down to the plains where his horse waited. "When I became the head of the arcanists, the council forbade me to contact you. I paid them no mind, of course, but they made it clear that if I pursued contact with you, there would be repercussions."

She looked at him curiously, a slow smile curling the corners of her mouth. He wanted so badly to kiss those lips, but knew if he started, he wouldn't be able to stop. "You have defied them?"

"I have on a number of occasions, and for lesser causes than you."

"But you're the Master of Kelos, the most powerful wielder of magic in all of Alba."

"Hardly the latter. In fact, I'd give you that title."

"My power has abandoned me," she said starkly.

"So you say. Come. We must hurry." He mounted and held out his hand for her.

"Why should I come when I have nothing to offer?" she demanded. He thought of all the things he could tell her, of the ways he could persuade her, and picked the one that he thought would resonate most in her. "What do you have here to stay for?"

She flushed angrily for a moment; then her shoulders slumped in acknowledgment. "You're right. There's nothing here but more isolation, more long years of being ignored and exiled and talking to the wind. Very well, I'll come with you, but do not expect miracles, Hallow. You must agree to take me as I am now, and not be disappointed later."

"You could never disappoint me, Allegria."

"Say it, Hallow." She had a mulish look that reminded him of her mount of old.

"Very well." He laid a hand on the top of her head. "I pledge to you that I accept you as you are and will never expect anything from you but what you freely give. Will that do?"

"Just remember it when you call on me to perform magic that has abandoned me," she said with a curt nod.

"So be it. Come along, now. My horse won't be too happy about it, but we can ride together."

"There's no need. We can take one of the temple's mules."

He was pleased to see the glint of humor in her eyes. "Not the infamous Buttercup, surely?"

"Of course. And I have no doubt she is as obstinate as ever." She hesitated a few seconds, then accepted his help to sit sideways across his thighs. "I might not be able to help you by means of magic, but I will admit to being pleased that you'd go against the council's dictates to find me."

"We shall see, Allegria. We shall see."

"Yes, we will, and I don't think you'll like what you see when I fail, but I've said enough about that for now. You didn't tell me why we are going to Abet if you are not under orders to bring me to Lord Israel."

"The council must meet and determine a plan of action. I wanted you to be a part of the decision-making process, since you will be a good part of the solution."

She said in exasperation, "I've told you and told you, I have no—"

"No power, I know. Let us deal with that once we have met with the council."

She shook her head sadly and said no more for a long while.

Chapter 16

We arrived in the city of Abet only to be greeted with dull skies, heavy rain, and sore behinds. At least mine was sore—Hallow hadn't been confined to a cave and cliff top for the last year, so I assumed he was used to spending time in the saddle.

"If I said this was an omen, would you mock me?" I asked when I limped away from the horse we'd rented along the road to Abet. We'd ridden so hard we had to change mounts several times, pausing only for brief breaks.

"I would never mock you, although I almost agree." Hallow glanced up at the leaden skies. "It seems our arrival does not have Kiriah's blessing."

"I told you that nothing connected with me would, but you insist on pretending it's just a temporary state." I realized just how grumpy I sounded and touched Hallow's hand. "I'm sorry, I'm tired and saddlesore. You know I will fight alongside whatever company will have me, assuming weapons can be found for me."

He flashed a brief smile, making my stomach turn somersaults. I marveled that even exile for eleven months hadn't changed my feelings toward him. He looked just the same—his eyes as blue as an early summer morning, his white-blond hair longer now, long enough to be caught back in a leather thong. The eye crinkles were still there, and still had the power to make my legs feel weak.

Blast the man! Why hadn't I gotten over him in my time of exile?

"As to that," he said, reaching for one of his saddlebags. "I have some good news—"

"Lord Hallow, at last you are come." A short little man with an unctuous smile hurried out to greet us in the stable yard. With a start, I realized it was Rixius. "Lord Israel has been most distraught thinking that your ship did not safely make it to shore, but when we heard from the captain that it had, but you left immediately—" He sputtered to a stop, having caught sight of me.

I curled my lip and gave as polite a greeting as I could manage. "Kiriah's blessings, Rixius."

"What is *that* doing here?" he demanded, pointing at me.

"Other than wishing I had a small beheading axe handy, you mean?" I asked, smiling sweetly.

He gasped in outrage and was about to unload on Hallow when the latter said, "Cease, Rixius. Allegria is here because she is a banesman, a strong warrior, and a clever priestess."

"She has been banished! Not even her temple would tolerate her presence because of the stink of Harborym about her. Lord Israel said so himself."

I sighed. I knew that I'd meet this very same reaction from everyone in the city.

Hallow wagged a few fingers at Rixius. The man was suddenly lifted a good four feet off the ground, hanging there as if held by an invisible hand. Beneath him, a ring of blue fire formed. "What was that you said about my good friend and sometime lover?"

Rixius squawked and wildly waved his arms in the air, his legs kicking ineffectually. "I take it back, I take it back! Please don't burn me, Master Hallow! I will say nothing more about the priest."

"Good." Hallow let the man drop to the ground, waiting a few seconds before quelling the arcane fire. "Is the rest of the council here?"

"No, my lord," Rixius said, hopping on one foot to examine the sole of his other foot. The soles were singed, but not burned through. Hallow might have a touch of the mischievous about him, but I had yet to see him be deliberately cruel.

Not that I'd realized that when it most mattered. I sighed to myself again and pushed back the guilty knowledge that at some point, I'd have to account for thinking the worst of him, but that time was not now.

Hallow frowned. "I thought Darius would have been right behind me. Surely he sent word of when to expect him?"

"No, my lord." Rixius studiously avoided looking at me as Hallow started for the interior of the great keep that housed Lord Israel and his court. I followed, pulling up the hood of my cloak, not due to a sense of inferiority, but because after my experiences with the people of my own town and temple, I preferred the shadows to the light. "Lord Darius is reportedly gravely ill, too ill to undertake the journey to Aryia. He promises to send an army as soon as one can be called, though."

"What's this?" Hallow stopped and for a moment, his eyes turned stormy. "What happened to the Starborn army?"

"There is no army," Rixius answered.

"Nonsense. I helped organize them myself some six months ago."

Rixius gave an oily smile that made me want to smack him on the back of his head. Then again, everything he did made me want to do that. I reminded myself that hitting others on the head, even if they were annoying and obsequious and reminded one of a steaming pile of cow manure, was not the way to prove my worth to Kiriah Sunbringer.

"What happened to them?" Hallow asked.

"I know not, my lord arcanist. Perhaps Lord Israel can answer that. He is awaiting news of your arrival in the war room at the top of the stairs. I must tend to procuring the supplies needed for Lord Israel's company, so I bid you farewell." Rixius bowed low and gestured for Hallow to climb the stairs. He did so with me at his heels. Rixius kept his head bowed when I passed, but I could feel his animosity poking at me with sharp jabs.

"I pray to Kiriah that you see through the flattery of that oily little blob of flyspecked cow dung," I murmured as we mounted the stairs.

"Tell me what you really think," he said with a little curl of his lips.

I pinched his arm.

The guards outside the war room bowed to Hallow, respect showing in their faces. I eyed them first, then Hallow, wondering at the change in the man who had dominated my thoughts for the course of my exile.

What was it that was different about him? He looked the same, although there were a few more lines radiating from his eyes. He held one shoulder a little higher than the other; it must have been broken during the battle. He was dressed in the same manner as he had been, although the black staff Exodius had given him appeared to have lost its bird. What was it, then, that brought such respect to the eyes of the guards?

He strode into the room, confident, easy in his own skin, and with a pronounced sense of purpose. That was what was different—he'd gone from being an apprentice, albeit a learned one, to a master of arcane knowledge.

He was a leader, and although he might balk at the title, he wore the mantle well.

"Lord Israel," he said, stopping in the middle of the round war room and giving a curt bow. Shadows lay heavily along the curved outer walls of the room, but I could see a number of laden bookshelves and tables, the biggest of which dominated the center, spread with large maps and scattered papers. The smell of incense hung in the air, making my nose wrinkle. "Rixius tells me that Darius's army is no more."

Lord Israel had been standing at the window, gazing out of it with his hands behind his back. He didn't turn at first, saying, "I gather the Starborn characteristic trait of thinking primarily of their own comfort has meant the army was dismantled. My own army is scattered across Aryia, although the troops were recalled at the first sign of the invasion. The full force should be assembled in a week or less."

"And Jalas?" Hallow's jaw tightened at Israel's words, but he kept control of his temper. I moved into the room behind him, putting a hand on his arm, more for my own comfort than his. "Where is the Tribe of Jalas?"

"They come, but it is slow going with the rift open in the pass between the High Lands and the rest of Aryia," a woman's voice responded. "I do not have my beloved father's way with the men, but they have heeded my call, and will be here as soon as they can."

Idril emerged from the shadows of the room, gliding forward in that annoying way she had (and which I could never duplicate, no matter how much I tried to get my hearty peasant feet to attempt it). She made me very aware that I had been living in a cave; my clothing was travel-stained and ragged, and since I'd lost my powers, I had nothing to offer anyone other than a reasonably strong sword arm, and a quick eye with the bow.

I disliked feeling inferior to anyone, but it really irked me that she could stand by, so coolly lovely and collected, while I had an itch on my back I couldn't reach, hadn't brushed my hair in two days, and had stepped in something foul-smelling in the courtyard.

"Allegria," Hallow whispered out of the corner of his mouth.

"What?" I whispered back.

"Stop growling. I'm sorry, my lady?" This last was directed toward Idril, who had asked him something.

She lifted a hand and brushed a dried leaf from his arm. "I asked where your army is. Do they remain on Genora?"

"No. Those arcanists I could recall from their various tasks are en route, as well. It was my intention for them to attack the southern rift while the other companies attack the northern two, but gathering them is taking time, and without the Starborn army, we shall simply have to make do with the forces we have. Once the southern portal is destroyed, we can turn our attention to the other two."

"An interesting plan, but not one that I believe holds much merit. I believe a better scheme is to combine forces now with the Tribe of Jalas—" Lord Israel turned as he spoke, stopping when he saw me standing next to Hallow.

I lifted my chin in response to the narrowed eyes he turned on me. "Kiriah's blessings," I said politely.

After a minute of intense scowling, he ignored me and turned his attention back to Hallow. "What have you done, arcanist?"

"I have brought you the one person who can give us a fighting chance to destroy the Harborym and their rifts," Hallow said simply.

"No," Lord Israel snapped, his gaze on me at once scathing and dismissive. "She has been rejected by her own temple. Kiriah has spurned her. She is an empty shell, nothing more."

His words pierced me deep, making me want to fight back, but a brief look at Hallow had me biting my tongue. Besides, I told myself with brutal honesty, there wasn't anything Israel said that wasn't fact.

"She is also the only one on Alba who can do what must be done," Hallow said, his voice strong and true.

It struck me at that moment that as irate as he was, Lord Israel sounded tired. His voice lacked emotion; it sounded as bland as the rainwater that streamed down the windows beyond him. He looked defeated. To be sure, his face was as impassive as ever, but he bore the air of a man who knew he was beaten even before the fight started. Though he belonged to a people who did not age for centuries, he looked as if he was at the end of his time.

"What must be done that only the priestess can achieve?" Idril asked, a little frown forming a wrinkle between her perfect pale blond brows.

In comparison, my own eyebrows, now as black as a raven's wing, resembled fuzzy caterpillars perched above my eyes.

"Yes, what can I do?" I asked Hallow. "I'm not quite as useless as Lord Israel makes me out to be, but you know that I can no longer wield magic."

He looked at Israel. "Do you wish to tell them, or should I explain?"

"Neither," Israel snapped. "You defied the mandates of the council by consorting with the priest. To bring her here was nothing short of treason; to suggest she can do anything to help is ludicrous in the extreme. The council will mete out punishment worthy of your crime once the invaders are dealt with."

"Really?" Idril asked, tipping her head to the side so that her shining silver hair slid like a curtain of silk. One rose-tipped expressive hand gestured at the room. "I see three members here, and I, for one, would like to hear Hallow out before deciding whether he is to be lauded or damned for bringing the priest with him." Her copper-colored eyes turned to me, making me feel even more itchy than before. I fought the urge to brush the wrinkles out of my tunic, instead holding her gaze with a look that told her I was a warrior, even if Kiriah had turned her back on me.

I went so far as to give her a little nod that acknowledged her hesitation to judge me, but all it did was elicit a slightly raised eyebrow before she turned back to her husband.

How could Deo have ever fallen in love with a woman apparently made of the ice so common in her native High Lands?

"You will leave my presence," Israel told me. "You will leave my town. If it were possible to banish you from Aryia itself, I would, but I swore to Lady Sandorillan that she should have the care of you. As for you—" He turned to Hallow. "You may think, because Exodius made you the Master of Kelos, that you have an influence on the path the council takes, but you are sorely mistaken. I lead the council, as I do all things. You would do best to remember that I, and I alone, allowed your master to raise you to this exalted position, and I can just as easily snatch it from you."

Anger roared to life in me, and with it, a slight burning sensation along the skin of my back and arms, as if I'd been out in the sun too long. "I'd call you an insufferable ass, but that would be doing a disservice to Buttercup and her descendants," I said acidly, my hands fisted.

Hallow, to my complete surprise, didn't look in the least bit outraged. He simply sighed and said under his breath, "Doing it too much," before adding in a louder voice, "If you will not tell them, then I must."

"I will not have my authority flouted in such a manner!" Israel bellowed. "Guards! Guards!"

No one entered the room. I cocked an eyebrow at him, and sadly, a little smirk curled my lips even though I knew it was unworthy of me to be pleased at his frustration.

"Blast them to Genora and back!" Lord Israel stormed to the doors and threw them open, shouting for the guards as he did so. "I'll teach them to leave their posts—"

Softly, the door closed behind him while he raged his way down the hall looking for the guards.

"Looks like you'd better tell us whatever it is he doesn't want us to know quickly," I said to Hallow, nodding toward Idril. "Before he comes back to throw me out of the city."

"Evidently," he said with a wry twist of his lips, before taking my hand and kissing my knuckles. I fought the brief spurt of warmth the gesture brought, oddly pleased that he had shown such affection in front of Idril. Her man might have treated her as coolly as she treated him, but mine wasn't afraid to kiss my hand no matter what the company.

"You asked me back at the temple why we were in such a hurry. The more time we delay, the more likely it is the Harborym will begin deploying their battalions through the rifts. The soul takers are easily overcome if dealt with quickly, but if they aren't, they will turn our people into Shades just as they did the Starborn."

"Soul takers?" I frowned. "I don't think I've ever heard of them. Wasn't it the Harborym who took the life force from the Starborn?"

"No. The Harborym used the Shades as servants, but it was the soul takers who turned the population." He must have noticed the confusion on both Idril's face and mine, because he added quickly, "They are monstrosities, resembling a cross between an insect and a giant dog. The Harborym have sent them through the rift ahead of their battalions, no doubt to enslave as many people as they can."

"They must be stopped," Idril said, brushing a speck of nothing from her lovely, pale, green and gold gown.

"They are being destroyed, but more continue to come. We are wasting time—we should leave now, before Lord Israel runs out of patience. We have precious little time to get to Enoch and back."

"Enoch?" I asked, wondering why we would be going there when the battle was on this continent. "Why would we want to go to the island where Deo was banished? Did you send the banesmen you saved there? You said there are only three of them left. Three are not enough to fight even a single battalion of Harborym, let alone however many might come through the rifts."

"I agree, and so I wrote to the council before I left Kelos."

"We have become weak since the dawning of the Fourth Age," Idril said, sitting gracefully in the nearest chair. She moved one of the papers on the table to examine the map beneath. "Peace has reigned in Alba since the closing of the rift, and that does not ensure an army is kept in top form. My beloved father's force had returned to their holdings and families before these three rifts opened, with only a small group remaining for the protection of the borderlands."

"We should go—" Hallow said, shooing me toward the door.

I dug in my heels. "I'm not setting foot out of this room until I know what's going on. You forget that I've been out of communication with literally everyone but Sandor for the last eleven months, and I'm not going to commit myself to anything until I know where we stand."

Hallow sighed heavily, but said, "Very well. You are owed that much, at least. I can only tell you what I know myself, however. The Starborn army barely existed before the fall of the Harborym. I tried to help them re-form and organize, but they lost their focus when Darius allowed the highborn to begin rebuilding their society, and training the remaining Shades as servants, rather than maintaining their army." His fingers gently stroked mine, causing little shivers to run down my back. How I had missed his touch, and how I wanted to topple him onto the nearest bed and reacquaint myself with that wonderful chest.

"And your people?" I asked in an attempt to distract myself from smutty thoughts. "What of them?"

"The arcanists were scattered by the invasion. They have been helping out as best as they could, wherever they could, but their organization under Master Exodius was lacking at best. I've tried to draw them together, but even now, they mostly go their own way and are slow to respond to my attempts to bring structure to the arcanists' guild. That is why there is only one hope of defeating the Harborym before they can bring forces too great to be overcome—the banesmen have to be restored."

"Restored how?" I asked, feeling hopeless. Why was he so focused on the power I no longer had? "They're dead, all but three, and you said you've lost touch with them."

He was silent for a moment, his eyes steady but holding a wary look that left me wondering what he was leading to. "We need Deo."

"Deo," Idril said softly, her gaze on the fingers that gently touched the map. "Deo is no more."

I gave a short bark of laughter at Hallow's words. "No wonder Lord Israel was so angry with you if you said that to him. I would love for him to realize now just how much he needs the son he killed."

"I did say it. He was not pleased, but not for the reason you believe."

The mocking smile left my lips, and at same the moment a suspicion crawled into the back of my mind. "Why are we going to Enoch, Hallow?"

"We're going to find Deo." He took a deep breath. "I will not defend Lord Israel's actions, because for the most part, I don't agree with them, but in two cases I did. The first was the way he dealt with the queen, and the second was Deo."

Emotion burned in me once more, growing until it spilled out into my limbs, leaving me flushed and hot with anger. I shot a quick glance at Idril, but she said nothing, her eyes on the table. "You agree with killing Deo? It's a wonder you wanted anything to do with me given that monstrous attitude."

"Deo isn't dead, my heart."

I stared at him for the count of thirty. "He is. Do you forget that I was there? We all were, all three of us. I saw what happened, Hallow. I saw Lord Israel encase him and the others in crystal. I heard him tell the guards to bury them deep where no one would find them."

"Nonetheless, Deo is not dead. Think, Allegria. If Lord Israel wanted Deo dead, he could have lopped his head off. Deo wasn't expecting an attack from his father, and was off his guard, not to mention being near the end of his strength after the battle with the Harborym. It would have been easy to kill him. Jalas and Darius both would have applauded Deo's slaughter, but instead of that, Lord Israel had Exodius use the moonstones to remove Deo and his men in a way that made the rest of the council believe they were dead, and no longer a threat to anyone in Alba."

"This is so," murmured Idril. "My beloved father would not have been happy with anything less than Deo's demise. His power was just too great to risk leaving him alive."

"Only Exodius knew the truth of what the moonstones would do, and he was very much devoted to Queen Dasa. He revealed the truth to me when he made me Master of Kelos because I had half guessed that the moonstones somehow teleported the men rather than trapping them in a crystal prison. They were intended to save the queen, but Lord Israel used them on his son, instead."

"But we *saw* Deo and the others trapped. We *saw* them encased in crystal."

"You saw their likeness only. I haven't seen the moonstones—Exodius hid them somewhere, saying they were too dangerous for anyone to use—but since that time, I've read of them, and I think that they hold the image of the being that is teleported."

"So when Lord Israel had them buried…"

"He buried nothing but a hollow image of his son, while the real man was safe on Enoch."

"He's alive? On Enoch?" I asked slowly, trying to readjust my thinking. Could Lord Israel really have saved Deo when I'd thought he'd destroyed him? It made sense that a father would wish to help his son, and yet, he was so violently against the banesmen…

"Yes to both."

"And the others? What happened to them?"

"I don't know. I haven't been able to find them. Lord Israel must know, but he refuses to speak on the subject." Hallow dropped my hand to rub a thumb over my cheek. "Now you see why it was so important that we come here. And why you are the only one left who can convince Deo to rejoin the people he believes betrayed him."

I shook my head at the idea I could convince Deo of anything. "Even if all this is true, he wouldn't listen to me. He never liked to take any counsel but his own, and I can't imagine that has changed in the last year."

"Then you will just have to convince him with magic." Hallow looked determined despite my resistance. "Normally I'm opposed to such forms of persuasion, but although I knew Deo for only a short time, I can't imagine he would back down from a battle."

"Nor can I," I said, thinking on the subject. If there was a way I could convince him... but I couldn't. "I just don't see how I can do anything when my abilities have abandoned me."

Hallow took my hand again, a little smile making his eye crinkles pop into life. He lifted my hand higher until I stared with wonder at my fingertips.

They glowed with a pale golden light.

"Your time in the shadows is over, my heart. Now we need all your strength, for we have hard battles ahead of us."

Chapter 17

"This might have been a pleasant voyage if not for two things," I told Hallow a few days later, as the ship navigated the great fingers of granite stabbing up from the sea along the best approach to the Isle of Enoch. It wasn't so much a port as a lessening of craggy, ship-destroying rocks. We stood together at the railing of the ship, watching as the captain piloted past them. Above us, the sky was a pale gray, washed with the faintest hints of blue, a dull brightness indicating where Kiriah struggled to burn through the high cloud cover. Seabirds wheeled and called over our heads, and the now-familiar tang of salt had me breathing deeply.

"I assume the company is one objection," Hallow answered, sliding a hand around my waist and pulling me against him.

"I can imagine people I'd rather spend time with than Idril and her gaggle of handmaidens, if that's what you mean." I tried to keep my voice neutral, but I feared a little bit of my true feelings snuck in.

"She does lead the Tribe of Jalas since her father has fallen ill," Hallow said, a smile in his voice even while his face presented its usual serene expression. "She has every right to come with us when it concerns the council, and releasing Deo very much does that."

"That's not why she's here, and you know it," I said. "You are aware that Deo wanted to marry her, but she married his father instead? And that when Deo was angry about the betrayal of his beloved and his father, Lord Israel banished him to this very same island? She clearly wants to be here to torment Deo. That or seduce him, assuming she has any passion in her icy veins."

"I have heard those same stories, yes," he said placidly, ignoring my slur. "But one thing my time with Master Nix taught me is never to believe something without first ascertaining whether it is true or not."

"And I agree with that principle in general, but if you think I'm going to march up to Lord Israel and ask him if it's true he stole his son's betrothed and got rid of him so he could thrust his lustful urges on her, you are quite, quite mad. Lord Israel wants me dead as it is—I don't think questioning him about his wife is going to do anything but ensure he adds torturing me to his plans."

Hallow laughed. "No, that would most definitely not be wise. However, you might wish to talk to Lady Idril before you damn her entirely."

I snorted softly to myself. The last thing I wanted to do was have a heart-to-heart conversation with the woman who made me feel awkward, unkempt, and unfeminine.

"And as for Lord Israel wanting you dead... I suppose I should tell you, lest you accuse me of keeping things from you, that if he had wished you dead, you would not be standing here now."

"Pfft," I objected, turning to face him, the tendrils of my hair whipping around my head like snakes. "The only reason he didn't kill me was because I closed the rift."

"And yet according to your beliefs, he was willing to kill his son for helping close the rift and defeat the Harborym?"

"But your point is that Deo isn't dead," I said, sidestepping the question.

"He's not." Hallow waited expectantly.

I puzzled over what he said. It didn't make sense. "You think Lord Israel doesn't want me dead, yet he banished me from his city and told you that he didn't want my magicless self helping to close the new rifts."

"He said that, yes. And then what did he do?"

"Had a fit? Stormed out of the room, calling for guards to do Kiriah knew what to me."

"Rather convenient, that, don't you think?"

"Convenient how?" I thought hard, a faint pattern starting to form in my mind. "You think... do you mean, that he left so that we could escape unharmed?"

"Despite all of his bluster and talk of beheadings, has he harmed you?"

"No," I admitted.

"And Deo? Did Lord Israel not save him from harm by preserving him the only way he could?"

"Well..."

"As he presumably also did for the other banesmen."

"You don't know where they are, though."

"No, but given the evidence, I don't think they were killed." Hallow gazed out at the cold, dark gray water. "I suspect that given enough time, with the right spells, I will be able to find them."

"Alive?"

"And well, though probably as isolated as Deo is. As you were."

"So Lord Israel isn't working against us?" I asked, trying to fit the puzzle pieces together. "Are you sure, Hallow? He certainly didn't sound like a man who was overjoyed to see me."

"He wasn't, because he knows you pose a problem. No, my heart, don't get your hackles up—I meant that you were a problem because now he must ensure your protection when others might wish you destroyed." He cast a look toward where Idril emerged from a cabin. "Although with Jalas confined to his bed, it appears a more prudent head now rules the tribe."

I was still trying to wrap my mind around the idea that Israel Langton wasn't the villain I had believed him to be. "But… he banished Deo in order to steal his beloved."

"I was there that night, you know."

I gazed at him in surprise. "I didn't know."

Hallow nodded. "I can assure you that the only reason Deo was sent to Enoch was to protect himself, and others who might be affected by the chaos power he'd consumed. He didn't have control of it at that point. He truly was a danger to others, and I assume if you ask him, he will admit that exile on an uninhabited island gave him the time and space he needed to perfect his control."

I mused over that for a bit, willing to agree it sounded reasonable. "You said Lord Israel had acquired the moonstones for the queen, but why did he use them on his son, instead?"

"Why should he not? He'd just learned that the queen was beyond the stones' reach, and he quickly realized they were the only way he could save Deo and the other banesmen."

"All because we did what he couldn't?" I asked, angry on behalf of Deo and the others. "And the council didn't like that fact?"

"No, because you and Deo were… You will forgive me if I use this word, but there is no other that suits. You were berserk. I can only imagine what the chaos power did to you, and how much strength you had to use to contain it, but the sight the council witnessed of you and Deo obliterating the Harborym could not help but inspire fear in them. If you could wield that sort of power, what threat would you pose should you ever turn against the council?"

"It was a horrible time," I agreed slowly, remembering well the sensation of being out of control, enraged with the lust of chaos magic flowing through me. It was the closest I'd felt to being consumed by it, and it was nothing I ever wished to experience again.

"That was why Lord Israel acted so quickly. He had to, lest the others demand you all be destroyed right then and there. You, he was quick to exclude, because he knew your head priest would keep you hidden and safe. But the others had no protection, so he changed his plans for the moonstones."

"Did he tell you this?" I asked, simultaneously annoyed that Hallow would keep this from me, and amazed that I could have—yet again—been so wrong in my assessment of Lord Israel's character. I would have to offer up several prayers of penitence to Kiriah for my hasty judgments.

"No, but if you think about it for a bit, I believe you'll realize it's the only reason for his actions that makes sense."

We were silent for a few minutes, Hallow deep in his own thoughts, while I was alternating between readjusting my view of the world and worrying about what was to come.

Idril moved toward us.

"What's the second thing?" Hallow asked suddenly.

"Hmm?" I asked, smoothing a hand down my tunic. I don't know where or how, but he had managed to find one of the Bane of Eris tunics, and although I'd had to alter it to make it fit, I was strangely pleased to once again be wearing the black tunic with the silver stars and sun. "Oh, uh…"

I coughed delicately and slid him a look from the corners of my eyes, aware that Idril and her ladies were now behind us. Normally I wouldn't have been so shy about making it clear that I desired Hallow, but given the limited accommodations on the small ship, and the fact that every time we attempted to take advantage of a moment's privacy, Idril managed to encounter us, we'd both had a pretty frustrating journey.

"It has been a difficult week, what with the long ride from the temple, followed by this trip," he said, his eyes crinkling in a way that made me want to throw modesty to the wind and disrobe him right then and there. "I am hopeful that Deo will have a building that will afford us some privacy."

"He'd better, if he wants to avoid my doing all the things I want to do to you right there in front of him," I murmured, then turned on the brittle smile I used whenever Idril blighted me with her presence.

"We arrive, I see," she said in her breathy voice, not one single blasted silver hair out of place. In contrast, I had hair clinging damply to the corners of my eyes, stuck to my nostrils, and in my mouth. I pulled it all free and ruthlessly bound it back with a cloth tie. "But what will we find? You are sure of the priestess's power, Hallow? You said she would regain the blessing of Kiriah during the voyage, and yet it does not seem to my eyes that she is graced with anything but a rather distressing libido."

"People who walk into cabins without first knocking should expect to see things not fit for public viewing," I said with as much dignity as I could find. Only that morning, she'd caught me without my tunic, and Hallow in the act of struggling out of his leggings.

"It was *my* cabin," Idril pointed out.

"We were just borrowing it for a little while," I began a bit tersely. I stopped when Hallow choked back a bubble of laughter. "Regardless, I would appreciate it if you didn't act like I'm not here when you're talking about me."

"Very well." She turned those glowing copper eyes on me. "Have you regained the grace of Kiriah Sunbringer?"

I glanced at my fingers. Not since the day we'd stood before Lord Israel had I felt even the remotest connection with the sun and Kiriah. "Not as such, but—"

"And the chaos power that Hallow informs me Deo bestowed upon you." Idril's voice, though soft, had an undernote of steel in it that made me pity the small herd of handmaidens who followed her around as if she were a rare flower that couldn't survive on her own. "Has it returned?"

I held out one of my wrists, the silver of the cuff as dull as the sky above us. "Do you see the runes etched upon this? No? Then there is nothing for the runes to contain. The chaos power has not stirred since I closed down the rift. You know, the one that was spewing Harborym of Eris into our world, the very same one your father and the other council members were unable to close in more than ten years of trying."

I felt ashamed of my outburst the second it left my lips.

Hallow raised both eyebrows, and my conscience got the better of me.

"My apologies," I said before Idril could respond. "That was unkind and conceited of me. I am well aware that I did not destroy the Harborym on my own. I'm sure the council and the Tribe of Jalas eliminated many Harborym over the years."

"It would, I think, be better if you remembered that more often," Idril said softly, then turned her face to the shore. "How do you expect to convince

Deo to fight if you do not possess either the grace of Kiriah or the tainted power of the Harborym?"

"Have no fear, she will," Hallow said, but before he could go on, he groaned aloud. "Blasted stars, moons, and planets. He found me."

"Who—oh. Thorn, isn't it? Is it bad that it's here?" I asked, watching the black wooden swallow that swooped and dove around the seabirds, heading straight for our ship.

"Only if I wish to remain sane." Hallow took a deep breath and pulled the staff from his back, holding it out. The swallow flew around his head six times before alighting on the top of the staff and taking its position. "Yes. Yes, I heard you. No, I'm not going to strangle anyone. I don't blame Darius for throwing you in the fire if you used that sort of language with him. What? You saw it for yourself?"

Hallow's face wore a decidedly martyred expression.

Idril gave the staff a curious glance. "Does it talk to you? I thought it was made of wood."

"It is. That is, his bird form is. I assure you that his spirit is very much still alive in there, and he talks nonstop to me."

She gave a delicate one-shouldered shrug. "That does sound annoying."

"You have no idea. However, it has one use—evidently he overheard in the queen's palace that Darius is not in any way injured, a fact that Thorn himself witnessed."

"Why would he say he was unable to come to Aryia with whatever Starborn he could round up if he was perfectly able to do so?" I asked, frowning over the puzzle. I had little to no knowledge of the Starborn, let alone the man who'd been chosen to lead them once the queen was taken through the rift.

"That is an answer I very much wish to know. Let us first address the situation with Deo, and once we are fully in force, we can turn our attention to the puzzle that is Darius."

I said nothing more, but I thought a great many things while the ship was docked, and a small rowboat ferried us to shore. I was troubled, not just because I sensed Hallow was concerned over the state of the Starborn army—or lack thereof—but because I was worried about what was to come.

How was I supposed to stir the magic that had remained dormant in me for so long? Hallow had no answer for me when I asked him, simply saying that when the time came for me to act, he had faith I would be able to summon the abilities I needed.

Hallow and I strode up a twisting path ahead of Idril, her swarm of ladies, and the few men-at-arms who protected her pristine self from any unpleasantness. Hallow spoke in a low tone with the captain of the ship. I gnawed my lower lip and sent up little queries to Kiriah to see if she wished to once again acknowledge me. Despite my glowing fingertips in Abet, I had no luck finding my lightweaving abilities, let alone feeling the chaos power.

The steely grip of worry deepened, leaving me feeling as if I couldn't take a deep breath for the vise that held me so tightly.

"There," Hallow said, pointing. I looked up the path to where it rose along a sheer cliff face. Topping it, almost invisible because it was made of the same stone, a building rose. It was three stories tall and had turrets on both ends, and a grim look that made little shivers run down my back.

"I didn't expect to find Deo living as wild as the goats," I said to Hallow as we climbed the path. "But that house is grand. It looks horribly cold, though. And sterile. And lonely."

"Still, it's shelter. No sign of a reception, which is interesting," Hallow said when we arrived at the door. It was wooden, with large black metal bands twisted and formed into fanciful shapes.

Topping the door, crescent moons were cut into the stone and filled with silver plates polished so brightly they shone even though the light of Kiriah was dulled by clouds.

Hallow rapped on the great doors, raising an uneasy feeling in me, one that grew with every passing minute.

"Hallow," I said quietly so that the others couldn't hear. "I've been thinking more upon this, and I know you believe that my powers will suddenly return to me, but if they haven't by now, I can only surmise that they never will. The situation in the war room in Abet must have been"—I raised my hands and let them fall—"an anomaly. I have said many prayers to Kiriah since then, and yet I remain without the sense of her, the feel of her power. The warmth of the sun, even."

"You mean when Lord Israel goaded you into anger so great that it stirred passions left untouched for a year?" he asked, his eyes crinkling at me.

"Blast your toenails, don't you dare tell me that he did that deliberately so that I would pull on Kiriah's power, because it makes no sense. Kiriah herself grants me her grace, and she's withheld it from me."

"Or perhaps you were so convinced of your own inability, you refused to allow her to grace you," he said gently.

I gaped at him, open-mouthed. "I *what*?"

"My heart," he said with a sigh, and took my hand in his. "Do you not see that in this, you have been your own enemy?"

"I have not! The power left me! You saw me in the throne room after Deo was killed... or taken away, or whatever happened to him. I had nothing, no power from the sun, no chaos magic."

"You were exhausted. You had completely drained your lightweaving abilities dry by closing the rift, and then when you ran berserk, you most likely depleted the chaos magic."

"It doesn't have a finite quantity," I argued. "It's just there. Or it was, but after Deo and I fought the Harborym, it was gone."

"Was it?" His eyes watched me with a gentle inquiry that made me want to both yell in frustration and kiss the breath right out of his lungs.

"I think I would know if magic was inside me or not."

"Or perhaps it had served its purpose and had no need to come when you called it. From what Deo said, the magic had its basis in the Harborym. If they were no more, if the rift was closed, would the magic still be active?"

I stared at him in amazement for a few seconds before admitting, "I don't know. I never... it never occurred to me that it might simply"—I gestured vaguely—"go to sleep because it wasn't needed."

"If chaos magic gains its power through the Harborym, then that might explain why you no longer feel it."

"If that is so... and I pray to Kiriah and Bellias both that it is... then how am I to find it now? Because without it, I don't see how I am going to be able to sway Deo."

"You will. I have faith that you will triumph."

"But what of Kiriah Sunbringer? Why does she shun me if I still bear her grace?"

"Only you can answer that," he said sagely. "But if I was to make a guess, I would reckon you overtaxed your strength, and when you couldn't immediately draw any more power from the sun, you believed you'd lost the blessing of Kiriah. From there, the doubt spiraled until you had convinced yourself that Kiriah had withdrawn herself, leaving you empty and bereft."

"I *am* empty and bereft," I insisted. "I told you that I can't even make a light animal, and that's the most basic use of her power."

He raised his eyebrows. "And yet the second Lord Israel enraged you, the power was there. Did you, perhaps, draw upon it without thinking?"

"I hate it when you do this," I said through gritted teeth.

"Do what?"

"Have insights into me that not even I know. Blast you, you're probably right. About Kiriah, that is. I hold little hope for the chaos power, though."

He gave my hand a squeeze before releasing it. "Courage, my heart. The time is not yet right for you to see what I see in you, although nearly so. Just be patient a little longer."

"Patience I have in abundance. Chaos magic and the ability to channel the strength of the sun, not so much."

"What is the delay?" Idril called from the path. "Why are you two standing there chatting when we should be inside, away from this cold and dampness?"

It was on the tip of my tongue to tell her that the man she had abandoned in order to wed his father might not wish to see her, but I kept my opinion behind my teeth, and resumed worrying.

It was all well and good for Hallow to say that something miraculous would happen when I came face-to-face with Deo, that the chaos power would return, but *he* would not be the one left standing there the subject of ridicule and failure when it didn't happen.

And as for the idea that I could be goaded into rediscovering my lightweaving abilities... I shook my head. I needed time to think on that, to offer prayers to Kiriah in hopes she would hear me.

Hallow banged on the door again and, when there was still no answer, turned the handle. It resisted, but after he worked a little magic on it, the lock gave way and allowed the door to swing open.

"I hope you know what you are about," Idril said as she marched past me into the entrance, her noble profile expressing no emotion stronger than a vague interest in Deo's home in exile. "We have come a long way and spent time we can ill afford, without any sign you will provide what is needed."

"Thank you so much for that show of support," I said, frustration tingeing my words with a note of waspishness. "It's been such a giddy nonstop cruise of pleasure and fulfillment that I had forgotten we aren't here to indulge in our most imaginative of vices."

Sarcasm was wasted on her. She simply continued to where Hallow stood at the bottom of a wooden staircase, her ladies filing past me with many pointed looks.

I stepped over the threshold, rubbing my arms against the chill. It seemed to be colder within. The hall was as depressing on the inside as on the exterior.

"I do not see the wisdom of disturbing the dead," the ship's captain was saying to Hallow when I was close enough to overhear. "Surely Lord Israel cannot wish to have his son exhumed."

"Would we be here now if we did not have his blessing on the pilgrimage?" Hallow asked smoothly. It was obvious that he hadn't taken the captain into his confidence, and the former believed we were here to see Deo's resting place.

"I suppose not," the captain said, but his face was filled with doubt. "I'll be at the ship should you need me."

He left the hall quickly, leaving me to wonder at Hallow's ability to lie so easily, a little stab of suspicion asking if he had lied thusly to me.

No, I told the suspicious voice. *He has no need to lie to me. He could have washed his hands of me and never seen me again.*

Except he wants something only you can do, the voice pointed out. *He believes you still have power. He knows you are the only Bane of Eris who is also a lightweaver. There is no doubt that you can do things the others cannot.*

"That way madness lies," I muttered to myself.

"So I would have said, but Hallow assured me that you are the solution to the problem," Idril said just as softly, then stepped forward with a gracious tilt of her head and accompanied Hallow up the stairs.

I was too worried to do more than grind my teeth for a few seconds. If Deo was alive, where was he?

Chapter 18

The ebb and flow of his mind disturbed Deo. At first, he wasn't aware of the disturbance, but after some time, he noticed that something was missing in the lucidity of his thoughts.

"I'm going mad," he said aloud. His nearest companion, a wild goat who would occasionally come around scrounging for food, lifted its tail and shat. Regardless, Deo continued to address him. Goat was, after all, his only friend. "I'm going mad, and there's nothing I can do to stop it. Not even if I wanted to, and now I'm not sure I want to. Talking to yourself in your out-loud voice is a sign of madness, isn't it? I'm sure it is. Then again, perhaps it's a sign of sanity. Who's to say?"

He lay back on the rocky outcropping that hung over the stormy gray waters beating relentlessly at an equally rocky beach and stared at the gray sky. His awareness moved on, rolling through memories of the past that seemed to blend seamlessly into an existence that he suspected wasn't his.

"Mad people think they are other people, I believe." That made sense. He tried to remember just who he was. Was he the young, cocky man who everyone thought was going to be the salvation of Alba? Was he handsome and tall, with his mother's coloring, and his father's wisdom?

Or was he a monstrous twisted parody of that man, tormented by a power he sometimes could not control, bearing unending pain in an attempt to protect those who had no protector.

"What is this madness, Goat? Is it truly insanity, or is it brilliance that other people just can't understand?" His father never understood him.

His father…

The madness sent his mind reeling again, protecting itself from the rage that had kept him as much a prisoner as the endless sea around him. For the first month after he had been imprisoned here for the second time, he'd raged against his father, against the cruelty of a man who would doom his son to an eternal living death, but slowly the madness drove the anger from him.

Yes, he was quite, quite mad, and there was comfort to be had in that.

A faint sound caught his attention for a moment. He stopped thinking about madness in order to focus on the sound.

No, there was nothing. Just the waves, and the wind, and the periodic bleating of the goats. Sometimes a seabird flew overhead and squawked.

"Mad people sometimes imagine sounds that aren't really there," he told Goat. The animal chewed on a bit of plant, then began mouthing the tattered bit of wool that Deo wore as a cloak. "Odd that I haven't heard noises before now. How long have I been here, Goat? A year? Twenty?" He'd lost count of time, since days, weeks, and months held no power once you were left alone. Utterly alone, with nothing but his own consciousness. His father had damned him to an eternal life alone, without even a jailer to converse with.

His father…

A dull thudding caught his attention again, followed by the faintest snatch of a voice.

"That's different," he said, and mused on the last time he'd experienced something like it. "The answer is never. I've been alone, trapped on this hellish nightmare of an island, banished from the race of Fireborn. Alone, alone, alone."

Goat, deciding the leather strap of Deo's belt held more attraction, began chomping on it.

Whump, whump, whump. "…he's alive…"

That was a woman's voice. What was a woman doing here? He shook his head. "Either I'm hallucinating or spirits have come to plague me. I wonder if they will mind that I'm mad."

Bang, thud, thunk.

Deo closed his eyes. Not even the lure of talking to a spirit could rouse him from his current depression. He'd just lie there for a few weeks and let his brain wander on its own.

A thin light caught his awareness even through his closed lids, starting at his feet and slowly moving upward. By the time he realized what was happening—a group of people had stumbled up to his perch and were standing around him—his mind moved from the simple comfort of madness into rage, savage and unchecked.

"Deo?"

Inside him, the chaos power, so long asleep, stirred, sensing its own kind. But instead of awakening in Deo the red-hot anger of his youth, it aroused a cold, enrobing fury. His hands formed fists. His muscles bunched.

"Goat. Invaders have arrived. Attack!"

"Deo," a woman's voice said in exasperation. "We thought you were dead."

"Did he just order that goat to attack us?" a man asked.

Deo recognized those voices even through the madness. Runes began to light up along his chest, and with each rune that came alive, so did the pain of controlling the beast within him. The chaos power, so long asleep, seared along his veins to his extremities, causing almost unbearable pain, but he welcomed it, for the agony gave fire to his rage. He struggled to gain the upper hand, but it was only when he stopped fighting the power and accepted it for what it was that he leashed it, and, with an agonized cry, leaped to his feet.

Ah, we are awake again. Good. We have been too long away.

Three people stood facing him.

Traitors, all of them.

Unreasonably, he wanted to lash out at them.

As you should. I can feel that you recognize their faces. These are the people who betrayed you.

The magic seeped into his blood, making him want to hurt them as they had hurt him.

Punish the guilty. Eliminate the weak. Establish your strength. That is the only way to triumph.

Before he could act, he was bathed in light. Not the harsh red light of pain that filled the corners of his mind, but the golden, warming light of Kiriah Sunbringer. He looked down to see two hands, glowing with the light of a summer sun, flatten themselves on his chest, and for a moment, the pain and rage faded away.

"Allegria," he said. "You've finally come."

Too late. Far too late.

The rage returned at the magic's words. Why had she not rescued him months ago, when his father had him teleported to this hellish nightmare existence?

He roared his fury and lunged toward her, but was suddenly flung backward by a white and blue light. He slammed into a wall of granite, knocking him senseless for a few seconds.

Don't just lie there like a landed fish! Strike now! Strike them down before they try to kill you again!

"Deo, you have to listen to us. I can see by the way your runes are sparking that the chaos magic is enraging you. You must control it. Don't heed its words. We are your friends, not it."

Slowly, he regained his wits, the red haze of anger fading enough that he could see the woman before him. She knelt next to him, the arcanist at her side.

He reached up and touched the circlet of black dots on her forehead. "Bane of Eris."

She clasped his hand in hers, warmth once again chasing away some of the pain. "That's right. You made me a Bane. Although the magic doesn't seem to be working now." She stopped and glanced to the side.

"Hallow," Deo said in acknowledgment.

"Greetings. I am glad to see you are back to your normal self. I'd hate to have to smite you again." He held out a hand of assistance.

After a moment's hesitation, Deo took the offered hand, and got to his feet. Allegria rose with him, one hand holding on to his arm lest, he assumed, he should topple. "I am... I am sorry." The words tasted like dust in his mouth. "I did not mean to attack you. The magic—"

I grow weary of these puerile beings' boasts. Eliminate them so that we might leave this blighted isle.

He straightened his shoulders, pain settling across them in a familiar mantle. The runes on his chest and wrists glowed a soft red as he faced Allegria, acknowledging his debt to her. She must be repaid, and there was only one way he could do that. "Goat, fetch paper and quill. I must write a betrothal oath to Allegria, who has rescued me. Once the terms are settled, we will wed at once, and I will raise you to queen of the Starborn when I take my mother's place." He put his hands on her shoulders and leaned in to seal the oath with a kiss.

"No!" she said quickly, backing up a few steps and looking at the arcanist. "Hallow—it wasn't me—Hallow... Hallow is..."

"Hallow is wondering about the goat, but I suppose now is not the right time to ask," the arcanist said.

Deo considered the man. "Very well," he said, and, before the arcanist could do more than open his eyes wide, kissed him. "But I refuse to marry him, no matter how grateful I am. He will be my trusted adviser, instead. Goat! Make note of that."

"Deo..." Allegria wrung her hands while the arcanist burst into laughter.

Deo narrowed his eyes at them both, fearing that somehow they were mocking him.

They are mocking you. As will I if you do not take steps to stop this foolishness!

Deo pushed down the impulse to violence, once again feeling master of himself.

"You don't understand," Allegria said, glaring at the arcanist. "For the love of Kiriah, Hallow, stop laughing. Deo, you misunderstand. You don't need to marry me or make Hallow your adviser. We don't expect any reward for rescuing you, and then... well... we're..."

"If she's going to wed anyone, it will be me," Hallow said, wrapping an arm around Allegria's shoulders and grinning at her.

She glared at him in response. "Is this your idea of a proposal?"

"No, but I thought it was better to make it clear that you and I have an understanding before your boyfriend marries you and makes you queen of Genora."

"There are times when you really are the most annoying man in the world—"

Deo, uninterested in their banter, allowed his gaze to rest on the third member of the group. He knew that face. He knew that silver hair rippling over her arms and breasts. For that matter, he knew those breasts.

A name floated through his mind, and with it, anger returned. Her name emerged from his lips as a low, guttural snarl. "Idril."

She dropped him a curtsy, her movements as lithe and graceful as a fine-boned deer's. "My lord Deo. I am pleased to see you again."

He fought a fresh wave of fury, one distracted, possibly still mad part of his mind wondering if that was all he was doomed to feel anymore— various shades of anger—and managed to say, "You were there when my father did this to me. It must have pleased you to see your husband remove the man whose heart you crushed."

"Husband?" Idril asked.

Another one who wishes you ill. I tire of telling you to destroy them before they destroy you.

"Do you deny that you wed my father when you were betrothed to me?" Deo roared the question, sending the goat leaping away with a squawk of dismay.

"Oh, him. No, I do not deny it," Idril said placidly. His fingers flexed, the chaos magic urging him to avenge his betrayal on her slender, pale neck. He wouldn't even need the magic to strangle the life from her.

You'll notice I'm making no comment here. I could, but I won't, because I don't want to appear boorish. Still, I like the way your mind is working.

He turned away, his jaw working silently as he strode down the rocky path that led back to his stone prison.

"Deo!" Allegria called after him the moment he left. She continued to call, catching at his arm when he entered the great hall.

He did not know where he was going—he simply knew he must remove himself from the presence of the woman whose hold on his heart was as cruel as it was unyielding.

Yawn.

"Deo, stop!"

"Why?" he snarled, continuing forward despite Allegria's hold on him. The arcanist grabbed his other arm, pulling him to a halt.

"Because we need you," Hallow said.

"We?" He looked from the arcanist to Allegria. "You made it quite clear you prefer the company of each other. If you expect my blessing, you will be waiting a very long time. I have vengeance to seek, and I cannot be bothered with trivialities like Allegria preferring a scrawny arcane wielder over marriage to me."

Allegria slapped him on the arm. He would have liked to be outraged over her lack of respect for him, but he'd allocated all of his anger to plotting how and when he would avenge himself on his father and couldn't spare any for her.

"First of all, you were just yelling at Idril because she married your father instead of you, so don't try to make me out to be someone who broke your heart. And second, Hallow is not scrawny!" she said, looking daggers at Deo. "He has a magnificent chest, and his thighs are… well, you probably don't care about them, but you can take it from me that I *do* care, and they're also magnificent. Stop running away and let us talk to you."

"No," he said moodily, and got three steps before the two pests (as he was coming to think of them) caught up to him. "I don't care what you need—I am busy. I have a father to destroy, and then possibly a woman to destroy, depending on how sorrowful Idril is regarding his death, and after that, I might be able to clear an hour or two for you. But not until then."

Hallow flashed by him at a speed too fast to see, and was suddenly in front of him, his staff at his side. "Thorn, take to the air. Do not argue with me, just do as I say." A martyred look crossed Hallow's face. "Because I said so. I'm the Master of Kelos, and you swore to aid the master."

The little black wooden bird poised at the top of the staff suddenly separated itself and flew around Deo's head. He swatted at it, catching it in midair, and snapping off one of the wooden wings.

"Oh, goddesses of day and night and all the hours in between," Hallow said, casting his gaze upward. At the same time Allegria, with an exclamation, dashed forward and snatched the broken pieces of bird from Deo's hands, murmuring softly to it as she tried to push the broken wing back onto the body. "He's not going to let me hear the end of *that* for centuries. Deo, if you take another step, I will be obligated to smite you again, this time with the biggest ball of arcane light I can summon, and I hate to do that, because not only do I rather like you, but also because we need you whole and unsinged if we are to triumph over the Harborym."

Deo, who had dismissed them from his mind, had turned and taken a step before the arcanist's words fought their way through all the plans of revenge that filled his thoughts. "Harborym?" he asked, turning back.

"At last," Hallow muttered under his breath, then, taking Allegria's hand, said louder, "They're back. Three rifts have been opened. On Aryia."

So, the masters have returned. I knew it must be something important to have awakened us. How very interesting. You will wish to annihilate them, of course. That will be most satisfying.

Deo reflected, not for the first time, what a fickle thing magic was.

"So far only soul takers have emerged from the rifts," Hallow added.

"They are a precursor," Deo said absently. "They weaken the population."

"The Council of Four Armies has gathered what forces are available, but they will not be enough."

"Of course not," he said, a little sneer gathering on his lips. "They fought for more than ten years and could do nothing but limit the growth of the Harborym. It took my banesmen to destroy them utterly."

"This is why we need you. If possible, we must find the remaining banesmen, and with your help—and Allegria's—we will be able to close the rifts before their armies begin pouring through."

Deo looked over Allegria's shoulder. Idril had come into the hall, and the shining light that made up her being smote his heart anew.

"No. Goat, heel!" he said, and pushed past the arcanist to the door, stalking down the path to his favorite overlook on this side of the island. There had to be a ship here. He would commandeer it, sail to Abet, and confront his father.

"Deo, please, stop being so obstinate," Allegria called, hurrying after him.

"Obstinate?" He spun around to glare at her. "Have they stripped the memories from your mind, priestling?"

"No," she said calmly, and, taking a deep breath, put her hands on his chest again, the glow from her fingers seeping through the pain and anger and betrayal that roiled inside him. "I will never forget, Deo. I lost much as a result of that day, not the least of which was the blessing of Kiriah Sunbringer. She has turned her back on me."

Don't believe her. She's dangerous. If she was spurned by your goddess, why does she now bear that power?

He looked down at her hands and cocked an eyebrow.

"Hallow helped me see that I wasn't completely denied Kiriah's blessing. At least, she forgave me when I needed her to calm you." She shot the arcanist a look of mingled gratitude and passion. "But you are wrong. None of us who were there for the destruction of the Harborym could ever forget what happened. That is why you must set aside your feelings and focus on what is important."

"Making my father pay for his cruelty *is* important," he insisted, unable to keep from leaning into her hands. The power of the sun flowed through her into him, chasing away some of the shadows and darkness. "Have you forgotten what they did to us? How we were repaid for our valor? Despite all that, you wish to help them?"

"Of course," Allegria said, her eyes full of so much hope, it almost hurt Deo to look in them.

Hope had been burned out of him long ago. Now there was only madness, and Goat. And the need to destroy the betrayers.

The chaos magic sighed into his mind.

"Allegria told me that you pledged yourself to rid these lands of the Harborym. Was that only a one-time oath, or do you still hold true to it?" Hallow said, drawing both Deo's attention and his ire.

"Of all of us who fought the Harborym that day, you alone did not suffer," he told the arcanist, suspicion stirring until it pushed out the light of Kiriah. Allegria stepped back, shaking her hands as if they stung. "In fact, it sounds as if the opposite is the case."

"Do you think that being parted from Allegria was not a punishment almost as great as yours?" Hallow asked quietly, but his eyes burned with a blue fire that oddly pleased Deo. If he couldn't have Allegria—and if he was honest with himself, he didn't really want her—then this arcanist would do well as his alternative.

"It's almost as bad as believing the man you were falling in love with had betrayed you," Allegria said, her gaze on the arcanist.

"*Were* falling in love with?" he asked her. "And now?"

She smiled. "You had better arrange for us to have our own cabin on the ship going back to Aryia."

"Most definitely."

Deo frowned at the sexual tension that charged the air. "Could you two stop gazing at each other as if you were naked and well-oiled and seated on a soft blanket before a blazing fire while outside the snow flies on a raging wind?"

Allegria blinked at him a couple of times. "That was strangely specific, but yes, I will attempt to keep from ravishing Hallow in front of you."

The arcanist rolled his eyes. "All right, but if I do this, you have to promise not to talk to me unless it's something of major importance."

Deo stared at him. Allegria looked startled for a moment, then said to Deo, "It's the staff. The bird talks to him."

"Does it urge you to kill everything?"

"No, fortunately."

"Ah. You're lucky. The voice in my head is always demanding the deaths of those around me." He frowned at Hallow. Perhaps he wasn't as ideal a candidate for Allegria's mate, as he'd first thought. Then again, if she'd chosen to fall in love with an arcanist—a group of people who almost always were insane on some level—then she must be confident in dealing with his oddities.

"No, that is not of major importance, Thorn. Nor is telling me what you think of Allegria. I don't care if her hands are nice—she's taken." Hallow took the bird from where Allegria had stuffed it in a satchel slung over her back, and spoke a few words over it, causing strange symbols to glow briefly in the air above it. He released the bird, once again whole, and it promptly flew twice over Deo's head before alighting on the top of the black staff.

Deo pursed his lips.

Hallow said in a voice filled with apology, "I am to inform you that you are to consider yourself shat upon. Now, if we can get back to the matter at hand—"

"I will not go with you," Deo said firmly, crossing his arms over his chest. "Not so long as she is involved."

Allegria and Hallow looked back at where Deo had nodded. Idril stood in the doorway.

"Since you were exiled, Lord Jalas has become gravely ill," Hallow said slowly, obviously picking his words carefully. "Lady Idril now leads the Tribe of Jalas in his stead."

"Those are my terms," Deo said. The chaos magic tutted to itself. Idly, he wondered if it was reacting to Allegria's nearness or the portent of doom that hung over the land like a shadow.

Oh, it is the thought of the battles to come. So much death. So much eradication. The priest has nothing to offer us. The arcanist might be useful. As for the other woman... she will only try to turn you against all you hold dear.

His gaze moved again to Idril, taking in her face, her lovely face so familiar to him, and yet that of a stranger. "Those are my terms," he repeated, turning his back on the sight of her.

"We accept," Hallow said quickly, and, with a loaded look at Allegria, strode away to converse with Idril.

The Harborym were back. A slow smile curved his lips as he touched the harness binding his chest. This time he would not fail. He would reclaim his mother from the invaders and prove his worth to his father once and for all.

He would be triumphant, or die trying.

Chapter 19

We sailed that night on the same ship that had brought us to Genora a year before.

"But the men are wary of leaving at night. It's bad luck," the captain protested when Hallow, Deo, and I arrived at the boat. The captain was overseeing the taking on of water and looked more than a little startled when Hallow asked to sail immediately.

"Tell them it's a matter of saving Aryia," Hallow said.

"They'll expect payment." The captain's expression turned canny. "We'll *all* expect payment for sailing through dangerous waters at night."

Hallow reached for the leather bag that hung from his belt. He opened it and pursed his lips, sending me a questioning look.

"Not so much as a copper coin," I told him. "I've been in a cave for the last year."

"Ah. Good point." He looked at Deo, who was staring moodily into the distance. "Do you have any coin?"

"Yes. Lots of them."

"With you?" Hallow asked, looking relieved.

"No. What is the delay? Why are we not sailing? *She* will not stay placated for long. I wish to be away before she demands we take her with us."

"Lady Idril understands that another ship will be sent out immediately for her and her entourage," Hallow said smoothly. "Thorn is even now taking a message to intercept a ship that set sail shortly after we left port."

"How much are you paying that ship to come here?" the captain asked.

"That is not pertinent. You and your men will be rewarded if we sail in the next hour," Hallow said sternly.

"I will fetch Goat," Deo said, nodding his head. "Then we will depart immediately."

"I cannot entice the crew if there is no evidence of this reward—" the captain said, blocking the small rowboat that would take us back to the ship.

Deo, his eyes lighting up red, picked the man up with one hand and gave him a little shake. "We sail in the next hour. Is that clear?"

"I cannot—"

A blue flame lit his feet.

"Aieee! I'll tell them!"

I slid a look toward Hallow. He whistled softly to himself.

"You've become incorrigible while I was in my cave," I told him when the captain rowed us out to his ship. It had taken some doing, but we'd managed to convince Deo to leave the wild goat behind.

"Good thinking," Deo said darkly, his eyes on his stone house. "Goat can keep an eye on *her.*"

We said nothing more about Deo's little touch of madness. I waited until we were urged aboard the ship by a limping captain to ask Hallow, "I thought arcanists took an oath to use their magic for the good of Alba?"

"We do. Why do you ask?"

I nodded toward the captain.

Hallow smiled and gently pushed me toward the hatch that led to the cabins. "I barely singed his stockings. Stop dawdling, or we'll lose the good cabin to your boyfriend."

"He's not my—Hallow!" I stopped, stomping my foot when my erstwhile lover dashed ahead, waving a hand to summon up a set of shackles that wrapped themselves around Deo's legs as the latter was about to enter the hatch.

"What is this magic?" Deo roared, growling when Hallow slipped ahead of him, "If you think to lay claim to the master's cabin, you are too late. I have already done so. Hallow! I demand you release me! That cabin is mine!"

"You haven't even seen it," Hallow's voice came from the innards of the ship.

"I don't have to see it to know it's mine! I am the leader of this battle force; it's only right that the best cabin should go to me," Deo bellowed back. He struggled against the chains, managing to get one leg free. The chains of the other kept his foot tied to the deck surface, but he dragged it along, yelling, "Come back here and face *my* magic, Hallow! Kiriah damn you, that cabin is mine!"

"It's going to be a long trip," I said to the stars faintly visible overhead and followed the two men inside.

By the time the accommodation situation was resolved (the captain refused to give up his cabin to Deo no matter how much he was threatened), and Deo had the second-best cabin, while Hallow claimed the last—and smallest—cabin for us, the ship's crew began preparations to leave. They weren't happy, but when they were told that Deo would pay them upon our arrival in Aryia, they took up their jobs, and we sailed before the moon rose fully.

Approximately two minutes later, I was headed for our tiny cabin tucked away behind the galley. I'd seen it briefly before we sailed to the Isle of Enoch, noting that the one bunk in it was barely big enough for one person, and that the two of us would be cramped, but it was our private haven, and I wasn't going to complain. It was better than sleeping down in the bowels of the ship with the sailors, as we'd done coming out.

I opened the door to the cabin to find Hallow in just his breeches, hopping on one foot while he pulled a boot off the other.

"Oooh," I said, my eyes trying to take in all that glorious bare chest. I was about to step in when the door to the second-best cabin opened and Deo stuck his head out.

"Allegria! Come."

He started to retreat into his cabin, pausing when I said loudly, "Are you insane?"

The look he gave me would have daunted a saint.

"Sorry," I apologized, then gestured toward my cabin, where Hallow had now sat down on the edge of the bunk to de-boot himself. "Not now, Deo."

"Now," he said, his voice booming around the lower deck.

"I've got better things to do—"

"Now!" he bellowed, and stalked back into his cabin.

I sighed and poked my head into our cabin. "Do you mind if I—"

"No," Hallow said, successfully removing one boot before starting on his crossties. "But if you don't get back in five minutes, I'll likely be asleep. I'm exhausted after arguing with Lady Idril that it was in her best interest to stay behind with her entourage for a day or two until a ship could be sent for them."

"Deal," I said, and, closing the door, walked briskly the ten steps to Deo's cabin. He was seated at a small table, frowning over a map of Alba that he had finagled from the captain. "Well?"

"Ah, there you are." He sounded more reasonable and gestured toward a three-legged stool. "Come in. Sit. Have some wine?"

"Deo, I have a mostly naked arcanist waiting for me—"

"And he'll continue to wait if the looks you two have been giving each other all day are any indication. Now, where exactly have the rifts opened? Where is the Tribe of Jalas? Did my father tell you his plans for attack?"

I looked at him for a good two minutes; then I rose and went to the door, pausing to say before I left, "I expected better from you, Deo. I know you've suffered more than anyone else, and I know you want to take charge of your life again, but I have not felt the touch of my lover's hands and his assorted body parts in almost a year, and by Kiriah's bright blazes, if I don't feel them in the next minute, I will expire. Good night."

He blustered a bit, but I paid no attention to it. I had far more important things to do.

"Hello, important things," I said, arriving at our cabin. I closed the door behind me, then, with foresight into Deo's behavior, shoved Hallow's leather trunk, the saddlebags, and the staff minus Thorn against the door.

Hallow was lying on the bunk, his hands behind his head, his feet bobbing to a tune that only he could hear. He was naked, and the sight of him spread out before me like a feast had desire pooling low in my parts, spreading a slow burn outward to my belly and breasts.

"Good evening." He waggled his eyebrows at me. "Are you planning on taking off that attractive tunic?"

"I am. That and everything else." I pulled the tunic off, posing provocatively for a moment before tackling the laces of my undertunic.

His eyes glinted in the dim light like blue gemstones in firelight. "Do you need help?"

"No, I'm fine." I pulled my undertunic off, shivering a little in the chill sea air that seeped in through the wood. I bent to pull off my boots and leggings, until I stood before him in just my linen breastband and underwear.

"You're more than fine. You're the loveliest woman I've ever seen. Your skin is as smooth as satin. The light glows off it like... like starlight on a pearl."

"A dusky, slightly blue pearl," I said, gesturing toward my belly as I sauntered toward him. I had never perfected the art of dalliance, but I did my best to be seductive. "One with freckles and forehead dots."

"I love your dusky blueness. I love the freckles. I love the forehead." He pulled me onto him, his hands sliding up my back until they untied my breastband. "I love everything about you. Goddess, it's been a long time."

The entreaty in his voice and eyes warmed me, driving out everything—all the worry, and fears, and concerns about Deo's sanity— everything but the pleasure I felt in his company. If this was love, it was a bittersweet emotion, since the joy Hallow gave me was so great, it threatened to overwhelm me.

"What's wrong?" he asked, his hands warm on my bare thighs, his eyes shrewd upon me. "Have you had a change of heart?"

"No." I leaned down to kiss him, savoring the sweetness of his lips on mine. "It's just that it's somewhat... overpowering, this feeling that happens when we are together, don't you think? It's like it will sweep us up before it, and we will never be able to separate ourselves again."

"Do you want to separate from me?" His voice was neutral, but a spark of pain lit his eyes. "Am I overpowering you? I assumed from the talk we had when I found you that you felt the same as I did, but perhaps you need more time."

"It's nothing to do with us, not in that way," I said, struggling to explain. My body ached for me to drop the conversation and get on with the lovemaking, but my mind wasn't willing to commit until I made Hallow understand. "It's this feeling that you stir inside of me. Before the rift closed, it was simple. I enjoyed you, and you enjoyed me, and that was all well and good. But then things changed.... *I* changed."

"I think I understand," he said slowly, one hand cupping my face. "Life has changed for us, and while you were sequestered in that cave, and I focused on bringing order to the arcanists, the thing that we are together has changed, as well. Is that it?"

"Yes. And it's big. Bigger than it was before."

He waggled his eyebrows. "I assure you it's exactly as you left it."

I pinched the skin on his belly. "I'm being silly, I know. I just wondered if you felt the same way."

"No," he said with an apology in his voice. "I wish I could say yes, but it would be untrue. I believe I know what it is you're feeling, however, and the reason why you feel overwhelmed, but short of changing the past, I can only promise you that not all emotion demands you lose control of yourself. You can love without becoming the berserker you fear."

"You *do* understand," I said, the feeling of relief making me sag down on top of him. "I didn't know how to explain it without sounding like the worst sort of coward... or an idiot."

"You are neither, my brave one. You are the strongest person I know, which is a bit intimidating when I think about it. I've never bedded a woman who could beat me into a stain on the ground if she chose to do so."

The twinkle of humor was in his eyes, causing me to bite his chin before sitting astride him again, my hands on his chest. "I don't know that I could do that, since you obviously have grown in your mastery of the arcane, but if you ever steal a runeseeker from me again—"

He laughed and flipped us over so that I was on my back, and his hands were full of my breasts. "Let us forget Exodius and the Harborym and everything outside of this cabin for a bit, shall we? Everything I want, I see before me."

I curled my toes into the linen sheet beneath me, running my hands down his sides, digging my fingers into the thick muscles of his behind. "That I can absolutely agree with. Love me, Hallow. Love me the way I've wanted for the longest time. Take me to Bellias Starsong and back."

"You've grown poetic in your old age," he murmured, kissing a path down my neck to my chest, pausing to pay tribute at each breast. "I must reward such a silver tongue with one of my own."

I watched with growing hope as he kissed further downward, my feminine parts feeling excessively warm in anticipation. "Oh, yes please."

His kisses and touches raised an inferno of sensation within me, the strokes of his tongue tormenting me until I trembled on the brink of an orgasm so great, I wanted to sing with the joy of it all.

And then he was there inside me, the sensation of being filled pushing me ever closer to the stars. I bit his shoulder, my legs wrapping around his hips as he began moving in a rhythm that consumed every thought I had. My body seemed to tighten until I couldn't hold back any longer and fell gloriously into waves of orgasm that rippled outward. Hallow didn't last beyond my inner convulsions and shouted his own completion into the pillow beneath my head.

I felt a pang of fear when I lost myself in the power of our physical acts, but it took only a few seconds to realize Hallow was right—I could give in to the intense pleasure that he brought me without losing control. It was not strong emotion that had made me a berserker so long ago, as I half feared.

"Still, the chaos magic didn't answer me," I said aloud some time later, when we had recovered. The fact that had been troubling me ever since we had rescued Deo came to the front of my mind. I'd pushed it aside once, but it couldn't be ignored any longer. "Deo was right there, but still it didn't waken. I'm afraid it's left me for good, Hallow."

"And therein lies your problem, my heart. You have given in to fear."

I tipped my head back and studied his chin. I like his chin almost as much as I like his eye crinkles. "Have you never felt fear?"

"On the contrary, I felt it my whole life, until the moment when I found the one thing that I knew would drive fear from my life."

"Arcane magic," I said, nodding.

"You," he said simply, causing me to push back on his chest until I could look down at him. He'd had his eyes closed, but at my movement, he opened them to watch me.

"Me? What are you talking about? Is this your way of declaring yourself? Because if it is, I'm not going to accept it. We're going to battle, Hallow, a battle that we don't know we can win. I refuse to let you pledge your troth to me now. Later, perhaps. But not now. You can just take back what you said."

He laughed, brushing my hair back from where it clung to one cheek. "I won't take it back, and furthermore, I'll stand behind it until the day I breathe my last. You changed me, Allegria—before you, I wandered the world craving something that I could never find. When I was young, I thought it was adventure and excitement. I had that aplenty with Master Nix, and later, when I was older, I decided that what I sought was to be of service. I wanted to make Alba a better place through the mastery of arcane practices."

"And after we met?" Despite my declaration, I was pleased and flattered by his words. The look in his eyes held passion, yes, but something more, something deeper that called to me.

"After you lipped off to Lord Israel and charged off to fight battles that I feared would consume you, I realized that what I'd been seeking all my days was you. You complete the world for me, my heart. You brought the sense of belonging that's been missing in my life, you eliminated the loneliness that is so often an arcanist's companion, and you presented a challenge that I knew I would never tire of trying to meet. In short, my lightweaving Bane of Eris, you give me a reason to be."

"By the light, Hallow," I said, rising onto my knees next to him. "I just told you not to declare yourself, and you've gone and done it, and now I have to face the fact that you're a much better person than I am, and I'm a coward and unworthy of you and you'll probably tire of me after a few centuries, and then I'll die alone in a ditch surrounded by Buttercup's descendants, and possibly a mangy cat or two."

He laughed again, his eyes crinkling delightfully, leaving me filled with the warm glow of love. "You can't possibly mean any of that."

"I don't," I said, snuggling back against his chest, reveling in the warmth of his arm around me. I'd never in my life felt so secure, and yet we were on the verge of what might well be our destruction. "But despite all that, I am still afraid, Hallow. If the chaos magic doesn't respond to the rifts... if the Harborym start coming through before we get there..."

"Don't borrow trouble," he said sleepily. "We'll face whatever the goddesses bring to us."

"Then there's Deo," I continued, stroking the soft hairs on his chest. "I hate to say this, but I don't think he's wholly sane any longer. The Deo I knew would never put his own purposes above others, and if you hadn't stopped him, he would have gone off to exact revenge even though he knew Alba needed him. All that time alone with nothing but goats… I don't know how he survived the first time he was exiled, but to be returned to Enoch a second time must have been intolerable. At least I saw Sandor and had some news of the world. It's no surprise if Deo's mind isn't quite right. Will we be able to count on him when we need to? Will the chaos magic sense the weakness, and use it to its own ends? Will he become more of a hindrance than the help we so desperately need?"

A light snore ruffled my hair. I sighed to myself, worried despite the warm emotions that Hallow stirred in me.

If only I knew the chaos magic was still alive in me.

If only I knew Deo could be relied upon.

If only I knew I could face the Harborym without losing control again.

Chapter 20

"Well, here we are again, fighting the forces of the Harborym. Allegria, to your left! No, your other left." Hallow jumped off the horse he'd rented in the port town of Siren's Lament and sent a bolt of pure arcane power into the lumbering soul taker that was almost upon her.

The monstrous being, approximately the size of a large dog, but resembling a beetle more than anything else, gave a screech and flipped over onto its shell-like back.

"Thank you," Allegria said, giving Hallow a grateful look. "I didn't even notice it because it blended in with the shadows. What... er... what exactly does it do?"

"Steals your will to live," Hallow said. "And if you're lucky, when it has all of your life force, kills you."

Would you like me to scout around? Thorn asked eagerly, his wooden body quivering with excitement. *I will determine the location of any other soul takers. Don't kill any Harborym without me.*

"Scout to your heart's content," Hallow told the bird and turned back to the rift that lay before them. "Prudence dictates that we remain here and destroy anything that comes through the rift, at least until the first of the armies finds us."

"That will be days," Deo said, tying his horse to a tree branch and stalking forward with a heavy gait.

Hallow glanced at him, a bit of Allegria's worry beginning to prick at his mind. Deo normally moved as silently as an owl, a feat considering his size. But now he moved awkwardly, as if he were struggling with his own body.

His runes were glowing a bright red, which confirmed Hallow's suspicions. He would have liked to offer his help in controlling the sentience that spoke inside Deo's head, but knew his offer would be useless. Deo wasn't the sort of man who accepted help unless there was no other choice.

"Lady Idril said she would have the Tribe of Jalas move the minute she reached Abet. They are three days' ride from here, but only half a day if they sailed as soon as they received her note." Hallow rubbed his chin and looked back to the rift. It was a mass of black and green, slightly taller than a man, twisting and turning upon itself in a never-ending action that raised the hairs on the back of Hallow's neck.

There was something wrong with that rift just hanging in the middle of nothing. That and the fact that it seemed to leech life from the very air.

"They will be too long. We will close the rift now," Deo said, his words slightly muffled.

"He's clenching his teeth," Allegria said, having examined the dead soul taker and moved over to Hallow's side. "I'm not sure about this. He seems to be struggling quite a bit."

"I agree, but I don't see any way we could convince him that it might be safer for him to remove himself from the presence of the rift."

"What are you whispering about?" Deo demanded, stomping over to them. "You were talking about me, weren't you? I can see you were. You think I'm mad. Well, I am mad, utterly and irrevocably, but that doesn't mean I can't see this rift closed. Allegria, you go around to the back of it. Hallow, you take the left side. I'll do the right. When I give the word, blast it back whence it came."

"Deo, wait—" Allegria said at the same time Hallow took hold of Deo by the sleeve and said, "Hold on, Deo. Let us consider what's best to be done. We have several options, since there appears to be little activity here."

The miasma spun upon itself and ejected two soul takers.

"Except for those, of course," he said, and gathered a handful of arcane power.

"Aiee!" Allegria yelled and pulled out the swords that Hallow had returned to her, attacking the first soul sucker. Deo started for the second, but checked himself, his runes glowing red for a second before they suddenly turned black.

"That's not good," Hallow muttered to himself, and leaped forward to blast the second soul taker even while Allegria was wiping her swords clean of innards.

"At least these are easy to kill," she told him, her smile lighting up his insides in a way he knew he'd be grateful for until the day he breathed his last. "It's nice having the swords back. Thank you for rescuing them." "You're more than welcome. Now, as I was saying before those blasted monstrosities ruined my nice speech, we have many choices as to our best course of action. If the Tribe of Jalas is here tomorrow, that would give us a sizable force to back us up should something go awry."

"I don't know that a bunch of soldiers are going to be able to take that down," Allegria said, nodding toward the rift.

"They won't," Deo said, moving alongside them. Hallow slid a glance his way, but he seemed as normal as he ever was.

"Perhaps not, but I also called up the arcanists. There are three who were in the area, and who should heed the call I sent out when we landed at Siren's Lament. I expect them in the next few days, or perhaps less."

"That seems like a better idea—Deo, no!"

"All this talk is a waste of time. We are the three most powerful people in Alba. If we can't close a single rift, then our world is doomed," Deo said, striding up to the rift. His runes glowed with a black light that gave Hallow a very bad feeling.

"He has a point," Allegria said, glancing upward. The sun was beginning to emerge from a thick gray covering of clouds. She lifted her hands to the sky, wordlessly intoning a prayer.

"Yes, but I'd be more comfortable if a few other arcanists were here as backup," Hallow said, worriedly dividing his attention between Deo and the rift.

"I understand, but look! Kiriah has blessed me again!" Her smile was almost as brilliant as the sun itself. Her arms glowed with the golden light of Kiriah, but it was the silver bands at her wrists and ankles that he looked at.

They, too, were now black.

His gaze moved to the rift. He had a *very* bad feeling. "I think, after due consideration, that we should wait until the arcanists or the Tribe of—"

Allegria had finished communing with Kiriah while he was speaking, and with a joyous smile moved toward the rift. Deo stood next to it, his head bowed, the muscles in his neck and arms tight, as if he were fighting something. Just as Allegria approached the rift, a little tendril of black power snaked out and grabbed her, jerking her forward until she almost toppled into it. She shrieked, losing her golden glow while a black miasma crept over her.

Hallow didn't wait to decide what the best action would be—he ran forward, pulling arcane power from the ground, from the skies, from the living things around him, from anywhere he could, and slammed it into the rift at the same time he grabbed Allegria's arm.

She screamed again, her body covered in a veil of blackness as she was pulled inward until half of her was swallowed up by the rift.

"Deo!" he yelled, throwing all his weight into pulling her free, while at the same time summoning up another blast of arcany. "For the love of the goddesses, do something! It's taking her!"

Deo swayed, roaring an oath, but his body remained locked in a battle against itself.

Hallow dug in his feet, trying desperately to pull Allegria back, but it was hopeless. The rift had a hold of her, and there was nothing physical strength could do to change that.

"Then I will use another method," he ground through his teeth, holding tight to keep her from being sucked in farther.

"Hallow, please!" Allegria said, her voice muffled and faint. "Blessed Kiriah, the chaos is alive! It's starting to consume me!"

Hallow summoned all his strength to hold her, while his right hand drew the spell in the air, his mouth moving silently as he spoke the ancient words. For a moment, he allowed his being to become one with the light of the stars and moon, their pure light morphing as it flowed through him into a physical manifestation of his intention.

Allegria was suddenly flung backward twenty yards, the protective transportation bubble taking her out of the reach of the rift and its insidious power.

The blackness that had enveloped her evaporated into nothing, leaving her stunned, floating about a yard off the ground, her face frozen in an expression of horror.

"Thorn!" Hallow bellowed. "We close this rift now!"

"Hallow, no, not by yourself!" Allegria called, struggling to get free of the bubble. "It's too dangerous on your own!"

"I'm not alone," he growled, and held the staff aloft, his gaze focused on the rift as once again, he called on Bellias Starsong to grant him her blessing. Power pulsed along his flesh, in little blue-white crests rising like floodwaters, snapping and growling to itself.

"Deo!" Allegria called. "Do something!"

Deo charged, roaring in anger, his hands thrust forward as he slammed chaos power into the rift. It shuddered, but didn't stop moving. Deo stumbled forward two steps and fell to his knees, his arms wrapped around himself as the black mist began to cover him, too.

Hallow had no time to think of Deo; he had to destroy the rift before it consumed them all. "Now, Thorn, now!" he yelled and, sending the arcane magic into the staff, slammed it to the ground at the same time the bird landed atop it, joining his power to Hallow's. A concussive wave blasted outward, focused by the bird into a cone before them, hitting the rift with wave after wave of pure starlight.

For one horrible moment, the rift absorbed it all, its pattern of twisting unfazed, and Hallow feared his magic wasn't going to be enough.

But then the twisting seemed to stutter, freezing for a moment, turning back on itself in the opposite direction before stopping again. The edges of it crumpled inward, compressing until all that remained was a fist-sized ball, and then with a deafening blast that sent Hallow flying backward, it imploded.

He was up on his feet in a second, dashing toward Allegria. Thorn darted ahead, chattering madly in his head.

I haven't seen a blast like that since the Ancient Ones stirred and came out from under the mountains. Did you see how I focused the magic? I used a spell that I learned from my master's master, before he turned himself into a dragonfly and was eaten by a frog. He didn't plan that, just in case you think he did. That's why I chose this form. Still, that blast was excellent. That fool Exodius would be proud, although I'm sure you didn't learn such skills under him. Why do you say nothing? The woman is alright, although she looks angry.

"My heart, are you hurt?" Hallow lifted Allegria from where the bubble had dropped her onto the ground, quickly checking her for signs of injury. "Did the blast from the rift closing—"

"I'm fine—it didn't hurt me." She did look angry, he reflected. No, she looked downright furious. "I am so going to have a thing or two to say to Kiriah, though. Did you see what she did? She withdrew her blessing from me the second that chaos power started to consume me. I won't have it, do you hear me? If I am to be blessed, that blessing should stay no matter what else is happening to me!"

Hallow held her to him, laughing with the sheer joy of her. "Only you, my love, only you would rail at a goddess while you were being eaten alive by death magic. Can you stand? Walk?"

"Of course I can stand and walk." She pushed out of his embrace, clearly annoyed. "I'm not hurt at all, although I will say that I've changed my mind, and I'm now glad that you know how to pop people out of bad situations, because it certainly came in handy."

Deo staggered to his feet. "You did it," he said, staring at Hallow as if he were a three-headed ghost. "I don't believe it. You closed it with arcane magic. That makes no sense. The rift is born of Harborym. They draw power from death. Your starlight should not have destroyed it, and yet it did."

I helped! Tell him I helped! Point out that it was my contribution that allowed the magic to focus, Thorn demanded. *You did it all, my shiny pink arse. I was clearly the most important part of the job. Oh, to be a real bird! I would befoul his head as it has never before been befouled!*

"What is starlight if not the light of a thousand stars' birth?" Hallow asked, feeling a little smug in his satisfaction. Allegria was safe, the rift was closed, and Deo saw that although Hallow might not be a Bane of Eris, there was value in being an arcanist. It was just about a perfect moment.

"Birth? It's the light of a thousand stars' death. Your arcane magic could have just as easily given the rift power and allowed it to consume us all," Deo said succinctly, and limped toward his horse.

Fool, Thorn said.

Hallow sighed and addressed the staff. "Why don't you fly on to Sanmael? You can check for soul takers along the way."

An excellent idea. I'm glad to see that you, at least, understand my value. With an injured sniff, the bird broke free of the staff and headed west.

"Was he causing problems?" Allegria asked, shading her eyes to watch Thorn fly off.

"Not yet, but he would if he spent any more time with Deo." Hallow shared an exasperated look with Allegria. "I don't expect a thank-you from him, or even an expression of gratitude, but you'd think he could tone down his disbelief that arcane magic managed to close the rift."

"With any other man, yes. But Deo never was happy when someone could do something he couldn't master. He told me once that as a child, he was furious when he found out that only women give birth. He thought that since men were stronger than women, they should be the ones to have the babies in order to produce the strongest offspring." She gave him a wry smile. "Expecting him to be happy about the fact that you, a Fireborn, can master arcane magic when he can't, despite having a Starborn mother, is like expecting Kiriah and Bellias to settle their differences. It will never happen."

Hallow pursed his lips briefly. "About that—"

"Are we leaving, or are you two going to dawdle here all day?" Deo bellowed, causing his horse, a huge black charger, to dance nervously. "If we change horses along the way, we can ride all night and be to Sanmael in two days' time. We'll have that rift closed before my father's men can drag themselves out of their comfortable beds."

He wheeled his horse around and let the animal have his head.

"Do you think we should let his horse tire out before we tell him he's headed in the wrong direction?" Hallow asked as he mounted. "Or try to catch him now?"

Allegria laughed and, putting her fingers to her lips, let loose a piercing whistle that had Deo swinging his horse in a wide circle when she pointed in the direction behind them.

"Do you want to talk about what happened with the chaos magic?" Hallow asked when they urged their horses into a brisk trot to follow Deo, now traveling on the correct road.

She slid him a look from the corner of her eye. He kept his expression neutral, not wanting to make her talk about the experience if it made her too uncomfortable, but feeling that it was important to ascertain just what had happened. If she was now at risk just by being near any of the Harborym or their rifts, then he would have to convince her to step back.

He knew in his bones that she'd never back down from a fight, not so long as there was breath in her body. Her tenacity—even in the face of self-destruction—was one of the things he admired most in her.

As if reading his thoughts, she said lightly, "What doesn't kill me had best run, remember? Hallow, you don't have to dance delicately around me like I'm going to break into hundreds of pieces. I know something went wrong—very wrong—back there."

"You were covered in a black haze," he said slowly, digging through his mental library for any reference to a similar happening. "You said the chaos magic was alive and consuming you. Are you certain that it was that magic, and not something within the rift itself?"

She was silent for a few minutes, the muted thump of the horses' hooves on the dirt track the only sound. There was a dull, oppressive sense that lay heavily upon the land, making Hallow feel as if he was fighting his way through something cloying and stifling, like endless bales of sun-warmed cotton. "It's hard to explain. It didn't help that at that moment Kiriah Sunbringer withdrew her grace, leaving me utterly powerless, but it felt to me as if the chaos magic within me was trying to absorb me, and make me part of it."

"Your runes turned black," Hallow told her. "As did Deo's."

She glanced at her wrists. The runes on them now were a dull pale gold, almost invisible. "The chaos power... when Deo first told me it was alive, I thought that was odd. Then when I underwent the change,

I thought that Kiriah's blessing had kept it from affecting me the way it did the others. My runes weren't the same as theirs, and I was marked whereas they were not." She touched her forehead before continuing. "I could feel the chaos power in me, but it never controlled me. It struggled to be free, but never fought against my wishes. The only time I really felt it at all were those times when we ran into groups of Shades and Harborym, and after closing the rift. And then when I went... when I lost myself."

"Berserk," he murmured to himself, nodding.

She flinched at the word. "But as soon as the Harborym were dead, that sense of being out of control died, along with the magic. This rift was different. It was as if I had been pulled into a land made up of smoke and shadows. The chaos magic leaped to life inside of me, Hallow. It didn't stir, then gain power—one moment it was dead, cold, utterly absent, and the next it had sucked me into this shadowland, and I knew if you let go of my hand, I would be lost to it. Thank you for holding on."

"Is it trite to say that my life would be nothing but endless misery if you were not in it?" he asked, his tone light despite the horrible mental images of the unthinkable happening. When he thought of how close he'd come to having her slip away into the netherworld, his skin crawled.

"Not trite, perhaps, but a bit cliché." She gave him a brilliant smile, one accompanied by a look that revealed a smoldering desire in her eyes that he very much wanted to satisfy. "Nonetheless, I appreciate it. What are we going to do?"

"About the next rift, about Deo, or about you?"

"The first. No, all of them. Deo was affected just as I was, although it appears he managed to break free." She was silent for a few minutes, her eyes scanning the horizon. "What good am I going to be if I can't be near the rifts? What if next time, the chaos magic wins?"

"I don't know," he finally admitted, having struggled to find an answer. Chaos magic was beyond his experience and knowledge, although he was beginning to feel that he had an insight into it. "But I will not let you be taken from me. Of that, I am certain."

She smiled again, but it lasted only a few seconds before worry returned to her eyes.

Hallow knew just how she felt.

Chapter 21

The rift at Sanmael was almost anticlimactic compared with the first one, despite being located directly in the middle of a thriving market town. The town elders had cleared the area around it, erecting barricades and setting guards to watch for soul takers, but even so, we were told there had been a few casualties.

"Allegria," Hallow said in a warning tone of voice when we approached the now-familiar sight of light twisting and turning and folding in on itself.

I lifted a hand to stop him. "I will stay back. Now that Kiriah and I have had a chat and we see eye to eye again, I will use the power of her grace to help you and Deo."

Hallow looked amused. "I wish you'd allowed me to witness your confrontation with the goddess. I can only imagine how... potent... your words to her must have been."

"She didn't smite me dead, if you're implying I was irreverent," I said with a lift of my chin, although I sent a quick prayer of thanks to the goddess for allowing me to tell her what I thought without turning me into a pile of unrepentant ash. "I will allow that I am mightily relieved to have my lightweaving abilities back. Even with Kiriah's whims, I can't help but think that it's much more reliable than the chaos magic."

"Most definitely. Deo, do you wish to approach the rift, or will you channel your magic from a distance?"

Deo, who rode next to Hallow, said nothing. I urged my mare forward until I could see why he was being so rude, but he wore the introspective expression that I was coming to learn meant he was brooding about events in the past.

I rode in front of him and turned my mare to block Deo's path. He looked up, the black expression clearing from his brow. "What is it?" he asked, glancing around with mild surprise, as if he didn't realize where he was. Ahead was the rift, set off by hastily made barricades. He dismounted, rolling his shoulders and flexing his arms in preparation for the battle to come.

"I know you want to seek revenge on your father almost as much as you want to rid Alba of Harborym, but if you could be a little more here and now rather than living in the future, I would be much easier in my mind," I told him.

He looked annoyed, which he frequently did when I spoke to him. "If I prefer my own thoughts to watching you and the arcanist make sheep's eyes at each other, then you have no right to complain."

"We do not make sheep's eyes," I said, giving him a quelling look that he utterly ignored. "Hallow has declared himself, although I told him not to, but he is a romantic man at heart, and he couldn't help himself. Not that I accepted him."

"You'd better do so," Deo said dryly, glancing at my midsection. "The way you two went at it on the ship, you're likely to be with child even now."

"Our private interest aside, can you please pay attention to what's happening? Hallow asked you a question."

I slid off the side of my horse, handing over the reins to one of the boys who darted forward to take them. Two of the town elders approached as Hallow dismounted, and they spoke briefly to him while Deo and I armed ourselves. Thorn had joined us just outside the town, evidently filling Hallow's ears with tales of the good people of the town, and how valiantly they had fought against the soul-sucking monsters that emerged with increasing rapidity.

Hallow joined us when we climbed over the wooden barricades. The rift had opened in the central square of the town, as hastily abandoned shops and a large well indicated. "They've lost seven people in the last ten days. The rate of soul takers is definitely increasing, and they are becoming harder to kill."

"The Harborym are preparing to send battalions through," Deo said, doubling over for a moment, his hands on his knees as he gasped for breath.

"Are you all right?" I asked, and started forward, but Hallow held me back, nodding toward the nearest of Deo's hands. The runes on the band were black, not bright, but dull and granular. It looked as if little bits of it were soaking into his flesh. "Give him a minute. If he doesn't master the magic, we'll have him pulled back. Regardless, I don't think you should go any closer."

I glanced at the rift. It hovered to the right of the well, little strands of it reaching out before folding into its center. It was an abomination of nature, but it didn't fill me with the same sense of destruction as the one that had almost pulled me in. I stepped forward until I was next to Deo, and instantly the chaos magic inside me came alive, filling my brain with a black wave of desperation. I gasped for air, but the magic held me in such a vise that I couldn't move, my muscles locked in a painful paroxysm from which there seemed to be no end. The blackness of the magic seeped downward, filling my chest and smothering me.

A blow struck me, knocking the blackness from me. I lay on the ground too stunned to do anything but breathe. When my vision cleared, Hallow was kneeling next to me.

"What... what did you do?" I asked, struggling to sit up.

"Pulled you back." He grimaced. "Well, knocked you back with arcany. Your color is returning. Will you be all right to continue, or do you want to wait a bit to catch your breath?"

"Oh, we are *not* waiting one second longer than we have to," I said, taking his hand to get to my feet. As usual, just the warmth and strength of him near me gave me a sense of security. Of unity. We were in this together, we three. I looked over to where Deo was straightening up, his battle with the chaos inside him won, for the moment at least. His runes were red again as he strode forward until he was about ten paces from the rift.

"Do I need to warn you to go no closer?" Hallow asked.

"No," I said, shaking my hands and gathering myself to commune with Kiriah. It was a struggle to quiet my mind while, around us, people had collected, calling to one another and to us, but I was well versed in meditation amongst chatty initiates. By the time I was pulling on the sun, weaving the power until it formed a golden net of Kiriah's grace, Hallow stood to the side of the rift, allowing us to target it from three different directions. Thorn took to wing, circling Hallow, clearly waiting to lend his assistance. As the people behind the barricades broke into cheers, Hallow began drawing his spell in the air, the purity of the stars gathering around him.

I threw the light of Kiriah onto the rift just as Hallow directed arcane power onto it. Deo bellowed something and spread his hands wide, causing red tendrils to emerge from the ground, snaking upward and outward until they spread across the rift.

It didn't stand a chance against the combined power of the three of us. Without the explosion of the first rift, it simply collapsed upon itself and disappeared with only a little sigh.

"That was very satisfying," Hallow said, nodding when the elders raised their hands in thanks. "Yes, Thorn, you were instrumental. I couldn't have done it without you."

The bird circled a few more times, then settled back on the staff.

"Where to now?" I asked two hours later, after we had been feted by the town.

"We go to Abet," Deo said, stomping past us to the stable yard, calling loudly, "Fresh horses! We ride tonight."

I looked longingly at the house of one of the elders, which had been offered up for our comfort. The thought of sleeping in a bed, a real bed, not a bedroll laid upon the stony ground for an hour's snatched rest, was almost overwhelming.

Hallow hesitated, as well, and I knew the thought was tempting him as greatly as it was me. But he sighed heavily and took my arm, leading me to the stable after Deo. "There will be time for bathing and scented oils later, after the last rift is destroyed."

"Oooh, is that what you were thinking?" I dwelled with pleasure on the idea of Hallow, naked, wet, and slippery with scented oil. It was almost enough to send me back to the elder's house, but instead, I accepted a new horse and mounted with a groan that was mostly inaudible.

To everyone but Hallow, who murmured, "Duty first, my heart, but once that is done, you and I are going to retreat from society for a long time."

"That sounds like heaven right now," I said, shifting in the saddle, my thighs and behind protesting at more time spent on horseback.

We arrived in Abet exhausted, our mounts—which we'd changed many times during the three-day journey—lathered and about ready to drop. We'd ridden hard through the nights, knowing we were so close to the end goal, and arrived on the cobbled streets of Abet just as Kiriah sent the sun above the horizon. Long peachy fingers streaked across the midnight blue sky, while the shadows of the night began to lift, the rosy dawn glistening in the wet puddles along the cobblestones.

The city was just waking up, but it didn't take long before the few people who were about saw Deo.

"Remember the plan," Hallow warned him when Deo noticed two stableboys bolting for the keep. "We deal with the rift first, then you do whatever you feel you must."

"You needn't remind me," Deo growled, pulling his great sword out of the scabbard and heading for the stone steps that led up toward the front of the house. "I know my duty well enough. You just keep an eye on Allegria. She doesn't have the mastery I have over the chaos magic."

Hallow said nothing, just helped me from my horse, holding on to my waist when I staggered a little.

"Tell me you don't mind if we walk back to Kelos," I said to him, trying to ease my cramped muscles as we followed Deo.

"I don't mind, but it might make crossing the sea a little difficult," he answered, his tone light, but his expression and eyes full of shadows.

"Are you going to be in very much trouble with the council?" I asked softly as we emerged into a dewy garden, planted with ornamental trees, decorative shrubs trimmed into animal shapes, and brilliant splashes of red, yellow, and blue overflowing the flower beds. "Even if Lord Israel didn't kill Deo, he's not going to be happy to see him here, in Abet."

"That can't be helped; we are obligated to go where the rifts open. Oy, lad! Yes, you." Hallow hailed a serving boy who was rushing by with two buckets of water. "Where in Abet is the rift that opened a fortnight ago?"

The boy looked somewhat insolently first at me, then at Hallow, but once he got a glimpse of Deo, his eyes widened and he backed away. "It's... it's in the war room. But you mustn't go in there."

"Why not?" I asked.

The lad looked even more frightened if that was possible. "It's dangerous. Lord Israel has forbidden entrance."

Deo smiled and marched past the boy, who stumbled and dumped both buckets on the cream stone steps leading into the keep. "That must infuriate my father to no end. Come along, you two, no dragging your feet. We have a rift to close."

"As much as I dislike surly and introspective Deo, a chipper one is almost a hundred times worse," I grumbled to Hallow.

He laughed, and slid a hand down to my behind, where he gave me a little pinch. "Just remember that as soon as we close it, we can demand a room, and I can give you the bath that for the last three days you've said you so desperately need."

I sighed at the thought of hot water easing my aching muscles and sore posterior. "That's almost enough to make me giddy."

"You make me gid—" Hallow stopped speaking when we entered the hall, expecting it to be the same as when we were last here.

Deo stood in front of us, his hands on his hips. Hallow moved alongside him. I stopped at the door, staring with growing horror at the monstrosity that seemed to seep out of the very walls. The rift might have started two floors above in the war room, but now it oozed out along the corridor, and down through the floors into the hall where we now stood. It was massive, at least three times as wide as the others, with long snakes of matter writhing and snapping. In the center of it, a black oval seemed to swallow the miasma that turned upon itself on the outer edges, the whole thing a massive blot on the existence of Alba.

There were no guards in the room, but if Israel had cleared the castle, there was no need of them. "Do you think…" I stopped, unsure how to put it into words. "Do you think that's…"

"Yes," Hallow said, placing a warning hand on my arm. He didn't need to. I wasn't about to step a single foot closer to that… thing. "Yes, I think it's different. It's not a rift so much as it is a… being."

"It's the threshold of Eris itself," Deo said. He took two steps forward, and the rift turned toward him. I swear, it saw him, recognized him. His runes lit up red, fading quickly to black.

"I don't think you should get too close," Hallow warned, moving up to him.

"You mind your magic, and I'll mind mine," Deo snarled and took another step forward.

"My son was never one to heed advice, arcanist. You are wasting your breath if you think to influence him."

The voice came from behind me and was slightly out of breath, as if the speaker had been running. I turned to see both Lord Israel and Idril come forward, the latter looking her perfect self despite obviously having been summoned from bed. A line of soldiers clustered behind them, but Israel waved them back.

"There is no need unless we fall," he said, closing the big double doors in their faces. Amongst them, I saw Rixius, his face red and twisted with anger.

I blew him a kiss right before the doors closed.

"I don't know why we bother having a council if you are going to ignore our wishes and simply go off to do what you want," Lord Israel told Hallow.

"I've told you before that if you wish for me to resign from the council, I will gladly stand down in deference to another arcanist," Hallow replied, a bite of frost to his words.

I hid a smile, but let Hallow see how proud I was that he wasn't in the least bit cowed by Lord Israel.

"And have another half-mad arcanist running off to fight his own demons?" Israel gave a mock shudder. "Preserve me from such horrors. You will stay as you are, although we will have a discussion later about your habit of disregarding direct orders. I refer, of course, to the present company."

"Nice to see you, too," I said smoothly, pulling a little light to form a lion that clambered up to my shoulder, where it sat and roared at Israel. His eyes widened ever so slightly at the sign of it, his gaze speculative. "It seems I was misled about you, priest. I will address that later, as well." He turned his eyes to his son. "And here we have the biggest question of all. What do you expect to accomplish here, Deo? Have you come to vent your anger upon me for saving your hide when others would have you dead? Or to continue to rail at me for the supposed slights you've suffered over the years?"

To my surprise, Deo didn't fall for his father's obvious bait. He simply looked him over as if he were a particularly uninteresting piece of mutton. "We are here to close the rift. As we've done with the other two."

That took his father aback, but only for a second or two. His eyes narrowed on Deo. "You closed them? You destroyed them completely?"

Deo looked bored. "Of course. It is why my banesmen were created, and although I'm told you saw to it that the others were banished to the far reaches of Alba, Allegria, Hallow, and I were able to handle them with ease."

I bit my lip to keep from correcting him. Almost being sucked into the black nothingness of the rift was not my idea of ease, but Deo deserved a little leeway when it came to bragging to his father.

"I see." Lord Israel was silent for a few moments before continuing, "I will call back both my army and that of the Tribe of Jalas."

"You speak for them now, do you?" Deo asked, and for the first time he looked beyond his father to where Idril stood. "I don't know why I'm surprised that once again you've usurped what belonged to another."

"Deo," Idril said then, sighing as she came forward to stand near Lord Israel. "You are being tiresome."

He bowed to her. "What the lady says must be so, since you once claimed never to have spoken an untrue word. If you would leave the keep with your lord, we will get to work on this rift."

"I have no lord," she said in a tone that almost expressed an emotion. She evidently realized her slip, because she said much more smoothly, "What you intend to do is too dangerous. Magisters from both Aryia and the High Lands have worked on the rift day and night for ten days. Half of them died in the attempt. The others went mad."

"No effect at all?" Hallow asked.

"None," Lord Israel answered, gesturing toward it. "I am about to raze the keep around it, with hopes that fire can do what the magisters cannot."

Hallow's eyebrows lifted as he considered the rift. I didn't like looking at it—it gave me the feeling it was looking back—and after a few minutes, he strolled up to it. I fought the urge to call him back.

"Go closer at your own peril," Lord Israel called. "It has a habit of snatching up those who are near."

Deo joined Hallow, almost instantly falling to the floor.

Idril exclaimed, while Lord Israel would have run forward if I hadn't stopped him. "No," I said, holding him back. "Leave him to his battle. He will triumph in the end. Just give him the time to master it."

"Thorn," Hallow said, turning his gaze back onto the rift.

The bird quivered.

"Yes. Are you willing to try? You know what it may mean."

The bird separated from the staff and flitted around the room.

Hallow gave it a dark smile. "I swear that your name will be remembered."

A little gasp escaped me when Thorn dove into the rift, causing the snaking tendrils to become agitated. One of them reached out toward Deo, but Hallow called down the light of the fading stars onto it.

Deo rose painfully to his knees, the black of the runes across his chest fading into a dark, shadowed red.

"There, you see?" I released Lord Israel's arm. "I know you think he is weak, but he is stronger than the chaos magic, no matter how much it tries to master him."

"I never believed him to be weak," Israel said, taking a step forward. "Just foolishly regardless of his own life. Deo, do not continue forward. You don't know the power of it."

"Stay back, old man," Deo said, his head partially bowed. Even so, I could see the red glitter in his black eyes as he held the rift in his gaze. "Take Idril and leave."

"We are not so faithless—" Israel started to say.

"For the love of the twin goddesses," Hallow snapped, looking directly at Lord Israel. I heard the latter gasp under his breath, and I had to say, I didn't blame him. Hallow's normally placid face was twisted with anger. "Get Lady Idril out now, lest you both be destroyed. The captain is coming."

"What?" I turned to look at the rift, the chill of the grave rippling down my back and arms as I saw what Hallow must have heard from Thorn. The black oval center was twisting until it turned into the form of the Harborym captain.

Deo roared in anger, but it was Lord Israel who charged forward, throwing himself at the captain. A dull throbbing sound filled the hall, and I realized the rift itself was laughing. Just as Israel was about to reach the captain, two tendrils reached out and grabbed him. Deo lunged forward, and the rift turned to him, slapping him with a force that sent him flying across the room into the doors. Idril screamed and ran to where he was slumped on the floor.

I didn't wait for an order, I sent a hurried prayer to Kiriah Sunbringer, and called down the power of the sun just as Hallow yanked Lord Israel from the grasp of the rift. He blasted the tendrils to powder even as I opened my mind and allowed the sun to flow through me to the rift.

"Do you think this makes any difference?" the captain said, looking around the room with mild interest. "We will take what we want. There is nothing you can do to stop us."

"Where is Dasa?" Lord Israel cried, trying to charge forward again. Hallow cast his bubble spell, sending Israel backward several feet before turning to narrow his eyes on the captain. I could see symbols on the air glowing for a fraction of a second as he cast spells.

"Dasa?" The captain looked thoughtful. "Ah, you mean Deva. That is her chosen name now. She is my queen, and is most pleased with being in Eris rather than this pathetic world."

Lord Israel uttered an oath that Sandor would be shocked I recognized, and tried to get forward to the captain again, but he was powerless against Hallow's spell.

"She will accompany me later, once I know it is safe for her," the captain said, his gaze lifting to Deo, who was groggily shaking his head and trying to get to his feet. "Once the last of the threats have been eliminated."

"Free me!" Israel demanded, swearing profanely.

I glanced at the man who held my heart, the man who wore responsibility and power with such ease, and yet still managed to laugh at himself. He was truly everything I could ever want in a mate, and I was suddenly possessed with a desire to tell him so. "I accept your offer," I told him.

He shot me a disbelieving glance. "You want to do this now?"

"No. But I wanted you to know I accept."

"I'm delighted to hear that, but I'm a little busy at the moment, so if you will excuse me for not kissing you, we can get on with this business."

I grinned at him. "I love you, too. Shall we?"

"Yes," he said, and we both turned to the captain, who was slowly advancing into the room. Behind him, in the rift, I could see the shape of a Harborym forming. I released the power of the sun that I'd been holding, directing it into the captain. It burned through him, causing him to cry out and half-turn toward the rift. At the same time, Hallow stepped forward and, with a spoken word of command, slammed down the staff, sending a ripple of arcane power directly into the rift. The captain toppled, and the rift itself gathered him up, sucking him into its depths.

"Again!" Hallow yelled, and I gathered up more light, but before I could send Kiriah's power into the rift, it swung around and lashed out at Hallow, catching him by one leg.

He fell and was dragged across the floor until his legs were both pulled into the rift.

"No!" I screamed, and leaped forward, throwing myself on him. The chaos magic in me roared to life, eating away at me.

"Allegria," Hallow cried, desperately casting spells, but they didn't stop him from being dragged into the rift. "Release the chaos into it."

"It'll just give it more power," I said, turning my head to squint into the rift, only a few feet from my face. Pure chaos energy poured out of it, making my eyes stream and my ears ring.

"Do it!" he cried and twisted to turn over in an attempt to claw the floor.

I didn't stop to question him. I took the light that glowed around me and, instead of sending it outward into the rift, poured it inward in an attempt to burn out the chaos. I felt as if I'd leaped into a bonfire, every inch of me alight with pain and heat, the fire within me turning me into a blazing inferno of anger. If I'd been berserk before, now I was wildness personified. I hauled Hallow out of the rift, snarling at it as rage and fury filled my burning self.

I was light. I was fire. I was the sun itself, and I would see everything before me burned to ash. A hand grasped my ankle as I prepared to throw myself into the rift, my madness demanding that I fill it with my wrath. Words filled my mind, foreign words, ones that echoed from the heavens. I chanted them as I struggled forward to the rift, dragging Hallow with me despite his attempts to stop me. The words rolled around the room, driving the chaos magic from my body.

The keep itself began to tremble and smolder, the stones burning with the intensity of my wrath. The floor quaked as I took another step, the words of the goddesses pouring from me and causing the very land to protest.

"Allegria, stop!" Hallow yelled above the noise that filled the room. "You must not go closer!"

He cast a spell to bind me, but I simply waved it off. I was the light that filled the deepest reaches of the stars—I would not be held back now. I had almost reached the rift, and the snaking whips of power from it tried to grab me, but jerked back in obvious pain.

Just as I reached it, a shadow flickered past me. Deo faced me, his eyes red, his runes glowing gold with the heat of... me.

"This is not your battle," he said, and then stepped into the rift.

The rift gave another one of its horrible chuckling noises; then suddenly it spoke, in a horrible voice that repulsed every iota of my being. "At last," it said, and then was gone. Completely gone, just as if it had never been there. I stood there, radiating the power of the sun, and the rift was gone.

And just as suddenly, the strange rage left me. Kiriah withdrew her presence, leaving me empty and cold and dark. I collapsed, hearing Hallow's voice before the blackness swept over me. "My heart, come back to me. Don't leave me now. Come back, Allegria. Come back."

EPILOGUE

"Allegria, you have slept enough. It is time for you to wake up."

I burrowed my head deeper into my pillow. "Just a little longer, Sandor. I'll stay for extra prayers later."

"She was ever thus," Sandor said. I snuggled into my blankets, wondering at a Sandor who would let me sleep when I ought to be up working at my chores.

"My heart, if you do not wake up, the water will cool, and you won't have the bath you have so long desired."

My heart? No one called me that but...

In a rush, memory returned to me, and I sat up in bed, pushing my hair back from my face. The first thing my bleary eyes noticed was that there were no silver cuffs on my wrists. The second was Hallow sitting at the end of my bed.

A surge of joy overwhelmed me, and I flung myself on him, knocking him backward against the wall of my room. "Hallow! I was dreaming I was back at the temple, and Sandor was nagging me to do my chores."

I kissed his chin, his nose, his lips, and all the while he was laughing and trying to speak.

"I never nag, child. I urge."

I froze in mid-kiss, looking over my shoulder to see Sandor standing with Lord Israel. The latter looked like a different man, his face gray and lined, his hair lank and laced with black streaks. But it was his eyes that would haunt me, eyes filled with despair and pain.

The joy inside me dimmed.

"Deo," I said on a breath, and sat back on my heels, allowing Hallow to sit up. "Goddesses of day and night, Deo went into the rift. I could have stopped him and I didn't. It's my fault he went into it!" Hallow's arms were around me as a lone tear rolled down my cheek. "You are not to blame, my love. He chose to enter the rift."

"He said it wasn't my fight, but it was," I said, clutching Hallow's arms. I turned my gaze to him, needing to make him understand. "It was my whole purpose! I am a Bane of Eris."

"No, you aren't," Hallow said, lifting my hand to his lips. He uncurled my fingers and kissed my palm. "The cuffs guarding you are gone. They fell off when the chaos magic was overwhelmed as you channeled Kiriah Sunbringer. You are as you were before you were transformed."

Sadness permeated every inch of the room. "But Deo... why did he do it?"

"To save his mother," Lord Israel said, his voice cracked and grating.

I slid off the bed to face him, feeling I owed him an apology.

"I'm sorry," I told Lord Israel. "Something happened to me. The sun... it was as if I had tapped directly into the power of the sun. I should have fought it to save Deo."

"There was no saving him," Lord Israel said in a toneless voice. His expression was as bleak as his eyes. "We can only pray to the goddesses that they will watch over him on Eris as they have on Alba."

"I'm sorry," I said again. There was nothing else to say.

Lord Israel took his leave shortly after that, Sandor escorting him out. While fresh bathwater was being heated, Hallow fed me small pieces of bread and cheese and fruit, and caught me up on the happenings after I'd swooned.

"We brought you here because Lord Israel said Lady Sandor was the only one who had the learning needed to treat you."

I looked down at my arms. The silver bands were gone, but my arms and hands were swathed in white bandages up to my elbows. "What happened to me, Hallow?"

He sat back in the chair next to the window seat where I was curled up, voraciously eating the tidbits he offered. "What do you remember?"

"I remember the rift laughing at us, and pulling you in. I remember the captain being hurt, and it sucked him back. And then, I called on Kiriah and... and it seemed as if I became the sun itself." I shivered and touched the bandages. "I felt like I was burning from the inside out."

"You were burning. The words you spoke, they were like nothing I've ever heard. I believe you were channeling Kiriah herself. I told Lady

Sandor a few of the words I recall you saying, and she turned whiter than your bandages."

I stopped with a grape halfway to my mouth. "How is that possible, Hallow?"

"For you to channel a goddess?" He shrugged and popped a piece of cheese into his mouth, saying around it, "I don't know. It is beyond my knowledge. After Deo went into the rift, and you collapsed, Lord Israel helped me bring you here."

"And Deo? What will happen to him? His runes... they were different."

"Yes. I think somehow he changed the chaos magic. Whatever he did to it, I believe that he survived the passage through the rift. If anyone can find his mother and rescue her, it is he."

"Yes," I said slowly, unable to shake the guilt that I bore in the matter. "If only I hadn't gone berserk again, I could have stopped him."

"Do you not think that, perhaps, the goddess chose that method to keep you from doing just that?" he asked.

I met his bright blue gaze, and once again, the lines fanning from his eyes made me feel warm inside. "You think Deo meant to go through the rift all along, don't you?"

"The last one? Yes." Hallow's jaw tightened. "He said himself that revenge drove him. We assumed he meant revenge on his father, but it was his mother's fate that he sought to change. I think he is where he wished to be."

I sighed and pushed the plate away. "It just seems like such a sad end. Lord Israel looks like a different person."

"We rode hard to get you here. On top of the shock of losing both the queen and Deo, he has had a hard time of it." Hallow gave me a little smile. "You've been asleep for almost a week. I was half-afraid you would not return to me."

I moved over to him, seating myself on his lap just as the door opened, and a handful of servants brought in a large copper tub and several leathers full of hot water. "And turn down such a promising suitor? The sun and moon would have to change places for me to do that. Did you tell Sandor that you are promised to me?"

"I did. She forbade it," he said, the lines from his eyes crinkling delightfully.

"Because you're an arcanist?" I asked, surprised. It wasn't often that priestesses left the temple to marry, but Sandor allowed it in certain circumstances, and I had a feeling she would be more than a little relieved to have me off her hands.

"Because I'm half-Starborn."

"What?" I asked loudly enough that the servants, giggling to themselves as they filled the tub, gawked at us.

"Like Deo, my mother was a Starborn. It's why I am able to master the arcane arts."

"But... you said you learned it from a Starborn master," I protested.

"And so I did. But I wouldn't have gotten very far if I did not have the blood of the arcane flowing through me. No, my heart, no more questions. Your bath is ready, and I know how much you were looking forward to it. You take it, and later, I'll tell you all about how my mother and father met and fell in love."

The servants filed out of the door, giggling once again when Hallow stood up and, with a gentle pat on my behind, followed them.

"You're leaving?" I asked, bemused to find out that the world I thought I knew was topsy-turvy. I gestured toward the tub. "It's large enough for both of us."

"Allegria," he said, *tsk*ing. "And you a priestess."

He closed the door behind him.

"Well, blast," I said, feeling distinctly let down.

The door opened and he popped his head in. "I'm just fetching the scented oil. If you're not in the tub by the time I get back, you have to wash my back first."

I grinned and started peeling off my clothing. There was sorrow in my heart, but Hallow filled the rest. I had a feeling he wasn't going to let the situation with Deo go, and I would be at his side, fighting with him to bring Deo and the queen back.

The future looked almost as bright as the sun that beamed down her love onto all of Alba.